Praise for Rambling into Madness

"This book does an excellent job of painting a first-person picture of the day to day life of a person struggling with a serious ment͟   ͘s. ... First person viewpoints of someone with a major mental ͘͘ protagonist are rarely this well written or this well ed͘

I would especially recommend this book to pa͘ of anyone with a serious and persistent ment͘ vivid and realistic descriptions of the pus͘   rela- tionship from parent to friend to thera͏   captures the frustration of parents and friends wh͘   ave but see the recurrent episodes of psychosis and seriou͘   ͘, and subsequent- ly feel thwarted in their desire to be helpful, or u͘   feel rejected or even abused.

Emmett (the protagonist) is someone that I felt sympathy for, then a great deal of empathy. I didn't have to go very far into the book before I found myself liking Emmett very much. I highly recommend this book as a lens into a way of living and being that few of us experience. The story is great, the writing is entertaining and educational. It's a great read."

Dr. Randy Stith
Ph.D., CEO and Executive Director
Aurora Mental Health and Colorado Crisis Centers
Member of the International Mental Health Coalition

"This book is amazing! It's great storytelling combined with honest and straight-forward insight into real mental illness. Chris Feld exposes the good, the bad, and the ugly of living with mental illness, pulling no punches, omitting any superfluous drama.

I recommend this book to anyone who would like to know how to effectively support a loved one with a mental illness, or anyone who is looking for some hope for a better life while suffering from a serious mental illness."

Tawney E. Bass
Past NAMI Affiliate President
Former mental health center executive
Mother of an adult with mental health issues

RAMBLING
INTO
MADNESS

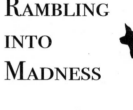

RAMBLING INTO MADNESS

A Novel
by

Chris Feld

Mostly Just Like You
Book One in the Series

High Prairie Press | Denver

HIGH PRAIRIE PRESS
6403 South Hudson Street, Centennial, CO 80121
www.highprairiepress.com
highprairiepress@gmail.com

Printed in the United States of America
ISBN 978-1-944868-07-9 (Paperback Format)
ISBN 978-1-944868-08-6 (Kindle MOBI Format)
ISBN 978-1-944868-09-3 (ePub Format)

Speaking engagements and other author events scheduled through High Prairie Press at highprairiepress@gmail.com or Chris Feld at chris.feld@gmail.com

For my dad.

"Violence is not the answer. Cellos is."

You ask me how I became a madman. It happened thus: One day, long before many gods were born, I woke from a deep sleep and found all my masks were stolen,--the seven masks I have fashioned and worn in seven lives,--I ran maskless through the crowded streets shouting, "Thieves, thieves, the cursed thieves."

Men and women laughed at me and some ran to their houses in fear of me.

And when I reached the market place, a youth standing on a house-top cried, "He is a madman." I looked up to behold him; the sun kissed my own naked face for the first time. For the first time the sun kissed my own naked face and my soul was inflamed with love for the sun, and I wanted my masks no more. And as if in a trance I cried, "Blessed, blessed are the thieves who stole my masks."

Thus I became a madman.

And I have found both freedom of loneliness and the safety from being understood, for those who understand us enslave something in us.

But let me not be too proud of my safety. Even a Thief in a jail is safe from another thief.

From *The Madman, His Parables and Poems*
by Kahlil Gibran

Foreword

By Tim Feld

While our society is very good at accepting physical ailments and diseases, it's scared to death of anything that suggests a disease of the mind. We'll happily accommodate folks with wheelchairs or canes, but look the other way if anyone appears to be hallucinating. We've convinced ourselves that these people must be dangerous and it's only a matter of time before they "snap." The truth is mental illness is no less treatable, and no less normal, than is physical illness.

Subtle signs of schizoaffective disorder began to manifest in my son Chris during his late teens. Looking back on that time, I wish this book had been available to me, to help me better understand what the world around my son was morphing into, hidden from my view. While we were able to successfully navigate some very difficult times as a family, that navigation would have been far easier with the kind of guide this book represents.

It was a blessing my son had a family who would love him unconditionally and support him through his illness and into a new life of living with schizoaffective disorder. His creativity was able to continue to blossom, finding new outlets, while his inquisitive mind expanded with a greater understanding of how this illness impacted his mind and the lens through which he could see and interact with the world.

That creative and inquisitive mind, and the road it travelled,

led to this book. While the story and the characters are fictional, they are inspired by life as seen through Chris's eyes. The reader is given a deeply personal and intimate sketch of life with an illness few people understand.

One of the treatments that eventually helped Chris move toward a more stable existence was ECT, or electro convulsive therapy. ECT is portrayed as a violent and barbaric treatment by the media. That portrayal was accurate in the early days of ECT but it is not accurate today. That is not to diminish the still present devastating side effects of the treatment. While it was no picnic for Chris, ECT helped to break the deep and dark depression. It pressed a reset button in his brain and allowed Chris to focus on moving forward rather than giving up. This story portrays ECT in a way that lets us experience a bit of it along with the main character, allowing us to feel the treatment from the perspective of the treated.

I believe this book will help reshape some of the inaccurate views society has regarding mental illness. It presents in an engaging fashion what it really is like to live with a mental illness. The reader will benefit from what one psychiatrist described as a genius-level insight into his mental illness. If you or a loved one suffers from a mental illness, it will provide hope that living a productive and purposeful life with a mental illness is possible.

Mental illness isn't something we want to talk about openly. Far more people are afflicted in one way or another than is generally acknowledged. With this in mind, there's a great benefit to be gained by coming to a better understanding of what mental illness is and how it impacts the lives of those who are touched by it. If you aren't aware of how mental illness touches your life or the life of a loved one, it may be only because you haven't talked about it…

Yet.

RAMBLING
INTO
MADNESS

Prologue

"Emmett, time to wake up. We're leaving in ten minutes," Dad said in a gentle voice as he came into the room and turned the light on.

Emmett's eyes opened immediately. Always a tense sleeper on the nights before the procedure. Always vaguely aware of his parents' alarm going off, unsurprised when one of them came into his room to tell him it was time to get up so they could go.

He struggled off the floor and went stumbling after his glasses.

It was still pitch black outside, maybe four in the morning. He peered out the window as he wrestled with his pants and saw, by the light of the solitary street lamp in the cul-de-sac, large white flakes of snow falling quickly to the ground, as if desperate to finish their descent. Several inches had already accumulated. Hopefully that didn't make them late. Not that it mattered if they were late. Dr. Romero would still see him, would still perform the procedure.

His appointment was for 6 a.m. in Louisville.

Mom and Dad always took care of the logistics, told him only minutes before they had to leave that it was time to wake up. All he needed was to put on his pants and swallow some of his pills—Mom and Dad would take care of the rest.

Pants on, Emmett made his way, in an automaton's haze, to the bathroom. He filled a glass with water and popped pills into his mouth one at a time, followed by a gulp of water.

He wasn't allowed to eat breakfast, wasn't allowed to drink anything, save for as little water as necessary to swallow his pills. Food or water mixed with the anesthesia would make him vomit.

Emmett had no opinion about this procedure, had no opinion about much of anything. The procedure was all he knew, was all he had to live for. Three days a week, Mom and Dad took turns driving him to Louisville to see the best ECT doctor in the country, where enough electricity was shot through his brain to give him a seizure.

Emmett headed downstairs to the kitchen where Dad was finishing up a bowl of cereal.

"RTG?" Dad asked. Dad's three-letter acronym comforted Emmett this morning.

Emmett yawned and gave his affirmation with a thumbs up; he was ready to go. Dad got up and put his cereal bowl in the sink.

Dad and Emmett got into the car.

Backed out of the driveway.

Dad's car made the first tracks on the snow-covered streets. The crunching sound of the tires compressing snow lulled Emmett back to sleep. The bumps and sways of the road, the sound of the radio tuned to a whisper to keep Dad company, the scraping of the windshield wipers clearing the falling snow away; it always reminded Emmett of going on road trips to Grandma and Grandpa's house when he was little. Being woken up early in the morning right as they had to leave; the gentle rocking of the car sending him and his sister, Clarissa, back to sleep; the same radio station keeping Dad company. All that was missing was Mom and her vacuum flask of coffee, the special Thermos only used on road trips.

◇◇◇

Emmett felt the car slow down in the brightening morning. They were pulling up to an unassuming hospital. The parking lot was mostly empty, only a few cars parked outside—one a tan Porsche with two giant bug eyes for headlights, in a reserved spot near the front of the building, covered by a blanket of snow.

They walked inside, and a nurse sitting at the front desk greeted them warmly.

"Just sign in and I'll let her know you're here," she said as she picked up a phone. Emmett printed and then signed his name on the sheet of paper.

Seconds later, another nurse appeared at the door. She too was friendly and greeted Emmett like they were old friends. Her name, Margaret, was printed on her hospital employee's ID tag. Emmett always forgot that—Margaret, Margaret, Margaret, he told himself. Next time he would remember.

Dad and Emmett followed the nurse through doors she unlocked by swiping her ID across a card reader.

"Feel free to sit down," she told Dad. "There are donuts and coffee if you're interested. Emmett, you can follow me."

"Hold on a sec," Emmett told the nurse, and she turned around to see him making his way over to give his dad a hug.

"I'll see you in a few hours, Emmett," Dad said as he returned the hug.

Emmett walked back toward the nurse, and she smiled at him and led him through the door.

The room was blindingly bright and smelled of overcooked

rice. Emmett took a chair in the first room directly off the hall-way where another nurse greeted him, again smiling warmly. Were they really this nice? Or was it just part of their job de-scription?

He knew from experience with the other patients the nurses didn't get smiled back at very often, so Emmett smiled back and greeted her in his usual friendly manner. He wasn't angry at anyone for what he was going through. It wasn't their fault. If anything, it was his own fault for being here.

"Life isn't fair," Mom had said frequently when he and Cla-rissa were kids.

Months ago, Emmett was supposed to be getting married. Months ago, he was going to school, he'd had an apartment of his own, he'd had a job he enjoyed. Months ago, he'd had a future. Maybe Lauren would have been expecting by now if things hadn't fallen apart. Mom and Dad would have been so excited to have had a grandchild. But things did fall apart, and he'd lost everything. He'd had to drop out of school, he'd lost his job, he'd lost his home, Lauren had left him for reasons he didn't entirely understand, and his future was looking more and more grim with each induced seizure.

Crippling depression had led him to try to kill himself mul-tiple times, to become obsessed with the idea of ending his life. Medication hadn't put an end to the suffering; neither had two hospitalizations. Out of options, Dr. Bogsdaughter had suggest-ed electroconvulsive therapy, ECT, as the only thing that could save Emmett from himself.

He felt like he was marching toward the executioner every time he was woken to have this done to him. But still he did it.

The nurse handed him a clipboard and a pen. It was a Beck test—a multiple-choice quiz that supposedly determined how depressed he was. It was a series of statements, each with a numerical value. For number one, the zero-point statement was

"I do not feel sad," the one-point statement was "I feel sad," the two-point statement was "I am sad all the time and I can't snap out of it," and the three-point statement was "I am so sad and unhappy that I can't stand it." Emmett couldn't identify with any of the statements ... except for maybe the zero-point statement. He didn't feel sad; he felt dead inside, he'd gone past the point of feeling anything, he was numb, he'd demitted his status as human.

So he circled the three-point statement and made a note, "I feel more dead inside than anything."

The rest of the questions were about his feelings about the future, the level of guilt he felt, his feelings about how much of a failure he was. He didn't feel guilt, he didn't feel like a failure—but he supposed he would, if he actually felt anything. Twos and threes for all of them.

Emmett always had to qualify his answer to the last one, whether he wanted to kill himself. He wasn't actively interested in killing himself, but death would be a welcome relief. He circled the two-point statement, "I would like to kill myself," and made another note that it came with the usual implication of, not so much a desire to do it himself, but strongly wishing his heart would just stop beating already.

Emmett looked up from his paper, finished. The nurse had her back turned, busy with some paperwork, so Emmett sat quietly.

It was a tiny room, more hallway-dimensioned than anything; crowded with him, another patient, and the two nurses. The patients never wanted to make eye contact with him—they each seemed to be in an even worse state than Emmett. He felt himself getting there, though. Every seizure chipping away another ounce of his humanity.

A counter occupied the opposite side of the room. On one side was the bottle of liquid Emmett loathed, next to a dispenser for plastic cups mounted on the wall—the same kind they use in psych wards and retirement homes. Probably prisons, too. There was a sink with soap and a paper towel dispenser on one side and boxes of nitrile and latex gloves on the other. An array of papers from charts in which the nurses were making notes lay on the counter.

Emmett waited patiently, stealing glances at the elderly woman next to him, thinking that maybe he could spark up a conversation. Talking to her would make her less scary. He could just see himself being her age and still getting ECT … having gotten it three times a week for sixty years. She probably hadn't been getting it that long, but she had been dealing with whatever it was she was dealing with for a long, long time. Oh, the stories she could probably tell. If she hadn't forgotten all of them, that is.

The nurse finally turned around.

"All done?"

"Yeah, I wrote a few notes to clarify, as usual." And Emmett handed her the clipboard and pen.

She smiled and turned around to put the Beck test in his chart, then turned back and said, "I'm going to ask you three questions."

"Okie dokie."

"Now, what floor of the hospital are we on?"

"The first." This was a trick question; there was only one floor in Mountain Vista Hospital.

"Good. What city are we in?"

"Louisville." And he pronounced it correctly this time, "Lou-iss-ville." The first time he'd come here, he'd pronounced it incorrectly and the nurse took him for a non-native, mostly because of his mispronunciation of Louisville but also because of his slight Midwestern drawl. Emmett was a native, but he'd still inherited a Midwestern accent from Mom and Dad and the rest of his family who were all from the Midwest. That peculiar extension of the vowels of certain words. Dad liked to make fun of it; "shoo-es."

"Good. What day of the week is it?"

"Wednesday?" Emmett wasn't entirely sure. There were ECT days, non-ECT days, and weekends, when he got two days in a row of relief from the cycle.

They were the same basic questions each time. They weren't designed so much to test your awareness of where and when you were as they were designed to test your memory—to make sure the ECT wasn't causing too much brain damage.

"Excellent. I'll get your sodium citrate ready for you."

"Wonderful … Puke Juice" Emmett cringed.

The Puke Juice, so named by Emmett because it made him want to puke every time he drank it, was easily the worst part of ECT. The irony of this was not lost on Emmett. Here he was, having lost everything he'd worked so hard for in life—having lost his ability to paint and draw and fix computers and read and everything else he'd enjoyed doing—getting enough electricity shot through his brain that it gave him a seizure. He was twenty-four years old and Dad read him a bedtime story every night like he was a little kid again because they'd fried his brain to a crisp. And the part he hated the most was … drinking a stupid cup of liquid.

The nurse handed the cup to Emmett. He grimaced at her. "I really don't like this," he said.

"You need to drink it; it'll settle the acid in your stomach so you don't get sick from the anesthesia."

"I know, and I'm going to drink it. I just need to complain about it, is all. It helps," Emmett told her.

Mom and Dad had started carrying around plastic bags with paper towels stuck inside for easy clean up in their cars. Emmett had developed the habit of randomly puking. He had vomited all over the floor of the car, right onto his shoes, when they were headed home from an appointment with Dr. Bogsdaughter; he'd vomited all over the side of his bed onto a stack of magazines he'd been saving to read; he'd even had to stereotypically roll down the window to puke out into the middle of rush hour.

The nurse smiled. "I can understand that."

"Thanks," Emmett said as he pinched his nose in an attempt to not taste it, and swallowed the liquid in one gagging gulp. It was awful stuff, a combination of the worst medication he'd had to drink as a child and the sweetest citrus juice he'd ever tasted. Its aftertaste had faint traces of a vomit-like quality, though that might be psychological. He swallowed, reflexively shaking his head from side to side and letting out a desperate gasp for air.

The nurse turned around. "You all right?"

"Yeah, I just really hate that stuff."

"Yeah, it's no fun. But I'm glad you take it; it's important."

"I know. I don't mean to be a bad patient," said Emmett.

"Oh, you're not a bad patient," she said with a laugh.

Emmett smiled.

"We're almost ready for you." She handed Emmett a large hospital gown and a well-used plastic bag with Emmett S. written on it, along with a nitrile glove and a little cup with the suppository which had some lube squirted onto it. "Take off your shirt and shoes and remove anything you have around your wrists or neck, and put it all in the bag. We'll put it back on you when you're all finished."

Emmett thanked her and headed to the next door down the hall—the bathroom.

The heavy door closed and Emmett locked it. He took off his watch, his bracelet, and his miniature harmonica necklace and put them in the bag. He took his shirt off and put that into the bag, too. He undid the button and zipper of his jeans and pulled down his underwear. Putting the nitrile glove on his right hand, he squatted to insert the suppository. It always felt weird going in there, suctioned up suddenly and feeling awkward until it had disintegrated. But it helped with the nausea and he was willing to do just about anything to help with that.

Anything but the Puke Juice.

Pants returned to normal, he tugged his shoes off and stuck them in the bag before finally pulling the hospital gown over his head.

It was a poor fit. Every hospital gown he'd ever worn had been a poor fit. The best hospital clothes he'd worn were the papery pants and oversized shirt they made you wear in the psych ward. The socks they'd given you were comfortable too, with little grips on the bottom like those he'd worn as a preschooler.

Emmett opened the door to the bathroom and stepped into the largest of the rooms.

He stood for a few seconds, observing the unwelcoming, clinical character of the room. No windows. Several hospital beds, all made up neatly and awaiting their next patients, lined three walls. Nurses busied themselves with papers. The two microwaves, where they heated up the rice bags that gave the whole place its characteristic smell, were busily a-humming. He wondered how many microwaves they went through a year. The room was sparkling clean and overly bright; the florescent lights reflecting on the white surfaces made it a little overwhelming to look at. Another nurse noticed him, took his bag of possessions, and placed a stool at the foot of the bed so he could crawl up into it.

"How are you doing?" the nurse asked.

"Oh, I'm doing just fine. It's snowing something awful outside, though." Emmett replied. The weather; you could always talk about the weather without offending anyone—a lesson

Emmett had learned from Mom.

"Oh really? I haven't been outside since I got here at four."

"Yeah. I was surprised I was here in time."

"Especially coming all the way from Aurora. Can I get you anything? Another blanket perhaps?" Emmett had pulled up the blanket to his chin.

"Yes, please."

The nurse walked off and got another thin, washed-a-thousand-times blanket from a heated container. She draped it over Emmett and he thanked her.

"Should only be a few more minutes," she said as she went to the end of the bed and pulled Emmett's right sock off. She placed the sock over Emmett's left foot so it wouldn't get lost.

The nurse walked over to a microwave and retrieved two cloth rice bags, placing the bags over the insides of his elbows.

"Are they too hot?" she asked.

"No, they're just fine. Feel good, actually."

They chatted for a while about nothing in particular—the nurse was well-versed in asking people whose lives were falling apart nonoffensive questions about their lives—until they heard the door bang open as another nurse, Dr. Romero's assistant, rolled a patient out of the operating room where the ECT was actually performed.

"We're next," the nurse said as she got up and unlocked the wheels of Emmett's bed.

Foreboding washed over Emmett whenever he saw what the patients looked like as they were wheeled out. This patient's hair was disheveled and frizzy, the hissing of the oxygen mask strapped to her face only adding to her otherness. He barely recognized her as the elderly woman who'd been sitting next to him when he'd arrived.

The patients were rolled out with an alarming necessitousness, as though their very lives depended on getting them to the reclining chairs that made up the entirety of the far wall, curtains allowing privacy so the nurses could monitor them and get their clothes back on them. He never remembered that happening to him. He never remembered anything after Dr. Romero injected the drugs into his system; he just woke up hours later back at Mom and Dad's house, completely exhausted, nauseated and famished.

"Here we go," and the nurse started rolling Emmett into the last room. Emmett felt a whoosh of cool air as the nurse wheeled him purposefully into the operating room. She maneuvered the hospital bed into position expertly so Emmett's head was within easy reach of the seated Dr. Romero, and left the room.

"Hello, Emmett," Dr. Romero said.

"Hey, Dr. Romero," Emmett replied.

An MP3 player was attached to a pair of speakers in the corner of the room, the calming rhythm of '40s cowboy music emanating from them. It was the kind of music you'd want to fall asleep to. Appropriate, given who-knows-how-many people Dr. Romero put to sleep in this room on any given day. He had two MDs—he was a psychiatrist and an anesthesiologist.

"Let's see how you're doing," as the doctor looked over what Emmett assumed were the results of his Beck test. "Still with the exceptions?" Dr. Romero asked with a chuckle.

"Yeah. I fear it's just genetics. My dad would have to have exceptions, too. Members of the Selv family are oftentimes too literal for their own good. Or is it our own good?" and Emmett paused to consider the grammar of the sentence.

"Tell me about how you've been doing," Dr. Romero said, ignoring the question as he removed the rice bags and began feeling for a vein, slapping at the insides of Emmett's elbows with the back of his absurdly clean hand.

"I don't know, life's been hard, but I don't really feel any kind of pain; I don't feel much of anything. I'm more just numb. The memory issues have been getting worse and I've been having some pretty severe difficulty reading. Everything fell apart and I ended up here. I'm sure you hear the same story a lot. So ... "

The "so" at the end of the sentence must be left over from some residual Door County roots; it didn't mean anything, people quickly found out—Emmett wasn't about to say something else, he was just finishing his sentence. Didn't Dad say he had relatives in Door County? Where they end sentences with "'N' so"?

"I'm sorry to hear that. This is a tough thing you're going through," Dr. Romero said. "When this is done, you'll get your life back. Your memory will return to you and you'll get everything sorted out. ECT is a drastic measure, but it's important. You've been making slow but steady improvements since we switched to bilateral."

Emmett remembered the switch from unilateral to bilateral very well—that was when the real trouble had started. Unilateral only uses one of the paddles, bilateral uses both. Twice the damage, twice the improvement, apparently. He hadn't noticed any improvement, though.

Dr. Romero had called Emmett's depressive condition, his seeming need to complete suicide, an "existential imperative."

This existential imperative, like all existential imperatives, is an ultimatum. A message from his subconscious to the rest of his higher-functioning brain, that said, "either you stop your heart from beating or you stop torturing me." So many people chose to stop their hearts; Emmett was fortunate that he had people around him who wanted him to keep his heart beating.

His plans had been more half-assed than decisive at first. He'd be riding his bike and would toy with the notion of riding headlong into oncoming traffic. The idea would scare him more than anything else, and he'd call Lauren, desperate not to kill himself. Lauren, who'd leave class early to come and pick him up while he sat at an intersection, desperately trying to distract himself.

He'd been at an appointment with Lacey the first time he'd gotten a more elaborate idea for how to kill himself. He'd told her about the plot, and that's how he'd ended up at the hospital. That's how the whole thing had begun, with one single fucking hospitalization. One cry for help and his house of cards had begun crumbling.

Over time, he'd become more obsessed; he'd had to call Lauren more often; plans had become more concrete, more plausible. And as he become more depressed, the idea of ending his life became more and more attractive. The voices had joined in, suggesting different ways for him to kill himself. Cutting sweet potatoes and asparagus to roast for dinner, they would shout out how he could just stab himself in the stomach. It was honorable, they'd argue; seppuku—the ritualistic suicide that had claimed the lives of so many samurai over the centuries. Honorable or not, what had been preventing Emmett from slicing his belly open or keeping all 120 pills in his stomach until they disintegrated was the thought of going to hell.

It was law motivation. Something Mom scoffed at. But there was something about that fear—a permanent miscalculation that would see him eternally separated not only from God, but from everyone and everything he'd ever loved—that kept him from stepping over that edge.

Now, laying on this hospital bed, feeling the weight of the ECT paddles on his shoulders, wondering if Dr. Romero did that on purpose to make his patients more aware of the weight of their decisions, he was answering that ultimatum, that fateful existential imperative. His ECT doctor, the best in the country, could see improvement in him even if Emmett couldn't. Whether it was the results of the Beck test or some kind of professional sensitivity to depression developed from long years of practice, Emmett didn't know. But the thought that he was making progress tore at him.

On the one hand, it would be nice to get back to a normal life. Maybe Lauren would take him back and they'd share in the same joy they'd had in the first year of their relationship, before the hospitalizations, before the haloperidol that had removed Emmett from the world of the heartfelt. To return to painting and school and the work he enjoyed so much. He thought that maybe he would take Greg up on his offer to make him the co-owner of the Cap Hill store. He could manage the store however he wanted to, fix computers the way he wanted to, do things right and maybe be successful in spite of the hell he was currently going through.

On the other hand, he couldn't see any existence other than this one here, in the hospital bed with the rice bags and the two socks on one foot. Severe depression was making him think small; he couldn't see six inches in front of his nose. And in a way, he liked being sick; he liked the idea of being the sickest person anyone knew, of living on that extreme edge of unhealthiness that would make people respect him for everything he'd gone through.

Either way, he'd finally answered the ultimatum. And though Emmett had full authority to stop Dr. Romero from injecting the drugs into his veins and placing the paddles along his temples to administer a seizing dose of electricity, he knew it wasn't possible. He knew he had to finish answering the ultimatum.

Dr. Romero found a vein to put the IV in and was trying to pierce it, but the vein kept rolling around.

"Looks like we'll have to try the hand," Dr. Romero said after a couple tries. But he didn't have much luck with the hand either. "Okay," he said in a voice that didn't betray any sense of frustration, "we'll have to put it in the wrist. It'll be quite painful; that's a tiny vein."

"That's okay. Pain doesn't last forever."

"Indeed it doesn't," and Dr. Romero fished a much thinner IV needle into the tiny vein on Emmett's wrist.

Emmett breathed to calm himself as the doctor started placing electrode patches all over his chest and face.

Emmett wasn't allowed to have facial hair because the patches needed to be placed on his face. He hadn't been especially fond of facial hair to begin with—he just wasn't much of a shaver. But Emmett promised himself he was going to grow a beard when this was all finished. He played the Bomb the Music Industry! song "Beard of Defiance" in his head to keep his brain occupied.

The nurse at the foot of the bed placed an inflatable cuff around his naked ankle. This would allow them to monitor the seizure. Dr. Romero used a drug that stopped Emmett from thrashing around when he had his seizure, but the cuff blocked that drug from getting to his foot so they could record whatever it was they needed to know about the seizure.

You need to be brave, he told himself. You'll get through this. Remember what Lacey told you—you're tough as nails.

Dr. Romero talked to the nurse about the five thousand milligrams of caffeine plus various other drugs whose names Emmett quickly forgot because of what was coming next.

The nurse started inflating the cuff and Dr. Romero started pushing the plungers of the syringes down. Emmett felt the tiny vein in his wrist expand and burn; it was much more painful than when the IV was elsewhere. Emmett concentrated on the song playing in his head.

It was time.

"Off to sleep." Dr. Romero's voice was gentle and calming.

The edges of the world started to go black. Emmett looked up at the bright lights in the ceiling, trying his best to keep his eyes open as the blackness moved to engulf his vision, his eyelids becoming impossibly heavy.

But try as he may to resist, and he tried every single time, he drifted off gently into blackness, as though embracing death.

He'd insisted he be the one to make the soup. Maybe so he could tell Jayne he'd made it himself, maybe to prove to himself he could still cook, to prove to himself he was still capable of doing something useful. It'd been weeks since he'd done anything useful with himself, and it was driving him crazy. Finally, Emmett had the opportunity to not only get out of the house but also do something useful, something besides sitting in front of the TV watching the same movie on cable day after day after day after day. Not that he actually watched the movie; he just lay on the couch, staring at the wall with the movie on, willing time to go by faster, dead eyes focused on nothing in particular. Minutes seemed to pass with great reluctance as Emmett thought maybe he should take one of his more sedating antipsychotics so he could just sleep away the rest of the day.

Mom said he just needed time to recover, to rest. ECT was over and he'd been through a lot. The hum of electricity had barely faded. His brain needed to repair the damage; it'd been reset by the ECT and he needed to be patient. Yet he was restless. He wanted his life back; he wanted to get back to his friends, to school, to his job. He wanted Lauren back.

But that wasn't going to happen by whining about it. He was going to have to gain his life back inch by precious inch. And maybe it started by making this sweet potato curry and bringing it to Jayne, who'd just had her wisdom teeth removed.

It was simple enough—follow the directions on the recipe Mom had left out for him. He remembered enough about cooking to know to read the entire recipe before starting to cook, and he was glad that he had, proud of himself for remembering this little tidbit of information. The kitchen was filled with the sweet aroma of the curry as Emmett busied himself, tasting the curry and adding a particular spice, stirring it and letting it simmer, tasting it again—it needed to be perfect. Recipes were always inadequately spiced for Emmett, so he always ended up adding his own, often such a complex blend of spices that he had no idea what exactly he'd added. Or how much.

"Ready to go?" Mom asked as she came into the kitchen.

Emmett was ladling the sweet potato curry into takeout containers. "Just about," he told her.

He put lids on the containers, sealed them in plastic bags, put those in King Soopers grocery bags, and carefully placed them in his orange messenger bag for safe keeping. He checked to make sure nothing else was in the bag save for the bare necessities ("the simple bear necessities," he sang to himself)—his bike tools, his metallic water bottle, and his map of Denver—and slung the bag over one shoulder. He was RTG.

They went out into the garage and Emmett checked the air pressure of the tires of his bike before putting the bike into the back of Mom's van.

"Where do you want me to drop you off?" Mom asked as they pulled out of the garage.

"Lemme see here." Emmett checked his map and found about where Jayne's parents' house was and told Mom a good intersection for her to drop him off. He didn't want to be dropped off too close, but also not too far away. He didn't know how badly out of shape he was or how lost he could potentially get as the Great Shock had wiped out his mental map of Denver.

He directed Mom to the location where he wanted to be dropped off, and she pulled over. He hugged her, got out, and lifted the bike out of her car. This was the first time he'd ridden his bike since Lauren broke up with him in the middle of treatment—when he'd had his last bike accident and broke his collarbone. Understandably, Mom was a little nervous about letting him ride his bike all by himself and had told him she was just going to stay in the area, go grocery shopping or something, until he was done giving Jayne her post-surgery cheer-up. She wouldn't let him bike any longer than a mile. It made Emmett feel like a little kid again, but there was nothing he could do about it—Mom wouldn't take no for an answer and that was final.

His bike felt unfamiliar to him as he mounted it and began pedaling. It was a fixie, the pedals fixed to the motion of the wheel, so there was no coasting. It was great for riding on snow where there was an added feeling of connection with the road, but when you were unsure of yourself on a bike it could be disastrous. Emmett was feeling a bit unsure of himself.

Emmett found his bearings and was soon biking down what he knew was the correct street. He looked for the street number, but when he found it nothing looked right. It wasn't the same house he remembered from years ago, when he'd first met Jayne. He looked about the street; he saw Fourteen Twenty-Four, but it didn't look anything like what he remembered Jayne's parents' house looking like, or anything like what he remembered the neighborhood looking like. Did he get the street wrong?

Uh oh. Dread washed over him as he began thinking he'd seriously screwed up. Or maybe he was having a bit of an episode and he needed to have Mom pick him up immediately.

Then it dawned on him. Fourteen Twenty-Four was his old street number from when he lived in Cap Hill before the Great Shock. He needed to go a few blocks north, past Colfax.

Feeling better that it was just his electricity-addled brain and not some terrible misperception, he pedaled off a few blocks north, crossing Colfax, and came to a much more familiar street.

Inside Jayne's parents' house, memories came flooding back—of the first time he met her parents and how dang nice they were and how nonjudgmental they were that a high schooler was hanging out with their middle-school-aged daughter.

Jayne was in the living room, propped up in the recliner, blankets all around, a crowd of people Emmett didn't recognize standing around her. Her dad was in the kitchen, working on his computer.

"Hey Emmett, come here a sec."

"What's up?"

Jayne's dad reached out to shake Emmett's hand and Emmett shook it.

"How are you?" Jayne's dad asked.

"I'm doing just fine. Jayne's got quite the crowd in there."

"She sure does, all for her wisdom teeth. Sheesh."

Emmett laughed; it was as though her dad had read his mind.

"I just got a terabyte hard drive," Jayne's dad started.

"Nice … "

"Yeah … and it's just about full. And I'm thinking I need to back it up. Would you know of any way I could back it up cheaply?"

"Just about full?" Emmett was surprised.

"Yeah, downloading music."

Emmett couldn't imagine having a terabyte worth of music. But Jayne's dad, whose name he couldn't for the life of him remember, was quite the talented musician … so Emmett figured it only followed. Emmett explained the virtues of various backup schemes—desperately sorting through tidbits of information in his disorganized, damaged brain.

Jayne's dad got distracted by something else and wandered down into the basement, shaking Emmett's hand one last time before making himself scarce.

Jayne was still talking to her friends in the living room.

Emmett wasn't sure she knew he was there, so he popped his head into the living room and told her that he's there and that he's brought her some dinner.

"Emmett!" her voice hoarse. She told him to put the sweet potato curry in the fridge.

He went back into the kitchen and opened the fridge. It was packed with all kinds of food, mostly leftover takeout food containers. He rearranged some things, feeling self-conscious—as though he were violating some host/guest laws by doing so. He heard Jayne's visitors exiting via the front door, and he closed the door to the fridge and went to take a seat next to her.

"I'm so glad you came," Jayne said smiling. "How'd you get here?"

"My mom brought me most of the way and I rode my bike the rest of the way."

"You rode your bike?"

"Yup," Emmett said with a grin on his face. "It wasn't very far though. And I ended up at the wrong address. Stupid ECT messing with my sense of direction."

"It'll come back to you."

"So Dr. Romero has told me."

There was a pause, during which Jayne watched the TV for a little while and then turned it off.

"I'm so glad you came when you did; I was getting sick of them."

"Who were they?"

"Oh, just classmates."

"Fellow philosonerds?"

"Yeah," Jayne said, chuckling.

"They know Lauren?"

"Yeah, she hasn't stopped by though."

"Good. I was a little worried that she might stop by."

"Oh, I wouldn't let her. I would much rather have you stop by."

"I figured as much."

Emmett and Jayne talked for a little while longer. Thunderclouds rolled in and Jayne's dad offered to let Emmett stay the night. Emmett politely refused, saying that his mom was coming to pick him up. He didn't know if Jayne had told her dad about Emmett's illness, so he didn't know if he could talk about needing to take his pills or not.

Jayne went into the kitchen to warm up some curry and complimented Emmett's mom on her cooking; Emmett had a proud smirk on his face when he told her that he was the one who made it.

On the way home, Emmett reflected on how much it hurt him to see Jayne with her philosonerd friends. There she was, recuperating from something so mundane, so routine, that she would be recovered from it in no time, and she had a roomful of visitors to wish her well. Heck, even he had brought her dinner. But he'd been going through six months' worth of hell—six months of getting his head shocked to oblivion three times a week, and no one had come to visit him. Not even his own fiancée had visited him; he'd always had to go to her.

He figured it had something to do with familiarity. People knew what getting wisdom teeth removed was. Even if you hadn't had it done to you, you at least knew what it was. It was much harder to relate to ECT. Most people didn't even realize they still performed ECT. It was much harder to understand the Great Shock—the ridiculous headaches, the constant nausea, the huge blank spots in your memory, the lost skills, the lost everything. People just couldn't relate. And when people couldn't relate, when people couldn't understand—they were afraid. No wonder no one had come to visit him. They were afraid.

It was a lonely car ride back to Aurora. Back to eat dinner with Mom and Dad. Back to be read a bedtime story by Dad because Emmett couldn't read very well for himself. Back to sleep in Mom and Dad's bathroom as he'd been doing for the past several weeks because it was the only place he felt safe, the only place where he knew they wouldn't get him. Back to the loneliness and isolation. Back to the day-to-day, minute-to-minute survival and trying not to break down in tears as soon as Dad came home for lunch.

So much had been destroyed in the electrical haze of obedience to the existential imperative and ECT. Life seemed to be defined by loss and limitation, and every day there was less and less. Emmett didn't know how much longer he could hold on.

So it goes.

2012

Chapter One

"You seem tired today," Lacey says, as Emmett takes a seat across from her and sighs.

"I don't think tired even begins to describe it."

"How would you describe it?"

Emmett cocks his head to one side and briefly meets his therapist's gaze. Her eyes are soft and kind, inviting any kind of answer he might come up with. "It's like," and he pauses. "It's like I've been running on empty for so long, I have no concept of what full is even like."

Lacey smiles sadly and nods. Emmett looks at a sleeping Kerrin laying on his lap, wondering how she manages to get so comfy so quickly.

Emmett's eyes open in the midmorning light of his bedroom. He knows he's late for pills without even looking at his watch. The lightness of his head, that familiar faint electrical humming about his body—the precursors of psychosis—let him know he only has so much time before bad things happen.

Fumbling for his glasses, he hefts himself out of bed and pads over to his drawing table for his pills. There, he swallows the contents of a little Tupperware cup full of pills in one big gulp, followed by several swigs of water from his metal water bottle. Checking his watch, he sees it's 10:30 a.m. Only half an hour late, not too bad.

He's still so sleepy he could go back to bed, but he's had enough. The room is much too bright, the day much too advanced to go back to sleep. He hates missing out on the morning. And besides, thirty milligrams of dextroamphetamine is making its way to his bloodstream right now; that'll wake him up. He just has to wait about a half hour to forty-five minutes for it to kick in. The pills are greatly affected by minute variables in his body—his metabolism, his body temperature, his level of hydration; the amount of food in his system. So he's learned to accept the inherent ambiguity of taking pills, and when exactly they'll kick in.

While he's buttoning up his shirt and tying his boots, Kerrinpuppy is stirring underneath the covers. Emmett sees the blankets at the end of his cot rise and a bulge make its way up to the head of the bed. Then his dog's head pops out and she shakes off the covers, greeting him by hopping off the bed and going over to him for some head scratches. Emmett unlocks his bedroom door and they both head into the kitchen, Emmett to see about some coffee, and Kerrinpuppy because she knows they're going outside soon.

Outside, Kerrinpuppy is doing her usual patrol of the yard, searching for a place to pee and for squirrels to chase. Emmett has a mug of French-press coffee and a perfectly rolled cigarette. He lights the cigarette and takes a deep drag, blowing out the smoke with a kind of whistling exhale he's extremely self-conscious of. He takes his phone out of his pocket and notes the time. Mom should be calling soon, as she does every morning, to check up on him; to make sure he's alive and that he's taken his pills. If he doesn't pick up she'll just call again, and keep on calling until he answers—there's no way to avoid this daily conversation.

And sure enough, two or three minutes later, his phone is ringing, the caller ID announcing it's Mom. Emmett dutifully answers and Mom responds in a cheerful voice. She always sounds more cheerful than Emmett thinks the situation dictates. She tells him about her morning and what's going on at the school/church where she works. Emmett never really has much to add to the conversation—he hadn't done anything the night before and he's just woken up, so not much has happened to him yet.

Inevitably the conversation falls into silence; neither one has anything to say, and neither one wants to hang up. Emmett listens to Mom talk as people come into her office to ask her things; he waits patiently when her phone rings and she has to answer it. The staccato-touch typing of Mom at her keyboard gets him thinking he ought to go and see what's happening with his computer.

He gathers his tobacco and coffee mug and calls Kerrinpuppy to him, and they both head into the house. Inside, Emmett puts his wireless headset on, stops by the kitchen to replenish his coffee, and sits down at his desk.

Emmett's desk occupies the corner of the living room nearest his bedroom. It's a fairly sizable setup, two computers and five monitors—Bluebeard, the Mac Pro he'd bought off of his semi-abusive roommate (SAR) and named after a Kurt Vonnegut novel, with two monitors connected to it; and Slaughterhouse, the PC he'd built with his first Social Security Disability Income (SSDI) check and also named after a Kurt Vonnegut novel, with three monitors connected to it. It's an impressive setup, with screens stretching from one end of the U-shaped desk to the other.

Slaughterhouse runs Linux most of the time, allowing Emmett to tinker with it incessantly. Any object on the desktop— from the order of the items in the menus, to what icons are displayed, to how the fonts are rendered on the screen—can be tweaked, and Emmett spends much of his time tweaking and tinkering and sometimes breaking the system with his incessant need to customize it.

It's an exercise in pointlessness that's not lost on him. Here he is with all the computer equipment one could wish for, and he doesn't do anything with it other than make it look pretty. Occasionally he gets a computer to fix and the setup comes in handy, but that doesn't happen very often.

To people who don't know about Emmett's illness or his status of being on SSDI, he owns a computer repair business. It's not a complete fabrication: he has business cards he can hand out, Dad has made a website for the company, and Emmett does take on computers as they come to him. But it's certainly not enough business to make a living off of; it's just a clever little ruse so he doesn't have to deal with the stigma and shame of telling people he's on SSDI.

What he really wants to do is paint. His easel and taboret are ready to be used in his bedroom, and he has a complete set of oil paints and brushes just waiting for him. But all he can seem to bring himself to do is sit in front of his computer and tinker away while he and Mom sit silently on the phone, saying nothing.

Emmett's psychiatrist, Dr. Bogsdaughter, tells him that mental illness often robs people of motivation. Lacey, Emmett's therapist, tells him that he's made a huge adjustment by moving back to Denver; that he just needs to give it time and soon he'll find himself painting. Dad likes to say that it's not a big deal Emmett isn't painting, that he can paint whenever he wants, whenever the inspiration hits him. This statement in particular angers Emmett. He knows if he's really going to make a living (more an existential living than a financial one) at painting he's going to have to instill in himself the discipline to paint every day, whether he wants to or not.

Emmett can be so hard on himself. Too hard on himself, one of his therapists was fond of telling him. He'll cut slack for anyone but himself. If he's not perfect then he's a failure, and he hasn't been perfect in a long time, not since attending school in Minnesota, when paintings just flowed out of him, one right after the other.

But that was before getting diagnosed, when life was easy, when life wasn't so bleak, when he was capable of getting up at a decent time, when he could actually go to school, when life was wonderful and he hadn't a care in the world. Lately, it seems, all he has are cares and those cares are exhausting him.

The dextroamphetamine finally starts kicking in and Emmett feels his mind begin to pick up speed, his body ceasing to resist his every movement. He finds himself thankful for his pills and almost says as much to Mom, but chooses not to disrupt the calming, awkward silence. He remembers, in the early days, telling Dr. Bogsdaughter he didn't want to be medicated too much—just enough to take the edge off. He'd assumed his illness was the key to his creativity, that it was the only thing he had going for him as an artist. Now he realizes he makes art despite his illness and not because of it. That is, when he actually manages to stand in front of his easel and put brush to paint and paint to canvas.

Emmett gets up from his desk, the sounds of general office activity buzzing in his right ear.

Into his bedroom.

Dirty clothes into hamper.

Pill cups hidden away in this week's hiding place so SAR won't find them.

Make the bed and return to the living room to refill his coffee mug with the last of the French press and then back outside with his tobacco and mug, Kerrinpuppy excitedly at his heels, to smoke another cigarette.

It seems this is just how his life is going to go. Endless, silent phone calls with Mom, nothing to do all day but smoke cigarettes and drink coffee; nothing to return to but a computer that doesn't offer any hope of purpose.

He whittles away the last hour of the morning smoking cigarettes and enjoying the brisk soon-to-be-fall weather. The light had changed this past Saturday. Going from the yellow light of summer to the cooler blue light of fall and winter. Soon it will be too cold to let Kerrinpuppy outside. Soon it will be too cold for even Emmett to sit outside and enjoy cigarette after cigarette; and he imagines that's when things will get really hard.

Emmett remembers how last year at this time, while things had certainly been hard, they hadn't been so bleak. He'd had a goal; he'd just recovered from the worst of the Great Shock, from ECT, and he'd had hope for the future. He'd had what Dr. Romero had called an existential imperative to face down, and he'd been victorious. Faced with life or death, he'd chosen life and paid a dear price for it. The price of his memories, along with his cognitive abilities, and even with his ability to go to school or hold down a job. Was it worth it? We cling to life so strongly, so desperate to take in another breath. But we never stop to think about what continuing to breathe will entail—will it be a good life? Will it be fulfilling? Satisfying? Rewarding?

He doesn't have any goals in life, nothing he wants to work toward. Just a general feeling of having failed. Even the victory of having moved out of his parents' house seems hollow in the face of SAR's oftentimes unreasonable demands and accusations. Emmett sits and contemplates this, the sound of Mom's typing coming through the wireless headset in to his right ear. He could ask Mom what she thinks, but she's focused on work. She has a job where she's important to the success of something, where people count on her. She doesn't know what it's like to just be drifting along, a complete accident, not knowing where she's going to end up or if she's going to survive it. Mom hasn't traded substantial pieces of her identity for the privilege of being able to continue drawing breath. How could she identify?

Emmett is tired. The dextroamphetamine only does so much. It can help with physical fatigue, but not with mental fatigue. He longs for a vacation, for his psychiatrist to prescribe him a vacation-from-his-problems like Bob Wiley's had done for him, but it never works like it does in the movies. Your problems follow you around wherever you go, and there's no place on earth Emmett can go to escape whatever it is that's haunting him.

Chapter Two

"What do you look forward to most in the day?" Lacey asks.

"It's kinda funny, actually. Maybe a sign that I've regressed somehow. But it's my walk with my dad."

"Why would that be a regression?"

"Because I remember recovering from ECT and making every passing minute about surviving until he came home for lunch. If I could just make it until he came home, I would be all right."

Lacey and Emmett are silent for a minute. Then Lacey speaks: "Your dad means a lot to you."

Emmett smiles. "He means everything. He's my best friend in a lot of ways. I know he'll always be there for me, I know he'd do anything for me. And it's always been that way."

Kerrinpuppy squirms with excitement as Emmett tries to get her E.T. tee shirt on her. It was a gift from the neighbors upstairs. Originally for a toddler, it fits her perfectly and keeps her warm enough for days like this. She loves wearing clothes. Whenever Mom sews her a new neckerchief, Kerrinpuppy dances around and does twirls as Emmett shows it to her. He wouldn't normally be the kind of person to dress his dog up in clothes; but Kerrinpuppy, being part Italian greyhound, has next-to-no body fat and so needs the clothes to keep her warm throughout the autumn, winter, and early spring.

Emmett rolls two cigarettes, Kerrinpuppy stomping the floor with her two front paws, and puts one between his lips and the other in the fold of the purple knit cap he wears almost all the time as soon as the weather permits. He clips Kerrinpuppy's leash onto her and they head out the back door and into the alley, locking the door behind them.

They have a ten-minute walk ahead of them to O'Fallon near where Dad works. Emmett takes a somewhat circuitous route, which adds about two minutes to the travel time. It has traffic lights at every intersection, and it's important he have those. Emmett's brain has a tendency to delete oncoming cars from his vision, or else add cars that aren't there, so having the extra safety of the little white walking person is crucial to them making it to Dad safely.

Kerrinpuppy, as always, leads the way, straining against the leash until they get to the large apartment building along Twelfth where she's nice enough to go to the bathroom right in front of a trash can. Emmett picks it up with a bagged hand, ties the bag up, and tosses it into the can. He then grabs two extra poop bags from the dispenser near the trash can, because you can pretty much count on her pooping again

She strains on the leash less now that she's gone to the bathroom, and Emmett is more insistent that she walk next to him, gently yanking on the leash when she gets too far ahead to keep her in line. But she pulls herself to the absolute limit of both leash and collar as soon as they're halfway down the block and she sees Dad standing outside O'Fallon. By the time they reach him, she's up on her hind feet, her front paws reaching out for her grandpa.

Dad catches her paws and she lets out some happy barks, completely oblivious to Emmett's calls of "no jumping." Dad scratches her behind her ears and wherever else happens to be most accessible as she dances around, barely able to contain her excitement or know what to do with it. As she settles down, Dad turns his attention to Emmett.

"Hi, Emmett," he says, half chuckling. Dad never tires of

Kerrinpuppy's antics.

"Hey, homie," Emmett says, and Dad goes in to give Emmett a hug, but Emmett gives a slight shake of his head.

"Doing all right?" Dad's brow wrinkling like it always does when Emmett isn't feeling well.

"Oh, I've been better," Emmett says.

"Anything I can do?"

"I think I might just need something to eat."

"Can I get you something?" Dad asks, meaning one of the vegan/gluten-free cookies inside O'Fallon that Emmett can actually eat.

"Oh, I can get it."

"You sure?" Dad commenting more on the crowded nature of the restaurant during its lunchtime rush than on the state of Emmett's finances.

Emmett looks inside the restaurant's glass front, sees the crowd of people and knows Dad is right. "Yeah, you should probably get it."

"Be right back," and Dad heads inside.

Emmett takes a seat at one of the benches outside and reins Kerrinpuppy in on her leash so she's not standing in the middle of pedestrian traffic. He sighs, relights his cigarette, and pats his dog on her side to reassure himself.

He doesn't do well in crowds. Hasn't for a long time. He remembers that shortly after telling Marta Lee about his illness, she told him a story about how she'd recognized him from Tag and Rag Church among the throngs of students on campus and had gone up to introduce herself. But he'd just kept walking and didn't even acknowledge her presence when she'd gone up to him. It wasn't that he was being rude, it was just that he'd been dissociating—completely checked out of reality because of the stress of the crowds on campus. He considered it a credit to

Marta Lee's character that she didn't let that interaction with him sour her to him completely a number of years later when he'd started talking to her at a party.

He'd been a little manic at the party. Sitting near the back of the yard, listening to the band play and smoking cigarettes. He always seems to make friends when he's a little manic. A little mania can be a good thing; it makes him more sociable, more talkative, cleverer, funnier. Marta Lee had sat down next to him and Emmett had immediately engaged her. Somehow they'd gotten on the topic of doing breakup lines instead of pickup lines and Emmett had come up with one that had endeared him to Marta Lee instantly.

She'd laughed and laughed and told him they were going to be friends from then on. And sure enough, they'd exchanged phone numbers and were soon hanging out.

Emmett likes to think back on that story. It was an exciting time to be alive. He was fresh out of the worst of his recovery from ECT and he was finally getting out into the world, meeting new people, and rediscovering things. It seems a nostalgic time for him, when he was a completely different person—before the failure and the resignation that brought him to sign up for SSDI.

Dad, bearing two cookies, appears before a preoccupied, nostalgic Emmett.

"Why two?"

"I figured you could save one for later?"

"You're the best," Emmett says, trying to put a genuine smile behind it, not knowing if he's succeeded or not.

"No prob, Bob," Dad says, and he waits for Emmett to put his cigarette out in the ashtray next to the bench before handing him the cookies. Emmett puts one cookie in the pocket of his peacoat and takes hold of the other one.

They start walking, Emmett less successful at eating and

walking his dog than he is at smoking and walking his dog.

"Want me to take Kerrin?" Dad asks.

"That'd be great," Emmett says, and he hands control of the leash to Dad. "TOP Protocol successful," Emmett says as soon as Dad has the end of the leash securely in his hand.

"TOP Protocol?"

"Transfer Of the Pooch, remember?"

"Oh yes!" Dad says, chuckling. "I remember that one now."

They walk down Sherman, a quieter street than most of the other streets in Cap Hill. It helps save Dad's voice and allows Emmett to be less paranoid about all the cars. They take a left at 7th and walk toward Governor's Park.

"Don't you want to stop at the bench?" Dad asks as Emmett passes it.

"Not enough time, I don't think."

"We have a few minutes."

"You're the man with the atomic watch," Emmett says. And they turn around and sit at a bench at the corner of the park where three trees grow out of blank spots in the concrete.

They sit for a few minutes, Emmett lighting his second cigarette.

"Weren't you telling me that a cheap Timex watch keeps better time than a Rolex?" Dad says.

Emmett starts talking, then stops. Pauses. Then continues: "I suppose it depends on your perspective. Rolexes are automatic watches that don't have a battery, so they depend on you moving your hand to wind a spring to keep them going. I've read there are certain inefficiencies in the design that cause an automatic watch to either gain or lose time over a period of a few days or weeks. A cheap Timex watch is powered by a battery and so has a constant supply of power; it doesn't gain or lose time at nearly the rate an automatic watch does."

"Huh, interesting," Dad says.

"Yeah. I don't think you buy a Rolex for it to keep accurate time. Unless maybe you're sailing? I've read some references about them being really good while sailing. But basically, if you want the precise time, you get an atomic watch like you have or just rely on your phone."

"What about—" Dad begins.

"I can't really explain it better than that," Emmett interrupts, a bit exasperated. "I don't know much about how they work. I'm at the level where I probably know enough to be dangerous."

"Gotcha. Should we change the subject?"

"Yes, please."

There are a few moments of silence; not quite awkward, but as awkward as it gets between Emmett and his dad.

"I've been thinking about this article that Dr. Lazarus sent in his newsletter a week or so ago," Emmett finally says.

"Which one?"

"My naturopath."

"No. I meant, which article?"

"Oh, duh," Emmett says, laughing nervously. "It's about tree bathing."

"Tree bathing?"

"Yeah. It's this ancient Japanese practice. I forget the Japanese term for it. But it's basically about going out in a forest and meditating to improve your mental health."

"Interesting."

"Yeah," Emmett says, brightening up. "They did a controlled experiment where they had people with diagnosed depression go out into the forest and either meditate or just sit and do as they please. I think the control group stayed in the city. There might have been other groups that went out to parks in the city.

"Anyways. They discovered that it's actually somewhat beneficial in treating depression. You don't even necessarily have to meditate. It's like being around nature is a natural improvement for people with mental illness. Or at least depression. I've been thinking about how we come here almost every day and sit at this bench among these three trees and wondering if they have any benefit for me."

"Hmmm, I don't know. But that's very interesting."

"Totally."

Their few minutes are up. Dad hands Kerrinpuppy back to Emmett and they make the climb back up the hill, the hill that Cap Hill is ostensibly named after. Dad tells Emmett about what he's been up to at work, the projects he's been working on and so forth. But Emmett isn't really listening. He's thinking about the garden he'd had before he moved out of his parents' house. The garden that Marta Lee had helped him plant. They'd put so much work into that garden, and Emmett had just abandoned it when he got the opportunity to leave.

He really enjoys looking after plants, taking care of them, nurturing them. He's thinking that maybe he'll tell SAR he's going to plant a garden in the spring. They certainly have the perfect spot for it. The only problem is keeping the squirrels away from it and making sure the dogs (Kerrinpuppy as well as the upstairs neighbors' dogs) don't trample over it. It'd be quite the project, but maybe just the thing he needs to get him out of this funk.

Dr. Bogsdaughter has told him he needs long-term plans, short-term plans, and medium-term plans in order to be successful. He'd had that at one time—with the garden, with going to school, with looking forward to getting on SSDI and moving out of Aurora and back to Denver where his friends are. But he doesn't have that anymore. A man can't live without hope. Plans are hope, and he has no plans.

Chapter Three

"Have the voices been especially bad lately?"

"I don't know about 'especially bad,'" Emmett says. "I hear them almost constantly, a kind of din that's hard to imagine living without. They're appearing more frequently, but I'm getting better at dealing with them. I have this whole routine down.

"I have noticed, though, they get worse when my roommate comes home," Emmett adds.

"You guys have lost a lot in your relationship."

"Yeah … " Emmett says, drifting off.

◇◇◇

Emmett presses the disconnect button after saying goodbye to Mom, glad to be free from the relative oppression of the silence of their non-conversation. He can't help but feel a little more drifty than usual. It's back to the same miserable routine—dorking around on his computer and, every two hours, going outside with Kerrinpuppy to take his smoke break. He eventually brings his laptop outside and sits at the little table he's borrowed from Mom and Dad's house, to customize the Linux installation on his laptop, smoking cigarette after cigarette after cigarette.

He pictures himself in a rat race, only instead of being given a lane with a tube and a piece of cheese at the end, he's been given a rodent wheel. It doesn't matter how fast or how long he runs, he's never going to get anywhere.

Something is going to have to give. And soon.

Around the time the sun is setting, he bids adieu to the day with another cigarette and he and Kerrinpuppy head inside to see about dinner. He preheats the oven and takes a pot pie that Mom had made for him the previous Sunday out of the freezer.

SAR comes home from work and Emmett feels his heart constrict. They exchange a few pseudo pleasantries, SAR with his self-satisfied smile that either comes from arrogance or all the weed he smokes. Emmett is relieved when SAR heads into the basement.

The pot pie has to cook for a full hour, so Emmett sets about to do something productive with the time. He might, at the very least, work up an appetite. The kitchen is always a mess. It doesn't matter how often he does the dishes, how often he sweeps, how many times he asks his roommates to please help out with keeping their place looking neat—the place is always a disaster. And Emmett cannot abide messes. SAR has a tendency to leave tools and bike parts lying around the house for weeks on end—just sitting there accumulating dust and being a major eyesore for everyone else (and particularly for Emmett). Emmett is on the verge of just taking all of the miscellaneous crap SAR has left around the house and putting it in the basement where it belongs. But Emmett also knows that'll cause a major confrontation, and he isn't so sure he can handle that.

So he does the next best thing and goes into his room to find his iPod and earbuds and takes sixty milligrams of ziprasidone so he can spend the hour doing dishes. It's absurd to him the number of dishes that can accumulate in just a day where he lives. It seems as though SAR gets a new glass every time he goes to get a drink. SAR also insists on reusing plastic bags and will even retrieve Emmett's old plastic bags from the trash and put them in the pile to be washed. Which would be fine except SAR never washes them—they just pile up and eventually Emmett has to throw them away because they start smelling, and then he and SAR have another confrontation Emmett has no hope of winning.

The feeling of hot water running over Emmett's hands as he washes the dishes is excruciatingly uncomfortable. If he had the money, he'd just buy a dishwasher to save him the potential psychosis-inducing pain that doing dishes sometimes causes. But he wants a clean kitchen, and he seems to be the only one who actually wants a clean kitchen (or a clean anything), so it lands on him to do them.

The ziprasidone kicks in pretty quickly and makes the task more tolerable, though he knows he's going to pay for it tomorrow by sleeping in even later than normal. He just hopes he doesn't get so sleepy he passes out while his pot pie is cooking, and then it catches on fire.

Emmett would live on his own, but he doesn't really have the money for it. Of the $735 he makes on SSDI, $600 of it goes toward rent, and Mom and Dad help him out with a bit of extra spending money. He knows he'd feel guilty asking for more, and even a studio apartment would be more than he's paying right now.

He can't help but feel he's stuck in a losing situation. He knows he can tell SAR at any point that living on his own isn't working, that he can give a month's notice and move back home. But it's either live in this dilapidated house in the neighborhood he loves—close to his friends and coffee shops and bookstores and record shops—and be miserable, or live in a nice, homey house in Aurora with his parents—far away from anything he might want to do—and be miserable.

A lose-lose situation.

Emmett measures his worth in productivity, in things done, in things accomplished. He hasn't accomplished or done much of anything lately; his incessant and heedless tinkering with his computer, his running around in circles, head cut off chicken-like, is making for some pretty pointless days.

What can you do when you can't do anything? He can't go

and get a job. He can't go back to school. He can't seem to bring himself to paint. When he tries he just sits there and grows more and more anxious, until finally the sickened side of his brain takes over and he suffers all the more for it. He thought SSDI would be his salvation, but he's beginning to realize he's traded one kind of purgatory for another. A meaningless, a pointless existence no matter what he does, no matter where he lives. It's no longer a matter of where will he be most happy and fulfilled, but where will he be less miserable and alone.

Emmett sits at the kitchen table next to SAR's circular saw and eats his pot pie, a hum of violent, hissing energy all around him. Pulses of electricity shiver from the tip-top point of his head down to the ends of his toes.

"YOU WORTHLESS FUCK. YOU ABSOLUTE TOTAL WASTE-OF-SPACE, NIGGARDLY SCUM. WOULD YOU GET IT PREGNANT IF YOU FUCKED A DUCK?" *Myra says in a sort of sing-song voice. She repeats herself, and the whole cadre, the whole happy family of voices occupying the trammels of Emmett's brain, joins in.*

Emmett thinks about the sixty milligrams of ziprasidone he took an hour-and-fifteen minutes ago, how it should be preventing this kind of attack on his psyche. But he's also resigned to this kind of thing, because he'd have to medicate himself into a stupor to avoid Myra and her cadre of clowns from ever showing up.

Responding to the voices in his head, telling them to shut up and go about their business (do they have business other than to do this to him?), he heads into his room to get his medication out of its hiding place, finds the risperidone among the heap of other medicine bottles, and pops one in his mouth. He chases it down with a swig of water and returns to his pot pie.

The voices laugh at him.

"PATHETIC, SIMPLY PATHETIC. YOU'VE ALWAYS
BEEN THE BIGGEST FUCK-UP LOSER THE WORLD
HAS EVER KNOWN. PUT EVERYONE BACK IN AN
ELEMENTARY SCHOOL CLASSROOM AND YOU'D
BE THE FOURTH GRADER WHO HASN'T FIGURED
OUT HOW TO SHIT PROPERLY—ALWAYS WALKING
AROUND WITH SHIT STAINS ON THEIR PANTS,
ALWAYS LITERALLY SMELLING LIKE SHIT."

They drone on, but Emmett just turns up the Pixies album
he's listening to. Nearly full blast. It doesn't drown them out as
much as give him something else to concentrate on. He focuses
the entirety of his attention on the presence of the music, every
nuanced detail his speakers can manage to convey to him. With
monk-like intensity, he maintains that focus until the risperidone makes its way into his bloodstream, thankfully faster than
usual, and the voices fade away.

A rush of fatigue washes over him. But he has to make it
until 10:00 p.m. so he can take the rest of his pills. Checking his
watch, the fatigue seems insurmountable as he realizes he has
about two and a half hours to go.

He always seems to be waiting for something. Waiting for
Mom to call, waiting until it's time to walk with Dad, waiting
until his dinner is finished cooking, waiting until it's time to take
his pills. Waiting for such insubstantial things but expecting
them to change his life.

He decides to risk a nap. A more productive way of waiting
than just sitting and trying to stay away. Coffee won't help. Coffee hasn't woken him up in years. Only a power stimulant like
dextroamphetamine will wake him up, and taking any amount
of dextroamphetamine right now will throw him off of his al-
mighty schedule.

He sets his alarm for 9:50 p.m. and lays down on his bed.
Kerrinpuppy comes trotting over from her bed in the living

room and makes herself comfy in the crook of his arm. He falls asleep almost immediately.

Chapter Four

"Routine is very important; when I deviate from the routine I get sick." Emmett stares at the floor. More is coming; Lacey knows this and waits for him to speak again. Finally, he says, "Sometimes it's hard to stick to the routine."

"How so?"

"Fatigue, for one. If I have to medicate myself with a PRN—you know, pro re nata, "as necessary"— it can ruin my entire day. Sometimes I sleep right through my walk with my dad. I've never known tiredness like this. It's exhaustion without reprieve."

"That must be tough."

"I don't know," Emmett says, sighing and scratching his dog behind her ear. "I guess it just is what it is. Why call it tough when I can't do anything about it?"

Emmett wakes to the annoying rhythm of an alarm trying not to be an alarm. It's a jingling kind of meandering music that sets him to a sour mood almost immediately.

He taps at his phone until the noise stops and is frustrated to see that he's just snoozed the alarm, so he closes one eye to better see the screen and navigates through the menus to turn the alarm off for good. He has ten minutes until he has to take his pills.

He totters, more exhausted from his nap than refreshed, into the living room where the remains of his pot pie have been sitting there for past two hours. His inner mom tells him to just throw it away. So, into the garbage can it goes.

He washes the plate and fork under hot water with a bit of soap and puts them on the overflowing dish rack. The dishes he'd done earlier this evening are dry now, but he doesn't have the energy to put them away. Emmett must conserve his energy toward completing his nighttime routine.

Normally his brain is more active at night. The bipolar aspect of his illness wants to turn him into a night owl. But sixty milligrams of ziprasidone and one milligram of risperidone will make anyone tired. He wonders if he ought to skip his dose of risperidone for the evening since he took one only a little while ago. A serious decision only he can make, and a decision that could have serious consequences for tomorrow.

He opens the backdoor to make sure SAR isn't outside on a smoke break, closes the door, and locks it. SAR isn't too concerned about locking the doors. But then again, SAR doesn't have a bunch of expensive computer equipment laying about the house waiting to be stolen. SAR had recently taken everyone's front door key because he'd been locked out of the house and didn't want it to happen again. SAR's reaction was so irrational. It seemed obvious to Emmett that the solution to the problem was to take your freaking keys with you when you left the house. Instead, SAR had compromised the security of the house by insisting it be left unlocked.

Going through the living room, Emmett turns off all of the lights save one, so people can navigate without bumping into stuff, and switches off the monitors of his computers. He's just trying to take up time until his ten minutes are up and it's time to take his pills. It seems to him that eating up this ten minutes is about as difficult as eating up the two and a half hours would have been, had he not decided to take a nap.

Finally, his phone goes off. He feels it vibrate and hears the telltale beep of a calendar notification, and he knows it's 10:00 p.m.

Into his bedroom, he closes the door and locks it. Taking the plastic bag full of pill bottles out of its hiding place and placing it on his drawing table, he gathers up his pill containers and takes a bottle of medication out of the bag and dispenses the appropriate amount into the appropriate container. There are two containers—one for his a.m. pills and one for his p.m. pills. He'll take the p.m. pills right now so they just go into a plastic cup, but the a.m. pills go into a tiny plastic container, mostly so Kerrinpuppy doesn't accidentally get into them. Emmett has no idea what would happen to her if she were to eat any of the pills, but he doesn't want to find out.

At the sound of the pills clinking in their containers, Kerrinpuppy perks up from the little nest she's made at the foot of the cot. She gets down and does a seesaw stretch, first the front legs and then the back legs, getting them limber for their foray outside.

Emmett wasn't too sure if they were actually going to go outside or not, but he figures they might as well. She probably needs to go potty and it's best to stick with routine. He downs his pills with a few slushes of water and seals the container for the a.m. pills. Then out with the cardboard tin of tobacco to roll a cigarette, so they can go outside.

Kerrinpuppy rushes outside past Emmett, committed to her usual patrol as Emmett sits on the front porch and lights his cigarette. He only gets a few drags in before the fatigue becomes overwhelming. Extinguishing his cigarette in the ashtray, he's afraid he sounds like a drunk when he calls his Little Girl back.

Inside, Emmett doesn't even manage to get his boots off or plug his phone in. He throws his peacoat over the rocking chair in the corner of the room and collapses onto his cot. He's fast asleep before Kerrinpuppy can even come and hop up to keep him company.

He'll wake up sometime near morning and turn off his bedroom lights, undress, and get into bed properly. All the while thinking it's amazing how doing so little with his day can make him so exhausted.

And his only response to such thoughts is the same response Kurt Vonnegut had to the deaths of so many people in Slaughterhouse Five:

"So it goes."

Chapter Five

"Emmett," Lacey begins. "It's important to remember that what you need most in your life is people who you can depend on."

"That makes sense. I think my life makes me more prone to depending on people, truly depending on people, more than the average person."

"Well, the other thing to consider is how easy they are to read."

"I'm not sure I understand," Emmett says, adjusting himself in his chair and causing Kerrinpuppy to squirm around a bit as she tries to sleep on his lap.

"If you can't read someone, you don't know how they're going to act—"

"And they become unpredictable, which feeds the paranoia and delusion factory."

"Exactly," Lacey says, and she leans back on her chair and they enjoy a pleasant silence.

Emmett fills the plastic bag with tobacco from his cardboard tin, then he checks to make sure he has everything: papers; iPod; earbuds; something to read; emergency daily doses of medication; extra risperidone, ziprasidone, and alprazolam in case he gets sick; and Kerrinpuppy's Little Red Riding Hood coat. He packs it all in his bag and turns his attention to Kerrinpuppy.

Kerrinpuppy isn't quite sure what's going on. She's learned by now to not necessarily get excited when Emmett starts packing his bag; it's not a sure bet she'll be coming along. Though it's curious that he'd put her giraffe costume on her. Something must be up.

She stares at Emmett as he putters about their bedroom from her post on their cot, a quizzical look on her face. That is until he goes and gets her leash. Then she knows that they're going for a walk.

It's Halloween, and Dad is particularly nervous about Emmett walking the half hour or so to Jayne and Rob's place by himself after the sun has set, mentioning something about people being out in costumes and how it could be upsetting. Emmett would like to think he has a bit more sense than that—he knows ahead of time it's Halloween and therefore he's more likely to run into people dressed up, and besides, there's an enormous difference between the things he hallucinates and some random bro dressed up in a Halloween costume he spent fifteen minutes making. But, just to be safe, Emmett took a small pre-emptive dose of ziprasidone to combat the inevitable heebie-jeebies from walking outside after dark and a smattering of dextroamphetamine to combat the inevitable sleepiness caused by the ziprasidone.

Everything is just a chemical balance, and Emmett just needs to be a bit more proactive in keeping his own chemicals balanced. Other people have it easy—their brains keep the balance by themselves. They don't have to think about when they're coming down off their medication or how much they ought to take to make it through a particular event. Such a carefree life it must be. Emmett's life is a constant assessment of the state of his mind. He tries to stay as many steps ahead of his brain as possible, but it doesn't always work.

Kerrinpuppy is festive enough in her giraffe costume. It's one of the first things Mom had made for her, before she realized how easily something that's simply tied to her will fall off. Eventually, Emmett stops and takes the giraffe costume off and puts her Little Red Riding Hood coat (another Mom original) on her, a process which takes a few minutes but they have plenty of time.

Dr. Dog's album We All Belong is playing through Emmett's

new earbuds. Lately, he's been discovering the beauty of high-fidelity music, and the earbuds (technically in-ear monitors) were a killer deal he'd found on Amazon. They've changed his outlook on certain songs. He's been hearing things in the music he's never heard through the speakers on his stereo, or through his larger headphones. It's amazing such little things could produce such large sound, and Emmett suspects he's been losing weight with all of the extra walking he's been doing just to have an excuse to listen to his new in-ear monitors.

He checks his watch and slows his pace a bit; he wants to make it to their house around the time the album finishes, which should make him just a couple minutes earlier than the agreed-upon time. He stops to roll a cigarette near the Safeway (the un-Safeway, as the new inhabitants of the recently gentrified Five Points are fond of calling it) and sits at the bus stop to smoke it. No one bothers him as he sits there. Emmett prides himself on always arriving on time; it's a dependability thing and he figures it's good for his mental health. If he's late, and someone knows he's always on time, then help can come sooner. He knows with Jayne it's best to be a little late, or that it would've been better to text ahead of time and ask what time they ought to meet. But they'd said 6:00 p.m. and it was in his phone as 6:00 p.m., so that's when he's going to arrive.

And sure enough, half a block away from Jayne and Rob's house, Emmett's phone vibrates in his pocket.

JAYNE:
I'm running a bit late, can I come pick you up?

Emmett shakes his head and smiles to himself, a smile of half amusement, half disbelief. It's like she doesn't know him at all. Doesn't she realize he has to walk there?

EMMETT:

Well, I'm basically at your house

Emmett leaves the period off his sentence because periods at the end of text messages always seem to convey a finality that borders on rudeness.

JAYNE:

Oh! Sorry, didn't realize you'd already be there or had even left

EMMETT:

Yeah. That whole walking thing :)

And Emmett is thinking to himself that of course he'd already be there, that he and Jayne had known each other for ten years, and while he had the really good excuse of getting his brain fried with ECT to make him forget most of their relationship, she doesn't have such an excuse.

JAYNE:

Duh! Sorry, my mind is a bit frazzled right now. Long day. I think Rob should be home soon, sorry!

EMMETT:

No worries. As long as I've got music and tobacco I'm good to wait for a while :)

He is, however, a little worried about Kerrinpuppy. It's getting colder and colder and she doesn't do particularly well in the cold. That whole lack-of-body-fat thing. She has her coat on, but that isn't enough if she isn't moving around. Rob isn't home yet, so Emmett rolls another cigarette, selects Cheeky's Choke on a Cheeseburger EP, and then texts Rob and Jayne to let them know he's going for a walk around the block. By the time he gets back to their front stoop, shortly after the EP has ended, his phone vibrates with a message from Jayne saying she's back home.

"I'm sorry, I just let time get past me," Jayne says, going in to give Emmett a hug before he can even get his coat off. "One minute it was like three and the next it was past time for me to go and get groceries."

"No worries, it was fun to hang out on a different porch for a change," Emmett says. It always amazes him how tiny Jayne is. Her hugs always seem so half-hearted, more a formality than an exchange of warmth.

"The good thing, though, is that I got the stuff we'll need for Rob's costume."

"Oh good," Emmett says, his Midwestern drawl showing through particularly well. "What are we making him into again?"

"The bear car from The Simpsons."

"Oh … I'm not familiar."

"Lemme see if I can find it." And Jayne gets her phone from the kitchen table and taps at it almost furiously. Soon Emmett is looking at an animated GIF of one of the earlier episodes of The Simpsons with a pink clown car driven by a bear. Emmett is supposed to recreate it using a cardboard box and some markers. And the party is tonight, so he has to do it all in one sitting.

"It's going to take quite a while to get it done with just markers. I shoulda brought some acrylic paint or something."

"It doesn't have to perfect," Jayne says, taking the phone from Emmett and tapping away at it again.

Emmett scratches his head, "Yeah. I know. It's just the whole perfectionist thing."

Jayne laughs and asks him if he wants a beer.

Emmett doesn't get beer too often. There's only one kind of gluten-free beer that's any good, but it's about $10 a pint at the liquor store, so he rarely if ever gets it. But it's this exact kind of beer that Jayne has, so Emmett can't turn down such a treat.

She takes down a glass and opens up the pint bottle of beer. She pours some out for Emmett and sets it on the kitchen table where Emmett is sitting; he takes a modest pull of the beer and wipes the foam off his mustache with his sleeve. He doesn't really drink very much or very often. One, he can't afford the only gluten-free beer he really likes, and two, a drunk Emmett isn't very fun; usually psychotic and difficult to manage. The last thing he wants is to be psychotic in front of Jayne, so he won't be drinking very much tonight.

Jayne starts pulling pots and pans down from the cupboards and Emmett gets up to help. He very much enjoys cooking but it's not the same when you're just cooking for one person. Cooking ought to be a communal activity—something done for a group of people. He misses the days when he'd have his ex-fiancée, Lauren, and their friend Maria over for brunch on Sunday mornings. He rarely goes over to people's houses for dinner. Given his food allergies, he doesn't trust many people to cook for him. But Jayne has the same restrictions he has—no dairy, no gluten—and while she isn't actually allergic to high-fructose corn syrup, he knows she doesn't keep it around. He knows he can comfortably eat there without fearing for his life. They've both recently decided to eat meat again, something which Jayne had actually convinced him to do; why restrict yourself even further by not eating meat? And to this end, Emmett's contribution to tonight's meal is some lengths of buffalo sausage.

Walking into the Whole Foods down the street to buy the sausage had been an ordeal. Grocery stores were probably among the top three worst places he could go. No one in the grocery store actually wants to be there, so Emmett just feeds off the energy of impatience, frustration, and the desire to just get home already. There's the harsh lighting, the constant beeping of the cashiers ringing up purchases, and then the sheer number of food choices—enough to overwhelm him with the magnitude of things he could possibly get to feed himself. So he doesn't go into grocery stores too often; Mom does his grocery shopping for him and it's a huge burden off of him.

But there were occasions, such as this impromptu Halloween meal/art party (which was probably going to be a one-man art party featuring only Emmett), where he had to go to the grocery store himself. He'd taken a small dose of ziprasidone, waited for it kick in, put Kerrinpuppy's service dog vest on her, told her to be a good girl, and prayed that nothing bad would happen while they were in the store. He'd walked the block and a half to the grocery store about an hour before he was supposed to walk with Dad. He figured if he made it close enough to his walk with Dad, then he could get access to help if he needed it without disrupting Dad's work schedule too much, though he knew Dad would take off of work at any time to come help him.

He'd made a beeline for the meat counter, ordered his sausage, taken it to the checkout line, paid for it, and was safely outside within five minutes. Then he'd gone home and taken a nap, nearly missing the time when he had to leave to go and meet Dad for their walk.

Emmett suspects that Jayne doesn't fully appreciate the mental work he's put into getting the sausage. In many ways, she just doesn't seem to understand the limitations his illness puts on him. She oftentimes compares herself to him—their living situation, the circumstances they find themselves in. While the facts of their living situations are similar—Emmett gets his rent and student loans paid for without working just like Jayne—there's a substantial difference. Jayne is perfectly healthy, perfectly capable. Of course, it's possible she's just trying to make him feel better about something he doesn't really need to feel better about. Or maybe she detects in him something he doesn't know about himself, a conflict or a neurosis that's plainly visible to everyone but him.

The front door swings open and Rob enters the apartment carrying a large cardboard box he's swiped from work. Kerrin and Resi (Jayne and Rob's dog) go over to greet him, Resi obviously much more enthusiastic about seeing him than Kerrin-puppy is. Rob stoops down and gives both dogs scratches and throws a nearby toy out for them to chase and fight over so he has room to put the box down.

"Hey guys," Rob says, "something sure smells good."

"Fennel," Emmett says, from his station at the stove where he's sautéing vegetables. "The best smelling food in the world."

"I believe it," and Rob goes into the bathroom to wash up for dinner.

Jayne combines the vegetables with the rice and buffalo sausage and they all sit down to eat.

"Is this going to be enough?" Rob asks.

"It'll be plenty," Jayne assures him.

Rob grabs plates for everyone and insists Emmett go first. "Do you want a beer?" he asks Emmett.

"Oh, no thanks. I think I've had enough for tonight."

"Coffee?"

"I don't think I've ever turned down coffee in my life and I'm not about to start now."

"Wonderful," and Rob sets about to make a French press.

Everyone gets to eating quickly and finishes by the time the coffee is ready; Jayne tells Rob and Emmett to split seconds. It wasn't really enough food and it occurs to Emmett that there's a fundamental difference between how his mom cooks and how Jayne cooks—Mom always makes way too much food and Jayne never seems to make enough. He usually finds himself having to eat again after he gets home from dinner with Rob and Jayne, though it's gotten better since the food has started to include meat.

Rob pours Emmett's coffee and offers him coconut milk creamer and sugar, then he feeds the dogs and washes the dishes.

"Show me some more pictures of this car," Emmett says, rolling a cigarette, taking extra care so as to not spill any tobacco on their nicely swept floor. "Well, actually, show me when we get back inside. That is if you want to come with me."

"Sure," Jayne says almost defensively, as though she's offended Emmett would think she wouldn't want to go outside and keep him company while he smoked.

"Well come on outside then," Emmett says as he gets up and goes over to put his coat on.

Emmett and Jayne head outside, Emmett in a heavy, U.S. Navy-issue peacoat he'd gotten from Dad at some point and Jayne in this dinky-looking fleece jacket. It looks like the kind of jacket you'd wear in the springtime, not on a night like this when the wind is blowing. But Jayne insists it keeps her plenty warm, that it's a good jacket, so Emmett tries not to press the matter. Though it bothers him to know how Jayne will go back inside before he's taken three drags from his cigarette because she's cold. And it bothers him that it bothers him; it's such a petty matter, why make it such a big deal?

Jayne taps away at the screen of her phone. The flurry of thumbs on the glass screen suggests to Emmett a kind of desperation, but he knows she's just a fast typist.

The dogs are out, sniffing around—Kerrinpuppy curious about the dismantled and harvested vegetable garden that one of Jayne's neighbors keeps, and Resi exploring the far end of yard.

Emmett is about to say something when Jayne announces that it's too cold outside and she's going back inside.

How typical, Emmett thinks. A $200 jacket that doesn't even keep you warm during the fall. He doesn't know if it's the fact that it's a $200 jacket that's failed to keep her warm or Jayne's refusal to be even mildly uncomfortable in keeping him company, but something about it bothers him. He distracts himself by taking out his own phone and looking at Facebook for a while, trying to keep one eye on the dogs so they don't discover the hole in the fence where they can get out into the alley. The worst thing in the world would be to lose Kerrinpuppy like that.

He heads over to the back of the yard to deposit what's left of his cigarette in the dumpster, calling the dogs to him, amazed that Resi actually listens to him. Jayne says Resi isn't the kind of dog to listen, blaming it on her being a stubborn breed of dog, but Emmett thinks part of it (even most of it) is because they don't seem to spend a lot of time trying to train her. They got her shortly after Emmett got Kerrin and he suspects she's more a "me-too" dog than anything else.

It's yet another thing that bothers him, and another thing that bothers him because it bothers him. He shakes his head to remove the sticky thought.

"Okay," Emmett says, coming in from the cold and depositing his coat on the back of a chair. "Let's see to this bear clown-car thing."

Jayne is over in the living room tapping away at her phone. Emmett walks in and she tells him "just a sec," and goes back to her phone. She pulls her laptop out from the bottom shelf of the coffee table and opens it. Her fingers are even more of a blur than they are on her phone—in no time at all Emmett is looking at a Google Images page full of pictures of the car in question. Emmett can type about eighty or ninety words per minute when he really gets going, when he knows exactly what he's saying. But Jayne is well over a hundred or more. Watching the veritable virtuoso yet chaotic-like approach Jayne has toward typing, he can see why she calls typing her best class in middle school.

The design is simple enough and shouldn't be too hard. He was thinking he'd have to fill in the entire cardboard box with color, but it looks like he can get away with just doing a line drawing and some clever cutting. Still, it would be nice if he'd brought along some acrylic paint—that would really take it to the next level and it'd dry quickly enough Rob would still be able to wear it. Emmett had packed everything he'd need in case of an emergency, but neglected the things he needed for the whole reason he came over in the first place: art supplies.

Emmett mumbles to himself, Jayne ignoring him because she knows the mumbles aren't directed at anyone.

"Okie dokie," he finally says. "Where dem markers?"

Jayne produces a Safeway bag full of the supplies she'd thought they'd need. It includes a package of assorted markers, an eight-color set of crayons, and a pair of scissors. The markers will be the most useful but there's only one of each color and Emmett knows he'll be using them up—probably better to stick with crayons.

"Do you have more crayons? Perhaps relics of a bygone coloring era?" Emmett asks.

Jayne gets up while Emmett has Rob trying on the box to get a sense of the scale, and returns a few minutes later with a much larger box of crayons—most of them in pretty good condition.

"This should be just about perfect," Emmett says. And he sets about working, he and Jayne talking back and forth about just about anything. Emmett tells her stories she's probably heard a million times before, but he likes telling stories. He figures if he'd been in a tribe a thousand years ago, not only would he be the shaman but he'd be the storyteller. If he's comfortable with a person he can keep them occupied for hours, and indeed that's how it often goes when he first meets someone.

He finally finishes, his hand aching from being used so much, and his back and knees aching from being in a crouching position for so long. He should have done this at the kitchen table; he's getting much too old for this.

"Wanna try it on?" Emmett asks Rob. And Rob gets up from the couch. Emmett helps him fit the box over his head and he carefully clips the suspenders to the cardboard box.

Rob goes over to the mirror and admires himself, a grin spreading across his face. "This is perfect," he says. "Thanks so much."

"My pleasure, sir." Emmett says. All Emmett can see are the flaws in the work—places where he'd started making the wrong line and had had to correct it, the parts where the color changed because he'd run out of a particular color. But for a quick job, ninety minutes' worth of work, it's pretty darn good. The bear with the bow tie in the front seat is especially endearing. "I've gotta have a smoke though, I think I'm past due for my mandatory two-hour-break smoke."

Jayne looks up at him. She's curled up in a blanket with her laptop. Emmett smiles at her—he hopes a warm and endearing smile, a smile that says he understands—and goes into the kitchen to roll his cigarette. Kerrinpuppy is there as soon as he gets a paper out of the package, tail wagging, waiting to go outside; and Resi is right behind, wanting to know what's up. People may not be reliable, but dogs are loyal almost beyond measure.

Emmett heads outside for one last smoke, keeping track of the dogs as they meander through the yard, checking his phone for interesting activity on Facebook, and feeling the chill of the night air, feeling more alive than he has in weeks—maybe because he's actually created something.

When he gets back inside, Jayne and Rob have changed into

their Halloween costumes. A glittery, golden leotard, tights, and a fake mustache have turned Jayne into a bearded lady and Rob is ready with a brown t-shirt, little fez, and his box which will turn him into the clown car from The Simpsons.

Jayne offers to reheat Emmett's coffee. She takes the mug, fills it with the rest of the coffee from the French press, and puts it in the microwave. She comes back a little while later with a steaming mug of coffee.

"Isn't science wonderful?" Emmett says, taking the mug.

"Science!" Jayne says, holding up her beer bottle triumphantly. Emmett tells her to hold that pose so he can take a picture, and he makes it the lock screen of his phone.

"Thanks for doing such a good job on the car," Rob says.

"No prob, Bob," Emmett says, channeling a Dad-ism. "It was fun. I haven't really done anything artistic lately so it was a good change of pace."

"Really?" Jayne says.

"Yep. Been going through a bit of a slump lately. Especially since changing bedrooms."

"Hmmm. That's odd. I thought you said the new place would be better for painting."

"I thought that too, but I'm also a very environmentally conscious artist."

Rob and Jayne both laugh.

Emmett smiles. "Dumb way to put it. What I mean is that I'm like hypersensitive to the environment where I paint. If I'm not comfortable in a space then I don't paint, and there's nothing I can do to force it."

"That's really interesting," Rob says.

"Yeah. I've kinda always been that way, I think. I need to have the appropriate environment to do just about anything. Get me the wrong kind of kitchen and I won't cook, get me the wrong kind of computer and I won't be interested in it. I'm just picayune."

"I'm sure it'll just take a bit of time to get used to," Jayne says.

"Hopefully," Emmett says. Then he adds, almost as an afterthought, "Probably."

There's a silence.

"Sorry. Didn't mean to kill the mood so much. It's just been a weight on my mind lately," Emmett says.

"No worries."

Emmett looks at his watch. It's 9:30 p.m., half an hour before pills. It'll take him longer than that to walk home. He has his emergency pills with him, but he'd rather not take them. It's always best to be at home where he can do his bedtime routine and stick to his schedule. If there's one thing that'd been drilled into him early on, it was sticking to the freaking schedule. "I should probably get going," he says. "It's almost ten, almost pill time."

"Really?" Jayne says.

"Yep."

"I had no idea."

"They make these things called clocks … " Emmett begins with a grin, and Jayne makes a face at him. "Do you suppose I could trouble y'all for a ride home, though? I don't want to be walking while drugs are kickin' in. Plus, there's the whole people walking about in strange costumes who are probably inebriated by now—tends to play tricks on the guy with the psychotic disorder."

"Sure thing," Rob says.

Emmett gets Kerrinpuppy ready and gives Jayne a goodbye hug then says goodbye to Resi, scratching her on the top of her head.

As he and Rob are heading out to the car, Jayne stops them and says, "I love you both," and then pauses, refusing to make eye contact with either Rob or Emmett before continuing: "In different ways."

"I love you too," Emmett replies. It was the first time either of them had ever said anything like that to each other.

On the ride home. Making idle chitchat with Rob. Getting his pills ready. Having his post-pills smoke. Trying to read before bed. Giving up and turning off the light and closing his eyes, Emmett is thinking about what Jayne had said and what she meant by it. And how she meant it. Why the pause? Was she hiding something? Had his paranoia factory just shifted into overdrive? There was something in the pause, in the refusal to make eye contact, that spoke of deeper, more substantial things.

He wouldn't be able to get the questions out of his mind. He'd have a quiet moment to himself and then the statement would pop into his head. He couldn't draw a bead on it, couldn't decipher its hidden meaning or if it even had a hidden meaning. What did she really mean? It was the first time she'd said something like that. What does it mean to be loved by Jayne?

2013

Chapter Six

"It just pisses me off," Emmett says, his words biting the air.

"Why does it piss you off?" Lacey says, her voice calm and even.

"I think it's because I've explained to my dad many times before that if you want to make a living at being an artist then you have to work at it every day, whether 'the spirit moves you' or not," Emmett says, using sarcastic air quotes. "It pisses me off because I come to him for help and he just placates me, he treats me like some little child—I'm a fully grown adult, I should have my shit together, and here I can't even do what's apparently my favorite thing in the world to do."

"Emmett, I need you to take a deep breath in through your nose and exhale slowly through your mouth," Lacey says.

Emmett obeys and he feels himself calming. He does it again, breathing with Lacey as he tries to get his racing thoughts back under control.

"Better?"

The place is small, only 350 square feet. And that includes the closet-of-a-kitchen and his unnecessarily spacious bathroom. Emmett feels as though they really should swap the two—make the kitchen the bathroom and the bathroom the kitchen. Maybe then the fridge would fit in the kitchen instead of hanging out into the living room.

But it's home, and it's freedom from SAR. Emmett doesn't have to worry about construction tools and bike parts and all sorts of trash accumulating throughout the house—every mess will be his mess and his mess alone. He doesn't have to worry about SAR disciplining Kerrinpuppy in front of him, or being called in the middle of the having dinner with a friend because

SAR wants to watch Breaking Bad and the Internet isn't working. Emmett is free, and he finds himself wondering why he didn't do this sooner; probably because SAR always cleaned up the house and made life so much more pleasant for him around the time the lease was due to be signed.

But it's also so small, smaller than the bedroom he'd had at his old place. Emmett tells himself it's okay though, there's a closet large enough he can hide his computer stuff in it. Not both computers, but one of them. Not all five monitors, but two of them. It's been the perfect opportunity to downsize on some of the seemingly useful but unnecessary computer stuff he's accumulated.

It's a chance to reduce the clutter in his life and live more minimally.

Emmett watches Jayne sitting at his workbench, trying for fifteen minutes to draw the plant he'd set in front of her. Seeing her sit there, so focused on the task at hand, he begins to see that the place might have some potential. With a little tweaking, he could turn this apartment into a home.

Jayne has wanted to have a drawing lesson from Emmett since the end of last year. Emmett had even made a list of drawing and painting supplies she'd need in order to take up art has a hobby, and he'd written a small booklet on the basics of painting. She'd gotten the painting supplies for Christmas and since then they'd just been sitting there, unused.

Emmett blamed the presence of SAR—he made Jayne uncomfortable. And Emmett couldn't blame her; SAR always said lewd things about her after she came over that made his skin crawl. Emmett didn't want Jayne around SAR anymore than Jayne wanted to be around SAR, so the drawing lesson had been put off and put off until finally Emmett was free from SAR's clutches and the drawing lesson could happen. He's shown her the basics—how to measure and judge the angle of something using her pencil, and how to sit far enough away from what she's drawing that she can do those things accurately—but other than that she's on her own. He wants to see how much of a knack she has for it. He won't know what she needs to be taught until he knows what areas she needs to improve upon.

The workbench juts out into the room directly behind the back of the couch, effectively cutting an already tiny room in half, and turning the apartment into an obstacle course of all of his stuff which must be navigated with deftness in order to get anywhere. But there's nothing he can do about it right now; it'll have to wait until later. He finds a lump rising to his chest at the thought of doing it later, the desire to do it now becoming more and more pronounced. He's finding that, more so than with his old living situation, he wants to take care of things right away. Having total control over his environment is making him somewhat anxious. Before, he'd had to submit to the desires of others; now he only has himself to answer to, so things must be done immediately or else the lumps he's increasingly finding developing in his chest grow into an anxiety he finds difficult to control.

Emmett tells himself it'll have to wait until later, pulls his phone out, and opens the Facebook app—mindless distraction awaits him. Jayne still has a few minutes until the timer goes off.

She sits at the stool in front of the workbench, sunglasses perched on top of her head, a light scarf wrapped around her neck, paying too much attention to the sheet of paper and not enough attention to the object she's drawing. That's the thing Emmett had also had difficulty with—he'd wanted to look more at the paper and less at the thing being drawn. But you can't draw what you don't see and you don't see what you don't look at.

Resi and Kerrinpuppy lie on opposite ends of the couch, exhausted from their play. Emmett takes a picture of his dog with his phone and then a picture of Jayne at the desk, the brightly lit windows behind her casting her into shadow and obscuring the features of her face.

Finally, the timer goes off and Jayne puts her pencil down. She takes her sunglasses off of their perch and runs her hands through her hair, exhaling as though she'd just finished a particularly hard workout.

"How'd you do?"

"Take a look … " Jayne doesn't seem too enthused with herself. That's pretty typical, Emmett thinks; you always have all kinds of expectations for your drawings, especially your first drawings, and reality never meets with expectations.

Emmett lumbers out of his rocking chair and makes his way through the veritable maze of furniture to come around behind Jayne to look at her drawing.

The key to giving a good critique, he's found (at least from the standpoint of not discouraging people who are first starting out) is to find two "good" things to say for every "bad" thing. People often forget that the so-called "bad" things said during critique are meant to make their pieces stronger, are meant to make them better artists, so saying good things about the piece makes them less defensive.

"Let's see here," Emmett begins, clicking his tongue. "First off, I like the confidence of your lines. So many people, myself included, start drawing by making a bunch of short strokes instead of one continuous line for each feature of the thing they're drawing. The confidence of your lines shows good intuition." One good thing down. Just need one more. "Second, your proportions are really good. You've managed to convey the mass of the leaves of the plant in relation to each other, a tricky thing to manage when you're first starting."

Jayne is nodding. Emmett imagines her smiling to herself.

Emmett wonders if he perhaps should have sandwiched his criticism between the two positive things, make it less of a blow to the fragile artist ego (and he knows all too well how fragile that ego is).

"But," Emmett pauses, placing his finger over the stems of the nameless houseplant he's had her draw, "this just doesn't do it for me."

"What do you mean?" her voice choking a little bit.

"These lines don't have any girth, any mass, they're far more than just a single line…you haven't conveyed the weight of the stems, ya know?" and Emmett does something he knows will make Jayne want to throw the drawing out, by taking a pencil out and drawing a second line parallel to the single line she's drawn for the stem of the plant. "See?" he says.

"Yeah."

He can tell Jayne is losing interest. Why? He's not so sure. In many ways, he doesn't know her at all. In many ways, it feels like he's just met her, though she insists it's been ten years.

Emmett remembers the day he'd taken her the sweet potato curry, when she'd had her wisdom teeth removed. He'd been genuinely hurt, quite a bit jealous, to see so many people crowded into her parents' living room, a luxury he hadn't experienced.

He remembers not blaming her for the fact that people visited her, and he still doesn't blame her. People understand what it is to have your wisdom teeth removed; they can relate to physical pain. But ECT? Psychological pain so excruciating they need to electrically induce seizures to get rid of it? That's not something people can relate to.

What he resents most is how he'd gone to great lengths to visit her but she'd never bothered to visit him. It'd been a huge deal for him, a massive undertaking to work up the nerve, the courage to visit her. Days of mental preparation leading up to it, working on visualizing himself getting out of the house and onto his bike, being out in public, feeling naked and exposed while pedaling through a city whose layout had been erased from his mind, navigating the complexities of riding a bike in traffic. He'd cooked again for the first time.

It would have been such a small thing for her to come visit. Just time out of her schedule—an hour-long ride, less if she pushed herself, and she routinely rode her bike much longer than that, much harder than that. She was a perfectly capable, completely healthy person, and still she never came.

Hardly anyone had come to visit him during ECT, especially while he was recovering. Not even Lauren, whom he was supposed to marry, ever found the time to come and visit. All Emmett or Mom or Dad could remember was her coming to the first ECT appointment and her riding her bike over after they'd broken up the first time and she'd decided it was a huge mistake and he hadn't been answering his phone because he was still sleeping off the anesthesia. He'd had no idea she was so distraught. He'd just been woken up from his drug-induced stupor by a crying Lauren who'd begged him to take her back, only to leave him again a month or two later.

Lauren had insisted he come to her, even on days when he'd had ECT that morning, days when what he'd needed most was rest. And he'd come. Because, if anything, he was loyal. Loyal to a fault.

Marta Lee had been the only one to come and visit him. But he'd only met her after the worst of the recovery time. She'd call him every so often to say she was in the neighborhood and ask if he'd like some company for a little while. He'd make them some coffee and they'd sit outside on the back porch, Emmett smoking his pipe and Marta Lee taking the occasional puff, and they'd talk and talk and it'd made Emmett feel like a worthwhile human being for the first time in a long time.

He also remembers Marta Lee later helping him with his garden. The garden that was abandoned as soon as he got on SSDI and moved in with SAR. She brought over compost and horse manure, helped him plant the seedlings he'd kept in his bedroom and watered so faithfully. She didn't pity him. She didn't question him incessantly about his illness like he was some kind of freak. She cared about him as a human being. She treated him as a person.

Emmett sighs as he looks at Jayne staring at her drawing, tapping his pencil on the surface of the workbench. He realizes he doesn't really understand her. She's more of a stranger than anything; a stranger with whom he has strong emotional ties. It's at least clear to him that she's done drawing for the day.

"Done for the day?" Emmett says.

Jayne stretches, lets out a yawn, nods her head.

Emmett starts gathering up the drawing supplies and putting them away. "Wanna grab some coffee?"

"That would be great. I'm so tired I could go to bed. I didn't think I would get so sleepy from that."

"It'll wear you out. But it's like riding a bike—your stamina increases the more you do it. Did you at least have fun?" Emmett says, holding up the drawing he'd modified and making a motion as if to offer it to her.

Jayne shakes her head and says "Totally."

But Emmett can tell this is probably the last drawing lesson he'll be giving her.

"Good," Emmett says despite himself. He turns to Kerrin-puppy and says in his sweet falsetto, "Kerrin, you wanna go on an a-venture?"

Her ears perk up at this word, "a-venture." She rolls over onto her feet, hops down onto the floor, and does her seesaw stretch. Emmett gets her leash from the hook behind the bathroom door and clips it onto her collar and they head down the hall, Jayne and Resi in pursuit, and start the shortest walk ever to a coffee shop.

Emmett isn't so sure how he feels about the coffee shop next door just yet. It's the sister location of his favorite coffee shop. But while the original location has comfy couches and an atmosphere that reeks of community, this second location makes him a little uncomfortable. It lacks comfortable chairs, and seems more setup along the thinking of form over function—the furniture chosen because it looked good, not because it was practical. This is most prominently proclaimed in the bench that occupies the north wall and the tables which are much too tall to be able to sit comfortably and draw or use your laptop; Emmett's hands inevitably go numb because of the awkward angle forced upon them. There isn't really a good place to spread out with a drawing and work for hours. The tables either force you to sit with your back to the entrance, or are too small, or are not set at the right height. He can feel it growing on him, though, and the commute is a heck of a lot shorter, being right next door.

He's had these grand plans of spending part of his day at the coffee shop: drinking a latte and reading a book or maybe doing some writing or a bit of drawing, maybe outside if it was nice so he could smoke cigarettes at the same time and have Kerrinpuppy with him. But so far, he's spent most of his time inside his apartment, hardly making use of the luxury of having his favorite coffee shop a 45-second walk away. When he has gone, it's been to meet up with someone, or to grab a cup of coffee and bring it back to his place, or to buy a pound of coffee. He tells himself this is because the apartment is still so new, because he's still adjusting to it, that he has at least an entire year to go and hang out and become a regular before his lease is up.

Jayne and Emmett tie their dogs up to the picnic tables outside the coffee shop, Jayne heading inside immediately and Emmett giving Kerrinpuppy some scratches and reassuring her that he'll be back in a few minutes before following Jayne inside.

It's one of those early spring days in Denver that sees people in all manner of dress: some in winter coats because it was almost freezing outside when they came into work in the morning, other people in short sleeves and shorts because it's Denver and Denverites like to dress to defy the weather, and still others, like Jayne, opting to mix it up with a combination of summer attire and a fleece vest to keep warm. Emmett remains consistent—jeans and a button-up shirt, preferably flannel, regardless of whether it's summer or winter. If it's cold he wears a jacket, if it's hot he rolls up his sleeves.

"How'd you like drawing?" he asks, rolling a cigarette.

Jayne sips her coffee, adjusts her sunglasses down over her face. "It was different than I was expecting."

"How so?"

"Harder maybe?"

"I can see that," Emmett says, nodding. "It's one thing to just doodle from memory and it's quite another to try to reproduce something from real life. Both are important, though. Good to be able to draw whatever it is you want whenever you want."

"How so?"

"It's like having tools. It's best to have the right tool for the job. Some jobs call for being able to reproduce something from life with precision, and other things call for being able to imagine something that doesn't exist. It depends on what you need to make."

Jayne looks at him, nodding placatingly. He continues: "It's like being a musician—sometimes you play what other people have written, and other times you play what you hear in your head. Both are important. It just depends on the circumstances."

"That makes sense. The last time I made anything close to visual art was in that 3D modeling class, and that was much easier."

"Yeah. Computers really simplify the process. But they also limit what you can do. Or maybe I'm just biased because I so often prefer analog to digital. I sometimes think that, for how much of a nerd I am, I'm very much the Luddite of my family."

Jayne laughs. "You think so?"

"Oh, definitely. I still prefer to write by hand, I like to listen to vinyl records as opposed to streaming it over the Internet, I hate ebooks with a passion, much preferring a real book. I communicate more frequently via handwritten letters than I do email, and I paint using a technique that's hundreds of years old.

"I've come across a lot of people, particularly at my church, who think I'm all about digital formats. And they're very much surprised to find out how much I almost loathe digital and how endeared I am to analog. I'd be all about a tube amp if they weren't so got-dang expensive."

"The Ludditic Nerd," Jayne says, laughing.

Emmett chuckles.

"It was fun though," Jayne says, as Emmett takes a drag off his cigarette.

"Drawing?"

"Yeah."

"Good. I was a little worried I scared you off."

"No, no. Not at all. It's just a very different way of thinking," Jayne says. She's got her phone on the table. It's not making any noise, but she's keeping a close eye on it ... pressing the Home button continually and picking it up every minute or so to type a quick message before returning the phone to the table and resuming her predaceous watch over it.

"Well, I suppose that being a philosophy major, you're not used to using the right side of your brain. Or is it the left?"

"Oh, I can never remember," Jayne says dismissively, tapping away at the screen of her phone.

"I remember that it's the right because right-brain dominant people are usually left handed and it's ironic that my dad isn't more overtly artistic, because he's left handed.

"I mean, he's certainly very creative," Emmett says to fill the silence as Jayne taps away at her phone. "Especially if you've ever read his Christmas letters."

"I didn't know he wrote Christmas letters," Jayne says, seeming to latch onto the last thing Emmett said.

"Oh yeah," Emmett says, his Midwestern accent showing through with particular gusto. "They're pretty hilarious. Parodies of the typical Christmas letter, kind of like something Mad magazine would have done back in the sixties when it was actually funny. Toward the end, he took it to extremes. Like the year he took an entire piece of legislation, a document hundreds of pages long, and changed random parts of it—I don't think anyone read it that year."

"He doesn't do them anymore?"

"No. He stopped around the time I got really sick. Said he just didn't have the heart to make them anymore," Emmett says, a sadness in his voice.

"Oh … "

Jayne nurses her coffee and Emmett rolls another cigarette.

"So when do you want your next drawing lesson?" Emmett asks suddenly, a little too loudly.

A pause, "I don't know if I'll have the time anytime soon, honestly. I'm literally up to my elbows in stuff to do."

"Oh no worries. Just whenever you have the time. I'll always be here."

"I know," Jayne says, smiling as she puts her phone down.

Jayne picks up her phone again. "I should probably get going."

"Okie dokie," Emmett says.

He walks her to her car and gives her a hug, then reaches down and gives Resi some head scratches. Then Emmett and Kerrinpuppy head back to their stoop. Emmett settles onto the ledge and rolls another cigarette while Kerrinpuppy makes herself comfortable in the grass next to him, turning a few times before finally finding an agreeable position. Emmett lights his cigarette, pondering the five inches of the screen of his phone; oblivious to the brilliance of the sunlight receding into night.

Chapter Seven

E Pluribus Unum. Out of many, one.

And that's how the monsters come.

Marching down the streets. A brigade of them.

Marching.

Waiting.

Marching.

Waiting.

Their footsteps coming from the worst nightmares he'd had as a kid.

Waiting.

For the proper timing, for certain ideal conditions.

Maybe for the Three Fates to let them go forth with their blessings.

In the dark of night. Coming. Coming. Always marching until they arrive. Pulsating in his eardrums; always awake. Thrumb. Thrumb. Thrumb. Pulses from his skull to the tips of his toes. Radiating like some kind of echo-location trick.

Always waiting. Always coming. Eventually crossing the no-man's land, past the psychological barriers he'd placed with such care for his general well-being.

"Be well," the barriers told him; they'd take care of stopping the monsters, the demons, whatever they were.

Until one night.

Liars!

One. Not two or three. Always and only one.

Peeling away from the eternal march ... to creep, to test the barriers and find them weakened.

Here to mount him like some drugged-out trophy woman.

The flunitrazepam willingly taken because of the promise of disconnection and rest.

Mounting, then exploring with cold, clever hands.

Its hands the temperature of the leftover baked fried chicken he'd eaten without warming up.

The microwave takes too long; he'd needed sustenance Now. Now. Now.

And, by the same merit, this thing had Waited. Waited and then Came and Came again, until at last arriving at his doorstep with its cold-from-refrigeration chicken hands.

Baked fried chicken hands, refrigerated; deftly searching among folds of clammy skin.

Down there, in the recesses between haphazardly lumped thigh meat and the guardians of his anus.

Past defenses, squeezing its hand through the narrow sphincter and Pushing. Pushing. Pushing. Deft baked fried chicken hands on their second exploration. Inside now, to the moist depths of the final steps of his digestive system. Searching for a handle, searching for something labelled "Remove Before Flight." Oh, it was going to make him fly, all right.

Deep. Deeper. Deeper. Spelunking the regions south of nether. Among folds of flesh, taking joy in the gasps of disbelief, the maniacally still attempts to move an arm, any arm. Frustration mounting as the victim is presented only with the pale white, ghostly outlines of hands moving. Neat trick. Buys it time.

Some grotesque pleasure, pure. Twisting its chicken fingered hand to leave an imprint visible from the outside. Fingers, chickened or not, shoulder deep; its arms carefully designed, or perhaps from accident, to get this far in.

"I'M IN," and that's all it says as it finds purchase among the twisting folds of interior flesh, the radial folds found far enough from the shitting part of digestion that it can do some damage.

Pulling.

Pulling.

Its grip more difficult to maintain as blood vessels, sanguine veins are torn asunder and hot blood complicates things. No matter, baked fried chicken hands are designed, or perhaps formed by accident, for this very thing. A gasp from the worthless paralyzed freak. It knows he can't scream out; screaming would relieve some of the pain, and his pitiful mind, the mind he has no control over, isn't going to give him an inch until he moves his damned arms.

Pulling. Pulling. Pulling.

His guts are endless, nearly thirty feet. It'll pull them all out before too long.

The insides come outside and the monster's, the demon's, the whatever-it-is's eyes, he's sure it has eyes, grow wide. Taking in the beauty of writhing intestines, evicted from their confines, and the white glow of his victim's face. There's feet and yards of them, and it can swear it sees the beginning of the stomach popping out his ass.

Piling the intestines on the man's stomach as if to say, "See what I did? I'm going to do it tomorrow too."

They're slipping off his stomach, off the bed, and falling to the floor.

Sickening liquid thump and the monster, just one of them—never two or three, only ever one—can see the man working; furious to move.

Move an arm. Move both arms. Ignore the pain, ignore the blood, the alarming amount of blood pouring out. When they're in front of your face, the game will be over. But the monster can hear, in the confines of the man's head, the shock, the screams of pain, and the too-much-sensation of utter panic.

The man still sees only the pale ghostly traces of his arms.

The monster, demon, whatever it is, is pleased. But the game is almost over.

There's no more to pull. Don't bother whispering threatening nonsense into his ear. Just watch, just wait. Maybe piss will mix with blood and guts. He knows it's there, knows it's just watching. Waiting. Waiting. Waiting. No longer Coming.

Patiently tapping its baked fried chicken fingers on the man's knee. The tapping somehow worse than the 30 feet of wriggling, bloody intestines.

It lives for the first moments, the sortie out of the marching brigade of its kin—the mission of such importance. The shudder as it mounts the man, watching the sweat coming out of pores to cover the man, making him sticky, ripening him. The tender moments of moving his fat, fleshy thighs away—his resistance to the chicken fingered hands, but powerless to stop. The shock from the first shove into the warmth. Past the sphincter, past the colon—shoulder deep, its arm growing longer.

Good rest for tonight. The monsters, demons, whatever they are always get a break from the continual marching when their sorties are successful. Thirty feet of intestines slowly flopping to the floor is certainly a success.

Savoring a job well done.

Suddenly. Happening so fast it didn't notice the first time it did this to him, Bolt Upright. The man goes shooting up and the monster transported where it Rests. Rests. Rests. and resumes its Waiting. Waiting. Waiting.

"SWEET DREAMS," sighs the monster as he barely catches

a glimpse of its impossible configuration. Gone in a flash. The man's nearly pissed himself and his anus, sphincter burn with the weight of his body, setting him on fire, doubling him over.

Into bathroom, check out the damage. None to be seen. The intestines back in place, though complaining passionately about their violation.

Moving gingerly, relieving the piss from his bladder, the piss that almost escaped.

Another night. Some ways from right now. The man, the farthest away he'll ever get. He'll enjoy sitting down.

The Excruciating Sit Down.

Chapter Eight

◇◇

"What happens when you get psychotic?" Lacey asks.

"It always seems to happen on the train ride home from Tag and Rag," Emmett begins. "I start out just fine, but by the time I get to Nine Mile, it's like there's nothing left of me. It's all I can do to get off the train, walk down the stairs and get into my dad's car."

"That must be awful."

"It is, and it gets worse. I can always hear my dad greet me, but I'm powerless to say anything back. I just get into the car and buckle my seat belt and I feel like I'm just dripping with a sick evil; I'm worried that I'll get it all over him and he'll be infected. He drives me back home, which is only about a ten-min-ute drive or so, and he tries to keep up a very decidedly one-sided conversation. Sometimes the voices are yelling at me; sometimes they're silent; other times I'm overcome with the creeping notion that I'm being driven to my death. Anyways. We get back home and I just break down crying. Dad pulls into the driveway and I just lose it. We sit in the car for a few minutes while I cry and sometimes wail on about making them stop, and then I compose myself and we go inside."

"What do you do when you get inside?"

"Usually my mom makes me some coffee. Coffee usually helps. And I go to the back porch to smoke a cigarette and my dad comes with me and we talk."

"What do you talk about?"

"Depends on how bad it's been. Sometimes I'm over it and don't want to talk. Other times I just rant about how my brain is torturing me and I want it to end."

Lacey is scribbling some notes on her legal pad. All Emmett can hear is the scribbling of the pen on the paper. Finally, she clicks the pen and says to him, "I think there's a pretty simple solution to this."

"Yeah?" Emmett says, adjusting himself.

"No more train. You've been describing before how the reflective surfaces of the windows on the train really bother you. Do you think you could get someone to

drive you home?"

"I don't know about that. I think the other problem is the crowd at Tag and Rag, too," Emmett says.

"Yeah. But if it's important to you, you should go. Unless there's somewhere else you could go."

"My parents' church, the church I grew up in, has a Thursday night service. Not too many people go there ... Emmett says, trailing off.

"Maybe that would be a better option then," Lacey says, always wanting Emmett to come to the final conclusion.

◇◇◇

Emmett is disobeying the decree he and Lacey had made a few weeks ago. Well, it was more Lacey's suggestion, which brought about the decree from Emmett. Specifically, he needs to avoid crowds.

It's Lent, Emmett's favorite time of the church year. Or, at least the one he remembers most fondly. It starts with Ash Wednesday and culminates in Holy Week, with a church service, called a Vesper, every Wednesday evening in between. Dad takes his car into work and they drive home, eat a quick dinner, and head to church for the service.

The Vespers replace the sparsely attended Thursday night service Emmett usually goes to, but they're also much more crowded. A typical Thursday has no more than fifteen people in it, while a Lenten Vesper fills the sanctuary. Mom and Dad have assured Emmett that he just needs to give them a signal and they'll head out and go back home.

The local Lutheran churches do a sort of exchange program during Lent, with a different pastor preaching in a different church every week. It's been this way since Emmett can remember, and it's part of what he likes about Lent—the variety, the fresh face behind the pulpit.

Emmett is proud of himself thus far. They've made it to the gospel reading and he's doing fine, though this particular pastor seems to like his congregation to feel the raw emotion of the Bible, and Emmett, being the kind of person who soaks up expressed emotion like a sponge, is feeding off of every word; taking every word, every shout, personally. The biggest problem so far is the sitting and standing. The nightmare psychosis from the other night has left a severe pain on his bottom. He feels he's ninety years old, the last one to finish standing and the last one to finish sitting, since he must account for paying special attention to the tender areas of his nether regions where the creature had torn out his intestines through his anus.

He's never experienced anything like it—a lasting physical pain from psychosis. Psychosis has always been painful, but that pain has never continued for weeks on end. He's taken to sitting on a pillow at his desk so he can continue working at his computer, and he has a tendency to sometimes hobble like an old man if he walks too far.

The pastor is standing by the pulpit, absorbed in the passion of his sermon, shouting "Crucify him! Crucify him!" His wild eyes look out at the congregation as his words echo off the acoustic tiles of the walls, irrupting Emmett's ears and filling his mind with images of the gore and suffering implicit in the word "crucify."

A familiar constriction begins to form around his heart, seeming to choke him. He starts to feel lightheaded, vaguely electric—everything more surreal than usual. Emmett taps Dad's shoulder and nods his head out toward the exit. Dad uncrosses his legs, stands up, and they both head out, Emmett hobbling behind; new surges of pain erupt from his rear as he holds his hand to his belt loop where his keys are attached to a carabiner so he doesn't jingle the whole way and draw attention to himself.

Out in the car, Emmett rolls himself a cigarette and sits smoking while Dad drives them the four minutes back home,

Emmett feeling guilty, like he'd faked the entire thing just to get out of church.

"Should I stay with you?" Dad asks.

"No, I think I'll be all right. I just needed to get out of there. That pastor is always a little intense just standing there, shouting."

"I know what you mean."

"I suppose if he wanted the congregation to feel the injustice of the whole situation, he succeeded," Emmett says, joking.

Dad chuckles and Emmett gets out of the car, putting his cigarette out against the brickwork of the house, tossing the butt into the trash can, and heading inside to a very excited Kerrinpuppy.

Chapter Nine

"I think you hold yourself to an unfair standard," Lacey says.

"Unfair?" Emmett says, pausing. "Maybe so. But then again, I'm supposed to be getting healthier, not regressing."

"Remember what you told me about progress with mental health?"

Emmett considers it for a while, "No. I think I say too much about that subject."

"You said it's like taking two steps forward and one step back. There's always going to be regression, life doesn't happen in a linear fashion. You arrive at the same destinations in your life again and again. But each time, you're a different person."

It's Easter Sunday. Emmett feels like a schmuck.

Things must be getting worse.

When he'd been getting ECT, he'd managed to ride his bike to church to surprise Mom before the Easter service started (Dad was gone at Grandpa Selv's funeral, which Emmett wasn't allowed to go to because Dad thought it would be too stressful—Dad's siblings were threatening to finally say all of the things they hadn't said while Grandpa was alive). He'd sat in a church so crowded they'd had to bring folding chairs in to the narthex; he'd sung the hymns and stood at the appropriate time and sat when he was supposed to; he'd listened to the sermon and even made small talk with people after the service was over.

Emmett figures if he's supposed to have improved since then, why can't he bring himself to go to the Easter service now, three years later?

Things change. He's learned a lot about his capabilities since then. And who knows, maybe he'd gotten really sick after the service and just doesn't remember it. Hindsight is not necessarily always 20/20.

So it goes.

Tattooed on his knuckles since last Thanksgiving are the words "So It Goes"; a Kurt Vonnegut quote lifted from Slaughterhouse Five. Every time a character dies, Vonnegut wrote "so it goes." Not only is Vonnegut one of Emmett's favorite authors and not only did the phrase happen to fit perfectly on his knuckles, but the phrase also happens to sum up his view on life perfectly.

Some terrible things had happened in Emmett's life, from getting ECT, to being hospitalized in the psych ward, to attempting suicide, to being medicated to a stupor, to losing everything he'd held dear; the list went on and on. Having gone through a period of his life when he'd gotten psychotic multiple times a day, he supposes one could say that terrible things used to happen to him all the time and, in some ways, they still did. But there was no use in dwelling on it; it's an aspect of his life he has very little control over, it's just how it is. So it goes.

You accept it and move on with your life, try to find the humor in it. Some might give him permission to be bitter, but Emmett isn't about to give himself such permission.

So it goes is periphrastic. His own sort of war cry. Whereas other people might be inclined to give up, to surrender, he refuses. At first stubbornly, then with a kind of defiant resolve, and now with a kind of lightheartedness and humor. So it goes is an acknowledgment that he doesn't have a choice in what happens to him, but he does have a choice in his attitude toward it. Life isn't fair was a phrase Mom had used on him and his sister, Clarissa, often; but it doesn't fit so neatly on your knuckles.

You can only make do with what you're given, you can only

make a life with the circumstances you've been presented with. Faced with your life, particularly if that life isn't especially enviable, Emmett believes you have two options. You can either ask "why me?" or you make the best with what you have, find the advantages in your life, find the joys in it. Emmett tries to embrace the latter.

He thinks back to when he'd first graduated high school—when his friends were going off to fancy schools to study more practical things like international business and law. He was going to art school, taking a year off to work so he could afford to go. His friends asked him a question his own parents never asked him: what are you going to do with an art degree?

All he'd wanted to do was be left alone to make his art. He'd wanted to live in a cool part of the city, make his art all day, and then spend the evenings hanging out with his friends and having interesting and stimulating conversations.

He's not quite there yet, but he's getting there. He feels himself at the cusp of achieving just that. Of course, he'd had to develop a severe mental illness and become disabled to achieve this goal, but God has a unique sense of humor. Emmett's beginning to rather enjoy his life most days, now that he feels removed from SAR's clutches. Even two or three years ago, Emmett couldn't have imagined living on his own, back in Cap Hill, close to his friends, no longer isolated in the suburbs.

He still calls Mom in a panic every so often, despondent over not painting, over not doing what he has all the time in the world to be doing. "It's a big adjustment; just give yourself some time," she assures him. And Emmett figures he has plenty of time. If time is the basic commodity that a person has to give in exchange for necessities, Emmett is one of the wealthiest people on the planet.

The tattoo reminds him of this. It reminds him to humble himself and be patient, that progress is inevitable and he's come a long way. It also reminds him that sometimes progress doesn't seem like progress, just like ECT and the loss of his memory and everything else didn't seem like progress, but that it'd been a very long time indeed since he'd gotten so depressed he was suicidal. It reminded him that even mental illness could be its own twisted sort of blessing.

Emmett sits on the back porch at Mom and Dad's house, smoking a cigarette, watching Kerrinpuppy on her vigil for squirrels (or any other small animal that might come into the backyard). His parents' backyard is Kerrinpuppy's favorite place in the whole wide world. When they'd lived here for the short couple months before moving out, he and Kerrinpuppy had spent almost all their time out here. Even now, when Emmett comes over for weekends, if the weather is nice enough, they'll spend most of the day outside—Emmett smoking, using his laptop, reading, and listening to music; Kerrinpuppy sunning herself, chasing after squirrels and bunnies, and cooling off in the shade.

He checks his watch occasionally, expecting Jayne and Rob to ring the doorbell any minute now. This is the first time the Selv family has had company over for Easter in quite some time. Clarissa can rarely make it home because of her teaching and church duties and Emmett has never been all that interested in inviting anyone over for Easter until this year.

"THEY'RE GOING TO BE EMBARRASSED THAT YOU'VE INVITED THEM OVER, YOU KNOW, MR. FUCKFACE," *the familiar purring of Myra coming from the back of his head.* "THEY THINK YOU'RE TRYING TO CONVERT THEM ... THAT IT'S SOME KIND OF FUCKING RETARDED CHRISTIAN SCHEME TO GET THEM TO GO TO CHURCH."

A wash of dread spills over him. There's never a good time for Myra to show up, but her timing always seems so ironically impeccable.

It's mere minutes before Jayne and Rob are due to arrive. Not enough time for him to deal with this particular voice in his head. He's got a conundrum on his hands: take sixty milligrams of ziprasidone? Or a quarter milligram of risperidone? Or maybe a cigarette would do it and he could listen to an EP? The thought crosses his mind that maybe Myra will just disappear on her own by the time Rob and Jayne show up, but he knows that's too much to hope for. Chances are she'll get worse if he doesn't do anything about it. She'll bring everyone, the entirety of her personal entourage, the cadre that always follows her around, and they'll explode in a fanfare of paranoiac thoughts and phrases, forcing him to chemically reduce himself to a drooling puddle on the cot downstairs just to survive.

Too many decisions, not enough time.

He leaves his cigarette burning on the ashtray and hustles inside to his black messenger bag in the basement. He immediately locates the bottle of ziprasidone he has stashed inside. He pops one of the tiny white capsules into his mouth and swallows it, then pockets the bottle in case he needs more. Grabbing his headphones and iPod from their compartments, he heads back up the stairs.

Back out on the porch, he puts the headphones on and selects Broken Arrow by Blackalicious, a hip-hop album he's come to rely on lately for its ability to make Myra and her cadre disappear. He hits play, grabs his cigarette to take another drag, and visualizes the tiny ziprasidone pill in his stomach, disintegrating, and tries to will it to enter his bloodstream faster. But realistically, he knows it'll be about a half hour to forty-five minutes before it kicks in.

He's sitting there, tapping his feet to the beat of the addictive hip-hop, when he feels his pocket vibrate. He fishes his phone out and checks to see who's messaged him.

JAYNE:
Hey Love! We're going to be a little late. Just thought I'd let you know

EMMETT:
No worries. See you soon :)

Perfect. Time for the ziprasidone to kick in, time for the album to work its magic, time for another cigarette. He stuffs his phone back into his pocket and rolls himself another cigarette.

Emmett gets to his feet, opens the sliding glass door. "They're running a little late," he tells Mom.

"Oh, okay," Mom says. "Did they say how late?"

"Nope. I can ask if you'd like."

"No. No worries."

"'K," and Emmett closes the door and heads back to his perch.

Dealing with a mental illness, you're at the mercy of certain chemicals. Whether those chemicals are dopamine, serotonin, norepinephrine, risperidone, or nicotine all depends. It's a fine balance between everything you put into your body. Too little, too much can mean dire consequences. It's far from an exact science.

Emmett is keenly aware of this; cigarette breaks every two hours, pills at exactly 10:00 a.m. and 10:00 p.m., and an almost preternatural awareness of the chemical needs of his body have given him an advantage over Myra and her troupe. He can somewhat predict oncoming psychosis, sometimes calling Mom and Dad from his apartment before it takes hold and renders him incapable of even operating a phone.

He'll call them and tell them he feels "funny," and then the conversation quickly deteriorates until Mom and Dad are getting into the car and telling him that they'll be there in forty minutes to offer what little relief they can, often in the form of a car ride back to their house.

Rob and Jayne ring the doorbell around the time Emmett can feel the friendly little chemicals making their way into his brain. He feels a release of pressure, imagining a fizzing like someone opening a two-liter bottle of soda.

Jayne apologizes for being late as they exchange a hug and Emmett tells her not to worry about it, leaving out any mention of how it's really just perfect timing because he would have gone crazy if they'd been on time, and not asking them what'd kept them occupied for the thirty-eight minutes it'd taken for the ziprasidone to kick in. He hopes it's enough of the drug to combat whatever it is that's trying to take hold of him, but not so much that it's going to knock him out before they finish dinner.

Resi darts inside and shakes herself out.

"Well hello there, Resi," Emmett calls down in his falsetto reserved exclusively for dogs. Resi gets up on her rear paws in an attempt to reach up to Emmett as he stoops down to her level to give her some scratches.

Kerrinpuppy and Resi greet each other briefly but enthusiastically.

"Jayne! Rob!" Mom calls from the kitchen. "Good to see you."

Emmett takes their jackets and they all go into the kitchen where Mom is taking food out of the oven.

Dad walks up the stairs, probably having heard the commotion of dogs running throughout the house. "Ned," Mom calls, "why don't you get drink orders?"

Dad shakes hands with Rob, and Jayne just waves. Emmett

asks for a Mountain Dew, thinking that he needs to get something in his system that'll combat the inevitable tiredness of the ziprasidone. Ziprasidone didn't used to make him so sleepy, but now it has a tendency to knock him out. He can never predict when that'll be. The caffeine in the Mountain Dew is a pittance of what he'd need to actually keep himself awake. He thinks about the five thousand milligrams of caffeine Dr. Romero used to inject into him before putting him to sleep, and that dose sounds about right. What Emmett is looking for is the sugar, a quick boost of physical energy that might just do the trick. It's either that or dextroamphetamine, and it's too late in the day to take dextroamphetamine and expect to get to sleep tonight.

Chemicals acting upon chemicals acting upon chemicals. We're nothing but sacks of chemical reactions, Emmett thinks to himself as he accepts the Mountain Dew, opens it, and takes a swig.

Jayne and Rob position themselves near the appetizers—veggies and gluten-free crackers with dairy-free dip. It's yogurt based, which Emmett doesn't care for. But Jayne absolutely loves it, so Mom always makes it when Jayne and Rob come over for dinner.

Emmett feels a little self-conscious eating in front of Jayne and Rob, though. They're both slender and muscular from long days spent riding their bikes. Emmett hasn't ridden his bike since he'd brought Jayne the curry after she'd had her wisdom teeth removed. Staying off his bike that long certainly hadn't helped him keep the weight off. Of course, the enormous bottles of Throwback Pepsi and Mountain Dew he drinks so consistently since moving back to Denver don't help him stay slender either.

Emmett was actually the one who'd gotten Jayne into cycling in the first place. It's something he takes pride in as it's one of the few things he actually remembers about their relationship prior to the Great Shock: it'd been the true start of their friendship. They'd known each other for a couple of years before that but hadn't hung out too much, mostly because of the significant age gap and Emmett's feelings about it: Emmett had been a junior in high school and Jayne still in middle school when they'd met, and he'd felt a little awkward about it. He still remembers getting an email from her. The subject read: "Will you?" and the body: "marry me?"

He still has the email. Not that he's saved it, but he hasn't deleted it either. It was just a young girl worshipping someone older because he actually talked to her. He could have been the biggest loser in the world and she would have idolized him purely on the basis that he was so much older than she was. Emmett stands there, thinking back on his past with Jayne, wondering if her comment the previous Halloween had anything to do with that email. He remembers getting into a series of car accidents shortly after graduating high school and, with him being too expensive to insure anymore, Dad had bought him a bike to get around. And while he loved riding his bike, his friends didn't appreciate having to come and pick him up. So he'd asked Jayne, not even old enough to drive yet, if she wanted to ride bikes with him. She'd agreed enthusiastically, and they'd met at a Starbucks about halfway between where they each lived, Emmett on his brand-new bike and Jayne on her old three-speed cruiser she'd fixed up hurriedly after it'd been abandoned in the garage.

He remembers getting into the best shape of his life, seeing Denver in a whole new way, exploring the city with Jayne. But he remembers it all in a very generic way, just still pictures in his head of scenes which must have come from his camera, from his memory of looking at those pictures later on. He'd have to look for those pictures later, see if they helped him with his memory at all. Jayne sometimes talked about the adventures they went on, the trouble they got into, always starring Emmett as her sidekick, but the Emmett she described always seemed like someone else—someone he'd never met, would never meet.

Memory is such a fickle thing in general, obfuscation seemingly its natural state. Add the electricity of the Great Shock three times a week for six months to the mix and memory is a veritable miasma, untrappable and forever eluding you. Emmett oscillates between a quiet confidence that he'll get his memories back and a roaring, underground panic that he'll forever drift without any such memories to ground him to where he is, to what's made him who he is. Jayne so often insists that he's the same person he's been since he was in high school. But though he has no proof, Emmett can't help but feel like a completely different person since the Great Shock. It changed who he is, his very substance.

Emmett calls Kerrinpuppy and soon she's trotting inside. Rob calls to Resi but there's no sign of her. Last Emmett saw, she was sniffing around in the lower part of the yard where a six-foot retaining wall separates one part of the yard from the other. Rob calls and calls, but Resi doesn't show. Finally, Rob heads out into the darkening backyard; down the path to the lower part of the yard. He comes back a couple minutes later with a squirming Resi in his hands. She frees herself from his grip and darts back inside.

Once they've gathered in the kitchen and Emmett, Mom, and Dad have prayed, Mom tells everyone what each dish is, which scalloped potatoes are for Jayne and Emmett and which are for everyone else, and tells Rob and Jayne to go first. They both motion for Emmett to go first. Not wanting to start a Battle of Politeness, Emmett takes his plate and begins to fill it. An itch is spreading behind his eyes, telling him how exhausted he is. He's not worried so much about falling asleep on everyone as what an exhausted state will do to his defenses against psychosis. Not much he can do about it now—he has to trust that the ziprasidone will do its job.

They sit down and eat their food, Emmett dreading what they're going to talk about, his mind a blank, relieved that they somehow make it through dinner; Jayne polite enough not to bring out her phone once.

Mom has set a collection of marshmallow Peeps in the middle of the table. Rob selects a few, puts them on his plate, and begins eating them.

"That's not what those are for," Emmett says, smiling.

"They're not?" Jayne says.

"Nope."

"Makes sense," Rob says, chewing, taking a sip of beer. "They're kinda stale."

"That's so they burn better."

"Burn better?"

"Yep!" Mom says, distributing boxes of matches and a candle to everyone and sitting back down. "It's the annual Burning of the Peeps!"

Mom explains that many Easters ago, Clarissa was trying to impress one of her friends and decided to set some Peeps on fire. Everyone had had such a great time (while Dad looked on in horror, thinking only of the fire hazard) that they'd turned it into a tradition. Emmett at one point had turned it into an art form with a crème brûlée torch, but the torch has since run out of fuel and Emmett admitted it hadn't been the same since.

"That's fantastic," Jayne says, somewhat in awe that Emmett's mom would encourage this outrageous activity.

They spend the next hour or so burning sugar-covered marshmallow effigies, Emmett carefully constructing a pyre of Peeps in an attempt to maximize the flames. Jayne and Rob, still new at the practice, burn each Peep individually and take pictures with their phones to post on Facebook and Instagram. Dad comes into the room to clear the dishes away, and upon seeing the pile of Peeps-to-be-burned, suggests they take it out-side so he doesn't have to call his insurance agent on Monday.

Emmett's funeral pyre doesn't burn like he wants it to and Mom denies his request for lighter fluid. The Burning of the Peeps always brings out his maniacal desire to set things on fire, this baser instinct for pyrotechnic glory.

They hadn't left them out long enough to dry, he explains to Rob and Jayne, and he settles for more ordinary kinds of burnings.

He has to stop, though. The innocent-looking Peeps begin to scream out in agony as he brings them to the candle flame; they beg him not to set them on fire. They turn their melting heads and ask Emmett why he would do such a thing. He can see their faces twisting and contorting in anguish—the usual two dots and half circle of their ordinary faces replaced with real faces, which writhe and struggle as the flames begin to consume them. The ordinary smell of sugar burning is replaced with the smell of fur and flesh burning. It sickens him. He sees their eyes turn to jelly from the heat, leaking out of their sockets and rolling down their charred bodies.

The pastel marshmallows accuse him, mock him, spit at him, curse him, damn him to hell until, finally, they breathe their last.

Emmett excuses himself and goes back inside.

A tightness constricts Emmett's throat, squeezes. Panic seizes him. He must gain control or else completely lose it. A distance erupts between him and everything else, the distance quicken-ing as he struggles to think of what to do while the tightness around his throat threatens to choke the life out of him. He's beginning to view himself as from a bastion inside his head, exerting less and less influence over his actions as each moment inexorably slips into the next.

He devises a plan:

He stops in the living room, Mom and Dad both entertaining themselves with their iPads, Kerrinpuppy snuggled up between them.

He asks Mom if she wouldn't mind making him some coffee. Pointing at his head and making a circular motion, the international sign of a looney.

"Sure, what kind?"

Emmett can't speak. He just shrugs and turns around to his next objective.

His boots make the basement steps creak heavily. Or it's maybe just his enormous weight. It's impossible to sneak into the basement, which is one of the reasons why he likes sleeping down here.

Turn on light.

Black messenger bag.

Inside compartment. ziprasidone gone. Only risperidone left.

He remembers the ziprasidone bottle, placed so long ago in his pocket.

Again he's faced with either sixty milligrams of ziprasidone or a quarter milligram of risperidone.

He already has ziprasidone pulsing through his system.

It's important that he not sleep; there are people to entertain. Though that might already be a luxury he can't afford; to entertain.

He checks his watch. Monday will be ruined if he takes the risperidone. He'll be taking his evening dose soon anyways, essentially doubling his dose. It's the same conundrum every time, and he's never been able to get a straight answer out of his psychiatrist, who always tells him to trust his gut.

His head swims with the cloud of the impossibility of the decision he must make.

What he really needs is to rest and be by himself. Would Rob and Jayne understand? They haven't even had pie yet.

He sits on the hard metal edge of the cot; an awkward spot to occupy, on the precipice, having to decide between accepting the rest the cot offered and being spilled onto the cold linoleum floor of the basement. Always, he's on a precipice.

There's even more medication upstairs in a case the size of a hatbox mom had made him to keep his pills organized. It zips up so he can take all of his pills with him easily, and not have to resort to a plastic grocery bag when he came to visit every weekend.

He likes for people to see the pill case open, to see how many pills he has to take; likes people to see him fill three small plastic cups' worth of pills and swallow the contents of one of them right there. It's something he does every day, but people didn't really know about it. They knew about it on an intellectual level but seeing him take them tended to put his illness in perspective for them. The sheer quantity of pills used to keep him sane.

So much of the suffering of the mentally ill is done alone, in isolation.

"Coffee's ready," Mom calls down from the top of the stairs.

Her voice pierces him, violates the calm he'd been surrounding himself with. Doesn't she know better than to yell? Doesn't she know better than to yell especially when he's sick? Anger consumes him and he takes the pill bottles, both in his right hand, and marches up the stairs.

Rob and Jayne sit on chairs at the kitchen table. A piece of pie in front of both of them.

Can't get angry in front of them, must maintain calm.

They greet him, unsure of themselves. He can tell, from their response to his response, he isn't doing too well. They go back to their pie.

Mom stirs sugar into an otherwise black cup of coffee, coffee she'd asked him to buy especially for tonight. She offers him the cup and tells him to sit in the other room when he accepts it.

Emmett obeys, juggling two bottles of pills and a mug of coffee. Hot liquid spills out the side onto the clean tile floor of Mom's kitchen. Mom comes to the rescue, taking the coffee mug and urging him to sit down.

Emmett sits.

Rob and Jayne confer with one another.

Mom doesn't apologize. Dad doesn't apologize. Emmett is the only one who wants to. Is the only one who needs to. Though why apologize for something you can't help? Do you apologize for having cancer?

Mom and Dad both trying to coax out of Emmett which pill he wants and how many. Emmett much too concerned about Rob and Jayne and who's entertaining them, much too concerned about the embarrassing scene he's making. He sits in the bastion in his head and watches the whole pathetic scene unravel. He hates the bastion, the place from which he observes the many things he does without his permission.

Further and further down a rabbit hole. Ironic. Rabbits brought him here in the first place.

Rob and Jayne announce they're leaving. Wave goodbye at Emmett. Something about wishing he feel better soon. Resi trotting over to nudge her head against his hand, as if giving her own well wishes. Emmett doesn't even so much as register the fact they're leaving as much as he does the failure at having neglected them for so long.

Mom leaves Emmett with Dad, hugs all around, leftovers dolled out, promises they'll come over again and finish burning the rest of the Peeps.

Emmett just knows soon Kerrinpuppy will be in his lap, soon he'll be getting headphones and music, soon drugs will be making their way through his system. More powerful drugs, a greater number of drugs.

Everything is progressing as it always does when he's sick, and things, he must admit, keep getting better, getting better all the time. Just like the man is singing in his ears.

Kerrinpuppy makes herself comfortable, letting out a sigh as she rests her head in his hand.

No thoughts of tomorrow. No thoughts of the past. He must live in the Now. Now. Now. Now he's okay, that's all that really matters.

So it goes.

Chapter Ten

"I've noticed this shift in me since I moved into a place of my own," Emmett says, changing the subject.

"What's that?" Lacey asks.

"I don't know if it's necessarily a good thing, either. But I've come to care a lot more about my space."

"What do you mean?"

"Like how the furniture is arranged and how neat everything is."

"I don't think that's such a bad thing. It was pretty bad at your old place."

"Yes. But I think my subconscious might be overcompensating for when I didn't have much control over a bunch of crap being left all over the place—I can feel myself getting so anal about my apartment. Nothing can be out of place."

Lacey makes a few notes on her pad of paper and looks at Emmett with those deeply sympathetic eyes. Finally she says, "It's always something, isn't it?"

◇◇◇

By the time Emmett gets out to the stoop, the day is already well underway. He sits there with his mug of coffee and rolls his cigarette, lights it, takes a drag, and pulls his phone out of his pocket. He needs to catch up. He busies himself looking at all the interesting things his friends have been doing without him, what they'd decided to do with their weekend.

Some of his friends had been to parties, some of his friends had been up to the mountains, hiking. Some of them had gone to shows. There were the inevitable pictures of plates of food and selfies taken in the mirror of the bathroom before going out for a night on the town. All things Emmett doesn't particularly care about, but all things that leave him feeling a bit empty.

He isn't invited to such things anymore.

Turn down enough invitations to go to shows, to go hiking, to go to parties, and people stop inviting you.

He has compelling enough reasons not to go. Namely, the serious consequences: the psychosis, the dissociation, the terrible psychotic scene he would inevitably end up making were he to find himself in a crowded bar listening to deafening music with people he barely knows. No, the better, the far safer choice is spend his Friday night with his dad. Order a pizza and go for a walk, have a good talk while Dad does the dishes because the feeling of water on Emmett's hands is oftentimes too overwhelming to allow him to do them.

Scrolling down his feed, it's the same sorts of things every day. He has his social justice friends, always commenting on the latest injustice, always so passionate on the Internet but whom he can't help but imagine absent from the actual protests. He misses protests, misses when he and Lauren had been street medics for the DNC in 2008.

Then there are his vain friends—always with the selfies and the posts saturated with thinly veiled attempts to get people to compliment them on their good looks. There's the adventure-seeking hipster crowd, always so smug and self-important with their weekend hiking, backpacking, and camping trips, always talking about how many miles they'd gone, their progress in conquering all of the fourteeners—mountain peaks with an elevation of at least 14,000 feet— in Colorado. They usually drove old Volvo station wagons, carried vintage camping gear, and took carefully composed pictures of their metal coffee mugs next to the campfire before they set off for the hikes, being sure to carefully document everything with the perfect Instagram filter so their trip would seem all the more … authentic.

Everyone fits into a stereotype so nicely. Everyone fulfills a role so perfectly. Everyone fits into a box so neatly.

He wonders which box, which role, which stereotype people assign to him. Emmett is one of those Facebookers who doesn't post all that much. He "likes" the occasional post, comments every now and then, but posts from him are rare. He'd had a series about his bizarre dreams for a while that garnered quite a number of likes (for him at least), but he isn't as addicted to the semi-anonymous praise as other people seemed to be. The psychological rush of a like isn't as satisfying to him as news reports would like to have him believe. Maybe he just isn't built to be an online socialite.

But maybe it's also that he assumes people won't understand about his victories, the things he has to be proud of; they're such minor victories in the grand scheme of things. It's not infrequent to come across posts from people talking about how the one thing all school shooters have in common was that they were taking psych meds, therefore psych meds (or perhaps psychiatric illnesses, the posts were never too clear) cause school shootings. It's disheartening to see, and he'd seen how other "discussions" often go on social media—ad hominem attacks, non-qualitative logic, a general lack of compassion and empathy.

He knows that when he gets people one on one, he can often talk competently to them, let them know about what it's like to actually live with a mental illness. But the Internet is a different story; its semi-anonymous cloak brings out the worst in people. It brings out the malevolence and the cruelty, the closed-mindedness and the bigotry. One only needs to look at any YouTube video's comments to see the effects of the anonymous Internet on people's behavior.

His cigarette has gone out.

He fishes his lighter out of his pocket, sets his phone down, and relights it. Picking his phone back up, he can feel the heat of it in the palm of his hand. His battery is at seventy percent.

Not even ten in the morning and he's already at seventy percent. He puts the phone back in his pocket; he'll have to charge it again when he gets back inside. Why can't they make phones with better battery life? Why can't he just be less anal about his battery?

Taking a sip of his coffee, Emmett takes stock of his neighborhood for the first time this morning. It's one of those beautifully bright winter mornings—warm enough to just sit and enjoy a cigarette. A group of tourists is standing outside the Molly Brown House Museum next door, taking pictures, consuming the entire sidewalk. The tourists always seem oblivious to the idea that people actually live on this street, so obsessed are they with getting the perfect family portrait in front of this famous house.

Emmett's coffee is growing tepid; he takes the last few drags of his cigarette. He feels the vibration of his phone in his pocket. It must be 10:00 a.m., time for pills. He extinguishes the now-sorry-excuse for a cigarette against the brickwork of the stoop, collects his coffee mug, gets to his feet, and heads inside.

Down the hall.

Deposit the cigarette butt in the trash can.

Open the door to lucky number seven.

"Hey Little Baby Kerrin," Emmett calls in his sweet falsetto.

Kerrinpuppy doesn't make a move; she just stares at him from the little nest she's made of the tangle of covers. Emmett gets his water bottle from the coffee table next to the futon that serves as their bed and heads into the bathroom. Unscrewing the lid of the metal water bottle, he pops the lid off the bottle of pills he'd prepared the night before, tips his head back, and washes the pills down his throat with a few chugs of water.

Then into the main room of the apartment to make the bed. Emmett can't do anything with the bed unmade. The order of operations every morning must be wake up, make coffee, go outside for cigarette, come inside, make bed, start day. There is, of course, the stipulation of taking pills at any point during the process; but the routine, the ritual must be followed without fail or else it throws the entire day off. Sometimes, like this morning, he dawdles and spends a good chunk of time in his chair or in bed staring at his phone, but the routine is still always followed; regardless of what he's planned for himself or how late he gets up, he must follow the routine.

Emmett unravels the mess of a nest of blankets Kerrinpuppy has created for herself; she lets it happen without protest. She doesn't mind.

"C'mon, get down," Emmett tells her, snapping his fingers. "Gotta make the bed."

Kerrinpuppy gets to her feet, stretches, and hops down.

"Good girl," Emmett drawls, and he folds up the blankets, depositing them in the closet one by one, and then folds the futon back into a couch. He shoves the couch against the wall and moves the coffee table back into place, and he's ready to start his day.

He was telling Mom the other day, he had no idea what he was thinking with his original furniture arrangement. Whenever he gets a new space, he always seems to have this vendetta against having furniture against the wall. Having the couch and workbench in the middle of the room just made the already tiny apartment seem tinier; there was no space to stretch out, no room to breathe. Since Jayne's drawing lesson, he's moved the futon along the long wall, with his newly purchased drafting table next to it, greatly opening the space and making his whole apartment seem not only larger but more inviting.

The drafting table he'd found on Craigslist for a hundred dollars was one of the best purchases he'd ever made. It offered tons of space to spread out and work on drawings— not quite as wide as the workbench but far deeper, and much cleaner looking. The old workbench had stickers and graffiti and paint marks all over it and just didn't look classy. Slowly but surely, he's building the kind of space he's always wanted. Though he can't quite put a name on the kind of space he wants: not quite modern, or Scandinavian, or industrial. Eclectic, he supposed. He doesn't stick to one particular style of furniture, and he theorizes this mixture of different styles is what lends his apartment its air of homeyness. Emmett sits on his chair and contemplates his tiny room. Everything must be arranged just so; everything has its place. He sips his coffee and waits for Mom to text him.

Chapter Eleven

"You look tired," Lacey says as Emmett settles into his chair and pats his lap for Kerrinpuppy to jump up.

"I feel like you say that every time I come here," Emmett says.

"Does that bother you?"

"No. Not particularly. I suppose it's nice, in a way, to have someone recognize how tired I am."

His phone, plugged into the wall so it can charge again after being used so much this morning, gives a ring like the bell on a bicycle, and he knows it's Mom checking in with him to make sure he's up and has taken his pills.

He likes this new arrangement better. He'd become quite frustrated with the old arrangement of her calling him. It'd often led to those long silences on the phone, neither he nor Mom wanting to end the conversation nor having anything else to say. He would want to listen to music or go read or do something productive but feel obligated to stay on the phone with her, and she would never end a phone call with her son because she didn't know how he was feeling.

So many things come down to simple communication, and it'd taken Emmett moving to a new place for him to realize that he didn't need her to call, he just needed a text message conversation, something low-committal, in order to make him feel connected to the outside world.

MOM:

Morning! Beautiful day today

EMMETT:

Good morning. Was just outside. Beautiful day
indeed

MOM:

What are you up today

EMMETT:

No idea. Don't really have a plan

Emmett knows he should have a plan. A plan for how to
spend his day is crucial for him to survive it. An idle brain
breeds psychosis, he's told Mom and Dad as much.

MOM:

What's on your to do list

A strange, familiar anger washes over Emmett, and he puts
his phone back on the drafting table. He doesn't want to answer
that fucking question.

Part of him knows he really ought to consult his to-do list.
He'd spent a good long while compiling a master to-do list—a
lengthy, color-coded spreadsheet of everything he could possibly do with his time. He only needs to read it and find something that appeals to him. But he knows reading it will only
frustrate him.

A couple-three minutes later, after the rage monster has
calmed, he feels guilty for his reaction. He hasn't expressed his
anger to Mom, which he's glad for. He hasn't sent the "fuck
you" message like he'd wanted to, but he still feels guilty for
thinking it. He still isn't going to actually consult the list; he
knows the list isn't going to be of any help. The list would only
overwhelm him—too many things to do. All he wants to do is sit

on a porch and smoke cigarettes. He doesn't want anyone to be practical, he doesn't want anyone to be proactive. He's suddenly and momentarily sick of fighting his illness, the stubbornly refusing to give up. He wants a fucking vacation from being a professional sick person.

But he's never going to get one, might as well face that reality now. Professional sick people are on the job twenty-four-seven, three-hundred-sixty-five days a year.

EMMETT:

I'll take a look at it after my walk with Dad.

MOM:

Sounds good. Preschool isn't in today. Enjoying the quiet.

EMMETT:

Getting a lot done?

Mom works at their church, where there's also a school. The same school Emmett had gone to for kindergarten through eighth grade, the same church where Emmett had been confirmed. Mom has worked as the secretary and then as the office manager for as long as Emmett can remember, at first just doing the bulletin and announcements and finally basically running the place, taking on task after task until it became a fulltime job. She loves doing it and it offers flexible enough hours that she can work whenever she wants or needs to, a big bonus when you have a son who needs to be taken to get bloodwork done or to doctors' appointments on a regular basis. The preschoolers are noisy and oftentimes a distraction and, while Mom loves them as she loves all little kids, she's thankful they don't meet on Fridays, as she's able to get a lot of work done for lack of the distractions they often bring.

MOM:

Lots. I should be done early today

EMMETT:

Good :)

MOM:

<3

Emmett doesn't reply to this one. Mom likes to be the last to reply in a text conversation.

Kerrinpuppy has moved to her bed on the floor, right next to the easel, which is getting less and less use these days. On the easel is a giant painting which Emmett last worked on when he was still living with SAR. The painting is huge—four feet by six feet—and it taunts him every time he looks at it. It's a constant reminder that he isn't working on it, that he isn't a painter.

It's just too much work to prepare his palette, the task taking up at least half an hour, and sometimes by the time he's finished he's lost his oomph and can't continue any longer. Painting is a physically demanding task and the illness or the pills or maybe both often don't allow him the luxury of taking on such a thing.

He turns his back to the easel and opens up the doors to the big closet in the corner of the room. His computer is inside; a much easier, less demanding thing to work on. He turns on the monitors, which occupy much of the tiny desk he's forced to use, given the dimensions of the closet. He's going to work on learning how to program Perl, the latest programming language he's obsessed with trying to learn.

Tobias has been encouraging him to learn a programming language ever since they'd started hanging out. Emmett had tried to learn Python first. MIT publishes their Introduction to Computer Science course, complete with lecture videos and a text book, for free on the Internet, and it seemed like the best resource for him to learn how to program. But he'd gotten lost not even two assignments into the class and had given up.

Emmett had been a computer science major the last time he'd dropped out of college. It hadn't been a good experience. Part of it might have been the professor, who'd put questions on the midterm without explaining what they were for or what they even represented, instead giving them the answers to the questions and telling them to figure out how those answers were reached. But it was mostly because Emmett just had no clue what he was doing or even why he was doing it. Computer science never seemed to explain the why, just the how. What was static void main()? No one had explained and no one seemed to care—it was just something the computer needed in order to run the program and that was enough for them, even for the professor.

Tobias is one of the smartest people Emmett knows and is incredibly encouraging of Emmett's darkening obsession with trying to figure out how to program, but Emmett probably hasn't done a good enough job of explaining why he wants to learn how to program. He doesn't have a particular application he wants to write, he doesn't want to become a programmer for a living; he simply thinks that learning how to code will somehow "complete" his knowledge of computers. Emmett knows just about everything about how computers work; he's rarely met a computer he couldn't fix. But there have been a number of times where people have come to him with an idea of a program to write and Emmett has been embarrassed to admit he doesn't know the first thing about writing software.

This is a bad way to learn how to program—to simply study it in a general, theoretical kind of way instead of having a specific task or problem to try to solve. Like the Eric S. Raymond quote says, "Learning how to write code by studying it is about as useful as learning how to paint by studying brushes and pigment." You have to actually do it.

Which is why Perl appeals to him. He often wishes he could automate certain tasks on his Linux machine, and Perl will let him do that; it was built specifically to automate certain tasks through scripts and what are called "one-liners." He hopes, since he has an objective, he'll take to it more easily. There are no free online MIT courses in Perl, but there are some great O'Reilly books (which, according to Dad, are the gold-standard in computer textbooks) on learning Perl. So he has set out on a quest to learn Perl, and it starts with this textbook. Learning Perl.

Emmett logs into his computer and pulls up his text editor, staring at the cryptic lines of code on his screen, trying to re-member what it is his program is supposed to do and referring to the careful notes he'd taken in the notebook he's specially designated for learning Perl.

A couple hours later, it's almost time for his walk with Dad. Emmett has made next-to-no progress on his program; he's barely grasped the purpose of his program. He's pretty sure he's used up his brain's juices for the day. He can feel his temper flaring as his frustration mounts, and the desire to throw his textbook through his very expensive high resolution monitor begins to rise inside him.

It's time for a break. That familiar electrical haze sending pulses of energy reverberating down the top of his head to the tips of his toes means psychosis is near.

He gets out of his chair, his knees making an awful cracking noise and throbbing in agony as he stands up. He bends over and rubs at them until the pain subsides; he really ought to take breaks more often. And this is his final cogent thought.

That familiar choking sensation is rising to his throat.

Power off the monitors.

Close the doors to the closet.

Position his chair in front of the closet doors, hiding the expensive computer equipment.

Over to his record collection. Selecting People Who Can Eat People Are the Luckiest People in the World by Andrew Jackson Jihad.

A relatively short album.

Onto the turntable. Plug in his headphones. Up goes the volume. Up goes the bass.

Little Baby Kerrin on his lap.

Side A has two gems right away: "Rejoice" and "Brave as a Noun." But what Emmett is really listening for is on Side B: "People II: The Reckoning," which oddly comes before "People." Emmett suspects this is an inside joke he'll never be made privy to. Andrew Jackson Jihad isn't exactly a huge enough band that they'll be publishing books about the inside stories on the creation of their records. The music plays, soothing him, returning him to the present, back to participating in reality with everyone else.

Side A ends, and Emmett snaps his fingers so LBK will get down. He flips the record over, hits the start button, gets back in his chair, and Kerrinpuppy hops back in his lap. Just before "People." the last track on the album, Little Baby Kerrin hops off his lap and heads for the door. A second or two later, the door opens and he sees Dad. Emmett waves at Dad and gestures that he's listening, holding up two fingers in an attempt to indicate that the song is two minutes long. That's the nice thing about Andrew Jackson Jihad songs; they're usually not very long.

This particular album always manages to calm Emmett down. That is, when he has the presence of mind to be able to put it on. When he doesn't, he has this tendency to take it out on the people closest him. He's never taken it out on Jayne, probably because he hasn't ever been vulnerable enough in front of her. He has no clue if he'd ever taken it out on Lauren or Maria, though he certainly was that vulnerable in front of them. The anger is a recent development—perhaps because he's been containing himself a lot more, recently, or perhaps because the illness is evolving like it's always evolving. He has no idea what to blame it on.

So it goes.

The song ends and the tonearm automatically lifts and returns to its resting position. Emmett lifts his headphones off his ears.

"Hey homie."

"Hey Emmett, you doing all right?"

"I've been better."

"I'm sorry. What's up?"

"Oh, just been banging my head against the wall trying to learn Perl."

Emmett goes to the kitchen and rolls a cigarette and Dad gets Kerrinpuppy on her leash and they head outside to go for their walk, Emmett explaining the whole way his experience with trying to learn how to program.

To him, it's nothing but frustration. Tobias and everyone else, it seems, talk about it like it's the easiest thing in the world. But Emmett feels as though there's some essential piece of information he's missing, something everyone else knows and he doesn't and that's what's holding him back.

He just doesn't get it, doesn't understand it. He reads the textbook, he watches the lectures, he's not a slacker. It seems to make sense; he seems to understand the information; he can even do the problems correctly sometimes, at least the easy ones at the beginning. But the information only seems to stick for twelve hours or so, because when he comes back to do more work the next day, it's like he has to start over from the beginning. Nothing has stuck, he's back to square one. Emmett explains his earlier frustration with even just trying to figure out what his program did.

They return home from their walk early so Dad can take a look at his code. Emmett opens up his computer closet and logs into his computer.

Dad looks over the code. He's not an expert at Perl; he last messed with Perl scripts some twenty-five years ago and hasn't written any code since then, but he knows messy code when he sees it.

"This is really neat code," Dad says. "Seriously some of the neatest I've ever seen. You even comment it really well. You say you don't know what it's doing?"

"I haven't a clue," Emmett sighing.

"You know," Dad says, straightening up. "I remember, when you were in high school, sitting at the kitchen table trying to help you with your chemistry homework. It was the first time I thought there was something 'up' with you—"

"What do you mean?" Emmett interrupts.

"Well, I thought that maybe you were just being lazy and not doing the homework. So I sat you down and figured I'd just make you do your homework—make it a habit. We worked through the first chapter together and you did just fine. You did the problems correctly, or what I assumed was correctly. And then we went through the second chapter and I thought everything was fine. But when it came time to recall the concepts from the first chapter, which you'd just read maybe twenty minutes prior, you didn't remember any of it, you were puzzled about what to do. We had to go back and read the first chapter all over again."

"Wow, I don't remember that."

"I sometimes feel guilty that I should have known something was up then. That we should have gotten you some help. Maybe things would have turned out differently."

There's a silence. Father and son considering the what ifs.

"You know," Emmett starts. "I've thought about it too. Sometimes I think it might have been nice. But then I think about how taking IB and AP classes in high school was my only shot at getting a college education. Sure, I did really poorly. Sure, my grades were abysmal. But I don't remember really suffering for it. I think it was good for me.

"I think of kids who're diagnosed early on," Emmett continues. "How they're often misdiagnosed. I think of how blessed I am to have only had one diagnosis and how accurate that diagnosis was—there hasn't been any time wasted on treatment that doesn't work or isn't targeted for what I actually have. Who knows what they would have diagnosed me with. Certainly not schizoaffective disorder. I know they say that getting help as early as possible is important, but so is getting the proper treatment. If they're treating you for high blood pressure when what you really need to be treated for is a brain aneurism, is the treatment really effective?"

"I think that's a good point."

But Dad is late for work. He's stayed fifteen minutes past when he's supposed to be back. He says a quick goodbye to Emmett and Little Baby Kerrin and heads back to work. Emmett is left with his thoughts and his little black notebook.

Small events like this can be blessings in Emmett's life—the hiccups that lead to him pontificating about the meaning and structure of life with a mental illness.

What's better? Early treatment or effective treatment? Is it better to get the earliest possible treatment even if it's not for an accurate diagnosis? Or is it better to wait until you know for sure what that diagnosis actually is? He can't help but feel fortunate not to have gotten an early, inaccurate diagnosis and possibly inappropriate treatment.

Of course you want to help someone as early as possible, of course you don't want someone to suffer. Of course you want to help someone as best you can with the information you have at the time. But doesn't that sometimes do more damage than good? Don't you want treatment to be effective as well as timely? Shouldn't effectiveness take precedence over timeliness?

Emmett writes page after page in his little black notebook on the topic, rambling, not quite sure where his opinion lays.

Around dinner time, his tummy grumbling, he decides it best to go to down the street to the deli to get a sandwich. He says a temporary goodbye to Little Baby Kerrin, locks the door behind him, and heads down the hall.

The deli is right next to the coffee shop. His new apartment might not have a porch, but it has most of his needs taken care of within a five-minute walk. Within this radius, he has available to him a convenience store, a coffee shop, a sandwich shop he can eat at, a record shop, and his favorite book store, Kilgore. Really, if he only had a porch, he wouldn't want to live anywhere else in the whole wide world.

He steps into the sub shop. They're playing The Specials, post-Terry Hall unfortunately, but at least they usually play good music. He orders the twelve-inch Homestyle (mayo, tomato, lettuce, avocado, and a ton of bacon) on gluten-free bread, and a fountain drink. He skipped lunch today and figures he could use the calories. Ordering it to go, he takes a seat where he can see the door. He pulls out his phone to see if anything new has happened in the world while he's been writing.

He gets his sandwich and takes it home. Eating it while listening to a Specials album featuring Terry Hall, the only music by The Specials he really cares for. He pours some dog food for Kerrinpuppy, putting a few stray slices of bacon in the bowl for her, and she gets to munching away.

Pulling his phone out for the umpteenth time today, he dials Dad's phone number and lets it ring a few times. Then he hangs up. But it's too late, he knows Dad will call back anyway.

His phone rings about twenty seconds later.

"Hey homie."

"You doing all right?"

"Yeah, I was just thinking and wanted to talk. Then I got to thinking some more and got to thinking that I didn't want to disturb you," Emmett says.

"Oh, you're not disturbing me. Mom and I were just watching an episode of House."

Which is just the kind of thing that makes Emmett feel as though he's disturbing Mom and Dad as they're relaxing after a hard day at work.

"I can call back later," Emmett says.

"No, it's fine. I'd rather talk to you than watch a dumb TV show."

"You sure?"

"Absolutely, you're much more important."

"Okay … "

"So what's up?"

"Well, I was just thinking about my frustration with computer science and programming in general."

Dad waits for Emmett to go on.

"And I was thinking about what a stupid, terrible, awful waste of brain juices it is—I'm just never going to get it."

"Emmett, I think—"

"—No, it's true. How many years has it been?" Emmett does a quick calculation. "Like two? Maybe three?"

"Something like that, yeah."

"So, two or three years, banging my head against the wall when I could have been doing something much more productive, when I could have been doing something worthwhile."

"Okay. But what would that something worthwhile be?"

"I'm not sure. But it sure isn't programming.

"You know how we've talked about how my brain works?" Emmett continues. "How I can just absorb stuff that I'm interested in but there's this huge mental block when I'm not interested? Like the story about my chemistry homework you told me this afternoon?"

"Yes."

"I think programming might be a bit like that. I have no idea what kind of programs I would even write—I'm learning it for the wrong reasons, and I don't know if it would even round out my computer education in the way I want it to.

"It was just so frustrating to sit there this morning before you came over," Emmett continues. "To try to figure out what I was trying to do with that fucking program. Sorry," apologizing for his language.

"It's okay."

"I just don't know if it's something I should be learning, or if it's something I'm capable of learning, or if it's even something worthwhile to be learning. I'm not as smart as I used to be—this illness makes me dumber, these pills make me dumber. I'm not the same brilliant kid I used to be. It's like I'm an athlete past their prime, having sustained a significant injury that means I can't be played as long or as hard. I'm thinking of that Whoopi Goldberg movie where she wins the contest to be head coach of the New York Knicks and ends up taking them to the NBA playoffs and there's the old player with his knees—he's past his prime, doesn't score the most points, but he used to ... he used to be great. But he's not some prima donna like the other guy who refers to himself in the third person all the time," Emmett said.

Dad chuckles, then says, "Why don't you talk to Dr. Bogsdaughter about it?"

"I don't know that he would know, either."

"Why not?"

"I dunno. Gut feeling, I guess. He just doesn't strike me as knowing about the capabilities of my mind. Seems like something a neuropsychologist would know about."

"Why don't we see a neuropsychologist then?"

"Sounds reasonable to me. I see Dr. Bogsdaughter next week, I'll ask him if he knows a good one then."

"Sounds good," Dad says. And then after a pause, "Are you feeling better?"

"Yeah, I suppose so. We've got a plan. And when we've got a plan I always end up feeling better."

"Good."

Emmett and Dad chat on the phone about other things, Dad on speakerphone, Emmett sitting in his chair with Kerrinpuppy on his lap, until his phone beeps.

"What was that?"

"Oh, just my reminder to take my pills."

"Is it ten already?"

"Yup."

"Wow, I had no idea it was so late," and Emmett can imagine Dad rubbing his forehead.

"Yeah, you need to go to bed. You've got to get up early."

"I can stay up with you while you take your pills."

"Nah, that's okay. I should probably get winding down anyways. Thanks for talking with me. I always have such good talks with you."

"No problemo," Dad says; and Emmett knows, if Dad were there with him, he'd be giving him a thumbs up.

"Good night, homie. I love you."

"Love you too."

Emmett prepares his pills for the night and the following

morning, the pills clinking as they hit the plastic containers.

Counting them out carefully but still completing the task of serving out nearly fifty pills in just over two and a half minutes.

Down the hatch, chased with a few gulps of water.

Outside with Little Baby Kerrin so he can smoke and she can go potty.

Placing his unspent cigarette on the ledge of a window near the entrance, to return to it after taking LBK back inside. It's much too cold for puppies to be outside not moving around. She'd be miserable, staring longingly at the door, shivering the entire time Emmett was smoking. So back inside she goes, where she has a warm bed waiting for her.

Back out on the stoop, collecting his thoughts in his notebook for Dr. Bogsdaughter.

Back inside, putting away programming books. All the way on the top shelf where he won't see them. Trying to think of something else to do with his time come morning.

Make the bed. Take his melatonin. Crawl into bed to read until he gets sleepy.

Waking in the middle of the night to eat two apples and just under half a jar of peanut butter. Hunger usually wakes him up in the middle of the night—it's just part of taking his pills, one of the side effects. An insatiable hunger, a hunger that makes him feel like he hasn't eaten in a week regardless of having eaten a foot-long sandwich a few hours ago, waking him up from his dreams and finding him sleepily marching toward the fridge to eat three or four containers of yogurt. He used to ask Mom for salami so he could cut off a few slices for a snack, until he started eating the entire thing in one sitting for a midnight snack. He can eat all the leftovers Mom leaves him with in one night and have to eat out the rest of the week because he doesn't have any food left. His hunger, it seems, is never satisfied.

His belly now mostly full, his beard and coffee table probably caked with peanut butter, he collapses back into bed to start the whole cycle all over again the next day.

2014

Chapter Twelve

"You've got it down to a routine by now," Lacey says.

"A routine?" Emmett chuckles; the word always makes him think of Dad and how he's had the same thing for lunch every day for the past fifteen years. "I suppose so. Or maybe it's more that I've just figured out exactly what I need. There's a careful order of operations."

"'Careful order of operations,'" Lacey quotes. "I like that. Do you ever vary it?"

"I suppose that's the thing about it. There's always a slight variation, always some tweak. But it almost always involves taking medication and smoking a cigarette. There's a mantra of sorts, though, a litany which must be performed in order for it to work."

"Care to share what this litany is?"

Emmett squirms in his chair, looks down at the floor. "I'll oftentimes remember my confirmation verse. I suppose it's not a direct recitation, just a remembrance of all it embodies. Here, I'll look it up," and Emmett fishes his phone out of his pocket and opens the Notes app where he's written the verse down. "It goes, Philippians 4:8—Finally, brothers and sisters, whatever is true, whatever is noble, whatever is right, whatever is pure, whatever is lovely, whatever is admirable—if anything is excellent or praiseworthy—think about such things."

Emmett and Mom and Dad sit in the waiting room of the neuropsychologist. His name is actually Dr. Brains, which Emmett finds a convenient enough title for the man. The office waiting room is littered with toys meant to improve cognitive performance, the loudspeaker in the ceiling playing music Emmett recognizes from when he was in middle school: "you don't know what you've got 'til it's gone. / They paved paradise and put up a parking lot." Originally done by Joni Mitchell, according to Dad, though this one, done by a male singer, is the first one Emmett remembers hearing. He has no idea who's singing because he'd never paid attention to such things when he was younger.

He pulls out his phone and does some quick Googling to put his mind at ease, give it something else to concentrate on. The song brings back vague, clustered memories of certain people from his childhood, of sitting in his childhood bedroom doing his homework or playing Need for Speed: Porsche Unleashed, of listening to the radio—having no clue who was singing what, but certainly having all of the songs memorized because they played them so often.

Turns out it's Counting Crows playing this particular cover, and that the song is titled "Big Yellow Taxi," at least according to Wikipedia. The song seems to him a premonition. Indeed, you don't know what you've got 'til it's gone. He remembers feeling so capable when he was younger, listening to this song. He could have done anything; he'd absorbed information like some kind of super-sponge back then.

Dr. Brains had put him through the ringer with tests—writing tests, math tests, memory tests, visual-spatial tests. They'd tested his ability to recognize faces, his ability to recall details from stories. It'd been a full two days' worth of squeezing every ounce of energy out of his mind as he could manage, and he'd paid for it with his sanity. Now he's going to find out if all the suffering has been worth it.

What Emmett wants to know is, is he capable of programming computers?

The thing is, though, he's already made up his mind. Just from trying to work out the logic problems. Just from trying to piece together the puzzles. Just from trying to hold little pieces of information while testing what Dr. Brains called "working memory" and failing miserably, he knows the answer. He isn't going to be programming anytime soon.

Part of him wants to do it anyway, just to prove to them (whoever they are) he could do it. Just to spite what he knows the expert is going to tell him. To be defiant to the end. And another part of him just wants to focus on what he's best at, whatever that is. Maybe Dr. Brains will tell him what he is good at so he can concentrate on that instead. He's been feeling lost these past few months—ever since moving out of SAR's clutches. Maybe Dr. Brains can provide him with some kind of guidance, some direction to point himself so he'll know what to do with himself.

Mom has her iPad out as usual, resting it against her purse—either playing Pet Rescue or reading a book, Emmett can't tell. Dad's checking his email; he's taken off of work to come to this meeting. Emmett wants a cigarette, though he'd already smoked one before coming inside; they always arrive early enough to appointments like this so he can smoke before they go inside.

Emmett checks his watch. Dr. Brains is running three minutes behind schedule … unless of course his fancy automatic watch isn't keeping accurate time again. Pulling his phone out again, he checks the time on his watch against the time on his phone and finds they're reasonably close together. Emmett pockets his phone again and thinks about the impending results; how Dr. Brains is probably in his office now, running the calculations to figure out how stupid Emmett is.

There's a part of him that doesn't mind being stupid, almost wants to be stupid. There's a part of him that would very nearly take pride in being intellectually disabled. Ever since moving out of Mom and Dad's house, Emmett has been giving speeches to NAMI Family-to-Family classes. The National Alliance on Mental Illness offers free classes for family members of those with mental illness so they can learn more about what their loved ones go through, and one of the last classes always features someone with a mental illness coming in to speak to the class. Emmett's speeches are nigh-legendary, apparently. People remember him and cherish his speeches. He's allowed to speak for as long as he wants, usually about forty-five minutes instead of the allotted ten minutes. He gives his entire story and expounds on his theories on how one lives with mental illness successfully.

He thinks to himself how remarkable it is to do something like that with an intellectual disability, smiling ever so slightly.

"What?" Mom asks with a nervous half-chuckle. Apparently he'd made a noise, too.

"Oh nothing, just thinking about something."

"Thinking about what?"

"Nothing," Emmett says, a little annoyed.

"Sorry," Mom going back to her iPad.

Now Emmett feels guilty. He doesn't want Mom to feel responsible for getting a rise out of him.

"Sorry. I was just thinking about how, if I have an intellectual disability, Dr. Brains would explain my ability to get up in front of twenty to twenty-five people and talk coherently and intelligently about my experiences with mental illness and how to best live with it; how he would explain my insight, is all."

Mom gives her nervous laugh. "Emmett. You don't have an intellectual disability. You're such an intelligent person. You're going to do fine."

"Mom, you weren't there for the tests. There's something fundamentally different about my brain now. I can't do what I used to be able to do. I'm not as smart as I used to be."

Sensing this is a losing argument, a discussion not worth having, at least not as this moment, Mom just nods her head and goes back to what she was doing.

Emmett opens his mouth to re-engage, offended that Mom is

just brushing him off like this, but Dad moves to intercept him. Luckily the door opens and Dr. Brains stands there to greet them.

"Hi, Emmett. Good to see you again. These are your parents?"

"Sure are," Emmett says. Mom and Dad introduce themselves.

"Follow me," and Dr. Brains leads them down the hallway into his office.

Dr. Brains has one of the more interesting offices Emmett has ever been in. Mom will later agree there's a lot of wasted space. All of the furniture is lined up against the wall and Dr. Brains has to pull a comfortable mid-century style lounge chair (which probably cost more than Emmett's rent) out to the middle of the room for Emmett to sit in and be a part of the conversation. Dr. Brains must do a lot of furniture moving in his daily life. Emmett remembers him doing it several times during the two days of testing.

Various neuropsych-y knick-knacks occupy a bookcase along one wall, things Emmett doesn't really recognize but, given their aged look, appear to be tools once used to determine the intelligence and intellectual capacity of individuals by Dr. Brains's predecessors. There are very few books, which Emmett finds interesting, even disconcerting ... books always comfort him. Dr. Bogsdaughter doesn't have too many books in his patient room either, just a few medical reference books and some books of Robert Frost's poetry. Emmett has never been in Dr. Bogsdaughter's actual office, only glimpsed the veritable fire hazard of piles of paper everywhere. Lacey probably has the largest collection of books, occupying a small bookshelf next to the chair she always sits in. But Dr. Brains's office has next-to-no books.

Emmett finds himself looking about the office, squirming in

his chair to see if there are any books hiding behind him.

"Something wrong, Emmett?" Dr. Brains finally asks.

"Oh, I was just looking for books," Emmett answers.

Dr. Brains gives a polite chuckle. "I replaced them years ago with a Kindle," he says, motioning to the little tablet on top of a pile of papers on his desk. "Much more efficient for looking things up."

"Ah," Emmett says, making himself comfortable.

"What do you think about that?" Dr. Brains says.

"I'm not sure," Emmett says. "I suppose it makes sense, in a way. Though personally, I'd prefer having shelf after shelf full of books. So … " his voice trailing off like it oftentimes does when he's under scrutiny.

"Why's that?" Emmett is feeling like the testing is continuing now, as Dr. Brains has a pad of paper and a pen at the ready.

"Books are comforting, they're peaceful."

"Go on," his pen moving across the page.

"I suppose at a technical level, they lower the ambient noise in a room," Emmett throws that out there, hoping it'll stick, hoping the inane questioning will end. Dr. Brains scribbles something down on his pad of paper, then looks up at Emmett, encouraging him to continue. "And I suppose a lot of it relates to my on-again off-again inability to read sometimes. When you lose something you don't realize you value so much, you hold on twice as tightly when you get it back, so … "

"That makes a lot of sense," Dr. Brains replies. He turns to Mom and Dad. Mom, who's been sitting there, erect with her purse held on her lap, has a notebook and pen ready to go like Emmett has asked. Dad has assumed his standard position: left leg crossed over right, hands folded over his knee. "What do you two think of his observation?"

Mom lets out a nervous laugh. "We had a hard time getting

Emmett to read when he was younger. I remember he liked the Goosebumps books for a while, but soon lost interest in them." Mom's words stop short as she searches for more. Dad cuts in:

"I think he was more interested in creating stories for himself. He was always playing with his toys, inventing stories, modding his toys, building with Legos—"

"- building with couch cushions," Mom says.

"Stuff like that," Dad says.

"He's always had a really rich inner world. But to go back to your original question—he has a fairly large book collection now." Mom goes on to explain about Dad reading to Emmett every night before bed during the Great Shock and in the months afterwards, and how Emmett has all of his books cataloged in a database.

Dr. Brains is amazed to hear that Emmett doesn't watch much TV—that he watches the occasional nature documentary while eating his dinner, and is known to watch a PBS documentary every so often, but for the most part abstains almost completely from TV.

"So what do you do for entertainment?"

"I read," Emmett says with a laugh, a little perplexed that Dr. Brains wouldn't have picked up on the fact that someone with a severe case of schizoaffective disorder would find something as stimulating as Game of Thrones or the newest Terminator movie too much to handle.

Dr. Brains writes some more comments on his paper and then notes the time. "We should get down to business. I've got the preliminary results right here. Bear in mind that these aren't the final results, and I'll be doing some tweaking to them, but these will serve as a guide for our discussion here today. Think of them as a general outline for the answer to Emmett's question."

He hands out a copy of the test results to each of them: several pages of a poorly formatted document with all kinds of percentages and terms Emmett is unfamiliar with.

Dr. Brains goes through each category—working memory, logic skills, math skills, verbal and writing skills, an IQ test, short-term memory, long-term memory, visual and spatial reasoning. Dr. Brains says Emmett is average in just about every category, with an average IQ, though Emmett doesn't consider being in the thirtieth percentile as average, especially given he was used to being in at least the ninetieth or ninety-fifth percentile in every category on the standardized tests he took when he was still in school.

What Dr. Brains is most concerned about is Emmett's memory. His long-term memory is largely fine, but it's his working memory, "his ability to hold tiny bits of information for short periods of time—we're talking just a few seconds, like the ability to carry a digit while adding or subtracting a number in his head," Dr. Brains explains, as well as Emmett's short-term memory, that concern the doctor. He says Emmett shows a marked deficiency in both categories, which probably accounts for his inability to remember what he reads sometimes.

As Emmett understands it, his short-term memory is shot, so he can't do math in his head anymore and can barely hold small snippets of information in his head—small facts, little assignments—no wonder he has to write almost everything down and only does things if they're in the calendar on his phone. Good thing his middle school teachers were wrong when they said he wouldn't be carrying around a calculator in his pocket in the future. He wants more of an explanation about how he can have a good long-term memory but not a good short-term memory, but there isn't time for that.

"As for Emmett's question of whether or not he can learn how to program a computer I would say 'yes, but not without great difficulty.'"

"Okay," Emmett says, simply.

Dr. Brains fortunately doesn't ask Emmett how he "feels" about this; they're too pressed for time from the little diversion about books. Emmett can feel a faint electrical buzz about him, things are beginning to get fuzzy ... a haze is drifting over him.

When the subject of painting comes up, Dr. Brains is surprised to find out that Emmett is a figure painter and not an abstract painter. Emmett explains the two are very similar: "It's just shapes, you just have to objectify them." He had done very poorly in the tests that should have been a piece of cake for an artist—taking smaller shapes and putting them together to mimic a larger shape. He'd been able to complete the first one (which had been incredibly simple) but not a single one after that. It's probably why Dr. Brains had come to the conclusion he was an abstract painter.

Emmett does tell the doctor that he paints mostly from his head and not from life—perhaps explaining part of his inability to mimic reality. But by then, checking item after item off the list as the clock marches ever so dutifully toward the time their hour was up, Dr. Brains is on to a new subject.

"I'm saving the most interesting part for last."

Emmett repositions himself in his chair.

"If you'll turn to page," and Dr. Brains thumbed through his own copy of the results, "mmm, four. You'll see the written and verbal scores. You'll see Emmett scored in the ninety-seventh and ninety-eighth percentiles. It's rare to see such unbalanced scores."

"Interesting," Mom says. Emmett looks over at Mom who's just beaming at him; Dad has that "proud of you" look to him. Emmett shakes his head. It isn't like he'd studied to score this well; this was just a fact of who he was as a person. He thought back to taking the test, when he'd been asked to define words and how he'd defined about a dozen words of increasing difficulty with hardly a problem, going from one word to the next and having plenty of time left afterwards.

"He took a little bit more time than usual writing his essay," Dr. Brains begins.

"Well, that's because I went back and re-read it to see if I made any mistakes, so … " Emmett replies.

"Interesting," Dr. Brains says.

"Yeah, wasn't thinking time was a factor at that point. So … "

"Anyway, that was about the only anomaly. Which apparently is easily accounted for by his re-reading his essay. But, as I was saying, it's interesting to see such unbalanced scores. It doesn't quite fit the colloquial (and you'll pardon the expression, Emmett) 'idiot savant,' as he isn't deficient in anything else—"

"Sure feels like it," Emmett interrupts.

"But, still. He isn't deficient in anything, simply average. Normally we see more balanced test scores. Whether it's the medication he's taking or the illness, it's hard to say. With regards to the working memory, Emmett did mention that the voices in his head were saying things to him to throw off his concentration, which certainly suggests the illness. But other times he said the item he was supposed to remember simply disappeared, unaccounted for, without a reason for disappearing."

"Yeah, it was kinda embarrassing. I like to have a reason and I just didn't have one."

"Well, in this case it's okay not to have one. This isn't a test of character, Emmett," Dr. Brains says.

"I know," Emmett says letting his hand with the paper slide off the arm rest of the expensive chair and onto the side. He's beginning to get antsy, ready to leave this room, process the results on his own, breathe some fresh air, get some freaking nicotine in his system.

"SUNSHINE AND RUN TIME. AND RUM SHINE AND
SOMETIMES.

"WE ALL WANT TO KILL YOU. AND WE ALL WANT TO
SPOON YOU," *the voices start in with their song.*

Emmett bends forward for his bag which contains his water
bottle and ziprasidone. No sense in trying to be sly about it
when it was obviously the whole point of why they were there.

He finds the pill bottle and pops two in his mouth, letting
them rest on the top of his tongue where they sit getting all
icky, thankfully not tasting nasty because they're capsules, not
tablets.

Unscrewing the lid to his metal water bottle, he takes a swig,
washing them down, and checks his watch to see about when
they'll be kicking in; a half hour from now, he hoped. The
thought occurs to him he should carry around some of those
single servings of peanut butter. Jayne carries them when she
bikes because they're pretty caloric for being so small. And Dr.
Bogsdaughter had said that taking ziprasidone with a bit of fat
means it's absorbed into his bloodstream better, thus making it
more effective.

He thinks about his confirmation verse. The voices in his
head want him to enter dark places, want him to go down a
path of violence. He can't allow himself to go to those places,
though they're so easy to fall into. If anything is excellent or
praiseworthy, he thinks about those things.

Mom casts him a concerned look and Emmett taps his watch
trying to indicate that it was about time for them to go.

But Dr. Brains is already looking at the clock. "But it looks
like we're just about out of time. I'll have the final test results
ready for you in a week or two, sound good?"

Nods all around.

"Good. Emmett, it was a pleasure working with you and nice meeting you."

"Good meeting you too," Emmett managing to still be polite and shaking the doctor's hand despite the chorus of voices in his head all singing different songs with similarly disturbing lyrics.

Dr. Brains says goodbye to Mom and Dad as Emmett hurries down the hall; he's out the door and rolling a cigarette waiting for the elevator by the time Mom and Dad get to him.

"You doin' okay, Emmett?" Dad asks.

"They're just singing to me."

"Anything we can do?"

"I just need to get outside," Emmett says. "Actually, here," and Emmett hands Dad his tobacco and half-rolled cigarette and fishes around in his bag for his headphones and iPod. Why hadn't he thought of this sooner? He gets the headphones situated on his head, connects them to his iPod and turns on Johnny Cash's American VI: Ain't No Grave, one of his favorite albums because Johnny Cash's voice reminds him of what he remembers his Grandpa Nyfjordeen sounding like. It also helps that the album in general sums up a portion of his life almost perfectly.

He swings his bag around to rest on his back, gets his tobacco stuff from Dad, and continues rolling his cigarette. Dad says something, probably apologizing for spilling tobacco from the rolling paper. Emmett just shakes his head and mouths the word "sorry," and Dad gives him a thumbs up. When the elevator comes, there're mirrors on all sides of the interior. Emmett had forgotten about the mirrors, which hadn't been a problem on the way up.

Years ago, immediately after ECT, Emmett had gone through a period of time when he hadn't been able to look in a mirror—Mom and Dad had had to cover up the giant mirror in his bathroom and he'd gone for months and months, if not over a year, hardly looking at his own reflection. And even now, when he wasn't feeling well, looking at a mirror was likely to make him feel worse.

So, Emmett does the only sensible thing and closes his eyes, searching for Mom's hand and gripping on so she can let him know when the doors open again.

Blind from shutting his eyes and deaf from the music, he rides uncertainly down to the ground floor. Time stretches out. But eventually Mom squeezes his hand and he opens his eyes and is greeted with a view of the lobby.

They step outside. Emmett lights his cigarette and inhales deeply. Maybe it isn't so much the nicotine fix as much as it is the inhaling and exhaling. Maybe it isn't so much the cigarette at all, as getting out in the fresh air. He feels better not being in the confines of the office. Not being around Dr. Brains, who treats him more as a test subject than a human being—something to be summed up on a piece of paper and made assumptions about. Why be so surprised he was a figure painter? Like it's some kind of holy feat to be a figure painter but not to be an abstract painter? But it's starting to make sense why it's so tremendously difficult for him to draw what he wants to draw: the test had been nearly impossible for him. He'd scored in the sixteenth percentile for something called Set-Loss Design and in the first percentile for Design Accuracy; most other artists probably got much higher scores than that.

Okay, maybe not Dr. Brains's fault for assuming Emmett's an abstract painter. And maybe he's already defying convention simply by painting, by doing what they say he can't do. He doesn't need to take up programming; he's doing it simply by painting, had already been doing it simply by painting.

"Feeling better?" Mom asks when he finally takes his headphones off to talk to them.

"Yeah. I think it's just hard to be the subject of all that scrutiny."

"I can imagine," Dad says. "He seemed like a pretty critical guy."

"Certainly very 'fact-based,'" Mom says.

"Shoulda brought Kerrin," Emmett says.

"Why didn't you?"

"Didn't clear it with the doctor first, and he proved to be pretty difficult to get ahold of."

"But she's a service dog," Mom says.

"Yeah, but it's kind of a tricky position with her. I feel a bit torn."

"What do you mean?"

"Well, she's a good girl. But she's not trained to be a traditional service dog. She's essential for me to be able to live on my own, but I'm perfectly capable of going places without her. And sometimes I feel as though she's more of a liability than a help."

"How so?"

"What if she has an accident? What if there's another dog there and she gets aggressive? What if something bad happens?"

"I can see that," Dad nodding.

"Is the ziprasidone starting to kick in?" Mom asks, seeing a more animated Emmett.

"Yeah. Pills started kicking in about five minutes ago."

"Amazing how you can time it like that."

"It's really anywhere from a half hour to forty-five minutes," Emmett says, taking a drag of his cigarette. "But I can definitely feel it when they kick in."

"It's a good thing we have them," Mom says.

"Yeah. Come on," Emmett says, tossing his cigarette on the ground and stomping it out with his boot, "I need me some quality Kerrin time."

Dad is the one to take him home. Emmett hugs Mom good-bye and she gets in her van and drives off. Dad and Emmett get into his Camry. It's just the kind of car Dad would drive—basic, maybe a little plain, certainly not stylish, but reliable. The kind of car you can always depend on. It only further confirms to Emmett that cars are an extension of who Americans are as people, which makes the car-less Emmett wonder who he is in the scheme of American culture.

They drive back to Emmett's house and Dad drops him off in the back alley.

"Say 'hi' to Kerrin for me," Dad says.

"Oh, I will," giving Dad a hug. "I'll see ya tomorrow."

"You got it," Dad says, giving Emmett his signature thumbs up.

Emmett adjusts his pants, grabs his bag, heads around the back of the car and opens the back door to his apartment building.

Down the hall. Key into lock. Hearing the jingling of Kerrinpuppy's dog tags as she trots over to the door to wait for him to open the dang door already.

"Kerrin! Your grandpa says 'hello,'" he greets her as she extends her front paws up toward him, tail wagging furiously. He catches her under her armpits on her descent and keeps her there, unaccustomedly upright, and scratches her behind her front legs. She isn't quite sure what to make of it—there's a queer look on her face. She's pretty sure she's enjoying it, but she's not sure as though she should be enjoying it.

Finally, Emmett lets her down and she jumps up at him excitedly. He tells her to sit and she does so immediately, looking up at him with eyes of unequivocal love and trust.

He scratches her until she collapses onto the floor and lifts her leg up for a belly rub. Emmett has never knowingly denied her a belly rub, having made the promise on the first day he got her when she'd lifted her leg a little apprehensively, unsure of whether or not a belly rub was in the terms of their relationship. Even when saying his sleepy goodnight to her, if he feels her leg lift beneath the covers, he obliges and scratches her until he's too sleepy to continue. It's the least he can do for the dog who's enabled him to do so much.

Chapter Thirteen

◇◇◇

"I suppose that part of being disabled is accepting that there are certain things I cannot do. But the things I can't do are so ... strange," Emmett says.

"How so?" Lacey says.

"Like sometimes I'm getting ready to get ready for bed—because I have to mentally prepare myself for just about everything—and it becomes impossible for me to make my bed."

Lacey shoots him a quizzical look.

"I sleep on a futon, so I have to make my bed twice a day," Emmett clarifies. And Lacey nods her head in understanding. "Anyways. I start thinking about how I have to get the blankets out of the closet and move the coffee table out of the way and move the futon out from next to the wall and how I'll have to put the blankets on the bed—all in all not a very complicated process—and it just becomes impossible. I just can't do it. So I start to get sick and I have to call my parents and it's this big production of them coming to get me and me getting ready to go to their place and it takes an hour and a half and if I'd just had the nerve to make my freaking bed in the first place I'd be okay."

Lacey breathes in deeply through her nose and exhales through her mouth slowly. Emmett follows suit and he feels the panic which was rising inside of him slowly fade.

◇◇◇

So it goes, Emmett thinks as he watches Dad doing his dishes. They were supposed to be out walking, getting exercise, taking Little Baby Kerrin outside so she can go potty. Instead, for reasons Emmett can't explain, Dad is up to his elbows in dish water, doing Emmett's dishes for him. Emmett just can't do them himself.

It reminds him of the story Mom likes to tell his friends about how he'd spent a part of his childhood wearing a black glove on his right hand. Mom always blamed it on him wanting to look like Luke Skywalker in Return of the Jedi, but that wasn't right. Emmett almost always has a good reason for what he does, no matter how weird it may seem.

He'd been maybe five or six at the time, old enough to be by himself while playing but young enough that they'd been in their old house. He'd been playing with his toy guns, his most prized possessions, a pair of metal six-shooters with plastic handles. He had holsters for them and took them everywhere with him. His pediatrician had even taken a picture of him with his guns because he'd found the spectacle so amusing. It was something which never would have happened these days—nor would him building submachine guns out of blocks during pre-school playtime be acceptable either.

During the course of his playing, he noticed that his guns and his hands were sticky. No big deal. He'd just go and wash his hands. He'd marched up the stairs and washed his hands with soap and water in the kitchen sink.

Back down the stairs to resume playing. Same problem.

Wash the gun with soap and water. Same problem.

Humph.

He went into the closet, found a pair of gloves, a pair of black leather gloves he'd never seen anyone wear, put them on, and resumed playing. He wasn't sure how long he went on wearing the gloves, but it was quite a while, to hear Mom and Clarissa talk about it. He eventually cut holes in the tips of the gloves, probably to more easily operate the guns. His winter gloves these days were also fingerless, but that's so he can smoke with them on and not set them on fire.

Dad had always thought it demonstrated Emmett's creativity and logical problem-solving abilities; Dad thought about how most kids that age wouldn't have solved the problem quite like that. And he was probably right.

Emmett was reminded of the incident with the sticky guns as he watched Dad washing his dishes, because he remembered what it was like to be faced with his guns failing him, how he couldn't bear, even to this day, to have certain of his things out of commission. He knew how anal he was and how anal he remained. His apartment was his new set of toy guns—it had to be pristine, perfect.

In some ways, living with SAR had been good for him; It had taught him to accept that things weren't going to be perfect, it had taught him to deal with the fact that sometimes there are going to be piles of dishes and messes on the floor. And maybe it was just retrospect being rose-colored glasses and all, but it seemed as though he'd done all right with it. But the panic he'd been feeling leading up to Dad coming over for their noon-thirty walk, knowing the dishes needed to get done and not being able to do anything before they got done, how crippling that was, made him long for all of SAR's petty bullshit once again. He couldn't remember getting like that before, he couldn't remember something like a pile of dishes crippling him and relegating him to sitting in his chair, unable to do anything. A pile of dishes might have annoyed him in those days, but it wouldn't have prevented him from doing anything.

Now that every mess is his mess and his alone, he feels personally accountable to it. It's as though the state of his mind and the state of his apartment are in direct correlation with one another. If he can only keep a clean apartment, then his mind will be clean, too.

If only it were that simple.

So Dad stands in the kitchen, happy to wash the dishes for Emmett while Emmett sits in his chair, trying not to feel guilty for making Dad do his dishes.

"There, all done," Dad says, walking into the main room.

"Did you still want to go for a walk?"

"Sure," Emmett says, that tone in his voice.

"You okay?"

"Yeah. I guess. No. Not really."

"What's up?"

"I just wish I weren't so picayune about this place," Emmett says.

"Picayune?"

"It means like, 'extremely picky.' Well, picky about petty nonsense. My math teacher said it a lot in math class in high school," Emmett said.

"Ah. I don't think you're extremely picky."

"No, I am."

"Well, how are you picky?"

"Just in how I decided to wash my dishes at about 11:30 this morning before you came over and ended up sitting in my chair until you walked in," Emmett says. Dad looks at him and Emmett continues: "I try to explain to people that it's hard for me to do things like the dishes, and they'll say 'oh yeah, me too,' but they really don't get it. I think they're just relating to it from the standpoint of laziness. They're thinking that they really ought to be doing it but they'd rather sit and watch TV instead. With me it's that I really want to be doing it, I'm actively trying to do it—I just can't. And I have no idea why. No fucking clue. It's not something I can explain. It's like I'm trying to climb a hill but no matter how hard I pedal there just isn't a gear setting that'll let me climb it. I can't believe I'm using a biking reference."

Dad smiles. "I don't know as if I'll ever really understand that, what it's like. But I'll always be here to help with what I can—dishes, taking Kerrin for a walk, whatever you need—I'm here to help."

"Thanks."

Emmett manages a moment or two of eye contact and sees the smile in Dad's eyes and hopes Dad can see one in his eyes. The eyes of the mentally ill, obfuscated, never quite communicating anything of value. He suspects that's what freaks people out the most about the mentally ill—the eyes. Not only the lack of eye contact but also the deadpan, expressionless eyes. The eyes that don't communicate anything, the eyes that don't reveal anything. It's the eyes he's referring to when he talks about the barrier between him and the rest of the world; the eyes that don't betray any emotion, the eyes you can't read any intent off of.

"Shall we go for a walk?"

"You betcha," Emmett says, getting out of his chair. He rolls a cigarette as Dad gets Kerrinpuppy's leash down from its hook behind the bathroom door. "You don't need to hook her onto it," Emmett calls from the kitchen. "She likes to run down the hall."

"Oh right," Dad says. Then Emmett hears Dad say something about getting to run down the hall to Little Baby Kerrin and he can't help but smile. Dad would make such a good real grandpa. Too bad neither he nor Clarissa are in any position to give Mom and Dad real grandkids.

Down the hall they go, Kerrinpuppy leading the way—racing down to the door, skidding to a stop. Turning around and running in place for a while, cartoon-style before finally gaining traction and running back to Emmett and her grandpa who're walking much too slowly. She lets out an excited, low bark as Emmett clips her leash onto her and they head outside.

Kerrinpuppy leading the way, knowing exactly where to go as always.

Getting out in the fresh air does wonders for one's mood. As they walk south on Pennsylvania, away from the busyness of Thirteenth and into the relative sedation of Twelfth and Eleventh and eventually to Governor's Park, Emmett feels as though he can finally think.

They walk in silence, Emmett appreciating the bond between him and his dad that allows them to do so. It's a rare thing to be able to hang out with someone and have a comfortable silence. He can have such comfortable silences with Marta Lee, but Jayne is a nervous enough person that long silences are always interpreted as awkward, to be filled up with something as soon as possible. But with Dad, walking in the cold afternoon air, they can both enjoy the slow walk to their bench at the park where they will "tree bathe" for a few minutes before it's time to head back.

"I've been thinking some more about the test results," Emmett finally says.

"Yeah?" Dad says, turning to face Emmett on the bench.

"Yeah. I think they're actually kind of comforting."

"Comforting?"

"That sound strange to you?"

"Yes. I was expecting them to make you feel worse."

"I could see that. But no, they make me feel better."

"Why's that?"

"They've given me permission to not be a genius." Emmett takes a deep breath and continues. "I was going along in my life thinking that I had a high IQ, either 163 or 136—surely vastly different scores, but still very high scores. And to have an IQ of—what was it? Like 110? Exactly average is really comforting.

"It's like now I don't have to master all of these things like Heidegger and phenomenology and quantum physics and calculus. I just get to focus on what I want to focus on."

"Couldn't you have done that before?"

"Yeah, I guess I could have. But it's like I felt this obligation or something. Like because I was so smart, it was something I really ought to know, like they were things I was supposed to have a handle on because people would expect me to know them. But beyond that, beyond just the IQ portion of the results, it's pretty clear what I'm good at and what I'm not."

"And what's that?"

"Well. All my life, taking standardized tests in school—I've scored in the ninetieth, ninety-fifth, ninetieth-whatever percentile in nearly every subject. It was like I could pick whatever subject I wanted and excel at it. But in my academic life I was failing at everything, I kinda wonder if I wasn't just overwhelmed at the sheer number of things I was supposedly 'good' at."

"Okay."

"And I know Dr. Brains said I was still average in everything, but thirtieth percentile is not 'average' to me, especially not compared to what I used to get in those kinds of tests. Thirtieth percentile is near the bottom of the bell curve, it's in the territory of 'hey, you suck at this, so don't make a career out of it,' and it included stuff like logical reasoning and mathematics and the kind of stuff I'd need for learning programming. Heck, it even included visual and spatial reasoning. Which I find really interesting," Emmett pauses, taking another breath. "But then I look at the verbal skills—ninety-eighth percentile—with the same reading comprehension as a graduate student getting a PhD. It's like God slapping me in the face with a cold fish."

Dad chuckles at the visual. Emmett grins too. "Okay, stupid image. But I stand by my argument. I know I'm one to doubt science a lot … but it was a powerful experience to go in there and take those tests, especially the visual and spatial reasoning ones. I remember Dr. Brains saying they should be pretty easy since I'm an artist, and I just couldn't figure them out. It made me realize a lot about why I'm so slow at making art."

"Why's that?"

"Because it's like banging my head against a wall," Emmett

says, somewhat louder.

"Why do you think that is?"

"When I'm drawing or painting, it's draw a line and erase, draw a line and erase; I just can never make the line correctly the first time 'round. Or the second time. Or the third. Or the fourth. Fifth. Sixth. Etcetera. Etcetera. Ad infinitum. The images I get are purely through trial and error. It's kind of like the whole 'putting a bunch of monkeys in a room with typewriters and eventually one of them puts out Shakespeare,' only I'm a much more highly trained monkey."

"I think I understand."

"Anyways. Back to God hitting me across the face with a cold fish," and Dad and Emmett break down into a fit of giggles. When they subside, Emmett has a look at his watch and discovers that they're late and need to get going. They get to their feet, Kerrinpuppy trotting along.

Emmett continues. "It's been comforting to know that there's a reason I haven't been able to pick up programming. It's comforting to know that I have some really severe problems with my memory and to know which parts of my memory there are problems with. Before, I didn't know there were essentially three parts to memory, I just thought that memory was memory."

"Same here."

"Yeah, I didn't know there was such a thing as working memory. I knew there was short-term memory and long-term memory. I just took it as something like RAM and hard drive storage, but I don't think it quite works like that. And working memory is fascinating."

"How so?"

"You can think of me like a computer that doesn't have cache," Emmett says, trying to be helpful.

"Interesting," Dad says.

"Yeah. Bummer, huh?"

"Big bummer. How do you get past it?"

"Well, they invented paper and pens a long time ago, and they have these things called 'calculators,' so I think I'm pretty good. I'm glad I got into the habit of carrying around a little notebook in my back pocket a long time ago because it comes in handy an awful lot. Without it I would be lost. I'm also glad I got into the habit of keeping track of all of my appointments in my phone years ago, because otherwise I would never know when I was doing what."

"Did Dr. Brains explain why your working memory and short-term memory would be affected but not your long-term memory?"

"No, we didn't get into that. I don't know that he would know. I suspect it's just a vicious circle of meds, illness, and ECT that cause it, and we'd have to have Dr. Brains, Dr. Bogsdaughter, and Dr. Romero in the same room at the same time for a few hours to get it all sorted out—which would probably be pretty expensive, as I doubt insurance would cover it."

"So we'll never know?" Dad asks, referring to the fact that it's been well over the promised two weeks and Dr. Brains still hasn't gotten back to Emmett.

"Nope. Probably not."

The Dr. Dog song "The World May Never Know" starts playing in Emmett's head and, when he and Dad part and Emmett gets back to his apartment, he turns his stereo on and puts on Easy Beat, the album which features the song. He doesn't own a physical copy of this particular EP because the vinyl, for whatever reason, is ridiculously expensive. Amazon wants a $120 for the vinyl and discogs.com wants $70 for the 2008 re-issue of the EP. Either way, far too much money for the album. Emmett may be a completionist when it comes to collecting records of bands he likes, but he isn't about to spend that much money on a single record, especially not an EP with only six tracks.

He invites Kerrinpuppy up onto his lap. She hops up, does a couple turns, decides against it, hops down, and makes herself comfortable in her bed.

Chapter Fourteen

◇◇◇

"When was the last time you painted?" Lacey asks.

"Oh, I'd say probably about a year ago. But I suppose it depends on what you mean by the word 'paint.'"

"What do you mean by 'paint?'"

"Well I've done a bit of drawing, and I'm still interested in doing so. But as far as oil painting, the full shebang, it's been a long time, and I've just lost my drive to do it, my love for it."

"How do you feel about that?"

Emmett pauses, considering. "Surprisingly fine. I don't know as if painting and I were meant to be together for life.

"I mean," Emmett continues, "it could just be the lack of space in my current apartment, or some other more practical considerations. But I just don't have it in me anymore. I feel like I have one last hurrah in me and then I'll be done forever."

"That's kinda sad."

"I suppose so. But I remember you telling me that people are in your life for a reason, a season, or a lifetime. And I suppose that applies to things like painting too, to vocations."

Lacey smiles at this.

◇◇◇

A few nights later, driving back to Emmett's house after an appointment with Dr. Bogsdaughter, Emmett announces that he would like to start a blog.

"A blog? Really?" Mom says from the back seat, putting down her iPad.

"Yeah. I think I have a lot to say about mental illness and I'd like to start saying it."

"I think that's a wonderful idea, Emmett." Dad says, in his 'I'm proud of you' tone.

"I was just thinking about how wonderful I feel after giving a speech, how much good I feel I do and how much hope I offer, and how I could do it consistently through a blog. There's also the issue of the depression afterwards."

"Depression?" Dad says.

"Yeah. I usually feel really great in the weeks and days leading up to a speech. It's exciting and I'm working on my speech, I feel like I'm doing something really worthwhile. And then ... I give my speech and afterwards, there's nothing else to do. I've given my speech and I have no more purpose. So I sink into a depression."

"So you're thinking this would help combat that?"

"Yeah—because there'd always be the next blog post," Emmett says.

"Well this is wonderful," Mom says. "I'm proud of you. Have you thought about what you're going to call it?"

"I was thinking Mostly Just Like You," Emmett says.

"That's interesting. Why that title?" Dad says.

"Because that's how I see myself; I'm mostly a normal person—I have normal aspirations, normal hopes and dreams. I'm just a regular person except with something extra, something which makes me a little different than other people."

"I like it," Mom says. "You remember this was my idea, right?"

"Really?" Emmett says.

"Yep, I've been suggesting it for years. Even since your first or second speech."

"Well I guess the idea finally took root," Emmett says. No one is sure if the comment is snarky or if it just came out that way. Emmett isn't always able to control the intonation of his voice—comments he makes that sound cutting or rude or otherwise hostile might not be intended that way at all. The illness just twists his voice, making it sound hostile. Mom's advice over the years, to "put the best construction on it," a good life philosophy in general, comes in handy in these situations.

They get home and, over dinner and after a brief post-meal-cigarette, they make a list of everything Emmett could talk about on his blog. A not-quite-three-page Word document full of stuff.

Later on, Mom asks Emmett what gave him the idea to start the blog. He explains it was at least partly the disparity of the results of his neuropsych testing—how it was patently obvious to him that he really ought to be writing. And what better way to start writing than with a blog?

"How often do you think you'll update your blog?"

"I'm thinking once a month, to start with. I don't want to stress myself out with too much writing, but I also don't want to bore myself with not enough, and once a month seems about right.

"I was actually thinking about posting it on the same day y'all have your NAMI Family Support Group meeting so you can advertise it for me. If you don't think that would be inappropriate," Emmett says.

"I don't think that would be inappropriate at all," Dad says.

"Okay good. Otherwise I don't know how I would advertise. Flyers maybe?"

"That's a good start," Mom says.

"I might start posting more often, but it'd be tricky to do it more than once a month—I want to focus more on quality than quantity. I was researching some other mental health blogs, particularly those done by people with schizoaffective disorder, and they're primarily personal blogs, more diary-like. Along the

lines of 'this is what happened to me today, blah-blah' and it's
not very insightful into the nature of the illness. I want to offer
practical advice and good insight into what it's like to live with
my illness. So people understand, ya know?"

Mom and Dad voice their agreements.

Later, over another after-dinner cigarette, Emmett is talking
a mile a minute. He hasn't been this excited about something in
a long, long time, and Dad is clearly enjoying it.

It's not a manic mile-a-minute, since Emmett has control
over what he's saying. He's not dominating the conversation,
he's not talking so much he's out of breath; he'll be able to get
to sleep that night just fine. He's just excited, and it's refreshing
for them, after such a long period of not so much sulking as just
plodding along, day after day, treading water, trying to keep
up with everyone else while the monsters attempt to drag him
down.

Mom and Dad leave at 8:30 p.m. as they'd agreed, leaving
Emmett and Kerrinpuppy alone in the apartment.

Emmett sits down in his chair and his gears are a-spinning.
He doesn't like the state of his apartment, the unsightly aspects
to it. He's recently purchased a new chair. Not a particular fancy chair, just one of those eighty-dollar Ikea easy chairs which
he can lean his head back against; a Pöang it's called. It's surprisingly well built for how inexpensive it is. He's folded up his
easel and put it away, next to the fridge. He hasn't painted in
quite some time, and getting the easel out of the way, not to
mention getting that giant six-by-four-foot canvas out of his
apartment, has gone a long way toward making the place feel
more open and capacious. He's reminded of the sticky-gun story from when he was little: his perpetual dissatisfaction with
his environment, his seemingly permanent quest to improve
his living conditions—always tinkering, never satisfied. Always
improving, never resting on his laurels; oftentimes obsessive in

his quest to have the perfectly arranged apartment. Was that something to bring up to Lacey or Dr. Bogsdaughter?

Probably not. It isn't affecting his life in a negative way. Just a character quirk. And really, it gave him something to do, and actually it ended up improving his life more often than not.

His need to be in a perfect environment usually brings about a positive change, though he does sometimes find himself in a position like he had the other afternoon with the dishes—paralyzed; consumed with the desire, the need, to get something mundane done; unable to move on with his day until he finishes with the mundane thing but unable to actually do it. That mundane thing could be doing the dishes, it could be making an appointment with his dentist, it could be any of an innumerable list of things everyone else takes for granted in the course of their day but which becomes an all-consuming roadblock for Emmett.

So maybe he really should mention his problem with the dishes, with accomplishing mundane goals, to Lacey and Dr. Bogsdaughter. He couldn't have done anything else until the dishes were clean.

But isn't that the point of being on SSDI? Isn't that part of the whole reason for his being considered disabled? This obsessiveness that oftentimes impairs his ability to function like a normal human being, this immobility when presented with certain tasks?

Of course it is.

Sometimes, not infrequently, Emmett feels like a fraud for being on SSDI, like he's cheating the system. So many people assume that the majority of people on SSDI are cheating the system. Emmett likes to point out that, with the rent of a one-bedroom apartment being 104% of the income one earned on SSDI, it isn't really a viable way of earning a living; it isn't like one is living in the lap of luxury off the hard work of the rest of the able-bodied tax payers. But he can't help but feel like a fraud—he passes so well; he seems to others so well-equipped to handle everyday life.

So he has his little "business" fixing computers. He even has business cards and handles the occasional computer. It gives him something to talk about with the baristas at the coffee shop (since people seem to like to talk about work) so he doesn't feel like too much of a liar, and it gives him some extra spending money so he can expand his book and record collection. He doesn't charge very much, partially because he's worried about getting too much business (and thus losing his SSDI), but mostly because he wants to be affordable for those people who can't afford to spend $250 to have their computer fixed like he'd had to charge at the computer repair shop where he'd worked before ECT.

Emmett often has to remind himself he is, in fact, disabled. That he does, in fact, have a severely debilitating mental illness.

He's reminded of Jayne's terrible habit of comparing herself to him. He never quite follows her logic, but maybe she's just trying to make him feel less alone. He also remembers Mom's phrase: "put the best construction on it." Mom is full of canned responses of incredible wisdom like that. Or maybe Jayne does genuinely think that Emmett is just mooching off of his parents and that he's perfectly capable of getting a job and living an independent life. Maybe it's all his fault for not being more vulnerable with her. He'll feel himself about to get psychotic around her, those signature electrical pulses, and he'll head home to suffer in isolation. Maybe if she sees that other side of him she'll realize how fundamentally different their situations are. How he isn't just cruising along, enjoying life, but that he's tortured by the demons who live inside his brain.

Chapter Fifteen

The decay surrounding him.

Not so much a stench as a basic olfactory sense,
a knowing,
following him down the street.

The street might as well be deserted.

No one seems to notice, no one seems to take heed, no one
seems to pay attention.

Just his Four-Legged Friend taking him home.

Leading him through the streets at once dank, at once dusty;
as they, the ominous they, closed in.

Their long searching claws probing blindly,
impossibly long—getting nearer and nearer.

A race he can't lose.

Following his Four-Legged Friend on faith alone. Willing traffic to work out in his favor.

Life (he knows) goes on around him.

People about them shopping: seeking meals, seeking quick
cups of coffee or an afternoon beer.

Him leaving someone,
someone important,
behind.

The lurking, lustful creatures aren't looking for the someone
important. Looking for me, he thinks, so some people get left
behind. Because you have to hold it together until you can
make it up the stairs and down the hall and into the room that
is your sanctuary where searching lecherous hands can't get
you; where capsules and tablets and the natural progression
of a digestion system will make them disappear.

What a mad, tender world.

Sometimes he wonders afterwards,
with a glass of water,
what would happen
if he let them take him?

Wonders if he were defiant,
if he were submissive.

What would the chicken say to the egg
if she got a chance to speak?

Would she be cordial?
Would she be derisive?
Would she be pandering like all mothers are wont to be?

Pick up the pace, it's not far now.

When you smell french fries it's never far.

Freedom fries, American bombs,
and their spindly, search-light
fingers never further, never closer.

Never look back, all too human
looking back—that's how you
turn into table salt.

Will you take a capsule or a tablet?

How long will you sleep?

Will your father tuck you in? wish you pleasant dreams and
lock the door against the spindly fingers?

Remember the code as your Four-Legged Friend leads you
up the stairs. And all you can remember is the Fifth of No-
vember, but it's much too warm out for that. It's always too
warm out.

Remember, remember the Fifth of Nov—

(Shut up. Shut up. shutupshutupshutup.)

Fingers automatically entering the code, never remembered
always just entered, automatic. Automatic like so many
things. Four-Legged Friend marching you down the hall and
its unfamiliarly twisting confines. No friendly faces whatso-
ever; all the better—you know what you look like. Twisted.
Insane. People liable to call the authorities, authorities who
couldn't care less about them or the one you left behind, who
wouldn't reward your Four-Legged Friend for bringing you
here. Only. Just ...

Get your keys out. You're at John Elway's apartment. Isn't
that what he joked? Laughing while you groaned at his nev-
er-ending panoply of jokes?

Find the right key (there aren't too many), into the apartment—Four-Legged Friend takes point, the first to enter any
room, always ready to take the brunt of any assault. Good

Girl. Such a Good Girl. Into the confines of a fortress the naked and the grotesque can't find their way into—except when they can.

Two capsules, one tablet.

The capsules work better when served with something fatty.

Just a spoonful of peanut butter helps the medicine go down.

Drink lots of water.

You've lost plenty through the millions of holes in your body, maybe that's what they're after, the millions upon millions of holes all over your body, which leak in the Hot Hot Heat of summer's glaring sun and freeze in the obstinacy of winter's curt production. Sit down in your chair. Drink lots of water. Offer the rest of the spoonful of peanut goop to your Four-Legged Friend.

Good Girl. Such a Good Girl.

Wait for the one you left behind to show up. Wait for the two capsules and a tablet to work their way down your throat, dissolve in your stomach, disband into your bloodstream.

Wait.

Wait.

Wait

Chapter Sixteen

✕✕✕

"So you go to your parents' house every weekend?" Lacey asks.

"Yep. It's kind of a necessity."

"How so?"

"Well there's practical stuff like doing laundry and getting my groceries and food for the week," Emmett says. "And then there's also the fact that my dad isn't at work on the weekends, so I don't necessarily have social contact on those two days unless I go over to their place. And then there's also that it's nice to get away from the city for a little while."

"When do you usually go?"

"One of them picks me up on Saturday around 5:00 p.m. so we're back in time for dinner."

"What about hanging out with Jayne or Marta Lee?"

"I don't know. I guess it's just not predictable enough. I'm at a point in my life when I need a consistent routine, something I know is going to happen every weekend like clockwork. Jayne has a tendency to flake out and never text me like she says she will, and Marta Lee doesn't strike me as the kind of person to have that consistent of a routine in her life right now—too much stuff to do, not enough time."

"I can understand that," Lacey says.

"I feel childish for always going over to my parents' house, but it's just kind of a necessary thing."

"Why feel childish?"

"Mostly because I'm 27 years old and I'm spending the weekends with my parents. I know I've got a really good reason, but sometimes it doesn't seem like a good enough reason ... I'm decently healthy, I ought to be able to handle two days alone by myself, I ought to be able to occupy myself at least that long."

Lacey smiles at him as he scratches the sleeping Kerrinpuppy on his lap. She stirs from her sleep, stretches, and closes her eyes again. It's not time to leave yet. She'll know when it's time to leave.

◇◇

He almost always regrets being taken back to Mom and Dad's house after a psychotic episode, especially on a Friday night. There's a certain cheeriness, a specific productive air about the house that immediately sours him to the experience of being around them on a Saturday morning.

Dad in the laundry room, checking the pockets of Mom's clothes for tissues so he can tease her later about her trying to sneak one past him. Mom at the kitchen counter watching one of those terrible cooking shows, still in her pajamas, foot bouncing up and down and up and down as she eats her eggs and bacon and stares at her iPad which is never more than a few feet away from her. Kerrinpuppy, his dearest friend, in the backyard, sunning herself and having the time of her life—so happy and carefree and eager to chase any small mammal that approaches the yard.

And then Emmett, beneath his five or six blankets to help him feel safe, not coaxed out of sleep gently by the pull of dextroamphetamine but yanked out of it by Guy Fieri and his nauseating optimism and the sound of the dryer door banging closed—the mere presence of other human beings in close proximity as Emmett's early warning systems try to kick him into high gear, getting him deeper and deeper into panic as he realizes he's in too drugged a state to defend himself, and then resolutely disappointed because it's just the TV. Because it's just Dad. No need to panic. Everything's okay.

Emmett waits for Dad to get out of the laundry room, staring at the blurry ceiling tiles, alternating squinting and resting his eyes to see what kind of a difference it makes. Squinting makes his eyelids quiver, just like smiling makes the edges of his mouth twitch. Both make him look like a drug addict or like a crazy person, so he doesn't do either very often. Doesn't have reason to do either very often. Glasses make it so he doesn't have to squint, and what does he have to smile about anyway?

Dad sits down in front of his computer, mouse clicking away. Annoyed, Emmett asks Dad to get out of there as politely as he can. He's been awake for five minutes and already his patience is worn thin; it's going to be a long weekend. But Dad understands. If only he could understand in the first place. He gets up from his chair and heads upstairs, the stairs creaking in a premature kind of way, the way you'd expect a house twice the age of this one to creak. They don't make them like they used to.

He changes into fresh clothes and heads back upstairs. As predicted, Mom is sitting there in her jammies, leg bouncing up and down and up and down, not in time to any music, more a genetic reflex—Emmett does the exact same thing when his leg is in that position, just like Grandpa had done. It's a proud family tradition.

"Morning Emmett," Mom says cheerily. "Kerrin's outside."

"Yep," Emmett says, about all the conversation he can manage. He so desperately wants to be polite, wants to be a morning person this morning … but. Fuck. What else is he supposed to do? He grabs a mug from the cupboard and begins to pour some coffee from the carafe.

"Good coffee," Mom adds. It's the cheerfulness that does it for Emmett.

"Okay … " Emmett's voice dismissive; how could she not know he wouldn't be up for conversation first thing in the morning?

Getting the coconut milk creamer from the fridge, he pours the tiniest amount into the mug and stirs it into the coffee; the coffee turns the color of a burnt Werther's Original.

He takes a sip.

"THAT LYING CUNT," *Myra says, incredulous.*

And Emmett can see Myra's point. The coffee is pretty terrible. It tastes less like coffee and more like coffee-flavored water.

"I DON'T EVEN UNDERSTAND WHY THAT BITCH BOTHERS TO BREW SHIT LIKE THIS, MIGHT AS WELL JUST DRINK HOT WATER WITH MILK AND SUGAR IN IT."

"Mmmhmm," Emmett says.

"What's that, Emm?" Mom says.

"Nothing."

"Good coffee?"

"Nope."

Mom gets an exasperated look on her face. Maybe she's tried extra hard to make good coffee for him this time and now he's just gone and insulted her coffee-making skills. But if the roles were reversed? He'd rather be told the truth than be lied to—better to know that your coffee is shitty than to go on believing you're making quality coffee and end up looking like a fool in front of company someday, right?

He doesn't know quite what to do. He takes another sip from his coffee. A chorus of voices suggest that he throw the coffee in Mom's face. He tells them to shut up in his mind, which just makes them laugh with glee. Mornings after psychosis at Mom and Dad's house often start out this way.

Maybe he ought to have this conversation with Mom right now. But with this chorus of voices chanting and singing and ranting there's no telling what might happen. He pours a measure of sugar into the coffee and stirs it in, then squeezes his way between Mom and the kitchen chair, saying "No, you're fine," when she tries to scoot forward, grabs his cardboard tin of tobacco, and heads outside.

He rolls himself a cigarette, lights it, and takes out his phone.

He feels better on the back porch—it feels more like home than any other space here, which is funny because it's probably the space where he spent the least amount of time as a kid.

Every other space has a distraction or a distraction in close proximity, most likely in the form of a TV. But the porch has no such distractions, save for their neighbor turning on his radio and blaring awful pop-country music in the evening as he sits in his hot tub.

It's the place where he and Dad have had so many of their wonderful conversations, the place where Emmett has done so much writing and thinking, and the place where he's watched Kerrinpuppy be her most satisfied: sitting out on the grass, alternating between sunny and shady spots, always on the lookout for squirrels. He reminds himself that, though it does frustrate him that oftentimes Kerrinpuppy isn't in bed with him when he wakes up in the morning, it's because she's in the backyard, a place she enjoys more than any other place in the whole wide world.

Sitting out on the porch, smoking his cigarette, finding himself paying less attention to his phone and more attention to what Little Baby Kerrin is so interested in, Emmett feels himself calm down. Bad coffee isn't the end of the world; Myra is just a spoiled bitch who needs to learn a thing or two about gratitude, and he needs to learn to stop listening to her quite so much. He finishes his cigarette and goes in to Mom, who's still in front of her iPad, playing solitaire and watching the Food Network.

"Sorry about the coffee comment," Emmett says.

"Oh, no worries, Emmett."

"It's just that Myra was trying to get the best of me and I think I might have said it a little rudely and I was just trying to say it matter-of-factly," Emmett goes on to explain anyway.

"I learned quite a while ago not to take how you say things

personally. But I appreciate the apology," Mom says, smiling.

"Thanks."

"But, by all means. Make your own coffee. I don't mind in the least."

"Okay," Emmett says, more an acknowledgment that he'd heard her than an agreement that he'd make himself new coffee.

He pours his second cup of coffee—the coffee is a weak light brown color. Next, the tiniest amount of coconut milk creamer into the cup, and this time he adds a few shakes of salt to the coffee.

"You know that's salt, right?" Mom says.

"Yep!" Emmett says, smiling. The salt will make the coffee taste more flavorful, his concession to not being able to drink coffee as strong as he'd like.

Mom just shakes her head as he heads back outside to enjoy the midmorning air.

Usually when Emmett stays in Aurora for a while, on his occasional vacations or when Clarissa is in town visiting, Mom has him buy a pound from the coffee shop next door—mostly because Emmett doesn't like the Starbucks coffee she buys and probably also because she doesn't want him to drink her completely out of coffee while he stays there. He can go through a pound of coffee in a matter of days, nursing a pot of coffee over the course of a few hours before brewing a new one without skipping a beat. It's a wonder to her he gets any sleep at all.

But coffee doesn't really affect Emmett much in the way of waking him up. The medication he takes is so sedating that he requires a powerful stimulant, dextroamphetamine, and quite a large dose of it (fifty milligrams every day as prescribed, though somedays a twenty-milligram pick-me-up in the early afternoon), to wake him up. Caffeine is a drop in the bucket compared to dextroamphetamine.

Emmett's taking about fifty-some-odd pills these days, though ten of those are a simple over-the-counter medication, completely unrelated to anything to do with mental health. Dr. Bogsdaughter's brilliant idea. Dr. Bogsdaughter had stumbled across the Finnish study and thought it was a low risk of a drug with such a large potential benefit that it would be dumb not to try it. So Dad had gone to Walgreens and bought a ton of it, enough for Emmett to work his way from twenty milligrams a day all the way up to the two hundred that the people in the study had been taking. He'd ramped up steadily, upping the dose by twenty milligrams every other day, and was soon at two hundred milligrams every night.

The results were dramatic. People started telling Emmett he looked much more present, looked much more put together. Much more … sane. He's able to maintain eye contact with people, no longer persistently staring at the wall, the floor, the coffee mugs in front of them, anything but the other person. He's able to relate to people more, to connect with them in the subtle body-language-type ways that make up most of communication. Emmett's become more human. Perhaps he fears less that people are capable of looking into his soul merely by looking into his eyes, so his eyes are less obfuscated, and so people can read things from them, people can access him now.

It's been the biggest improvement Emmett has ever seen with any medication he's ever taken. And the best part is there aren't any side effects he can detect. It's such an innocuous drug that he has no problem taking it. All of his other drugs come with terrible drawbacks. Some of them mimic the negative symptoms of the illness by making him subhuman: unable to touch other people, unable to relate to other people; putting up a barrier between him and the rest of the world. His other drugs make him fat and stupid and uncoordinated; they affect his balance. One of them gives him seizures. They all seem to make him so unbelievably tired he'd come to accept that getting up at 11:00 a.m. would be normal for the rest of his life. But with this drug, he's been able to reduce his risperidone, which is one of the worst of the sedaters, to a quarter of what it had been, and now he's getting up at more reasonable times, eight-thirty or nine in the morning, sometimes earlier. He has time for breakfast, a meal he'd thought he'd never eat again.

The medicine has given him an extra three hours—an extra three hours he oftentimes doesn't know what to do with, but he's going to figure something out. Coffee has become an important part of his morning routine, something he just barely remembers from back when Lauren was a part of his life. When she'd come over before they both headed over to work, and he'd have a French press of coffee and some eggs and toast waiting, and they'd wolf it down so they'd have time to enjoy their coffee, her feet in his lap, before they took off speeding through Denver morning traffic for the bus that would take them to Wheat Ridge, another French press of coffee safely hot in a Thermos in Lauren's bag.

This morning, Emmett goes downstairs and gets his laptop while waiting for the coffeemaker to do its thing: groaning and gurgling and making odd digestive-type noises. Mom goes upstairs to change out of her PJs, Dad lamenting that today won't be an all-day-jammie-day after all, as he carries a load of laundry down the stairs.

Everyone with their tasks for the day except for Emmett. He wonders what in the world he'd actually taken to occupy himself when he'd left his apartment the night before, half-crazed, to spend the night at Mom and Dad's and thereby ruining his Saturday schedule.

It always seems like a good idea at the time. To wake up with people in the house after being psychotic, to have someone to talk to, to have that kind of support. But in practice, it rarely works out as nicely as it does in their collective imagination.

Mom and Dad (Dad in particular) have their weekend routines, and Emmett feels as though he ought to stay out of the way. He doesn't want to intrude any more than absolutely necessary. His own Saturdays are usually dedicated to trying to clean his tiny apartment in the morning and then hanging out with Tobias for a few hours in the afternoon where they talk endlessly about just about anything, flowing easily from one topic to another as one does when stream-of-consciousness takes over. At five, Dad picks him up and takes him back to Aurora where he'll stay until just after dinner Sunday evening before returning to his apartment to start the week all over again.

On the occasions that he finds himself at Mom and Dad's house on a Saturday morning, it's hard for him to know what to do with himself, and it often means he gets sick. Even now, he can feel a slowly plodding monstrous sickness coming his way in the form of a dull electric ache behind his eyes and a certain lightness to his heart. It's signaling: do something with yourself now or there will be serious consequences to pay later.

He really ought to tell someone about the slowly plodding monster, but instead he takes a sip of his coffee and opens up his laptop—maybe there'll be some kind of salvation waiting for him after he enters his login password and takes a peek around.

Pill time comes and Emmett dutifully swallows his morning ration. All in the same cup, swallowed at the same time, followed by a swig of water.

The slowly plodding monstrous sickness is still making progress a couple hours later after Emmett has exhausted the interesting-ness of what his laptop can provide: the email to be checked (none of it from a real person) and the RSS feeds to be read, none of it really interesting enough to be commented upon. He just needs a jump start, a little spark to get him writing. If Emmett can start writing, then he'll be all right; it can keep him occupied for hours and hours and he'll be all right. All right. All right. That's what he needs. He doesn't need perfection. He doesn't need extravagance or anything otherworldly. He just needs "all right."

The default is always a cigarette.

There's a certain calming ritual to rolling your own cigarette. It requires a level of precision that only the human eye can offer. And, while there are certainly tools that can aid you in your endeavor to get the perfectly rolled cigarette, these tools are more of a hindrance than a help, an unnecessary burden, because your hands are perfectly capable of making the perfect cigarette. It's best to be calm, to be purposeful, to be present when rolling the cigarette—rush any part of the process and you're liable to end up with a cigarette that bulges in the middle; or you'll rip the paper; or you'll apply too much spit and it won't burn evenly, or not enough spit and the cigarette will unravel as you smoke it.

Emmett is an expert roller; in many ways it's his form of meditation, his own Zen-like practice. People compliment him on his rolling abilities whenever he finds himself rolling a cigarette for a passerby on his stoop. He still screws up from time to time (usually if he rolls while standing or if both of his hands aren't free or if he rushes himself) but a good 90 percent of the time he gets a perfectly rolled cigarette that smokes just like a pre-rolled cigarette, but without it tasting like complete rubbish.

He rolls himself another perfect cigarette and takes a half-second to appreciate it, the craftsmanship that went into it—the untold legions of cigarettes that went before it, informing the creation of this particular cigarette—before lighting it and taking the first drag.

Mom comes out and asks him questions about what he wants on his sandwich. Emmett just agrees to anything she says. She can make him whatever kind of sandwich she wants and he'll like it, he doesn't care. Oftentimes, with clothes, with food, he just wants what he's given.

Pulling out his phone, he checks his email once again, then Facebook, Instagram, etc., etc., even though he just checked them a few minutes ago. The screen is more entertaining than the veritable desert of the suburbs of Aurora. Kerrin might find the place endlessly entertaining, but Emmett doesn't have her sense of hearing or her sense of smell. Neither does he have her prey drive, her dedication to the eradication of small mammals. He needs social media because life doesn't seem interesting enough without it. Though it might someday occur to him that people have existed for tens of thousands of years without social media just fine; that there might be something more out there worth paying attention to.

Mom finally calls him in for lunch. Not yelling from the kitchen like she used to. She knows that Emmett finds the yelling grating. He's a sponge for yelling, even the kind of yelling that promises food. She opens the sliding glass door to find Emmett, with the cigarette burning down nearly to his fingers, staring at his phone, and tells him that lunch is ready.

He looks up from his phone, nods, extinguishes what little is left of his cigarette into the overflowing ashtray, and calls Little Baby Kerrin in for lunch.

They pray and then dig in.

It's simple food—just sandwiches and chips, but delicious. Somehow, food always tastes better when it's prepared by your mom.

"Emmett, what do you say to a W-A-L-K after lunch?" Dad says, spelling it out so Kerrin doesn't hear, in case Emmett doesn't want to go on one.

"Sure thing," Emmett says. "I think I'm starting to get a bit of cabin fever so it'll be good to get out of the house."

"I've got some checks to deposit if you're looking to go to the bank."

"Hmm, maybe," Emmett says. The ATM at the bank is a long way. About a mile and a half one way. It always leaves him exhausted afterward. But, considering the state of his belly these days and how out of shape he feels, he could probably use a walk to the bank every day.

"Up to you."

"Yeah, let's do it."

Dad gives him a thumbs up.

"Can I accidentally drop a chip on the floor?" Mom says, that look in her eye.

"Oh, I guess," Emmett says. It immediately sours his mood. Mom knows he doesn't like to give Kerrin table scraps, but the look is like one of judgment, one that suggests he never gives Kerrin food that she likes, never gives her treats, and that Kerrin really ought to be getting treats all the time.

"SLAP THE BITCH UPSIDE THE HEAD, SHOW THE CUNT HER PLACE," *one of the many unnamed voices suggests. This goes on for some minutes as conversation between Mom and Dad, seeming even more distant, continues.*

Emmett excuses himself from the table to go to his messenger bag in the basement where he takes out two white ziprasidone pills and tosses them down his throat, swallowing them; returning to the kitchen table to wash them down his throat with a swig of his Pepsi.

He glares at Mom with that "don't think of fucking with me or even opening your mouth" look in his eyes as she turns to him with a bit of cheese in her hands. She smiles and says "okay," and then turns to Dad and offers him the cheese. He really needs to talk to her about that. If only he could hook up an amplifier and some speakers to his brain so Mom and Dad could hear what the voices tell him. It was much worse before the over-the-counter medication; then it was almost constant—

the din of voices.

Dad clears the lunch table and Emmett goes outside to smoke his after-lunch cigarette. The ziprasidone kicks in pretty quickly, the voices in his head promising they'll be back with plenty of "fuck you"s all around and kissy noises and the like. And then it's time for Emmett to go. Sleep dowsing his consciousness, like any second could be his last, he calls Kerrinpuppy inside, as impatient for her to come inside as she is reluctant to go inside.

He passes Dad, still cleaning up after lunch. Dad asks him something—probably about going for a walk—to which Emmett mumbles something back; not so much words as noises meant to convey tiredness. Down the stairs to his cot. He finds enough energy to make up his cot since he doesn't like to sleep under the covers with his boots on. He lumbers onto the cot and Kerrinpuppy is just getting herself settled into the crook of his arm when he falls asleep.

Emmett's first thought upon waking up is that he needs a soda. He gets to his feet, Kerrinpuppy jolting awake, and wanders over to the mini fridge in the store room, where he finds a cold Pepsi. Opening it, he takes a long drink from the cold can—thankful that the executives at the Pepsi-Cola company saw it fit to make Pepsi with real sugar, since he's allergic to high-fructose corn syrup.

He looks at his watch, it says he's been asleep for four hours—he checks his phone, doubting this. Nope, more like thirty minutes, and he sets his watch to the correct time. He loves this watch, it's just about perfect … if only it would keep accurate time. He can actually read this one. Digital watches don't give him any sense of time; the numbers aren't meaningful in the way an analog watches hands are. But traditional analog watches make you do math, which is troublesome for him. This watch face has minute markers on the outside and hour markers on the inside—hardly any math involved in telling the time. It also has a sweep motion second hand so he doesn't get so anal about the second hand not lining up with the tick marks.

If only it would keep accurate time.

He's still pretty tired from his ziprasidone, but he can at least function; it's the familiar dry-eyed, back-of-the-eye itchiness that used to only accompany long nights doing homework but is now a near-constant sensation letting him know he's about as energized as he's likely to get.

Kerrinpuppy gets to her feet, doing a seesaw stretch and yawning loudly. She looks ready, willing, and able to go anywhere, any time. Emmett appreciates this about her—his little Navy SEAL, ready to deploy at a moment's notice, so well rested from her constant napping that she's in go-mode at all (waking) times.

"Come on, let's find Grandpa," he calls to her as he starts lumbering up the stairs.

She jumps down from the cot and bolts up the stairs, heading around the corner before trotting back and looking like, "You coming?"

They find Dad also napping, in front of an episode of Northern Exposure, the DVD from Netflix set to autoplay. Emmett snaps his fingers by Dad's lap and Kerrinpuppy jumps up on his lap and starts giving her grandpa kisses.

Dad wakes up with a bit of a start but is immediately laughing at Emmett's ridiculous dog licking his face with such enthusiasm.

"Well hello there, Kerrin," he says between chuckles.

"Hey homie," Emmett says.

"Hi there," he says, still laughing, Kerrinpuppy's tongue tickling his face.

"I think I'm ready for a walk."

"So, to the bank?"

"Yep, to the bank."

"To the bank, to the bank, to the bank bank bank. To the bank, to the bank, to the bank bank bank," Dad starts singing to the tune of the William Tell Overture.

Dad and Emmett have been singing that song ever since they started walking to the bank, which was well before Kerrinpuppy was even born. Emmett sometimes got the song stuck in his head in a bad way and they'd have to turn back so he could get some medication in him, a cup of coffee, and his headphones to combat the litany of voices singing the song to him. Fortunately, this is not one of those times. He's never mentioned to Dad the song sometimes causes psychosis, because Dad seems to enjoy the song so much. Emmett feels he has to draw the line somewhere on how much his illness limits other people's fun—and the line is at the stupid song they always sing before departing for the bank.

They get back from their walk, sweating profusely, Dad heading upstairs to take a quick shower and change into clean clothes before supper, and Emmett to the porch to let Kerrinpuppy run around the backyard (her stamina for the backyard seemingly inexhaustible) while he smokes another cigarette.

Sweat is dripping off his forehead and he botches his first cigarette with a drop that lands plunk in the middle of his near-perfectly rolled cigarette. Nothing he can do but tear the cigarette apart and start fresh.

Dad joins him, barefoot—a rare sight on any occasion. Emmett always marvels at Dad's toenails. His own toenails are disgustingly misshapen. He occasionally but obsessively rips his toenails off, searching for tracking devices, and they always grow back a little funny. Dad's toenails are nearly perfect. Emmett, like Dad, almost never goes around barefoot. Dad never goes barefoot because once he'd accidentally stepped on one of Mom's sewing needles and it'd gone straight through his toe.

Emmett's reason is more vain: his own toenails are frequently bloodstained and next-to-nonexistent, only thick, sickly stumps of what they're supposed to be.

Mom brings them each a glass of water. It hadn't gotten all that hot out, but they'd over-dressed and hadn't been smart enough to layer their clothes. Not that Emmett would have layered much anyways. He feels fat enough these days that he wouldn't be caught dead outside in just a tee shirt; that was a sight he only put his family through, and even then, only for the first couple cigarettes early in the morning.

Some days his weight, his disgusting belly, is on the forefront of his thoughts, and other days it doesn't even compute; he just goes on living and it doesn't matter. He wishes he'd exercise more, he wishes he could get on his bike, he wishes he were as skinny as he'd once been—but most of the time it isn't that big of a deal to him.

He remembers telling Dr. Bogsdaughter long ago that he'd rather be happy, functional, and fat than miserable, psychotic, and skinny. It'd seems as though that was the choice at the time, and that it's still the choice. The reality is simply that the pills make you fat, and that's all there is to it. Clozapine still makes him feel as though he hasn't eaten in two weeks every night about an hour after taking it, as do a number of the other medications he's taking, and he's also convinced the calories he eats count more than the calories other people eat. But the clozapine works; it's the most effective antipsychotic they have, and if he wants to be a functioning human being that's what he's going to have to take—it's another existential imperative: be fat and functional or be skinny and crazy. Seems like a pretty obvious choice to Emmett. Seems like most of the choices he's made so far due to having a mental illness are, though quite unfair, painfully obvious.

So it goes.

Chapter Seventeen

"I never know how to feel about summer," Emmett says as he sits down in the chair opposite Lacey, perspiration streaming down his face.

"How do you mean?"

"Well beyond just this," Emmett says gesturing to his face as he takes a towel out of his bag and begins drying his face off, "it's also that Jayne is out of school for a little while and therefore has more time to hang out, at least theoretically."

"Theoretically?" Lacey says.

"It's like when she took the semester off. She promised we'd hang out all the time, and we didn't see each other hardly at all. Maybe even less than when she was in school."

"Jayne doesn't keep her word," Lacey offers.

"Not at all," Emmett says as he puts the towel away and tells Kerrinpuppy to hop up in his lap. "But I've been writing, like you asked."

"Come to any conclusions?"

"Mostly that my feelings factory is pretty messed up. Which is interesting because we always talk about gut feelings as being just that—feelings."

"There are many kinds of feelings," Lacey says.

"Precisely. It's our failure to grasp the English language which enhances this misunderstanding. I may not have much in the way of emotions, but I have plenty in the way of feelings.

"Anyways. I came to the conclusion that Jayne isn't going to be one of those people who'll support me in my illness. Not fully."

"How so?" Lacey is scribbling down some notes now.

"I think it goes back to when I was recovering from ECT. She never came to visit me, plain and simple. And I think she's lying about Lauren chasing her off because, while I don't remember exactly when Lauren left me, it was pretty soon into it—my mom thinks right after Christmas. So why didn't she come then?"

"This is a difficult conclusion for you to come to, isn't it?"

"Yep ... " Emmett sighs and looks down at his puppy; the sweat has started to stream down his face once more. What to do? What to do?

◇◇◇

Emmett sits down on the stoop and begins to write. Writing helps quite a bit—processing through his appointment with Lacey in his little black notebook. Page after page of what he imagines is nonsense, just rambling about what he can remember of his relationship with Jayne. Which isn't much. The more he writes. the more he feels deceived, as though Jayne has been taking advantage of his memory loss to create a bond between them that just isn't there.

More and more he's relegated to intuiting his way through a problem. His brain is a trash heap, a pile of refuse he hasn't bothered to clean up yet, perhaps one that can't be cleaned up at all—beyond all hope, and therefore one that needs to be abandoned for another base camp. Ever since the neuropsych testing, he's come to think of his brain as less and less a tool and more a liability—this broken machine he wants to use as little as possible. Still essential in some fashion, but not one you want to be depending on for truly crucial tasks.

Lacey, Dad, Dr. Bogsdaughter, and Emmett himself have grown to understand that Emmett's gut is the new processing center, the new thing-he-must-trust. If his gut tells him something, chances are it's true, while his brain is the stumbling, mumbling, bastard grumbling drunk uncle who yells from the porch about conspiracy theories and alien abduction stories wearing nothing but a wife beater and stained boxer shorts.

Lacey encourages him to write his way through his feelings, because she knows that writing is one of Emmett's only ways of processing through the myriad thoughts and feelings that are building up about Jayne. Is it because of his attraction to her? What kind of love does he feel for her? Is it a romantic kind of love? Is it a brotherly kind of love? He doesn't feel especially attracted to her per se, but he knows he won't necessarily feel anything in that blackish wasteland inside of him. There will be other signs of his emotions ... emotions and severe mental illness, especially with the addition of all those chemicals to treat the illness, don't often mix.

But the writing is a jumble; he just keeps going back and forth and back and forth. Trying to figure her out, trying to pick apart everything she's doing to him. That Halloween, all those months ago: her "I love you both ... in different ways," haunts him—especially when combined with the letter she'd sent him a few weeks later in which she'd told him she once had feelings for him, before he'd met Lauren, before she'd met Rob. Why tell him now? What purpose did it serve? Surely she doesn't just want to torture him. There must be a reason; there's always a reason.

Their hangout time is getting shorter and shorter. It seems that ever since she'd revealed her old feelings to him, ever since they'd started telling each other "I love you" at the end of their hangouts and conversations, something has changed.

The situation makes him feel like he's in high school again, though he'd never bothered with anything like this in high school, because he'd felt high school relationships were pointless.

But now he finds himself sitting on the porch on Saturday evenings with Dad, trying to process what he's been writing throughout the week; only able to come to the conclusion that "one ought to be with their best friend." He's ashamed that he'd seen it on a meme on Facebook, so he doesn't say that part to Dad. But it makes sense to him ... why wouldn't you be with your best friend? Why wouldn't you spend the rest of your life with them? A couple at his old church, Tag and Rag, who're now pastors there, had started out as simply friends, became best friends, then best friends who'd married each other, and now they were the church's marriage counselors—he and Lauren had gone to them for their own premarital counseling before everything fell apart.

The afternoon sun beats down and the cigarette Emmett drags from is hot and miserable. Little Baby Kerrin strains against the leash to get to the one little section of shade produced by the awning by a window. It just isn't worth it.

He puts the half-smoked cigarette out on the brick work of the stoop and calls her over to him. She doesn't budge. He gives gentle pull on the leash and she gets to her feet and mopes over beside him.

Down the hall, depositing the cigarette butt in the trash can. Kerrinpuppy too tired and hot to go running down the hallway.

Into their wonderfully air-conditioned apartment, for which they spend an extra twenty-five dollars a month in rent.

Emmett hangs up the leash and takes a lemon seltzer water out of the fridge. Opening it up, he takes a long drink and sets the can down on the table beside his chair. The easel, folded up next to the refrigerator, is collecting dust, having not been used since January. He sits in the chair and thumbs through the latest issue of Maximum PC. The magazine, dedicated to the fastest computer hardware available, is interesting Emmett less and less these days; he's often giving issues to Dad after barely reading them, having mostly just looked at the pictures.

The air conditioner is a small window unit, but it's highly effective; much more effective than the window unit they'd had at his old place, which more often than not just blew hot air in—another point of contention between him and SAR, Emmett turning off the air conditioner because of the hot air and SAR turning it back on. Why? Because it was an air conditioner, so it must be cooling the air. The benefit of living in a tiny space, Emmett has discovered, is that it's incredibly easy to heat and cool; the air conditioner hardly needs to be on at all and it keeps his little apartment at a comfortable temperature. He can turn it off completely most nights and sleep through the night without waking up in a sweat.

It's about appreciating the small things, he's sure Mom would say.

He finishes his lemon seltzer water and checks his watch. Jayne said she'd be texting him this afternoon to see about hanging out with him. It's been this afternoon for about three hours and still no word from her.

It's really dumb how he can't just get on with his life while waiting for someone to get back to him. Everything must be on hold while he waits; he doesn't want to be in the middle of something important when they finally do reach out. He figures he's gotten some writing done in the meantime, but it's mostly just processing his thoughts on Jayne, and he can do that any time—easy enough to just pick up and put down. It certainly won't be going on his blog.

He's been having a lot of fun with his blog. It's a good fit for him, this writing thing. He's about five posts into his posting-once-a-month plan, and it's going really well. He's writing almost obsessively for it, knowing he'll probably throw most of the writing out. One particularly embarrassing essay about picking out a psychiatrist was actually based on the Bill Murray comedy What About Bob? But there's always going to be trash among the treasures, and one has to start somewhere. His biggest embarrassment is that he'd shared the article with Marta Lee. She'd never read any of his writing before, and that's what he'd chosen to share with her.

Emmett has been telling Lacey, Dr. Bogsdaughter, Mom, Dad, Jayne, anyone who'll listen really, that writing seems to be a better fit than painting—it's so much easier than painting. He doesn't have to prepare for forty-five minutes just to start doing it. All he has to do is whip out his notebook and start in on writing any time he feels like it. He can do it in the car, sitting on the toilet, in church, at the dinner table, while out smoking, in the middle of the night. With few exceptions, it doesn't matter where he is or what he's doing; as long as he has access to pen and paper, he can write.

He feels more and more like he's been a writer all along and never actually a painter, though he keeps these feelings to himself for now. It's just so easy—sit down in front of a computer and start letting your thoughts fly out instead of spending some inordinate amount of time preparing a palette or whatever to struggle through trying to make the correct line. Make-a-line. Erase. Make-a-line. Erase. Make-a-line. Erase. Over and over and over again. Unto sickness. It was always so frustrating, and he'd always felt like a fraud when around other artists, like they were going to find him out because he couldn't just whip out a drawing. He'd always needed to carefully plan it out and execute it in private. Forget about impromptu drawing sessions, forget about drawing with other people—he couldn't be found out, he couldn't be exposed. It was nerve-racking to even think about doing it in public, to be denied the careful calculation afforded by privacy—the patient erase, re-draw, erase.

There's a difference between doing what's easy because you're lazy and doing what's easy because you're good at it. Emmett is so used to his thing, his job or profession or life's work or what-have-you, being so enormously difficult, that writing almost seems like cheating. He's used to painting, to his own Sisyphean task; always pointless labor, never producing anything appreciable. A day's labor always needing to be redone because he'd inevitably made too many mistakes, progress being so slow as to be only microscopically detected. Emmett has finished very few paintings since leaving college and has called a few unfinished paintings finished just so he could get them out of his sight. Some of the paintings have made it to the walls of his apartment, but most are in storage in the garage of his parents' house, protected in plastic for no one to see. But his writing is being read by a growing audience. Dad is sending him the Google Analytics reports every month, and each month more and more people are reading his blog. His writing is doing something his paintings never did: affecting people's lives.

Another hour passes. Soon it's 4:00 p.m. and Emmett thinks his chances of Jayne actually texting him are nearing zilch. He can text her now and remind her that she was going to text him, or he could just let it go. She'll probably say that she's been so swamped with something, that she couldn't find the time to text him to let him know she was too busy to hang out with him, that she's super sorry but she'll make it up to him.

Mostly he doesn't want to know what she's been up to.

Sometimes it's better not to know.

He's been listening to an album with headphones on. The Big Come Up by The Black Keys. Their very first recording, and one of his favorites. SAR had liked to comment that you could tell they could barely play their instruments. But Emmett has to disagree, and he sometimes wishes he still talked to SAR so he could tell him he was full of it. They played just fine. Maybe not as tightly as they do on later recordings like Thick-freakness and Chulahoma, but not to the point of "can barely play their instruments." Sometimes SAR had impossible standards, and sometimes he just liked to say things to get a rise out of people.

Emmett figures the sun should be behind the office building across the street by now. Or at the very least, there should be some shade on the right side of the stoop. He'll gladly settle for the lesser part of the stoop if it means a cigarette.

Up onto his feet, depositing his headphones on the head of the phrenology bust Mom had gotten him for Christmas, the same one Gregory House has on the TV show Emmett never watches anymore.

Into the kitchen to roll a cigarette. Kerrinpuppy stirring to life as soon as she hears the cardboard tin of tobacco open, Emmett hearing the jingling of her dog tags as he imagines her stretching with a little smile on her face.

He gets her leash down from its hook behind the bathroom door. She does a twirl and a happy bark and jumps up at Emmett, far too excited to contain herself or remember her manners.

"Sit," Emmett commands, repeating it with increasing authority as she ignores the command and barks back at him.

Finally she sits, stomping the floor impatiently with her front paws, and Emmett gives her a scratch on the top of her head. He opens the door and she goes bursting down the hall, Emmett far behind, Kerrinpuppy running back and forth and back and forth as Emmett lumbers behind her, far too slow for her liking.

Clip her onto her leash. Out the door. Into the entryway. Outside.

Immediately Kerrinpuppy is barking at a passing dog. The kind of vicious bark that he knows means business.

"Hey! Hey! Hey!" Emmett yells as he tries to get his dog to stop barking. But his dog isn't having any of it. This other dog is encroaching on her territory and she needs to chase it off. Emmett's voice gets louder; he tugs on the leash, making the collar tighter, as his dog ignores his commands and barks as viciously as she knows how.

Emmett has had enough. He pulls her inside. Pulls her down the hallway. Drags her inside. Yelling at her the entire way: "NO. BAD GIRL. NO!" He doesn't even bother to take her leash off. Just pushes her inside the door to their apartment and closes the door. Then outside to smoke.

He's livid going down the hallway and then feels despicable.

Like the worst person ever. Like he's abused the sweetest dog in the whole wide world. He replays the whole scenario in his head over again.

Emmett knows, intuitively, that he didn't harm her—that he didn't kick her—that he just pushed her, not even all that hard, inside the door. He knows that she needed to be shown that her behavior was unacceptable. But his mind doesn't afford him that logic. Soon, replay after replay, his mind has him beating Kerrinpuppy with the leash, driving her down the hall and kicking her into the doorway. There's no way he can go back inside to face his puppy now.

Out comes his phone.

Text to Dad:

> EMMETT:
>
> help

Of course Dad calls; why wouldn't he? Emmett rejects the call.

> EMMETT:
>
> Just come now

DAD:

I'm on my way

This is the first time, at least in Emmett's memory, that Dad has had to come to be with Emmett since Dad has started working so close to Emmett. It's an eleven-minute walk; Emmett needs to last for eleven minutes.

Lighting his cigarette, Emmett takes note of the time; it takes about ten to twelve minutes for him to smoke a cigarette, sometimes fifteen if the tobacco is fresh. He tries to think of something else besides his dog barking at the other dog. He tries to think of her as Kerrinpuppy, as his Little Girl, remembering the day he got her, the very first picture he took of her—looking so intelligent standing on the console of Dad's car, a place she's stood he-doesn't-know-how-many times, as if giving Dad directions on where to turn. Remembering how he couldn't get her in the car afterwards, he imagined because she thought he was going to take her away to another home.

His cigarette is a few drags away from being spent by the time Dad arrives. Dad has his case with him; the day is nearly over anyways.

"Hey Emmett, what's up?"

Emmett takes a deep breath, his first in quite a while, and explains the entire situation.

"I'm sorry. That sounds awful. How can I help?"

"I think … " he starts. "I don't know," Emmett says, trying to think of what exactly Dad can do. "Maybe if you could just go in there and make sure she's okay. Make sure I didn't actually do those things—I don't think I can go in there and face her by myself."

"Okay. We'll do that. Do you want to wait out here or in the hall?"

Emmett pauses, thinking. "Hall."

Emmett stands a little way off and Dad opens the door. Little Baby Kerrin comes trotting out, making a beeline for Emmett who stoops down to receive kisses from her.

"Little Baby Kerrin. Ohhh, my Little Girl," Emmett says, a rush of relief coming to him. Kerrin is totally fine, not a scratch on her, and she loves him just the same as she's always loved him.

They go inside and take her leash off, and Emmett gets some ziprasidone into his system for good measure. "Kerrin, you can't go yelling at other dogs like that … you just can't," Emmett says as she settles into her bed and gives out a sigh.

"I think she heard you," Dad says.

"I doubt it. She'll do it again," Emmett says, his demeanor instantly serious again.

"Yeah," Dad not knowing how to respond to that.

"I just don't know the best way to deal with it. I suppose there's really nothing I can do when it's just barking first thing when I open the door. Took me by total surprise to see the dog. And it was huge," Emmett says gesturing vaguely to indicate something of considerable mass. "It just reminded me of the time she got attacked, and I don't think I can take on a dog that large. Though it might just be my imagination making the dog larger than it really was. Pretty soon it'll be as large as the dog in The Sand Lot."

Dad chuckles at this; they're always finding the humor in any situation. "Funny how it works like that. You'll figure something out; you always do."

"Yeah ... "

The pills had kicked in a while ago and, invariably, Emmett has become a bottomless pit. His stomach starts grumbling loudly.

"Hungry?" Dad asks.

"Starving. It's a little early though, isn't it? And don't you have to be getting home?"

"I can stay and eat with you and then I'll get going. If that's okay with you."

"Sounds good. I think I need some dextroamphetamine in my system though, or else I'm going to be conked out from the food," Emmett says. And then he adds, "I'm a walking chemical reaction, I wonder if someday they'll make me explosive with the chemicals they put into me—I'll eat the wrong thing and BOOM! I explode."

Dad chuckles.

They say goodbye to Kerrinpuppy.

Out the door. Lock it.

Down the hallway.

Into the deli.

Emmett orders a twelve-inch sub with a bag of chips and a soda, since they have soda without high-fructose corn syrup—might as well take advantage when you can. The corner convenience store also has this, so it's actually not so much taking-advantage-when-you-can as making-a-habit-of-it. Emmett ends up devouring his sandwich before Dad can finish his half-a-sandwich, Emmett almost wishing for more and then remembering his ever-expanding gut and how much bacon he's just consumed as well as the bag of chips he'd worked through while waiting for their sandwiches.

He and Dad go out on the stoop one more time so Emmett can smoke his after-dinner cigarette and then say goodbye. Despite an extra twenty milligrams of dextroamphetamine in his system, which should be kicking in about now, Emmett needs to take a nap and passes out on the couch shortly after Dad leaves, Kerrinpuppy squeezed up next to his legs and pushing against them for more space. There's little enough space as is, but Emmett will give her all the space she wants.

Chapter Eighteen

"I'm convinced these cortados symbolize something," Emmett says.

"Okay. Symbolize what? And what's a cortado?" Lacey says with a quizzical look.

"I'm not totally sure what they symbolize. Maybe it's a lack of commitment, or a lack of the kind of commitment I need. I know that sounds conspiratorial, maybe even a little crazy; but if I'm not allowed to sound crazy, who is?

"And," Emmett continues, "it's like a shot of espresso, with half espresso and half cream. Really kind of a dinky amount of coffee."

Lacey chuckles at this and says, "Emmett, I think maybe you're reading too much into the existence of these cortados. Life doesn't reflect literature; it's not chock-full of symbols and the motifs and leitmotifs you've been talking about. Sometimes things simply are."

"Yeah," Emmett says, though in his head he's thinking that while life doesn't reflect literature, literature reflects life. But he doesn't want to appear too crazy in front of his therapist. He knows she's right; he just has to get to the point where he sees things from her perspective. The cortado as just a cortado, nothing more.

Waking up, he needs to find something to do with himself. He searches for his glasses on the coffee table, finds them and goes to roll a cigarette, the pull of sleep still tempting enough that he might just give up on staying up.

Kerrinpuppy is alert now, wondering what might be important enough to trump bed. She can sleep eighteen hours a day, according to what Emmett has read on the Internet, and he supposes this is what makes her a good apartment dog.

He finishes rolling his cigarette and goes outside. No taking Kerrinpuppy with him this time—he needs to be alone for a while. He pulls his phone out of his pocket to find a text message:

DAD:
I'm home and I love you and Kerrin!

Emmett replies and thanks him for coming over on such short notice. Has he really been asleep that long?

The sun is beginning to make its descent past the mountains. He wonders how much time the mountains subtract from the amount of daylight. But he also knows, if he were to have an actual view of them, the sight would be worth it. Unfortunately, with tall buildings everywhere there's no way he's going to see one of the sunsets Colorado is so famous for. No wonder the people in the high-rise apartments spend so much more money for a west-facing apartment high enough to see the sunset, and all the more a pity that they have to work so much they don't get to see the sunsets very often—the brilliant oranges and reds fading to purples and greys, the occasional magenta, a slow chiaroscuro of color that's impossible to get sick of. It was the first thing he'd missed upon leaving Colorado for his year away while attending college.

Emmett takes deep drags from his cigarette, thankful that the sun isn't beating down on him anymore. Nearly finished with it, he walks down the stairs of his stoop, takes a left and finds himself in front of the coffee shop. Taking one last drag, he deposits the cigarette butt in the little metal container they have for them out front and heads inside.

"Hey Emmett," the barista says.

"Hey," Emmett says, forgetting the barista's name.

"Large latte?"

"I hope so."

The coffee shop is nearly empty, just a couple people sitting together, talking with each other. There's no Wi-Fi here, so it's a safe bet they're actually working. Every so often you'll get someone who hasn't been here, who doesn't read the sign on the front door which says they don't have Wi-Fi. They come in, order a drink, sit down and pull their laptop out. And, before their drink comes out, they ask for the Wi-Fi password and leave in a huff when informed that they don't have it.

Inevitably a Yelp review comes in complaining that they don't have Wi-Fi, the review saying something about how one would think that a coffee shop would lose too much business not having Wi-Fi these days. But the coffee shop is doing just fine; they do a steady enough business. It's nice to come to a coffee shop where not everyone is glued to their laptops browsing Facebook, where people are there to talk, to congregate. Or, if they are on their laptop, they're actually working on something. Though the cynical part of him can't help thinking they've just turned their phone into a wireless hotspot.

He chats with the barista about his day, mostly making stuff up. Emmett can't really tell the truth; he doesn't know this barista well enough to tell them about what happened with Kerrin-puppy or about how Dad had to come over to comfort him. To the barista, Emmett runs his own computer repair shop out of his apartment, and it's an essential cover for him to have, a protection of sorts.

Emmett is a superhero with a secret identity. In public, the mild-mannered, utterly relaxed computer repair guy. In actuality, the sometimes-crazy guy with a mental illness who's trying to dedicate his life to helping out people like him, to helping so-called normal people understand what it's like to live with a mental illness.

A superhero. Emmett likes that.

He gets his coffee and thanks the barista, picking up a sleeve and top for the coffee. He stops at his stoop to roll another cigarette. He can't help but pair a good cup of coffee with a ciga-rette; the combination is just too perfect not to.

Taking out his little black notebook from his back pocket, he writes down the superhero/secret-identity thought to save for another time and waits for more thoughts to occur to him. Perhaps a blog post will come out of it, or maybe that's as deep as the thought will go. He wants the thought to be deep and powerful and moving, to perhaps have a book come of it … but no, it's just that simple thought. Emmett Selv as a superhero with a secret identity, no more, no less.

Smoke cigarette.

Back inside to Kerrinpuppy.

She's moved back to her bed, nose tucked in to the fold of the bed, the bed having been designed for just this purpose. He greets her in his falsetto reserved exclusively for dogs; her ears perk up and she looks up from her bed. Emmett squats down and scratches her behind her ears. She likes this.

He spends the rest of the evening trying to clean his apart-ment.

Trying.

It's one false start after another. Working up the courage, if you can call it courage—the gumption, if you can call it gump-tion—to clean and make his place as spotless as he'd like it to be. There's sweeping to be done, dishes to be washed, a floor to be mopped, a bathroom (particularly a toilet) to be cleaned; he tries to make a list of everything he needs to do. Mom says that lists oftentimes help her, but the longer he makes this list the more daunting the task seems.

Finally, he just settles for sitting down in his chair with a Pavement album and his headphones, listening to Side A on repeat and browsing Facebook, Little Baby Kerrin on his lap. He opens the text messaging app on his phone:

EMMETT:

Hey you

He puts his phone back on the table next to his chair and lets the music wash over him

Eventually, through the muffle of his headphones, he hears the notification of Jayne's reply.

JAYNE:

Hey love! How are you?

EMMETT:

I'm okay, had kind of a shitty day

JAYNE:

I'm sorry. What happened?

EMMETT:

Long story, I'm actually a little too wiped to tell it
by text

JAYNE:

I understand. Would you like to tell me about it over coffee sometime at the end of the week?

EMMETT:

Sure thing, that's what I was going to suggest
anyways :)

At the end of the week, Emmett is sitting in front of Jayne with a cortado. Jayne has told him she really likes them, though to him they seem like a crummy deal—more expensive than a regular drink but significantly less coffee.

He takes his first sip.

Pretty good. At least it's good quality coffee. He still wishes he'd ordered a latte, though.

Jayne is explaining that she doesn't have much time to hang out, and Emmett is trying to mentally adjust his schedule. He's figured on two hours hanging out with Jayne like usual. He doesn't do well with unexpected changes like this, doesn't do well when things don't go according to plan.

But outwardly he's Mr. Understanding. "No worries. I understand," he says, all smiles. And he supposes he does understand, it's just that he's worried about how he's going to make it through the rest of the day when he has a whole hour and a half where he has no clue what to do with himself.

He's not even sure he quite understands why Jayne needs to leave. He's just woken up from a nap. Didn't get the dextroamphetamine in his system soon enough and he's paying for it—still a little delirious; calling his brain "fuzzy" is a compliment. Jayne is urging him to drink the coffee, telling him it'll help him feel better. He's chuckling at her; if fifty milligrams of dextroamphetamine didn't help him this morning, there's no way this little bitty cup of coffee is going to help him now. Nope, he's going to have to wait for the additional pills to kick in.

Jayne's attention is on her phone. Emmett's attention is on trying to detect when the dextroamphetamine starts to kick in.

It's probably for the best anyway, he tells himself. This way I can take a nap and feel rested for going to sleep tonight. He smiles as Jayne is draining the last of her coffee, gesturing for Emmett to do the same. He picks up the lukewarm cup and swallows the concoction. It's good; he's just not sure it's three-and-a-half dollars' worth of good, especially since it's about two fingers' worth of coffee. But he feels as though he and Jayne have started a new tradition: getting cortados.

Jayne takes the glasses over to the bus tray and they head outside.

"Okay, love, I've got to go," she says, putting on her sunglasses and dropping her phone in her bag.

"Okie dokie. Sorry I was such miserable company."

"Oh, you weren't," she says, smiling. "Go take a nap and feel better."

"Thanks."

"Love you. I'll call you this weekend to see what you're up to."

"Okay, sounds good. Love you too," Emmett says, turning to head back toward his apartment. Back to his couch, to take a nap so he'll be well rested in time for bed. She'll call this weekend. Heh. Funny.

Chapter Nineteen

◇◇

"I think sometimes the bipolar side of me is expressed rather literally," Emmett says.

"How do you figure?" Lacey is contemplating Emmett across the top of her newly acquired glasses. Emmett thinks that when he'd first started seeing her she hadn't needed the glasses; she also hadn't needed the pad of paper. She also didn't have kids—a lot can change in eight years, including your therapist.

"I think mostly in how I dress. I've got some clothes I suppose you could consider neat and clean and others that I haven't washed in a good long while. My normal clothes and my crust punk clothes," Emmett begins. "I think, depending on the day, I oscillate between my old identity as a crust punk and my new identity, which I don't think has a name."

"How is that a literal expression of your bipolar illness?"

"It's a literal expression insofar as they're opposite ends of extremes. One is grungy, dirty, and probably somewhat repulsive, and the other is normal and acceptable."

Lacey scribbles down a few notes. Emmett wonders what exactly she writes down, thinks to maybe ask to see his files. Finally, she speaks: "That's an interesting thought. Do you think that maybe you're just in transition? That maybe you're easing into no longer identifying as a crust punk?"

"Oh, I was a lousy crust punk. I just wore dirty clothing. It was really a blessing that crust punk was so fashionable when I was going through the worst of not being able to clean myself or my clothes, because otherwise I would've been even more of an outcast. But, yeah. It could be a transition. Maybe I'm just easing myself into being a normal person."

"How is bathing for you?"

"I think we're going on month six of not having taken a shower. But I've been washing my face almost every day—taking better care of my beard and cutting my hair more often."

"So showers are still noxious for you?"

"Probably. It used to be really bad, I'd get psychotic if I was even caught out in the rain. But I don't know about now. I think I've just gotten out of the habit. A shower has been on my mental to-do list for a long time now. They're just such a hassle."

"How so?"

"I have to take sixty milligrams of ziprasidone half an hour before I shower, I have to make sure it's kicked in, then I have to shower, gradually introducing myself to the water. I tend to stay in there for a long time because I want to make it worth it. And then, usually by the time I'm done showering, I'm so exhausted from the ziprasidone that I have to take a nap."

"That sounds rough," Lacey says, concern and a sort of love in her soft voice. She always drops the volume of her voice when she says stuff like that. Emmett has always found it comforting.

E mmett is having a particularly difficult time deciding what to wear this morning, a rarity for him. His small collection of button-up shirts is piling up around his feet, as each one fails in some specific way to meet some impossible standard of making him feel the way he wants it to make him feel. He picks a shirt off the rack, pulls it on, buttons it up, walks over to the mirror in the bathroom (which is just a vanity mirror and not really suited for checking out your outfit) and the reflection looking back at him is just abhorrent. There's no way he's going out in public looking like this.

He takes it off and throws it onto the floor. Then the cycle starts all over again. Trying on a shirt, being disgusted, throwing the shirt into the pile. On and on. Making a circuit around the apartment as Emmett chases his shirts around the apartment, never quite satisfied.

Eventually his phone starts ringing and Emmett knows who it is. He finds his phone, still plugged into the wall in the bathroom, the caller ID announcing it's Mom.

"Hey Mom," his voice a little distant.

"Hey Emmett, just making sure you're up."

"I am, just a little frustrated."

"Why's that?"

"Nothing fits."

"What do you mean?"

Emmett explains about the shirts, all the while examining his belly in the mirror; how did it get so huge so quickly? He downs the pills he's forgotten to take in the frustration of trying to find something to wear.

"I think you might just be a little bloated," Mom says. "Do you still have some of that Metamucil?"

Emmett heads into the kitchen, examining the neatly arranged shelves of spices, teas, and the like. "Yeah, I've got it right here."

"Take some of that, it should help you."

Emmett thanks her, hangs up, drinks a glass of the fiber powder, rolls a cigarette, and heads outside after donning his hoodie, despite the fact that it's over eighty degrees outside, his level of self-consciousness about the sheer enormity of his body outweighing any thoughts of being comfortable out in the hot sun.

He smokes his cigarette, texting Mom all the while and checking Facebook. Social media has, for Emmett, devolved even more into an observation, a mere looking at what the people are up to; he doesn't really know if most of them are actually his friends or not. He doesn't talk to them anymore, doesn't really interact with them. He hasn't seen them in a good three or four years. And even back then, he just existed in their presence—merely available for them to talk to, having never shared with them his darkest secret, having never trusted them enough with that information.

Forty-five minutes later, he's on the toilet. Fifteen minutes after that, he's found a shirt he's comfortable wearing—feeling like a million bucks.

EMMETT:
You're a miracle worker :)

MOM:
Glad that worked :)

Their chatting brings them to the weather, as it always does. It brings back memories of Emmett trying to talk to his grandma while manic—rambling on and on about something and Grandma asking about the weather and Emmett feeling deflated. Whenever they start talking about the weather you know it's all over, he remembered someone saying once. And soon enough the conversation was, indeed over. He's been writing letters to Grandma ever since, thinking it a better way of conversing anyway because he doesn't have to get paranoid about where in the house grandma was or worrying he was interrupting her from something important. One time his Aunt Metsy had been visiting and Grandma had been away shopping or something. Metsy had answered the phone and he'd told her who it was. "I don't know an Emmett," Metsy had said.

"Of course you do," Emmett had said. "Your sister's son, Emmett Selv?"

"Of course!" Aunt Metsy had said. And she apologized profusely and they'd gone on to have a wonderful chat Emmett hasn't been able to recall since.

Dad is due at Emmett's apartment for a walk in about half an hour, and Emmett's clothes are still strewn all over his apartment. Not wanting to miss an opportunity—perhaps divinely called by constipation—to clean his closet, he empties it of the rest of his clothes. He may not have very many clothes, but when they're crammed into a tiny closet meant more for a few coats than for the bedding and entire wardrobe of an individual, it can get messy and disorganized pretty quickly.

Refolding his tee shirts, jeans, and underwear again and putting them back in their appropriate spots takes longer than he thinks, and soon there's a knock at the door. Kerrinpuppy gets up from her bed, stretches, and is just heading over for the door when it opens.

"Kerrin!" Dad calls out as Emmett's dog, tail wagging back and forth furiously, goes over to greet him. "Hey Emmett."

"Hey, homie," Emmett says, folding a tee shirt and going over to give his dad a hug. "Sorry, I thought I'd be done with this before it was time to go on a walk."

"NBD," Dad says. He takes his accustomed seat in the chair at the corner by the computer closet and starts playing Squirrel with Kerrinpuppy: Dad throwing one of her stuffed squirrels in the air and she catches it, makes it squeak for a while, and then drops it at his feet, looking up at him expectantly.

Emmett tries to hurry up his closet cleaning without rushing it too much. He can't leave the job unfinished; nothing would be worse than coming back to his apartment, soaked in sweat, faced with a mess.

Kerrinpuppy and Dad are in the middle of their game when Emmett finishes, and they go for their walk, taking a left after going down the stairs. They take another left on Tenth, sticking to quieter streets for the sake of Emmett's fragile mind.

Fortunately, Emmett is in high spirits today as Dad tells Emmett the latest on the infrastructure project—his work's project wherein they're replacing all of their servers and network equipment. The project is going surprisingly smoothly in Emmett's opinion; he was expecting something to go horribly wrong, but nothing has. It has him a little suspicious, but he's cynical like that. Years of experience with fixing computers, not to mention years of listening to Dad's stories from work, have taught him that massive undertakings like this rarely go without a problem.

He remembers going over to Dad's ex-coworker's house

when he was little. Clarissa was having a sleepover, and Emmett had this annoying tendency, being the little Casanova he was, of injecting himself in the middle of Clarissa's friends, so it was pretty convenient that Dad was going over to help his ex-coworker with her computer. Emmett figured it would be a quick job, an hour maybe two and they'd be on their way. He doesn't remember now what they were doing, installing a printer maybe, probably something network related; he hates network problems. At any rate—they were there for almost five hours, with one thing after another going wrong, this being back before you could Google your way out of a problem.

Emmett couldn't remember if he'd been much of a help, but he'd certainly learned a lot from the experience—chiefly, how to manage expectations for how long a particular project was going to take. When an hour and a half had passed and he realized they weren't even close to fixing the problem, he'd had to set his mind to the mystery of the unknown—to not knowing how long it was going to take to fix the problem.

Computers, in the sense of how they broke, hadn't changed all that much in the eighteen-some-odd years since his first house call. But the tools to fix them certainly had. Now, he took his laptop so he could Google the problem when he went on house calls. Because of the magic of Google, and his proficiency at using Google, he was able to take a house call that would otherwise have taken a similar five to six hours and reduce it to maybe half an hour or an hour. It felt like cheating, but it meant a lot less work.

He and Dad often lamented the good old days and then laughed about what old fogies they must sound like. But Emmett feels like they have a point. When Emmett first started, before Google, one really had to know their way around a computer; one really had to figure out a problem, and because of that, a person really learned. You don't learn from Googling a problem; all you learn is the fix and not the reason behind the fix. You don't earn the knowledge, and therefore the computer remains as much a mystery as it was before. Dad often comments that Emmett is the last of a generation of old-school nerds—the nerds who got into the guts of the computer, who really knew the computer, who could fix the computer without the aid of Google. Emmett more feels trapped between generations— Googling because it saves time, but more than capable of figuring it out for himself if Google proves to not be able to help him solve the problem (and those sorts of problems do still exist).

But feeling trapped between generations, being caught in a sort of nerd purgatory, has him feeling like less and less of a nerd with each passing generation of Intel processor. Google has removed a lot of the magic of computers, the mystery, the challenge. He's no longer a wizard with some secret knowledge; anyone can look up the same fix to a particular problem as long as they know what to search for. The only difference is there are some fixes that require a bit of specialized skill after you've Googled it, and there are some fixes that require knowing exactly which terms to Google.

Dad very much agrees, but unlike Emmett he doesn't take it so personally. Dad has invested over thirty years into his career in IT, and Emmett is still young enough that something else more interesting might pop up. Besides, Emmett is in a unique position: unable to get a job, it's not like he's had the opportunity to really get into IT. All he can do is hear stories from the trenches; all he can do is imagine himself doing the job but never actually do the job himself. He has to relegate himself to repair-shop-type fixes—the type of stuff he's been doing his whole life—and the thought of removing viruses and recovering data from crashed hard drives just doesn't seem like the kind of thing he wants to be doing for the rest of his life. It isn't the kind of "life's work" he wants to look back on at age sixty and feel proud of. He wants to leave a legacy behind: something important, something substantial, something with meaning.

They say goodbye at the bottom of the stairs leading up to the stoop, Emmett's forehead glistening in the sun, his hair matted down to his scalp; he should have remembered to wear his hat.

"Say goodbye," Emmett says to Kerrinpuppy. And she dutifully goes over to her grandpa to receive some scratches.

Up the stairs, hoping for packages, though he doesn't think he's ordered anything.

Down the hall, Kerrinpuppy running up and down its length.

Into the apartment.

Fresh shirt. Cold washcloth on the face in an attempt to cool off.

Sitting in his chair to feel the wind of the air conditioner blowing around the apartment, Kerrinpuppy checking out the contents of her food bowl and eating a bit of kibble before settling into bed to meet her eighteen-hour sleep quota for the day.

Chapter Twenty

"Sometimes the voices are just commentary, not really a bother," Emmett explains.

"What do you do about them?"

"If it's just commentary, I usually just thank them silently in my head and they seem satisfied with that.

"It's funny," Emmett continues. "I think sometimes they just get lonely and need someone to pay attention to them. I pity them every once in a while."

"Why would you pity them?" Lacey asks.

"Well ... they're stuck up there in my head all day and all night, they don't have the same power over me they used to—it must get boring, they must get lonely. I wonder what they do with themselves when they're not bothering me. Are they having committee meetings to see how to drive me over the edge?"

"That's a very interesting perspective."

"What's interesting to me is how they operate. What they are. How I can conceive of them, in a perfectly rational state of mind, as completely real, as having their own agency. I know on an intellectual level they're just subconscious expressions of myself ... but it's like my gut wants to treat them as whole persons sometimes, like maybe I have the power of sucking people's souls up and they get trapped in my head and their only way out is to torture me."

Every once in a while, Emmett has run across memes criticizing smartphones for their lack of durability and battery life. They're definitely fragile, dainty little machines, especially compared to the early cell phones which you could chuck across the room and still expect to be in perfect working order when you went to retrieve them after your little outburst. But what the meme fails to recognize is just how much more capable a smartphone is, compared to those Nokia phones of the early two thousands. His very first Nokia cellphone was more powerful than the computer Apollo 11 had used to land on the moon, and his current smartphone was probably more powerful than the desktop PC, lovingly referred to as ROD (Rig of Death), he'd built the summer before starting high school. Just thinking about it blew his mind. The meme just didn't account for all the additional features a smartphone has that those Nokia cellphones simply weren't capable of offering. And for them to be able to last all day on a single charge was pretty remarkable.

Maybe that's why Emmett is so enamored with his smartphone, so nearly addicted to it. Chances are, if he has a still moment in his day, his phone is out of his pocket and he's doing something on it. It's just such an amazing piece of technology.

Jayne had texted him earlier in the day and he's still processing the information, having texted Mom to tell her the news.

Rob has gotten an offer for a paid internship in California, so they would be moving there in about a month so Rob could finally get started with his career. The thought of living in Denver without Jayne leaves Emmett with an empty feeling inside. He's been half-tempted to tell her that he's going to break his lease and move out with them. Forget about his doctors and the support of his parents and the rest of his friends; all he needs is Jayne in his life, and he would go wherever Jayne goes.

But that's the irrational part of his brain talking, the damaged part—it isn't his gut telling him to do that, the part he can trust.

He'd texted Marta Lee almost immediately to tell her about the news.

MARTA LEE:
How do you feel about it?

EMMETT:

Not really sure. I know that sometimes I need a while before feelings start to actually set in. I suppose maybe a little empty inside?

MARTA LEE:

I can understand that. She's your longest-running friend, isn't she?

EMMETT:

Yeah. Almost ten years, I think. But sometimes it feels like it hasn't really been that long

MARTA LEE:

What do you mean?

EMMETT:

It's kinda like that with most of my friends who were there before ECT. I don't really have a whole lot of memories of being with them from beforehand. Kind of like how I don't remember a whole lot about Lauren; she's just lost to the ether or whatever you want to call it

MARTA LEE:

Makes sense

Emmett arranges a time to meet with Marta Lee in person. It's been much too long, anyway—sometimes he feels like he can manage only so many friends at a time, so some friends inevitably get pushed out of the picture. There're only so many days of the week, after all, and he needs downtime. He's continually amazed at how therapists manage their own schedules, how they find consistent times to fit in their clients. They must learn it as part of their training: Scheduling 101.

It's about thirty minutes of walking for Emmett to meet with Marta Lee at the little paleo coffee shop where they'd started meeting every so often since he'd moved back to Denver. Marta Lee has a car, but he's told her he wants to walk—he's still enamored of his earbuds and doesn't often get a chance to listen to them while walking, since he's most often walking with Dad. The bummer thing about living next door to your favorite coffee shop is that you don't get much of an opportunity to listen to music on your way there.

He'll probably get a ride back with her, though.

He's early, as usual, and stands outside the entrance to the coffee shop smoking a cigarette. It's in the Santa Fe Art District, pretty well hidden from most foot traffic and so is only known to locals. There's limited indoor seating but it has a courtyard with additional seating and this is where Marta Lee and Emmett prefer to sit, at least when it isn't too cold outside.

Marta Lee comes walking up the street. "Heeey!" Emmett calls out, in what's his approximation of a catcall. Marta Lee does a little strut and smiles, stretching out her arms for a hug.

Emmett would never turn down a Marta Lee hug. Her hugs are among some of the best he ever gets.

"It's been much too long," Marta Lee says.

"I know, right?" Emmett says. "And I feel like we always say that. I think it's mostly my fault … I just turn into a bumbling idiot when it comes to my schedule."

"Bah. Doesn't matter. As long as we get to see each other."

"True that."

They walk into the coffee shop. Marta Lee orders a cappuccino and Emmett orders a mocha with coconut milk. They use real coconut milk here, and it's makes for one of the best dairy-free coffee drinks one's likely to have in Denver. It's a little expensive, but worth it, Emmett tipping more than usual because he believes such quality should be rewarded.

"Where would you like to sit?"

"Preferably where I can smoke," Emmett says.

"Outside?"

"Outside!" Emmett in a mock yell, able to be goofy around Marta Lee.

The proprietor of the coffee shop tells them she'll bring their drinks out to them, so they head outside and set up shop, sitting next to each other since they both like to keep tabs on who's entering and exiting the courtyard. It's something Emmett very much appreciates about Marta Lee, that she understands, on a more substantial level than his other friends, the need to see the exit; they don't have to explain to each other the why behind it.

Their drinks arrive along with a tray of chocolates, the proprietor explaining that they're all vegan, and gluten free. Emmett especially thanks her because he doesn't often get treats at coffee shops because of his food allergies.

"So, tell me about Jayne moving," Marta Lee says; taking out her crocheting and setting to work as Emmett brings out his sketchbook and halfheartedly sets to drawing, something he hasn't done in months. He's not sure why he brought his sketchbook—tradition, maybe?

"BECAUSE IT'S EASY TO TALK AND DRAW AT THE SAME TIME BUT NOT TALK AND WRITE, DUMBASS." *And Emmett thanks the voice silently and goes on talking with Marta Lee.*

"I don't know if there's really any more to tell. I think the desire to move out with her has subsided. I think I decided a while ago, when they were thinking about moving to Portland, that it would be a bad idea to leave Denver. There are too many good things happening here for me to leave."

"Yeah? Like what?"

"Well there're my parents, who can come and get me anytime. My dad working an eleven-minute walk away, that's a huge one. There's Dr. Bogsdaughter who's proven to have found some really beneficial things for me. There's Lacey whom I've been seeing for like eight or nine years or something like that. I've been seeing her since before I was diagnosed, and that means a lot to me. Then there's my involvement with NAMI and how that might lead to something important.

"I don't know," Emmett continues. "It just seems like God is telling me Denver is the place to be. Besides, it's not like Jayne invited me or anything. Sometimes I get the sense that she's trying to distance herself from me."

"You think?"

"Just a gut feeling. I can't think of anything specific," Emmett says, Jayne's hawk-like predation of her phone and the briefer and briefer hangout sessions escaping his mind like they tend to when he's asked to recall crucial information on the spot. He really ought to write this information down. He does say, "I also don't think I could really depend on her to take care of me if I were to go with them, ya know? I'd basically have to put my life in her hands, and I'm not so sure I can do that."

"Yeah."

They work in silence for a while. An altogether pleasant silence; Emmett drawing and erasing, drawing and erasing. For once he's not working on a drawing of a hallucination—of something that's been haunting him as he walks down the street or inside a coffee shop or a doctor's waiting room. It's a picture of a babirusa, a strange four-tusked, pig-like animal indigenous to Indonesia. Emmett has always wanted to draw animals realistically, recalling sitting on the floor of his parent's living room, trying to draw orcas for his Grandma Selv but failing miserably. It's still with great difficulty that he's drawing, but he's seeing much greater success; he's got this plan to create a whole series of weird animals.

Marta Lee asks him about what he's drawing, so he shows her and tells her about his lack of drawing his hallucinations. She doesn't fail to recognize the significance of this. He tells her how he's recently moved his easel, taboret and the rest of this painting stuff to his parents' house, having decided that oil painting isn't for him. She's understandably shocked; she had always thought of him as an oil painter.

"It's not an irrational move," he assures her. "I've been thinking about it for a while. I haven't actually touched oil paint since January. And I figured it was just taking up space; and space in my tiny-ass apartment is at a premium."

Marta Lee laughs and nods her agreement: "Your place is pretty tiny."

"I just feel a lot better just doing these small projects, ya know? I think I'll get a lot more of them done. Working with gouache, doing smaller stuff—I think I'll get a lot more of them done and feel more productive … maybe even get a show out of them and sell some of them."

"That makes me feel better," she says. "Just as long as you're not giving up on art."

"Oh I don't think that's going to happen," he smiles.

Marta Lee drives Emmett home, Emmett a little reluctant since he has about thirty minutes left on the album he was listening to. Marta Lee tells him about a guy named Owen she went on a date with.

"You have to meet him. I think you'll like him."

"I hope he's better than the other guy," Emmett says. "He was nice and all. But when he came over like three hours early to hang out before watching The Walking Dead, I thought I was going to have to gouge my eyes out."

Marta Lee laughs, "You should have told me that."

"I was going to, actually. But then you came over for dinner a little while later and told me that you'd broken up with him and I figured it was taken care of, so I didn't have to say anything."

"Well, it's a funny story is what I meant."

"Oh," Emmett chuckles. "Well, I suppose I just told you, didn't I? Also, he owes me like twelve dollars for dinner."

"I can tell him to pay you," Marta Lee offers.

"Actually it's not a big deal. I just mentioned it because I thought it was funny. Especially since it was like General Tso's Chicken or whatever. Which I didn't think anyone actually ordered because it's such a stupid name."

Marta Lee laughs. "Really?"

"What?"

"Really?"

"Okay. Stupid joke. I think the sugar in my mocha might have been cocaine. I'll go inside and listen to some Johnny Cash."

"Hmm?"

"Oh that whole line, how does it go? 'Lay off that whiskey and let that cocaine be,'" Emmett sings, doing a pretty good baritone impression of Johnny Cash. "Yeah. Really bad joke. Shit, two bad jokes in a row ... I'm losing my touch."

"Oh right. What song is that?" she asks, kind enough to ignore the terrible joke.

"Don't remember the name of it. But I do remember the guitar's chord progression." And Emmett mimics it in the same baritone.

"I totally know what you're talking about but can't name the song."

"I'll tell you when I get inside."

"Sounds good."

They pull up to Emmett's apartment building. Hug. A car hug from Marta Lee isn't as good as a sidewalk-greeting hug, but you have to take what you can get.

"I'll talk to you later," Emmett says.

"See ya."

Emmett shoulders his bag and walks across the street, up the stairs, and into the entryway, pausing to check his mail. Nothing there.

Down the hall to open the door.

The most excited puppy in the world waiting for him. But he has to pee like nobody's business.

Kerrinpuppy bringing her squirrel into the bathroom for him to throw for her.

"In a second; you have to be patient, Little Girl," he tells her.

Between rounds of throwing the squirrel for Kerrinpuppy he turns his TV on and looks at his iTunes music library, searching his Johnny Cash collection for the song he was quoting.

Finally he finds it and sends a text message to Marta Lee.

EMMETT:
Cocaine Blues

About twenty minutes later,

MARTA LEE:
That's a pretty obvious title

EMMETT:
Isn't it?

Chapter Twenty One

"How are you today?" Lacey asks.

Emmett sits down, sighs and smiles. "I'm doing just fine, better than I have been in a long time."

Lacey, getting her pad of paper and her glasses from her desk, turns around and smiles at him. "Good."

E mmett watches Jayne pull into the driveway leading up to the lofts above the deli and coffee shop. She's a clumsy driver, but he forgives her that; she hasn't been driving for very long and Pennsylvania Street is narrow, oftentimes unforgivingly so. She waves, smiling her awkward smile from behind the cracked glass of the old squealing BMW Rob somehow manages to keep running, and Emmett waves back, tossing his cigarette to the ground and stomping it out with his boot. He grabs his black messenger bag and gets into her car.

"Heyyy," she calls out and leans over for a hug.

"Hey you," he says, trying to be as enthusiastic as her. Not that he isn't happy to see her; he's just dead tired—waking up in the middle of the night to psychosis tends to have that effect on a person.

He pulls on his seat belt as Jayne pulls out of the driveway and away they go.

"I thought we could go to Stella's," Jayne says.

"Oh, that would be wonderful," Emmett says, his voice perking up. "I haven't been there in years." He imagines, if they're going that far, Jayne must be planning on them hanging out for quite a while.

Jayne turns right onto Fourteenth. "I just need to figure out how to get there ... "

"Hmmm, I'm not totally sure. I think Washington will take you most of the way there. But I'm a pedestrian these days so ... " Emmett's voice trails off. "You realize you just blew through a red light, right?"

"Did I?" Jayne looks into the rearview mirror.

"Sure did."

"Shit."

Emmett laughs nervously and repositions his bag onto the floor, so that if the airbag goes off (assuming it still works) he doesn't end up getting squished to death by the contents inside.

Jayne and Emmett eventually find their way there; Washington takes them most of the way and they wind their way through the side streets the rest of the way, just like they would have if they'd been on their bikes all those years ago. Memories are flooding back to Emmett and he starts telling Jayne about them—about the girl he had a crush on with the "troubled artist" friend he'd had back in high school. A guy who'd been so stereotypical in every way, Emmett hadn't batted an eyelash when he'd found out he'd joined the Marines. The girl, who was the more important part of the story, had told Emmett he wasn't her type, had called him too "well fed" for her taste, and then had thrown his address out the window as she drove away; he'd never seen her again.

"Were you heartbroken?"

"I don't really remember," Emmett says. "I suppose so. But not really desperately so. She'd just called me fat, remember. And I have this history of being completely enamored with girls-dash-women up until a certain point and then it just vanishes. And I think her calling me fat was when it vanished. Calling her on the phone had been pretty hilarious too."

"Why's that?"

By then they have their coffee and are sitting among the books in Stella's, both with real cups of coffee this time ... no dinky cortados.

"It was early on in our 'relationship,'" Emmett begins, using air quotes. "She'd given me her phone number and I figured I'd call her. Her father was eastern European and answered the phone. I very politely identified who I was and asked if I could talk to her and he just flipped his shit: 'How dare you call my daughter! Who do you think you are?' On and on just yelling at me for calling his daughter."

Jayne giggles: "What did you do?"

"I think I ended up just apologizing profusely and hanging up, thinking that she must get a lot of calls from some real a-holes for him to flip out like that. And then being a little offended for being lumped in with them. She found me at school the next day and apologized profusely for his behavior, saying that her dad thought that every boy who called her was trying to impregnate her. And all I could think was that she must have some pretty lowlife-type boys coming after her."

Jayne has a puzzled look on her face.

"You remember the first time I came to pick you up when we hung out, right?" Jayne half nods, half shakes her head. "In high school, whenever I picked up a girl, I always made a point of going inside her house to go and meet her family. Even if it wasn't a date, and it wasn't ever a date, because I thought dating in high school was pretty stupid. I made a point to not be the prick in the car with the loud music who pulls up to some girl's house and honks the horn until she comes out. I was the picture-perfect wholesome all-American high school boy. I went to church every Sunday, took IB and AP classes, didn't drink or do drugs, didn't wear eyeliner or strange clothes like girl jeans or anything, made eye contact when I spoke, wasn't sketchy in the least bit—I figured, if there was one person this girl's dad shouldn't just be randomly yelling at for calling his daughter, it would be me."

"I get what you mean. So you were a little offended?"

"I suppose so," Emmett says. "Speaking of wholesome activities, wanna move outside so I can inhale some nicotine?"

"I was just thinking that it's really much too nice to be cooped up inside like this."

"Excellent," and Emmett reaches for his bag as Jayne grabs their coffees and they wander around for a spell looking for a spot to sit so Emmett can smoke.

Out on the front porch of Stella's, expanded since Emmett had first started going, they sit for longer than Emmett has sat in recent memory. He wants this afternoon to just go on forever and ever. Jayne seems less interested in her phone than usual.

"Do you talk to Lauren much anymore?" Emmett asks.

"Lauren? No, not too much. She Facebooks me every so often to see if I want to go on a bike ride, but we have much different styles of cycling and I don't find her much fun to go on rides with."

"How's that?"

"I'm more of a leisurely pace-type person," Jayne says. "Lauren just wants to push herself as hard as possible. She's into racing, she's into going as fast as possible."

"That sounds about right; Little Miss Competitive."

Jayne laughs. "See, you do remember something about her!"

"I can remember things in context. I remember that she can be more anal than me sometimes—and now that you've mentioned it, I remember that most everything was a competition. Especially when it came to supporting each other. Yeah. That's probably what it was."

"What do you mean?"

"Well, my mom has been telling me that her theory as to why Lauren left me is that she was keeping track, however mental, however abstract, of how much support she was offering me versus how much support I was offering her—she saw it from a bookkeeping standpoint. One day I just borrowed too much from her savings-and-loan department and then I defaulted. I never really saw it from a competitive standpoint though, who could be more 'independent,'" using the air quotes again. "I've always figured you just love a person and that's that … you accept them for who they are, flaws and all."

"Interesting," Jayne says. "Hold on a sec. I have to pee."

"Sure thing." Emmett reaches into his shirt pocket and rolls another cigarette. He's smoking it, politely observing the other patrons of Stella's, by the time Jayne gets back. He tells her, "You know, one of the last 'fights,' if you can really call them fights—since I don't really fight with people, at least not really shouting-and-name-calling fighting … Anyways, one of the last arguments or discussions or whatevers I remember having with her was over how often we could say 'I love you' to each other."

"Huh."

"Our families have vastly different approaches to the phrase. In her family it's a rarity, a treat to be dispensed only on special occasions, whereas in my family, we say it all the time: at the end of every email, at the end of every telephone conversation, every time we say goodbye, it's 'I love you.' And, to Lauren, me constantly saying it to her was cheapening its meaning, was stripping it of its worth, whereas to me, I meant it every time, so I was simply reinforcing my love for her."

"Interesting."

"I think it just shows where her heart was."

"Definitely."

"Here I am, getting my brain shot with enough electricity it gives me a seizure three times a week, just knowing that I love the poor girl—just trying to love her the best I know how. And she doesn't want to take care of my cat, she doesn't want to come over for dinner, she doesn't want me even touching her—"

"Wait, she didn't want you to even touch you?"

"Nope, couldn't touch her. No kissing, no hand holding, no cuddling, no hugs. Nothing."

"Wow. That's kinda fucked up."

"Yep. And I just went along with it. Because I myself was pretty fucked up.

"But I think it shows where our hearts were, you know," Emmett says, Jayne nodding. "It's like I knew I loved her. According to my mom I demonstrated it by showing her family around town when they came to visit, despite my getting psychotic in the middle of it, despite having gotten ECT that morning. I think she felt grated by the phrase because she knew she didn't love me. I have this theory that it was the repeated phrase that led her to leave me."

"Which, if you think about it, was a good thing. You know that, right?"

"Oh, absolutely," Emmett says. "I read a study," he begins, "or did I hear it on the radio?" he says more to himself. "Anyways. There was this study they did on our generation that more or less came to the conclusion that millennials are pretty messed up because of the constant reassurance we received as kids."

"I don't think I need constant reassurance," Jayne says.

"I don't think many people need constant reassurance. What the study was talking about was authority figures like teachers, principals, youth pastors, guidance counselors, parents, camp leaders or whatever they're called—people who lead groups of kids, essentially—always saying that they're doing a great job, that they're sooo awesome, that they're sooo great, and so on and so forth. It's like the theme song to the LEGO Movie, you know 'Everything is awesome, everything is cool when you're blah diddy blah'" and Emmett mockingly mumbles more than sings the first line to the song that had been stuck in his head during the week that Clarissa had been home earlier in the summer.

Jayne has a look on her face Emmett can't quite read, it's either shocked or nauseated; he waits for her to speak. She finally shakes her head and asks, "They have songs like that?"

"They really do. Look it up when you get home. But not now. The song is on the tip of my subconscious and I don't want it to actually get into my conscious because then it'll get stuck there for who knows how long."

Jayne laughs, "Okay."

"Anyways. It's like our generation was told that everything was so awesome so often that we became cynical about it. We weren't given a realistic view of life. Because in real life, only a few things are awesome, most are mediocre, and a few things, though more plentiful than the things that are awesome, absolutely suck. In real life, there are few winners and not everyone gets a trophy. We were taught standard distribution, the bell curve, but not shown its real-world application because, you know ... everything is awesome. It makes for a pretty screwed view on life when you grow older and encounter things like racists and rapists and all of the other things kids would encounter if they were raised on Andrew Jackson Jihad albums."

Jayne laughs at this and Emmett realizes his voice is getting progressively louder and louder. Mania is starting to settle in. He rolls another cigarette and steadies his breathing. If only weed weren't so bad for him, that would chill him out immediately.

"I think that's an excellent point. Do you happen to still have the link to the article?"

"Probably not; I don't even know what one would Google to

find it. I do know that I'm not pulling it out of my ass though. At least I'm about 93.8 percent sure that I'm not. It might be knowledge divinely inserted, though."

Jayne lets out a laugh and says, "Oh I believe you, it sounds totally plausible and true. I'd just like to read the entire article. Do you remember the source of the article at all?"

"It's that whole memory thing. Sorry, love."

She lets her face go into a frown.

"But my long-term memory is pretty good. So maybe ask in a year and I'll remember?"

They sit there as Emmett smokes one last cigarette. Emmett is satisfied. Lately, they haven't been hanging out long enough to warrant even a single cigarette for Emmett and today it's been a four-cigarette hangout. He's enjoying himself so much he even blows some smoke rings and allows himself to look like a tool. Jayne has kept her phone in her purse almost the entire time but brings it out to take some photos of Emmett.

He always feels so self-conscious having his picture taken, but he allows it; Jayne and Rob are leaving next week and soon they'll be reduced to Google Hangouts, text messaging, and good-old-fashioned letters for communication. That's probably why today is so good—because Jayne knows it's going to be the last time she'll see Emmett for a long time.

Walking in the door to an excited Kerrinpuppy, Emmett feels appreciated for a second time. He sits down in his chair feeling exhausted, patting his lap for Little Baby Kerrin to hop up so she can give him kisses.

He takes her outside so she can go potty and then back down the hall so Emmett can think about some dinner and how to best occupy himself for the rest of the evening.

Chapter Twenty Two

◇◇

Emmett and Dad sit at their bench at Governor's Park, Emmett rolling a ciga-
rette while Dad holds onto Kerrinpuppy.

"You know, I like visiting Lacey a lot more than Dr. Bogsdaughter," Emmett
says.

"Why's that?" Dad says.

"Not as much of a production. I much prefer the twenty-minute walk to and
from her office to going down Colorado Boulevard to visit with Dr. Bogsdaugh-
ter."

"Less stressful?"

"Much less stressful," Emmett says. "And while I like our tradition of you and
Mom having dinner over at my place afterwards, it's also a drain on me—I feel
like I've lost an entire afternoon because of a freaking doctor's appointment."

"I can understand that. Do you want to stop doing dinner?"

Emmett licks the rolling paper and folds it over to complete the cigarette, puts it
to his lips and lights. He takes a drag and exhales, that odd double whistle he
can't seem to get rid of. He says: "No. It's a good tradition. Dr. Bogsdaughter
himself is also a bit more stressful than Lacey. I can't quite pin down why it
is—maybe because I focus on more negative stuff with him. All of the psychosis
and dissociation and such, it's like poison that gets dragged to the surface."

Dad looks at Emmett, about to say something, but Emmett beats him to it: "It's
necessary to drag that poison to the surface. He needs to know about that kind
of stuff. It's just hard, ya know?"

"Yeah," Dad says.

And Emmett changes the topic to something less depressing so he doesn't ruin his
own mood: computers. Computers are always less depressing.

◇◇

Kerrinpuppy sits at Emmett's feet, looking up at him with longing in her eyes as he tries to concentrate on his notebook, hurriedly writing everything he wants to talk about with Lacey. LBK wants nothing else in the whole wide world but to sit in Emmett's lap.

Finally, Emmett relents, sticking pen and notebook back into their respective pockets and patting his lap with both hands so his Little Girl can hop up on his lap. She gives him two quick kisses and settles down.

He's always fifteen minutes early, simply because Dad needs fifteen minutes to be back to work on time. And so he sits there, looking at the various covers of the magazines on the table next to him, waiting for the time to pass.

Finally, Lacey's office door opens and a woman comes out. It's the same woman who's been coming out of her office for the past few weeks. He doesn't know her name and she doesn't know his but she sure knows Kerrinpuppy's name.

"Kerrin!" she exclaimed. "Can I come say hi?"

Emmett nods, smiling.

The woman, looking like the yuppie outdoorsy type one finds in the Highlands or Boulder comes over and greets Kerrin who, with wagging tail, sits up on Emmett's lap to receive the attention. Kerrinpuppy might not be much of a dog's dog but she loves people, women especially, which makes Emmett suspect she'd been mistreated by men in the past, as she usually takes a while to warm up to them. All men but him; she's been licking his face since the moment they'd met.

The woman says her goodbye, and Emmett wishes her a pleasant day and soon Lacey is there.

"Hey Emmett, hey Kerrin," she greets them in her warm, even, and friendly manner, Kerrinpuppy already hopping off of Emmett's lap and stretching to get ready to greet her. "Come on back," Lacey says, gesturing with her head toward her office.

Emmett gets to his feet, grabs his bag and follows Kerrinpuppy and Lacey down the short hall and into her office.

Lacey's office hasn't changed very much since he first started seeing her when he'd just turned nineteen. There are a few new paintings on the wall and he seems to remember her having gotten either a new chair or a new couch, or maybe she's just switched their position. But for the most part it's stayed the same. While Emmett is one to appreciate and even need a fresh environment in his own quarters, he likes that Lacey's office has stayed largely the same for all these years.

"How've you been?"

"Oh, pretty good," Emmett says. And he launches into a brief overview of his mental health over the past couple weeks. Not much of anything to note—depression about the same, nothing major. Psychosis about the same, nothing major. In general, just a little thoughtful.

"Thoughtful? About what?" Lacey says, reaching over to her desk—one of the biggest changes in her office having been the removal of the hutch which used to rest over it—to grab her glasses. "By the way, would you like some water?"

"No thanks," Emmett says. "Well, this blog of mine has had me writing what seems like nonstop for the past few months. It's just come, like ... gushing out of me."

"Well that sounds nice."

"It is nice. Really nice. To actually have something to work on. To have a purpose, to feel like my life has meaning. I think that's one of the biggest reasons I've been doing so well—just having something to do with myself."

Lacey takes down a few notes and Emmett waits for her to stop writing.

"Anyways. I started writing this post; which I don't think I'll actually put up, because it's not really pertinent to anything, just an interesting tidbit of a story I remembered from high school. And maybe an interesting factoid for you to put in that therapist file of yours ... maybe if you have some kind of psychological profile of me for when I get famous."

Lacey laughs and tells him she really doesn't have anything like that and it doesn't work that way.

"I know. But it's funny to think it works that way ... just like it does on TV. Because, you know, TV is reality, right?"

"Right," Lacey says, grinning.

"Anyways. It's about my handwriting."

"I don't think I've ever seen your handwriting."

"I'm actually pretty proud of my handwriting. At least most of the time. My letter-writing handwriting, at least. I spent a lot of time trying to develop it. I think handwriting is a lost art—kind of like how they aren't teaching cursive in Holland or whatever country it is because they figure kids will be using a keyboard so much they won't have to write quickly by hand anymore."

"I heard about that, kind of sad."

"I know, right?" Emmett raising his voice a little. Kerrinpuppy stirs in his lap and he scratches her neck until she settles back down to her nap.

"Anyways," Emmett says, sighing. "When I was a sophomore in high school, we had some assignment—or maybe it was that the kids who were taking psych had an assignment—and my friend, I don't remember her name, but she was very nice and had auburn hair, came up to me and asked me if she could analyze my handwriting."

"Okay ... " Lacey says.

"So I write the test sentences or whatever. Actually, I don't remember what the test even entailed. I just remember the outcome.

"She comes to me later on, a little worried look on her face," Emmett continues. "And tells me that the analysis says that I'm a lunatic. Mentally ill. Batshit crazy. I think she used more PC terms than that."

"Interesting. What do you think of that now?"

"Well it's interesting. Because I recently came across some of my handwriting from that time period, and it turns out that my handwriting from sophomore year of high school, when I wasn't diagnosed with any mental illness but was surely developing one, isn't anything like my handwriting now, when I actually am, quote-unquote, 'batshit crazy,'" Emmett says.

"Yes, and there's also—"

"Hold on," Emmett says, holding up his free finger. "From what I can remember I was almost excited that I had the handwriting of a lunatic; it was kinda cool. I remember it was about that time that I learned what schizophrenia actually is and I remember wanting to actually experience it, just try it out because it seemed so interesting to me.

"But, that aside, a person can change their handwriting. It isn't like their fingerprint or their DNA or something like that. It's like a drawing technique. Sure you have a way you're naturally inclined toward drawing, but they have whole schools of thought toward drawing—design schools instead of fine arts schools where they teach you how to draw in whatever style you need to in order to please the client. So how can handwriting analysis be accurate in predicting what kind of personality a person has?"

"Those are interesting points," Lacey says. "Kind of makes you wonder about the whole concept of psychological profiling in the first place, vis-à-vis your earlier joking comment about my psychological profile on you."

"Exactly," Emmett says, triumphantly. "Only," his voice deflated, "I suppose I really ought to track her down, or someone who does handwriting analysis, and have them do the analysis again. Maybe my handwriting still suggests that I'm crazy."

"But do you really need a handwriting test to confirm that?"

"Oh no," Emmett says, much louder than necessary. "Sorry. This is just a line of thought I'm having at the moment and choosing to pursue, and you happen to be here. Just an interesting thing for me to talk about. I know I have a mental illness."

"So it's not a path you're taking where you think you'll end up thinking you're faking it?" Lacey says, referring to Emmett's persistent delusion that he thinks he's just making his illness up to get attention.

"Probably not; it's just an interesting thing to think about. A philosophical carnival ride. Fun for a while but not really an effective means of transportation."

Lacey laughs. "So how are you doing with Jayne and Rob moving?"

"Well she promised me that we'd text a lot while they were driving through to California, but I didn't get a whole lot of messages," Emmett says, sighing. "And Resi is supposedly going to stay at my place at some point, but I never got her parents' contact information to set that up ... though I think that might end up being a good thing. I just wish it'd been directly addressed instead of passively ignored."

"Jayne makes a lot of promises like that and doesn't keep them," Lacey says, a ruthful tone in her voice from which Emmett has come to find great solace.

"Yeah," Emmett looking at the floor. "I mean, I'm used to it. But that doesn't mean I like it, so..."

"Of course not," Lacey says.

"But it's also not like I'm going to change it. I don't know if I ought to confront her about it. Especially now, when she's going to be like thirteen hundred miles away."

"Is that how far it is?"

"Yeah."

"That's an awfully long way."

"Yeah, I've already started saving up money to go out and see her."

"Have you made a plan on how to stay in touch? I know that you're pretty iffy with phones."

"Yeah, we're going to do Google Hangouts every so often, try to write letters as often as we can. I explained to her about the phone stuff—about how I really need to be familiar with the space someone is occupying so I know where they are before I can really talk to them for very long, and that pictures don't really help. Google Hangouts aren't much better. I can chat for maybe thirty minutes or so; at least that's how long I last with Clarissa, so…"

"It's important for you to stay in touch with your friends though, and you've always made it a priority. Like with your pen pal, I forget her name, when you were going through ECT."

"Totally," Emmett perking up at the mention of Nicole. "Nicole was her name. And we often joke that we're closer the further apart we are. I think with Jayne it might be different, though. I don't know; we've never been this far apart. And I'm not sure how close we actually are—like our relationship is just mostly vague blurs, so … "

"That whole ECT thing, huh?"

"Yeah."

"And you don't have as much of a history with Nicole," Lacey says.

"That too. I can actually remember most of my relationship with Nicole, and most of that relationship exists in letters we've exchanged—so I can go back and review that relationship. I have to rely on what Jayne has told me about our relationship and the bits and pieces I can reconstruct myself and from the pictures I can find on my hard drives.

"Things can just seem so fragmented sometimes," Emmett says. "Like I'm a five-million-piece jigsaw puzzle that I'm trying to assemble without a reference picture."

"That's a pretty good analogy."

"Yeah. And I fucking hate jigsaw puzzles."

Lacey cocks her head to one side to match Emmett's perpetually cocked head and smiles—it's a motherly smile and it always makes Emmett feel better, to know that someone out there, however much money Dad pays her, wants to scoop him up and protect him.

Emmett walks home as the heat of the day is at its worst. He's got his earbuds in, listening to Songs of Our Soil by This Bike is a Pipe Bomb. Feel-good music to walk your dog to after a particularly good session with Lacey.

He's walking up Logan because Logan has traffic signals. It's safer for him to walk with traffic signals. Obi-Wan Kenobi was right: your eyes can deceive you; don't trust them. At least when you've got a mental illness. And it's better to have something you can put faith in, like the authority of the green light and the little white walking man, than to gamble on your brain not just completely eliminating a car from your vision. Anything can happen.

He turns right at Twelfth because he has the right-of-way at Pennsylvania and because the corner of Logan and Thirteenth is busy and stressful. Though if he's completely honest with himself, it's also because the homeless man at that intersection makes him uncomfortable. Which is strange, because usually homeless people don't make Emmett uncomfortable at all.

Walking in front of the coffee shop, Emmett finds himself with a hankering for a cold coffee. He ties Little Baby Kerrin up to the picnic table outside, says goodbye to her, pulls his earbuds out of his ears, and enters the establishment. The 3:00 p.m. rush is going on and Emmett has to wait in line for a little while. No time to chat with the baristas like usual—they have too many coffee orders to fill.

He gets his large iced latte, properly bitter with a bit of a bite to it and refreshingly cold, and goes out to greet an ecstatic LBK.

Then inside his building.

Down the hall.

Key inserted into lucky number seven.

Kerrinpuppy making a beeline for her water dish, taking a long drink.

Emmett making a beeline for his letter-writing supplies: the special paper and his fountain pen. Then to his drafting table, to write his first letter to Jayne—to maybe just get his thoughts in order.

Chapter Twenty Three

"How are you preparing for your flight?" Lacey asks, as Emmett takes his seat and pats his lap for Kerrinpuppy to hop up.

"Well, Dr. Bogsdaughter and my parents seem to want me to take one of those cart things to my gate," Emmett says.

"I take it you don't like that idea?" Lacey says after a pause.

"Not in the slightest. I'm perfectly capable of walking, and I think I can match up some numbers on my ticket with some numbers on the wall, I'm not that disabled."

Lacey chuckles and says, "I don't think you are either, but it's at least worth considering."

"Oh, I considered it. I just came to the conclusion rather quickly that it's not necessary."

"Why's that?"

"I just don't see myself as that disabled. Sure, I've got some handicaps. Sure, I have problems with grocery stores and crowded places … but the airport? I can't imagine it being busy enough to make me psychotic. It's a weekday, it's not a holiday, it'll be in the afternoon. Though I'm going to take some risperidone anyways."

"Why not ziprasidone?" Lacey asks. Emmett always takes ziprasidone, it's been his standard issue PRN antipsychotic for years, why would he take something else?

"Ziprasidone's been making me super-sleepy lately. I'm thinking if I take half of one of the quarter milligram risperidones, I should be pretty good."

"Gotcha," Lacey says, as she writes more notes down and then sets her pen down and looks up at Emmett, smiling in a way only Lacey can smile.

◇◇

Emmett hadn't been too surprised when his first letter from Jayne in California wasn't all sunshine and beach weather.

She's always had this remarkable gift for finding the negative in everything. He can't help but notice the irony of the role reversal: Jayne trapped in the suburbs with nothing to do and feeling suffocated by it, just like he'd been a couple years before.

According to her letters, she doesn't do much of anything but drink coffee and listen to NPR and go for her daily bike ride (already three times as many things as he'd done). She avoids her roommates, who're more into partying and smoking pot than anything. She barely sees Rob, and as their letter conversations continue, Emmett grows more concerned. Until, in one of her letters, Jayne admits to Emmett she thinks she's depressed. He reads the words and sees the monster rear its ugly head for a brief moment before dipping back beneath the surface—it's the last thing she needs.

Thinking about the letter, he doesn't know if it's quite depression or if it's just that she doesn't know what to do with herself. Sometimes there isn't much of a difference. Emmett can remember this from when she took a semester off of school, a mental break where she'd promised they'd hang out all the time and go on adventures, the always-promised, rarely-delivered shenanigans. They'd gone for a hike once, but beyond that he hadn't seen much more of her than when she'd been in school. Jayne needs to be busy, she needs structure, she doesn't do well providing her own structure. Heck, most everyone needs structure, most everyone does poorly on their own. It's taken Emmett years of being left to his own devices to come up with his own structure for occupying himself throughout the day and he's still getting the hang of it.

Life improves for Jayne when she insists she and Rob move out of the suburbs to a coastal city about forty-five minutes farther away from where Rob works. It means a longer commute for Rob, but it also means they can live together (up until this point Rob has been living in the corporate dorms where cohabitation isn't allowed). But then Jayne breaks her collarbone in a bike accident, something Emmett himself had done years ago, which means she isn't going to be able to ride her bike for a number of weeks, and the one thing that's been keeping her sane is taken away from her.

Rob starts texting Emmett, asking him for advice on how to handle depression, asking him for all the little tricks Emmett knows for how to survive day to day with little-to-no hope, and now Emmett finds himself boarding an airplane, having spent money he doesn't really have, to spend a week in California with Jayne in an attempt to cheer her up and remind her of how much she's loved.

Flying is a big deal to Emmett, a monumental feat in will-power; it usually requires weeks of building himself up to it, and here he's doing it with hardly a week's notice. The first time he'd flown after ECT, before Kerrinpuppy, on his way to visit Clarissa in Wisconsin, he'd been so nervous he'd thrown up his breakfast. He and Dad had had to stop at Starbucks so Emmett could get some peppermint tea to calm his stomach—he was mostly worried about TSA, worried they'd peg him as a terror-ist. This time he's mostly worried about navigating the airport by himself. He has to take the in-airport train to get to his flight because he's not flying Frontier for once, which has the easiest gate to navigate to at Denver International Airport. Emmett has left with plenty of time to get lost.

It hasn't necessarily been a piece of cake, but he's gotten to the correct gate, and now he's on the correct plane and they're taxiing to the runway, and Emmett is thinking about Kerrin-puppy and how much he'll miss her and trying to think if he has enough medication to make it through the next several days, if he has enough tobacco and rolling papers, and what he'll do if any of those things go missing. Clothes he can do without; he's worn the same thing day-in, day-out for several days before. His laptop he can do without. He has his little black notebook and a pen in his pocket, so he can at least write and draw to some extent. He can always buy a book at a bookstore; California is sure to have a myriad of bookstores with something he'll like and, if he can't find anything, Jayne will have something he can read. But the pills and the tobacco … he really needs those. Traveling in general has always been done with a great deal of planning, and doing it last minute like this is risky—leaving Kerrinpuppy behind, something he's only done once before, leaving his entire support system behind and going to a new one that may not be able to support him. If something goes wrong he'll be in real trouble; Jayne and Rob have never seen him psychotic before, and he doesn't know how they'll react. They might be champs; they might make things even worse. Too many unknowns, not enough planning. But Emmett is nothing if not loyal.

The flight is uneventful. He finds himself with his tray table pulled down and his hand moving furiously over the page, trying to get his thoughts down before the plane lands, as though the two-and-a-half-hour flight will be over at any minute and he'll have to pack up and leave thoughts unexpressed.

Depression is tricky because, to him, there's clinical depression like he has, and then there's simple situational depression (as if there were ever anything "simple" about depression). It doesn't help that Jayne has been decommissioned from riding her bike by getting into that accident and her break was bad enough it'd required surgery.

But it'd been wonderful that she'd ended up flying home to get the surgery. After a mere six or seven weeks without her he'd found himself sitting at the coffee shop with her, having a cortado, her dad taking a picture of the two of them, Emmett feeling self-conscious about his belly, Jayne telling him he looked great. She'd stayed in Denver for a week or so to recover from the surgery and then headed back to California.

But Jayne stuck all alone in a strange town with nothing to do and no bike to ride—even if it was "just" situational depression, it's a miserable way for her to be. And he figures his mere presence, however stressful him getting there might be, however expensive it might be to fly out immediately instead of waiting a month or so, might be enough to lift her spirits, to get her into some kind of routine and help ease her out of the funk she's found herself in.

He finds himself writing about how he wishes she'd come to his rescue when he'd been going through ECT and needed someone to come get him out of his funk. He crosses it out, but not fully—just enough to let his future-self know that he'd scratched the idea, but not enough to totally obscure the idea. It feels a selfish thing to write, to have Jayne suffering so and him only thinking of himself. But the idea is out there, black ink on cream-colored paper.

Emmett knows now's not the time to find himself in a pity party, but he figures if he is, it might as well be a pity party directed at this notebook while he's trapped thirty-some-thousand feet up in the air and not when he's at sea-level with his best friend, who doesn't need him whining about how unfair life is.

Life isn't fair; his mom's old phrase.

He ends up filling about twenty pages of his notebook. Word vomit this time instead of actual vomit. He feels better having gotten the bile-like contents of his brain onto a piece of paper where they won't poison him or his relationship with Jayne. As the plane lands, he mostly just wants a cigarette. He keeps himself to a strict, every-two-hour smoking regimen, and it's been a good four hours since his last inhalation of any kind of smoke. He's hoping Rob and Jayne will be running behind schedule so he can have a cigarette before their car comes rolling up and they drive him out of San Francisco and down the highway to their house.

Chapter Twenty Four

◇◇◇

"Why do people have to use the word 'crazy' all the time?" Emmett asks, changing the subject.

"I suppose it's just a word we're comfortable saying," Lacey replies.

"Like a default word?"

"Yep," Lacey says, nodding her head. "Does it bug you when people say it?"

"Only when certain people say it. I suppose I have a double standard," Emmett says. "I've asked certain people not to say 'crazy,' and generally speaking they're pretty good at not saying it. But Jayne never seems to get it."

"That hurts, doesn't it?" Lacey says, her voice getting softer and quieter.

Emmett sits there for a couple seconds. "I suppose it does."

"Is there anything you suppose you could do about it?"

"I've thought about making anti-Semitic jokes every time she says the word crazy, since she has Jewish heritage," Emmett says, joking.

Lacey laughs, sets her pen down and says, "I think there's such a thing as accepting people for who they are, and trying to decide if a person's behavior is bad enough that you don't want to be their friend anymore."

Emmett looks at his favorite spot on the carpet, right next to Lacey's chair, where the red of the rug meets the beige of the carpet meets the golden-brown color of her chair. He nods his head and says: "Yeah, I get that. Sometimes people don't change."

◇◇◇

A cigarette proves impossible. No sooner has he lit up and had the first dizzy-head-inducing drag, then the familiar whining of their 1970s BMW, which he imagines has barely made it all thirteen-hundred-some miles, gives them away. It sounds like some kind of belt is coming loose; Emmett doesn't know—he doesn't do engines, he does computers.

Jayne waves her one good arm, and Emmett smiles at her. Rob slows the car to a stop and Emmett opens the door, tosses his hiking bag and black bag inside, and climbs in. Rob is already punching the accelerator and merging back into traffic by the time Emmett gets his seat belt on.

"Hey y'all," Emmett says.

"Hey love!" Jayne says, flipping down the visor and peering into the mirror to give him a huge smile.

"Hello, sir." Rob says, his attention mostly on the traffic around him. "How was your flight?"

"Oh, it was a flight. Much better than last time I flew."

"Oh yeah?"

"Yeah," and Emmett tells them about the vomiting and general anxiety of the last time he flew and how this time he'd basically kicked its ass. Emmett has his phone out and is texting Mom and Dad and Clarissa back home to let them know he'd been picked up and was on his way to Jayne and Rob's home.

They're all dead tired, Rob having gotten up before dawn to make it to the car pool that would take him to his job, an hour-and-a-half-long commute each way. They'd had just enough time for a quick bite to eat before having to get in the car to pick up Emmett. Unfortunately, no dinner for Emmett.

He's a little disappointed, had been hoping for a nice dinner like Mom would have provided. He tells himself that with Jayne only having one functional arm it's a lot to expect of her. He's brought along a stash of chocolate-covered walnuts to tide him over and isn't particularly famished, so he decides he'll make do with whatever he can find at the grocery store Jayne has suggested they stop at on the way home from the airport.

Emmett peruses the aisles, conscious of his belly in the presence of the fit and trim Rob and Jayne. He'd been like both of them once—slim and muscular, able to justify eating just about anything he wasn't allergic to because he'd burn off any calories he consumed by riding his bike. The sandwich station is closed, but they have Virgil's Root Beer on tap, his absolute favorite, so he orders a huge glass of that and settles for a junk-food-supper, JFS as Dad would put it.

Outside, Emmett remembers his nicotine habit and his desire for a cigarette becomes overwhelming. "Mind if I partake?" he asks them.

"Not at all," Rob says, and Jayne says she's going to go wait in the car and eat her kale chips.

Emmett sits on a bench, rolls his cigarette, and lights. The tobacco seems to have grown moist, as dragging on it doesn't produce the kind of smoke Emmett prefers in his tobacco.

"How close are we to the ocean?"

"Less than a mile; it's within walking distance from our house," Rob says.

"Well fuck," Emmett says.

Rob laughs, "What?"

"My tobacco is never going to dry out. Means goodbye, pleasantly half-dry tobacco. Might have to put it in your oven."

Rob laughs again. Then, seeing Emmett's face, says "You're serious?"

"Oh, I don't know. Just never particularly cared for moist tobacco. I don't feel as though I'm getting enough smoke. If I'm going to be putting myself into an early grave, I want to do it the right way. My parents raised me to always try my best."

"I'd forgotten how ridiculous you can be," Rob says, chuckling.

"Just when I'm nicotine deprived. So, how's Jayne been?" Emmett says.

"About the same. She's been super excited for you to come, of course. I just don't know how bad it actually is."

"You know; I was thinking about it on the flight over. Thinking about how bad it got for me, when I was recovering from ECT. I don't think even I knew how bad it was for me at the time. It's like—every day becomes about survival, just making it from day to day, hour to hour … the more time gets divided, the worse it is. Shit, depression sucks."

"Yeah."

Emmett discards his cigarette early, giving up on it because it just isn't satisfying. He thinks that maybe living near the ocean would be enough to get him to quit smoking. Or he'd just switch to smoking pre-rolled cigarettes. "Ready-rolls," a cowboy would have called them.

The guys get back into the car. Jayne is busy with her phone, Emmett getting the feeling that maybe she's worse off than he thought.

"They have you on pain meds?"

"Yeah, but I'm not taking too many. I don't like how they make me feel."

"Oh, I used to love that feeling," Emmett says, referring to his previous addiction to painkillers, which he sees more as God having given him something to self-medicate with early on in the development of his illness, a necessary step in his path to recovery.

"Not me. You can have the pills if you want."

"Ha! Not on your life. I wouldn't touch that shit with a ten-foot pole," Emmett says, almost offended that she would offer. Would she offer a former alcoholic a pint of whiskey?

When they pull up to the house, it's a few minutes past Emmett's pill time. He's already taken pills from his emergency stash, but he replenishes his pills as soon as they get inside.

Rob goes to get ready for bed—washing face, brushing teeth and so forth. And Jayne sits at their tiny kitchen table, watching Emmett count out all his pills, about fifty of them, putting them in either the a.m. or p.m. bottle. Emmett looks up occasionally from his near-automatic dispensing of the pills, watching Jayne's reaction.

"That's a lot of pills," Jayne says.

Emmett realizes that she's never actually seen how many pills he takes. It's one thing to be told it's fifty pills, and quite another to see them. "Yup. But they work. I wouldn't be here right now if it weren't for them."

"That's crazy."

"No, anti-crazy. Sane." Why do people have to use that word so often?

"Yeah. I suppose so."

Emmett finishes up with the pills, puts the tops on the bottles, and puts the pill case away in a corner. "Imma get ready for bed."

"I'll get your blankets and pillows and stuff out."

Resi is playing with her toys, having immediately greeted Emmett with the kind of enthusiasm only a dog can muster. Emmett had been hoping that she'd sleep with him, but of course she'll be sleeping with Jayne and Rob.

Jayne gets his bed ready as Emmett washes his face and attempts to brush his teeth—he always seems to manage to put on more of a show when in the presence of other people.

He'd told Jayne that his only request for sleeping arrangements was having several heavy blankets, so he's a bit disappointed to see just a sleeping bag and a comforter. He's told her that the more weight he has on top of him while he sleeps, the safer he feels, the less prone to psychosis he is. Oh well, no sense in bringing it up now; not much anyone can do about it at 10:30 at night, and they probably don't have any other blankets anyway.

He says goodnight to everyone and they retire to their bedroom, Resi along with them. Emmett finds an outlet and plugs his phone in. He pulls his book out of his bag, Ulysses by James Joyce, something he's been told he has to read and figures now is as good a time as any. He has a backup Kurt Vonnegut book just in case he doesn't like James Joyce.

Chapter Twenty Five

"It felt a little strange, being with Jayne for a week," Emmett says.

"How so?"

"I dunno. Maybe it was that it felt like … home."

Rob has to work most of the time Emmett is over visiting. They manage to go on a hike the first day, as it's a weekend, but Emmett will be gone by the next Friday, so he'll only be seeing Rob at night.

The days are oddly spaced, with Emmett sleeping in until about 10:00 a.m.—11:00 a.m. Mountain Standard Time. He thought he'd be getting up earlier than usual, given the time difference, but he seems to have acclimated to Pacific Standard Time immediately.

Jayne seems about like her usual self, a little reserved at first, maybe a little short with Rob, but by Monday they're back to inside jokes and are even cooking together. They visit the poor excuse for an art museum and go to a bunch of coffee shops. The local record store seems to have about as many records as Dad and Emmett have combined. Emmett thinks about buying something but then realizes how awkward it would be to carry the record home with him and finally decides against it when he sees how expensive the record is.

A kid comes up to Emmett while he's outside smoking, asking him if he as any methadone, explaining to Emmett that he's been sleeping on the streets, which is a little suspicious to

Emmett since the kid is wearing cleaner clothes than he is. They later see the kid talking on an iPhone at the coffee shop they've come to prefer, the one that reminds them of Stella's, only full of crust punks instead of DU law students.

Emmett sees the ocean for essentially the first time in his life—he's technically seen it two other times, but he doesn't remember either time. It's not an especially moving moment for him. He and Jayne have taken Resi for a walk to the local park where there's a bench that overlooks the beach and the ocean.

"Oh, so that's the ocean," Emmett says.

"Yup," Jayne replies.

"Looks wet."

"Yup."

And they continue their conversation about nothing in particular, shooting the breeze as homeless people take naps and old ladies walk their tiny, well-bred dogs along the paths.

Emmett can't remember having such good conversations with Jayne before, probably because he's never had her undivided attention for such a long stretch of time before. The two of them being stuck together for the next few days means they have lots of opportunities for such talk.

When Jayne does her homework, Emmett breaks out his laptop and manages to accomplish a bit of programming. Nothing major, just a shell script he found on the Internet and has been meaning to modify to make work on his system. It'll automatically mount network drives every time he logs in—it's an essential script to have, because one of the biggest reasons he refuses to reboot his computer is all of the labor that goes into manually mounting all five network shares. With this script, all he has to do is set his computer to run it, and it'll take care of the rest.

He's able to remote into his computer back home and test the script, making the necessary changes on his laptop and retesting it, marveling at how cool it is. He thinks of how many people take this kind of thing for granted, and how he's sitting there like some kind of caveman gawking at fire or the wheel and its many uses. Still, it's nice to appreciate things that didn't used to exist but have since become commonplace.

Chapter Twenty Six

"Of course, then she decides to go back to Denver, and I feel as though I've failed somehow."

"How would that be a failure?" Lacey asks.

"Because I saw her moving out to California as her opportunity to do some major growing, to really spread her wings, so to speak. And then I come, and I feel as though I convinced her to just move back to Denver, a place where she might just be stagnant and never grow because it doesn't challenge her enough."

"What about the depression?"

"That's a fair point," Emmett says. "And it makes it all the trickier. But it's not like she's heeding my advice to go see a doctor or anything. I dunno. I just look at how much I grew, having been put in such a difficult position, and I want the same for her."

As the time of his departure draws nearer, Jayne seems to have returned to her normal self—instead of going out to eat, she's cooking meals, screw her one-armed confinement. She's getting feisty again, and Emmett is glad to see that but worried that it'll disappear as soon as he enters the airport.

Denver comes up more and more in conversation, especially when Emmett starts sharing the pictures of Kerrinpuppy that Mom and Dad are sending every day to put Emmett's mind at ease. He calls Mom every morning when he goes to smoke his first cigarette of the day. Sitting on the stoop, he talks to her for a few minutes and smokes a wholly unsatisfying cigarette to tell her about what he did the day before, but he seems to not need to talk to her as much with Jayne around and an adventure to look forward to, even if that adventure is just hanging around listening to Dr. Dog on his crummy laptop speakers while Jayne does her online homework.

Maybe it wouldn't have been so bad to move out here with them. Maybe Emmett could weather just about anything with them. Perhaps they're more family than he thought, perhaps he just underestimated them in his occasional-though-not-infrequent bitterness at the world.

Everything feels all right, and he's half-dreading, half-looking-forward-to Friday when his plane takes off and he returns to Denver.

He'll be back with Kerrinpuppy, he'll be back to his regular routine, cigarettes will be back to normal, but it'll be bittersweet—he'll miss them and he doesn't know when he'll see them again. Thanksgiving he supposes, or perhaps Christmas.

But around Thursday night, as Emmett is scanning their living room for his possessions, making sure he isn't forgetting anything, Jayne is in plotting mode. Emmett gets like this, too. When in plotting mode, little can stop them, little can stand in their way. They're both schemers by nature, and he supposes at least this quality would make them good businessfolk. Jayne has had enough; Emmett was enough of a taste of Denver that she wants to be back, she needs to be back. Not exactly the kind of reaction Emmett was hoping for. He was hoping to be like the methadone the cleanly-dressed-homeless-kid was asking for: not quite the full fix, just a taste to ween you off.

He's been talking to her for a while about how good of an experience it is to go to a new place and actually live there. Not just visit, not just live out of a suitcase, but actually live there. It's an opportunity to grow, an opportunity for new adventures. He feels as though he doesn't have to tell her that adventures aren't always good and fun and awesome; but, then again, maybe he does. Maybe it's her lack of experience, the maturity she just can't fake her way into having, that she doesn't realize it's the dark times, providing the contrast, that make the good times all the better.

Emmett sometimes carries an awful lot of guilt when it comes to Jayne. She's only twenty-one years old, and he'll be turning twenty-eight this year. Such a huge age gap, and he doesn't often consider it because Jayne has always just been there; she acts so grown up that he usually forgets that she isn't actually grown up, that she still has a lot of learning to do. There's a lot about life he can't assume she doesn't already know. Maybe part of the problem is that, in acting like she's so much older, she assumes she knows more about life than she really does—assumes the responsibility without having earned it, and that's how she ends up thirteen-hundred-some miles away from home, poorly equipped to handle it and scheming for a way to get home and tear Rob away from a good internship that could potentially mean a lot for his career.

Emmett listens to Jayne's profluent scheming as she becomes more and more enamored with the idea of just leaving California and coming back to Denver. Always going for the quick fix, he thinks, his generation plagued with thinking that moving someplace new means they'll leave their problems behind; not realizing problems are just as mobile as they are.

Should he say something?

Probably not right now. But if it really is depression, it ought to be sorted out, because it will rear its ugly head again. Depression is a potentially fatal illness, something to be taken seriously. He might be proven a fool; she might go to a therapist and find that she isn't depressed in the least. But it's like getting a biopsy on a lump—you want to know what you're dealing with. Is it simple melancholy brought on by boredom or lack of structure? Or is it actual, ugly, real clinical depression?

A couple days after Emmett lands in Denver, Jayne and Rob have broken the lease on their apartment, sold their furniture, packed up what they want to keep in their little BMW, and are headed back to Denver.

Emmett will go so far as to get a list of therapists that are covered by Jayne's insurance and give it to Lacey so she can see if any of them are any good, or if she even knows any of them—but that's as far as it'll go.

Jayne will immerse herself in work. Distracting herself instead of facing the problem head-on, trying to move away from the problem instead of dealing with it. What the problem actually is, Emmett will never find out.

If there's one thing Emmett has learned about life with a severe mental illness it's that you have to face it head-on—you can't avoid it, you can't try to dodge it. You have to be brave and confront it in all its ugliness. It hurts him to say this to Jayne and see her smile and nod her head, totally agreeing with him and then completely ignoring his advice. Mental illness is what he's good at, it's his area of expertise; if he can live so successfully with such a severe mental illness, then he must be able to impart some pretty good advice on someone like Jayne.

But people don't deal with problems when they're small and reasonable; only when they get too big, too out of control. He'd done the exact same thing—ignoring all of the tiny signs and only dealing with his mental illness once it'd become too enormous to handle. Heck, even then he still ignored it. People are irrational, people are lazy, people are stupid. But just like the Andrew Jackson Jihad song, he loved people, because people were so very, very special.

Chapter Twenty Seven

◇◇

Emmett looks at the clock next to Lacey. Every therapist he's ever met with has two clocks: one right next to where the client sits and another one right next to the therapist, so everyone knows when the hour is up. The clock next to Lacey is showing he has about a minute or so left.

Lacey must be thinking the same thing. "Anything else before we stop for the day?"

Kerrinpuppy starts stirring in Emmett's lap, gets to her feet, hops down and does a stretch.

Emmett searches through his brain and it comes up a total blank. Not that they'd talked about everything; it was just that he always comes up a blank whenever someone asks him a question such as this.

Lacey bends over to give Kerrinpuppy some scratches as Emmett says, "No. I think we covered everything."

"Awesome," Lacey says in her gentle voice, smiling at Emmett as Kerrinpuppy licks her hand. "So I'll see you in two weeks?"

"Most definitely."

◇◇

Out on a walk, just as the weather is thinking about be-ginning to turn. Emmett can smell it in the air between the clouds of cigarette smoke he's producing as they walk, Dad talking some nonsense about something he'd heard on conser-vative talk radio.

Emmett tries not to get too involved in politics, tries not to listen to the radio other than NPR because at least NPR isn't constantly telling him the world is going to end and then trying to sell him concealed carry permit classes and ten years' worth of nonperishable food during commercial breaks. NPR just wants you to feel intellectually superior, and Emmett figures it's better to be arrogant than paranoid.

Mostly it's the calm voices, the near-whispering of the NPR radio hosts. No turning up the volume suddenly during commercial breaks (because there are no commercial breaks), which always puts him on edge. No thundering voices, no tyrannical rants, no manipulating of emotions. Emmett is an emotional super-sponge, sopping up whatever expressed emotions he's exposed to and taking them on as his own. Dr. Bogsdaughter implores Mom and Dad to remain as calm and even-keeled as possible when dealing with Emmett, because even a small amount of stress from them can affect him greatly. He needs to be handled with kid gloves—don't yell at him, don't raise your voice, don't even approach him with a tense voice. Save your emotions for the privacy of your own room, away from Emmett.

He and Dad are completing their usual circuit, Emmett's mind off somewhere else. Not a dangerous somewhere else, he tells Dad; he just happens to be in a thoughtful mood. The silence is serene; Eleventh Avenue is strangely quiet today as they make their way east.

Kerrinpuppy is on the trail of something and straining against the leash, Emmett and Dad walking too slow. "Calm down there, Corporal McSniffers," Emmett says, giving a gentle but firm tug on the leash to remind her of her manners. It doesn't work very well. Emmett repeats the same firm but gentle tug a few more times before she either finally comes to her senses or they've left the trail behind.

They complete their circuit, arriving back home with time to spare. The barometric pressure is changing and Emmett's knees are throbbing. Walks are getting shorter.

Up the stairs.

Punch in the door code.

Down the hall, Kerrinpuppy racing up and down: "Follow me! I know the way!"

Inside, Emmett offers Dad a glass of water. He relegates himself to the remnants of a lukewarm cup of coffee.

They sit there for a little while, chatting about nothing in particular, Kerrin sniffing at her food bowl, Emmett rubbing his knees, thinking about when Dad leaves and how he's going to put his knee braces on, watching Kerrinpuppy eat her lunch.

She only seems to eat, at least at home, after she's played with her squirrels—"killing" them by making their seemingly indestructible squeakers go off incessantly, and placing them around her food dish as though she were pretending to eat them.

"Dogs are mysterious animals," Emmett says.

"What do you mean?"

"Just with how much routine is in her life. Like her eating schedule," Emmett sits and ponders for a while, Dad nodding, knowing there's more coming. "I think what's especially impressive is how she knows when an appointment with Lacey is done. I don't have to tell her to get down or anything. I don't know, maybe she can tell from the tone of Lacey's voice or how I shift in my seat, or maybe she's just got a really good internal clock. But after that hour is up, she hops down and stretches and is ready to go without so much as a comment from me. It's uncanny. She's often the one to end the appointment, and she's almost always dead-on with the timing."

Dad chuckles. "She's an amazing dog."

"Very true. Baxter was amazing, too. I remember Lauren used to sometimes go to my apartment to wait up for me to come home from work and she said that Baxter knew when I entered the building. He would hear the door open, all the way at the end of the building, and know it was me walking down the hall and would get up and wait for me by the door. He just knew."

"Well, Baxter was pretty amazing too."

"Yeah, my little one-eyed wonder kitty. I miss him."

Baxter had been Emmett's very first pet. A fluffy white cat with one eye who'd been rescued from a medical testing facility. He'd been a bit of a grump and very timid. You had to really earn his trust and affection. It'd been a great honor when Baxter had finally decided he trusted Dad enough to sit on his lap. Come time for the Great Shock, when Emmett had had to give up his apartment, he'd had to let Lauren take care of the little guy, as Mom was allergic to cats.

Lauren had done a terrible job taking care of him, neglecting to brush him (as a one-eyed cat can only do one side), and adopting a feral cat who'd terrorized poor tenderhearted little Baxter. So Baxter had gone to Maria and with Maria he'd stayed until he'd died earlier in the summer. Maria and her family had loved him and taken good care of him. Emmett hadn't taken Baxter back after moving out of Mom and Dad's house; by that time Maria had had him longer than he ever had. But when he came to visit, Emmett could still find the spot on Baxter's head where he loved to be scratched the most, leaning his head into it so hard he didn't have space or strength left to scratch anymore.

Baxter had died with Maria holding him, not in any pain, well-loved and taken care of. And that's all Emmett had ever wanted for him.

"He was in a good home," Dad says.

"Oh, I know that. I just miss the little guy is all."

"Yeah, he was a great cat."

Emmett looks at his watch; it's five minutes past the time Dad had to leave. "You're late."

"Oops, gotta go." And Dad gets to his feet, waving his hands about in feigned panic like C-3PO might. He takes his sweet time saying goodbye to Little Baby Kerrin, whispering softly to her.

"Come on, dude," Emmett's voice thin on patience, as Dad bends over his granddog, whispering sweet nothings.

"Sorry," and giving a hug to Emmett, he puts his coat on and heads out the door. Emmett closes the door and cusses to himself, shaking his head. He spent more time saying goodbye to a fucking dog than he did to his own son.

Emmett breathes deeply and collects himself; no sense in getting all worked up about this.

He checks his phone—just enough time to put his knee braces on and take a quick nap while the dextroamphetamine in his immediate future kicked in.

Into the bathroom.

Knee braces on underneath pants.

Pop a quick twenty milligrams of dextroamphetamine. Two moderately sized peach-ish-colored pills and a swig of water.

Stretch out on the futon and close eyes. A quick nap. Twenty minutes.

Chapter Twenty Eight

"If you may allow me to complain for a minute," Emmett tells Lacey.

"Of course," Lacey says, smirking.

"Yeah. Dumb thing to say. I suppose what else is therapy for but to complain?" Emmett pauses. "Anyways. I've been getting up earlier and earlier lately, like two hours earlier than usual and it's sometimes a problem."

"A problem? How so?"

"Because I have no fucking clue what to do with myself," Emmett says, almost giddy. "It's a good problem to have, a really good problem to have. It's better than how I thought the rest of my life was going to be."

"Because you're getting up earlier?"

"Exactly. It's really hard to understand how demoralizing it is to need so much sleep, to not ever be able to do anything because you're always so tired. So this is great. But I also just need to adjust to it."

Emmett's quick nap ends up lasting about an hour. He tries to tell himself that that hour wouldn't have been very productive anyway, had he tried to stay awake through it, and it probably would have led to a much lengthier nap.

There are consequences for every action, and the accounts must be balanced in every column, including restfulness. Sooner or later it catches up and it's best to pay before too much debt accumulates.

He's made major strides in improving his quality of life in the past year, and getting up earlier is one of the biggest and most recent ones. He suspects it's going to be huge during the winter, when there's so little daylight.

Emmett still needs the occasional nap, still needs to boost himself in the afternoon with some dextroamphetamine, but he hasn't missed a walk because he's slept through it since the reduction of risperidone. He remembers having times when he'd just slept all day—gotten up at one in the afternoon, taken his morning pills, made coffee and smoked a cigarette, but the cigarette had made him tired again, so he'd taken a nap, and, upon waking in the dark, found it was pill time again and thus just prepared his pills and went back to bed. It's taxing on a person to do so little with their day.

Sitting up from his futon, Emmett stretches and tries to identify his glasses. His blurry vision doesn't let him see anything further than a couple inches away from his face; how can he hope to identify his glasses? But he likes to play this game from time to time, remembering Mom playing games on her iPad. Mystery games where you're presented with a picture of a room full of objects and you have to find specific objects from a list. It's one of the few things they can do together besides cooking (and cooking is getting iffy-er and iffy-er). It's a mindless game, not particularly challenging to Mom but actually pretty taxing for Emmett, whose brain is confronted with a particular challenge when presented with crowded spaces filled with objects.

This is different though; this picture is blurred, terribly blurred, to the point Emmett is sure there are objects that're totally obscured from his vision, cloaked and simply unseen because his eyes are so unfocused. But still he plays the game with himself, searching for his glasses on the coffee table. It isn't like he has anything better to do.

Finally giving up.

Searching with hands on the flat surface.

Finding them.

Clear vision at last.

He should really get new glasses; the anti-reflective coating on this pair is starting to peel off.

Over to the kitchen, to finally tackle the dishes.

Dishes at Eleventh and Washington had been an ordeal, a Trial by Ordeal. He remembers telling Mom on the phone one night that all he had to do was put on an album that lasted forty-five minutes and he'd be done with dishes. Then an EP that lasted fifteen minutes and he'd have the kitchen floor swept and countertops wiped and he'd be done with all the kitchen cleaning. He'd taken great joy in deleting his kitchen cleaning playlists from his iPod when he'd moved out; an hour to clean the kitchen every night. How absurd.

This mindset, that it took an hour to clean the kitchen, when his current kitchen is smaller than his last bathroom, still permeates his thinking somewhat, intimidating him into thinking he'll never finish the pile of dishes.

Luckily, even if he lets the dishes pile up for a couple days, it only takes a maximum of twenty minutes to clean the kitchen. He simply doesn't have enough dishes to dirty, the kitchen simply isn't big enough to make that much of a mess, and he also doesn't cook all that often—in fact the most cooking he does is make his morning French press or percolator of coffee.

Prior to ECT, Emmett had done a lot of cooking, —inviting Maria and Lauren over most every Sunday morning to make them brunch, Lauren specializing in making Bloody Marys and mimosas (often with way more alcohol than Emmett could really handle) and Emmett making vegan/gluten-free pancakes, waffles, or other such brunch items. He'd even had his own recipe for tempeh bacon, because the store-bought tempeh bacon has gluten in it. People said his tasted better, though his was a much more complicated recipe. He'd enjoyed coming up with his own recipes and experimenting; he was the vegan/gluten-free version of his Mom, in the kitchen, cooking for everyone. But after ECT, that changed.

He didn't know why. He just couldn't do it anymore. Mom has tried any number of things to get him into it again—cooking with him, giving him a rice cooker that doubled as a crock pot so he could make easy meals for himself. The most he's really managed to make on his own is grandma noodles or eggs and bacon for breakfast in the morning on rare occasions. Usually he settles for heating up leftovers or baking something Mom has made for him. He just can't do it anymore.

This is a major experience of his in living with mental illness—loss, often for no particular reason. The loss of skills, the loss of passions, the loss of friendships, the loss of loves, the near-loss of his faith at one point. So much loss, and not a whole lot has been gained. Mental illness is a life of reduction, a constant abatement—those accounts that need to be balanced forever hungry with new debts created for no particular reason stated or implied.

He goes into the kitchen and moves all of the dishes out of the sink and onto the counter.

Hot water on, testing the temperature until it's hot enough.

Too hot. His hands probably overly sensitive to the temperature of the water.

Cold water to compensate.

Play with it until it's the perfect temperature. Hot enough to kill germs. Not so hot that he can't work with it.

Dish tub out from under the sink. Dish soap and sponge from underneath the counter.

Fill the dish tub with water. Measure of dish soap. Dishes into dish tub.

Wipe the meager counter while the tub is filling.

Scrub the dishes; this isn't going to take long at all. Pile the clean dishes off to the right.

Rinse the dishes with cold water. Pile them in the dish tray mounted to the wall just above the sink.

Wash out Kerrinpuppy's food and water bowls. Fill the water bowl. Dry the food bowl.

Empty out the dish tub, careful not to do it too fast; the sink is illogically shallow and the drain ill-suited for the volume of water.

Rinse the suds out of the tub and put it back underneath the sink.

Dry hands.

Ten minutes have passed, but Emmett finds himself wishing it had been forty-five minutes. It's really not so bad once you get started. Kind of meditative, actually. There's a method to it. It's the kind of work one can get lost in. He can maybe understand a person wanting to wash dishes for a living because it gives you space to think, space to ponder; it gives you a clear objective and clear standards for meeting that objective—either the dish is clean or it's not.

Chapter Twenty Nine

"*Your mom can be a real source of frustration, can't she?*" Lacey says, sensing Emmett's nauseating angst in what he'd just told her.

"*Yeah. And it's hard. Because I know she just means well. I know she just wants to help me. I know that sometimes, even oftentimes, I can be too demanding. But it comes across as her not paying attention to me. As her just fucking placating me. I hate that word, 'placate.'*"

"*Why hate?*" Lacey is ignoring her notebook and pen now and is giving Emmett her full attention.

"*Because of an email Lauren sent me. The subject of the email was 'I'm at my wits' end.' She unloaded all of the stresses she was going through and how unsupported she felt in the midst of all the ECT garbage, and when I responded saying I was going to try harder and asked specifically what I could do, she told me to stop 'fucking placating' her—her words.*"

"*That's a tough thing to deal with.*"

"*Yeah.*"

"*But your mom and Lauren are in totally different leagues. You've said before that there are a lot of things your mom doesn't understand about you.*"

"*Sometimes we're like strangers. But I know that doesn't mean she doesn't love me. Not like it did with Lauren where soon after that she left. My mom will always be there for me. I just wish her being there wasn't so frustrating.*"

"*I think that's one of the most common themes in any family,*" Lacey says.

"*I don't doubt it,*" Emmett says.

Transitions are perhaps the hardest part of life, but they're also a constant part of life. And with age comes a certain awareness of their constant presence. Even just the continual (as without your consent) march of the seasons. Time is a fugitive, constantly fleeing and never resting, never sitting to enjoy a moment's rest. There's a huge difference between being twenty-one and twenty-eight; less of a difference between being twenty-eight and twenty-nine. Emmett's spent his whole life growing up, and now that the growing-up phase of his life is slowing down, the other transitions are becoming more apparent. The changes in weather that his knees are now complaining about. The utter lack of daylight that has him so desperately longing for summer again, though he's torn because he knows that winter has its own joys—the snow, his own and Dad's birthdays, Thanksgiving and Christmas and Clarissa coming home to visit. Less welcome is the inherent loneliness of the season: people holing up for the winter and spending more time secluded from each other, and the crushing isolation because the streets are less likely to be occupied—fewer people riding their bikes, fewer people out walking their dogs. It seems everyone just disappears in the winter. Where do they go?

Dr. Bogsdaughter always asks him about light therapy this time of year, and this year is no different. Emmett has never seen much of a difference from sitting in front of a lamp that mimics the sun for ten minutes every morning before getting up. He knows he needs to get up and going immediately or else drift into melancholy, which his mind is wont to do if left to wander without purpose as it sits in front of that lamp.

He's got full-spectrum bulbs in all of his lamps, and his fluoxetine, oxcarbazepine, and lamotrigine do a pretty good job of keeping his mood stable. His main problem is the doldrums: the late afternoon, the early evening, these extra hours of time he wishes he could just excise and insert into the morning when he finds himself the most productive. Maybe he can convince Dad to walk with him at 2:00 p.m. instead of 12:30 p.m., but Dad has meetings then and it probably wouldn't be convenient.

Listless, restless—he feels the need to explode and implode, to collapse and relapse all at once. He wants to be around people and be alone at the same time. Maybe it's because he's trapped in his tiny 350-square-foot apartment all day, with no clear separation between work and play. His work is his play and his play, his work; no distinguishing between the two.

He's jealous of Mom, who wakes up in the morning and brews her pot of coffee, eats her bacon and eggs, and drives to work. She drinks her coffee and works all day and then comes home to relax and take a nap before making dinner and then retiring to rest and relax some more, perhaps working on some project, but having the benefit of a very clear separation between work and home life. She doesn't take her work home with her. Sometimes she works from home, when she has something she really needs to concentrate on and knows the school will be particularly noisy, but work is where work is and home is where home is.

It's the same for Dad.

But Emmett works and lives and suffers in the same tiny room every day. His only break is when he goes to Aurora on the weekends, and there he finds himself missing his minikin apartment terribly. He longs for release from his prison during those listless, restless, doldrum-y lost few hours and then craves it when he finally is released.

His solution is usually to call Mom or Dad, but he feels tremendously guilty for doing so; he knows that they both work hard and just need to relax, that they need some downtime from helping him out.

But what if he doesn't call and it gets worse? What if he doesn't take care of these feelings right away? He might get sick; he might get psychotic. Then it's late at night and they're piling into the car to come and get him and the next day Dad is operating on very little sleep and Mom is skipping lunch to bring Emmett home to walk with Dad and everything is thrown off and everything is out of balance and the world is put into a precarious state and if only Emmett had just called the very moment he'd started feeling weird and they'd just talked for an hour or two until the doldrums passed and he got the inkling to listen to a record or look at pictures of himself as a little kid or go on a walk with Little Baby Kerrin and this whole thing could be avoided if only Emmett had nipped this thing in the bud whatever that phrase means Mom could you please Google that?

The slippery slope argument always works best on Emmett and his family. What if this gets worse? What if this turns into something no one can control? What if this turns into a hospitalization? What if this turns into another round of ECT? What if? What if? What if?

Still, he feels guilty as he fishes his phone out of his pocket and dials the number so familiar to him. He pauses before hitting the green button which will connect him to his mother. What if he calls Clarissa? One day she'll be the one to take care of him; one day she'll be the one he'll be looking to for support. Wouldn't it be best to start training her early?

But then he remembers her homework load, how she's working on getting her master's degree, how she's always out someplace, playing piano for or singing in a choir, out doing good things for the community, and how Mom and Dad are just sitting there, essentially on call for him. Is it good for him to think of Mom and Dad like that? As on call?

Green button not so much pressed or pushed as touched. Not too many buttons are actual buttons these days.

Two rings and Mom's voice is on the other end.

"Hi, Emmett," her voice is clear and bright. Emmett knows she's always nervous answering a phone call from him—he can call anytime day or night, in any state of mind. He might be bouncing-off-the-wall happy, talking a mile a minute; he might start cussing her out; he might be so scared, so frightened, so paralyzed with fear and psychosis that he doesn't say a thing, or he might simply be calling her to ask her something about a cooking term or to tell her something interesting he's just read.

"Hey Mom," Emmett says, voice not altogether there, but not so far gone she fears he's dissociating or psychotic.

"Not doing well?"

"I don't know, I guess not. Who knows?" Emmett stumbles, trying to think, it's a harder question to answer than one might think. "Things are just hard," he finally settles on.

"I'm sorry. Want me to come get you?"

"No."

Fortunately he's not angry this time. It's a dangerous question to ask, but a question Mom gambles on asking every time because it's an important question to ask. Oftentimes the process of angering Emmett with asking the question is part of the diagnostic in and of itself.

"Okay, we'll just talk then."

"Okay."

Mom proceeds to tell him about her day, the bulletins she finished, the finance report she's had to do, all things Emmett really couldn't care less about. Then she tells him about how one of the second graders at the school where she works asked the preschool teacher if Mom owned the school.

Emmett laughs: "I suppose you're really the only one who takes any kind of pride of ownership in the school, so it makes sense if you think about it."

"You know, I didn't think about it like that. Is it okay if I put you on speaker? It's just Dad and me."

"Sure thing."

"Okay, you're on speaker."

"Hey Emmett," Dad calls, his voice sounding distant though he's probably just right next to Mom on the love seat in the chick cave.

"Hey homie."

They talk for a little while longer. Around nine or so, Mom changes to get ready for bed. Dad's still in the chick cave watching a documentary about the history of rock 'n' roll.

"He said he was going to watch it until it was done," Mom says.

"Yeah. I think the entire documentary is like fifteen or sixteen hours long."

"Hmmm," Mom says. "I guess he's not going to work tomorrow then."

"Nope, and he'll miss our walk. Kerrin's going to miss him."

The topic of transitions comes up. And Emmett talks about the nature of time changing, the lessening of sunlight. But what it really comes down to is that any change, good or bad, usually has a negative effect on him.

"Really? Even good things?"

"Yeah. Like moving to my new place; it's been a really hard transition. It's been well over a year and I'm still not used to it."

"Things like that take a while, Emm."

"I know that. I'm just using it to illustrate my point," Emmett says, temper flaring at the lecturing. Then he immediately calms down. "It was such a good thing to get away from that place ... but even with how careful we were about transitioning me into this new place, I've had a hard time of it. It's been getting better, though."

"Good. Things like this take a while, they do for anyone. But remember, God's got a plan."

Mom has this special way of completely ignoring what you're saying, ignoring the more philosophical point you were trying to make and focusing only the practical, the mundane. Emmett suspects this is because she's playing a game on her iPad or browsing Pinterest or something.

He chooses to not let this piss him off and just go with his line of thought—even if she isn't interested in pursuing this train of thought with him, he's going to go on regardless. Otherwise he'll have to hang up and worry himself sick about what would happen if Dad dies before Mom and he's stuck trying to have these discussions with just Mom. A morbid line of thinking, but the line of thinking he knows he'll be reduced to if he lets himself be angered over what he perceives as her inattention to him.

"Just transitions in general. Maybe I should keep track of it, but I'm pretty sure I call y'all at about the same time every day. Around seven or eight o'clock. I sometimes feel like a day school teacher who has to schedule activities to keep their students occupied throughout the day—only it's not just from eight-thirty until three-fifteen. It's every waking moment. I'm pretty good at it for most of the day, but I just get exhausted at some point.

"I become aware of the transition that's been made," Emmett continues. "The sun has gone down; the day has ended. The coffee shop has closed, suddenly I don't have the solace of a coffee shop to go to—"

"Do you go there often?" More of that same focus on practicality. Almost like a machine that catches key phrases and asks canned questions.

"To sit down and just hang out? No, not very often. It's more just comforting to have that option. But that's not the point. The point is, that I come to this crossroads of sorts. It's like a little kid being left with a babysitter and suddenly realizing their parents are gone; the world has ended. It's like I know the day has ended so I feel as though I can't work anymore, I essentially ban myself from doing anything you might call 'productive,' but I'm so work-philic that it leaves me with little else to do. Or maybe it's just that I'm so exhausted from my so-called 'working' that I can't do anything else."

"What about reading or listening to the radio or something like that?"

"I'm not trying to be practical here, Mom," Emmett said, warning in his voice. "This is different."

"Okay, sorry."

But Emmett has had his fill. He'll get more out of a piece of paper than he will his mom. Mom isn't interested in participating in a conversation … she's just sitting there giving him an excuse to talk out loud and a piece of paper at least has the decency to record everything you have to say.

"I think I'm going to get going," Emmett says with a sigh.

"Oh, okay," Mom says, surprised.

"Sorry, I think I'm just boring you."

"No, this is all very interesting."

"Well, I think I need to write it all down."

"You can write it all down while you're talking to me."

"No. No I can't," his voice denouncing her as the stupidest person on the planet. "Anyways," trying to make up for himself, "I love you and I'll talk to you later."

"Love you too. Good night, God bless you."

"Bye."

Emmett touches the red button on his phone and wipes the screen off with his shirt. Why haven't they made oil-phobic glass yet? he thinks. But he discards the thought, just a momentary distraction. He's got something more important to write.

In his chair, he opens the drawer of the table next to him and pulls out the notebook and pen inside. He flips to the next blank page and begins writing, recapping what he can remember of what he'd told Mom. He supposes the nice thing about talking to Mom was that he only has to remember his own points and not anything that she'd said. His mind wanders a bit, since this is his third time going over the material. He writes in the margin to have a little more compassion for people: she's worked a long day and just needs to relax; she's said before she doesn't have the mental capacity after looking at little numbers all day to talk about something like that, and he really ought to cut her more slack.

Emmett's self-absorption often leaves him racked with guilt. He feels as though Dr. Bogsdaughter and Lacey have led him down a path wherein his needs always come first. If he needs to talk at two in the morning, of course he calls; Mom will always gladly answer. They'll gladly come pick him up at any time of day, no matter the reason. It's always Emmett first—he's encouraged to put his needs before anyone else's.

But it's also necessary. His illness affects not just him but everyone around him: Mom, Dad, Clarissa, Jayne, Marta Lee—everyone. Mental illness is a communal illness. It takes a whole support system to treat it and so, in a way, he's thinking of others when he thinks of himself. Not attending to the needs of his brain would have disastrous consequences. The slippery slope argument actually applies to mental illness: it always gets worse when left unattended, so sometimes the best thing he can do is be responsibly self-absorbed.

In the course of his writing he finds himself longing for a period of time earlier in the summer, when he was listening to A Song of Fire and Ice by George R. R. Martin on audiobook and drawing pictures of animals. He'd made a number of finished drawings out of the sketches he'd been doing while visiting Jayne and had ended up giving two of them away—one to Grandma and another to Dr. Bogsdaughter. He hadn't been able to give any of his previous work to Grandma because his artwork usually had a nude figure in it, and because it was usually macabre enough to scare the younger grandchildren, but the musk deer he'd drawn wasn't nearly as creepy; in fact, it was beautiful. He'd given another drawing of a musk deer, in the same pose actually, to Dr. Bogsdaughter as thanks for improving his life so much by finding the trick with the famotidine, as well as for being such a great psychiatrist for the past seven years.

He'd thoroughly enjoyed listening to those books, sitting there making those tedious lines, working his right hand into tremendous cramps that were barely relieved by the cigarette breaks he'd taken every hour instead of every two hours in an effort to not do permanent damage to his hand. He'd felt so much like an artist then. It was perhaps the first time he'd felt like an artist since his first full semester in college—he'd sat there for hours, toiling away, and the results had been worth it.

His assumption had been that, since he'd stumbled across this new style, his new mojo, so to speak, he would be drawing for good, for the rest of his life. Stooped over his drafting table with his inks and his gouache, drawing strange animals and having art shows and finally being the artist he'd always wanted to be. He'd made more drawings in six weeks than he'd made in the past five years combined, and then he'd stopped. And he was satisfied with that.

Now he's beginning to think that the drafting table is taking up space that could be used more efficiently. And the thought of making those drawings is more a fond memory than something he wishes to repeat, much like one has fond memories of playing with childhood friends—not something you'd like to repeat as an adult, but something you like to think about warmly.

Soon his hand is aching from the writing, and 10:00 p.m. is drawing near. He gets up and asks Little Baby Kerrin if she wants to go outside. She looks at him with that "holy crap" look she always gets when he asks her such a question; she hops down from the futon and starts stomping her feet on the floor, barely able to contain her excitement.

Leash her up.

Down the hall.

Kerrinpuppy's a little incredulous about being on her leash instead of bolting down the hall, but Emmett doesn't want to disturb his elderly neighbor, who's told him he goes to bed at about nine-thirty.

Outside, Kerrinpuppy quickly finding a place to go potty.

Down to the intersection to throw the bag out.

One last excursion to the grass to pee. She always does this—the large rocks in this particular patch of grass are a veritable Facebook for dogs.

Up the stairs, Little Baby Kerrin once more incredulous at having to be on the leash, and inside.

His phone vibrates and beeps, informing him it's time to take his pills. Emmett goes into the bathroom and has all fifty-some pills counted out in no time. He texts Dad to let him know he needs more ziprasidone eighty-milligram pills.

DAD:
Done!

And Emmett texts his thanks.

Then outside for a cigarette.

He makes the bed and climbs in to read for a little while, waiting for the pills to kick in. He carefully times when to stop reading so the second wind doesn't hit, and so he'll remember his place in the novel he's reading. Sometimes he has to backtrack a little bit the next night, but it's better than starting in the middle of a section or paragraph.

Chapter Thirty

The concrete looks as water.

Can't be trusted, can't be treaded upon.

Waves of it buckle, by forces unknown.

The poor, miserable sidewalk.

A construction trailer parked on the street bulges outwards and sucks itself inwards as though breathing.

The grass stays still, nature eerily calm among the torrid of man-made objects gone amok. Motionless among the tyranny of tidal-force waves of concrete and asphalt. Emmett won't walk past the stoop, his hopes of a quiet cup of coffee dashed.

Back inside, to the bucking and whipping of a hallway under similar forces; a prayer quickly made that his home, and his Little Girl in particular, are safe from the devil causing this.

A neighbor walking down the hall.

Emmett knows he'll make a fool of himself, be mistaken for drunk in the middle of the day; a hard-won reputation ruined by a brain gone haywire.

The salvation of his phone, steadying himself against the wall, drawn quickly from his pocket and fiddled with, greeting his neighbor as he steps aside to let him pass through the door.

An awkward fist bump; how's he doing? Fine. How are you doing? That's good. Have a good time at work. Hope you have a good one too.

Down the hallway. Down the unsteady, unnaturally situated boards of the wood floors. Objects not otherwise found in the hallway of an apartment building—coils of rope, barrels, pallets—appear in his path for him to dodge as though his brain is treating this like some cheap arcade video game. He stumbles down the hall, insulted on his landlubber legs, unaccustomed to this sudden squall at sea.

Safely inside, the doorknob not quite working like it ought to but easy enough to figure out—just missed a cannon, weighing God-knows-how-many hundreds of pounds, as it careens down the hallway.

Peace and quiet. The turmoil outside still rages. Something pounds at the door. The squall or something more? Salvation in pills or salvation in something more substantial? Both, perhaps? All his tricks at once—lie under every blanket he owns and perhaps some borrowed from neighbors (if he can get hold of them). Drugging himself to oblivion, coffee surging into his bloodstream, music pounding through his ears, a root beer splashing into his mouth, what else can he do? Everything all at once. All to avoid a panic.

No. He must remain rational. He's safe in here. Safe because he knows it cannot reach him. Safe because he knows this place is sacrosanct, protected.

Dad will be here at some point, inevitable and unaffected by the torrid outside, somehow immune to the powers of Emmett's brain.

Jealousy sets in.

Two pills, and a glass of water to wash them down.

He sinks into his chair and waits out the storm.

Chapter Thirty One

Lacey takes a deep breath, inhaling through her mouth and exhaling through her nose—her private signal to Emmett to do the same. Emmett follows suit and feels better.

"That was a lot to tell me," Lacey says.

"Yeah, I suppose so," Emmett says quietly.

"You know what I think?"

"No, what?"

"I think you're tough as nails," and Lacey smiles at him as Emmett makes eye contact with her briefly, his eyes smiling more than his mouth.

The mail comes at three o'clock. Baby Steps to three o'clock. Bill Murray is probably unaware of the wisdom of the "baby steps" mantra of his Bob Wiley in What About Bob? that helped Bob break down big tasks into smaller, manageable ones ("Baby Steps through the office. Baby Steps out the door"). Emmett is reminded of four, five years ago when everything really was Baby Steps. Baby Steps Survive. Baby Steps Go Downstairs, maybe feed yourself—he could at least fry an egg or two back then, toast bread, smother it with veganaise (was it pronounced "vej-an-aise" or "veeg-an-aise"?) and ketchup and eat it like a sandwich.

Baby Steps Survive until Dad came home for lunch. Sometimes Dad would find him on the back porch, not doing anything in particular, certainly not smoking yet. Emmett would see Dad and break down—whether from relief at having survived or for some other reason, he can't remember. And Dad would stay; stay until Emmett had calmed down and seemed to have pulled himself together. Seemed. Seamed. Always bursting at the seams, always on the verge of breaking down, in need of being sewn back together.

Baby Steps Survive until Mom came home from work. They never really left him alone for more than a few hours at a time. But they were never really with him because he was always somewhere else. La-la land. Did you take your pills? Yes, Mom. Did you eat breakfast? Lunch? Yes. Yes. (Though oftentimes one or the other or both were lies.) What did you do today? Nothing. (That was never a lie.) All he ever did was survive. Baby Steps Survive.

His objective for each day was to make it to the next. Maybe tomorrow would be better. Try to have hope. Tuesdays were something to look forward to: Vegan Community Dinner, get out of the house for a few hours, though sometimes they'd get to the train station and he couldn't bear the thought of being around people. Overwhelmed by the loneliness, overwhelmed by the thought of being around all those people who hadn't a clue his life was Bob Wiley's personal game of Survival. Maybe he should have told them, maybe they would have understood—they didn't ask him why he'd just disappeared one week and hadn't returned again until six months later.

Sometimes he'd get a text message and his heart would leap with joy. He'd devour it hungrily, all the while trying to savor it. Maybe keep his phone in his pocket until it notified him a second time he had a message. Sometimes it was Jayne, and they'd talk for a while and he'd feel normal, it'd feel like old times, he'd forget about Baby Steps Survive—but then she'd disappear, stop messaging in the middle of a conversation, and Emmett would remember back to their AOL Instant Messenger days when "brb" usually meant goodbye. It was text messaging, it wasn't supposed to be taken seriously, and no one knew it was one of his only connections to the outside world, to that land of milk and honey he'd had to leave after only living in it such a short while.

But he didn't hold grudges; he couldn't afford to—too many other things to sort through with Lacey, things left unfinished with Lauren, things he couldn't remember because ECT had taken away his memories along with what seemed like everything else.

He had picked up paint brushes, but they felt alien in his hand, keyboards felt foreign to his fingertips. Everything once familiar to him had become strange, bizarre; a sense of foreboding occupied every corner of the house. When he tried to read books, the books that had once brought him so much comfort a mere nine months before, he found only disjointed words that made no sense at all, a collection of nonsense. He knew it was his fault, not the book's—the book hadn't changed, he had. And so he lay on his floor mat every night, because he was afraid his bed was going to eat him, while Dad read to him. He was twenty-three years old, being read a bedtime story because he couldn't read by himself; was he going to have to start over at the very beginning with everything?

Baby Steps Try Not To Be Overwhelmed.

Baby Steps worked for Bob Wiley and it worked for Emmett, though Emmett wasn't consciously channeling the cheaply-wrought Hollywood-peppered advice of a Bill Murray comedy, meant more to comment on the nature of self-help books than offer any kind of practical advice. If he'd had Kerrinpuppy at the time, perhaps the point his cognitive and behavioral therapist had been making would have been all the more effective—she could have told him to emulate his dog, because that's what she meant by "living in the now."

Hung up on a past that evaded him like a shadow in the dark, he had been simply existing with the hope that tomorrow would be better. But his CBT reminded Emmett that he had the power to do something to affect the future, to actually make tomorrow better. For something so obvious having eluded him,

Emmett could only blame Dr. Bogsdaughter's chemical cocktail and Dr. Romero's electrical irruptions—pulling blouses over his eyes and obscuring rational vision and, okay, now that he'd used the term 'rational,' perhaps it could be the illness itself, too.

She'd asked him what he wanted.

To be happy. To not be lonely.

Two good things. But you must be more specific.

He'd told her he would have to think about it.

It was just as well. The forty-five minutes were up. She'd see him next week. He'd think about what he wanted.

A week passed and something huge had happened. Not Baby Steps. Adult Steps. He'd gone to a coffee shop. No, not that. He'd been asked to fix a computer. No, not just that. He'd fixed a computer in an extraordinary way. Yeah, that, but also not quite that.

He knew what he wanted. He wanted a PhD in computer science, perhaps with a focus in biomedical engineering. And he wanted to live in Cap Hill again.

Now, four or five years later—my how the fugitive time flies—half the stated goal has been accomplished and the other half largely forgotten about, only recalled when trying to remember how he got out of his Baby Steps mentality when he slips back into his Baby Steps mentality and uses it to survive from day to day or from evening time to pill time. Maybe it had been the Bob Wiley Method all along, nothing but that awkward stumbling from day to day, hour to hour, moment to moment. Stumbling on infant feet, too insignificant to be of much use or to impress much of anyone.

But he's not here to impress.

Isn't everyone here to make it from day to day? Doesn't the prayer go "give us today our daily bread"?

It isn't like he feels like a failure for not having a PhD in computer science with a focus on biomedical engineering. He doesn't much care about that. He suspects he never really cared about it in the first place; it was just a goal, because a person has to have a goal, a person has to have a purpose, a reason to get up in the morning.

He thinks of an unemployed Dad, of Valentine's Day when he got laid off—the relief Emmett felt and his guilt at feeling relieved as he saw Dad break down in tears.

Then the prayer Emmett prayed, asking for strength and guidance—for Mom and Dad and Emmett to put their trust in God that everything would be okay. Because deep down, Emmett knew it was the best possible thing, because he knew he just couldn't survive anymore by himself, he just couldn't do the Baby Steps Survive 'til Dad Gets Home for Lunch anymore; he had to do something more substantial, and he needed someone home to help him do that.

Sometimes Emmett has this calm wisdom about him, this secret confidence. One would think that with mounting ECT bills and all of the other expenses that came with his illness— psychiatrist and therapist bills not to mention the cost of his prescriptions—that he'd be breaking down too, wondering how Mom and Dad would manage to afford to keep taking care of him. But somehow he knew it was supposed to happen, knew it was part of God's plan, and that, if it were part of God's plan, then he would be taken care of throughout its duration.

And he was. He found his footing, and Baby Steps slowly turned into more adult kinds of steps, and it's not like he was running or jumping or anything, but he was at least making appreciable progress.

Then Emmett got Little Baby Kerrin and a month later Dad found a job working near downtown Denver. Then Emmett got on SSDI and found a place to live a few blocks away from where Dad worked. They were able to go on walks every day, and Dad was close enough that if the proverbial feces ever hit the fan, he could be there relatively quickly.

Emmett still sank into Baby Steps every so often, but he knew how to pull himself out—it didn't go on for days and weeks and months. His CBT had given him tools. Lacey and Dr. Bogsdaughter helped him maintain these tools, so he could walk like a person.

Baby Steps was a concept developed from a need to have a comedic device to make fun of the self-help book industry. This cadre of authors who all have a different spin on saying the same thing. Emmett had never read an entire self-help book, though SAR had certainly urged him to read several throughout their time together as roommates, SAR thinking they'd really help Emmett through his life, Emmett fully knowing that a self-help book was just watered-down, generic advice that didn't apply to him because the book would assume he was mentally healthy. He'd perused the books, but never dedicated much time to them; the kinds of self-help books SAR prescribed were largely about manipulating people into giving you things, or how to make money quickly, things Emmett didn't have half-an-ounce of interest in.

But Baby Steps was different. "It means setting small, reasonable goals," Dr. Leo Marvin explains to Bob. And Bob takes it literally, taking the smallest steps possible throughout Leo's fancy office as the good doctor does absolutely nothing to try to correct him.

Baby Steps are always awkward; they land where they may and never where intended. They can't be executed with precision; baby feet are too unwieldy, too awkward, too undeveloped. And maybe that's what Emmett likes about the image. In trying to just survive from day to day, hour to hour, he wasn't doing it gracefully. He was just fumbling along, doing it however he could; if it meant sitting there and staring at the wall and willing time to pass by, that's exactly what he did.

Anything in the name of survival.

Chapter Thirty Two

Emmett heaves a sigh in response to Lacey's question about how he's doing. He sits down in his usual chair and invites Kerrinpuppy up onto his lap by patting it with his hands.

"That bad, huh?" Lacey says.

"I wouldn't say 'bad' necessarily. It's just such a hard question to answer sometimes."

"What do you mean?"

"Well. Like I've had a pretty shitty week, but I think things are still improving. At least, they're improving when you look at the big picture. I'm not in the hospital, I'm not suicidal, I'm not getting ECT—but it's still hard," Emmett says, scratching Kerrinpuppy's neck and trying to avoid her kisses as he speaks.

"That makes sense; it all depends on your perspective."

"Exactly," Emmett says, shifting in his chair to make a more comfortable space for his beloved dog. "What scale do I rate myself on? The old scale from before all this madness? Or the new scale from ECT and hospitalizations and suicide attempts and my life falling apart?"

"So they'd be two different ratings?"

"Indubitably. But they'd both be low scores, 'cause life kinda sucks right now and all I can do is tread water." Emmett pauses for a bit, looking at Lacey's shoes. Finally, he says, "I don't think I even know how to swim."

Emmett's pills have fully kicked in, so he ventures to set his notebook down and look out into the hallway; he badly wants a cigarette. Cracking the door open, all looks at peace. The chaos that had enveloped the hallway forty-five minutes before seems forgotten, so he bids Kerrinpuppy goodbye and makes his way cautiously down to the entryway door.

From what he can see through the glass doors to the world outside, all looks calm there too, so he steps out into the cool of the day and sits on the stoop and rolls a cigarette, lights it, and takes a drag, checking his watch to see what he can expect to happen next. It's twelve-thirty; Dad will be arriving by the time he's finishing his cigarette. Should they hazard taking a walk on the potentially unstable sidewalk which at any moment could turn into a torrent again? It's always a gamble to go on a walk, and the stakes are always higher right after a psychotic episode.

He watches the people go by: businesspeople hurrying off to lunch or meetings; women dressed in yoga pants, their yoga mats rolled up in bags, hurrying down the street to the yoga studio located next to where the computer repair shop he'd worked at, before ECT, had been located before it'd closed. He wonders whatever happened to the people that'd worked there, what his old boss is up to these days. He's seen the kid he'd worked with there at a local computer store one time, applying for a job. Maybe he got it. But Emmett doubts his former coworker would recognize him now; too much weight gained, too much facial hair. A lot of people don't recognize him these days.

Emmett consciously rejects his phone right now; he knows a screen would only serve to remove him from reality. He needs to feel grounded. He does his inventory. Starting with his feet and working his way up his legs, to his buttocks, to his stomach all the way up to his head, he tries to notice the sensations that every part of his body feels: the pressure of the ground on his feet, the smell of the McDonald's up on Colfax, the taste of smoke as he takes a drag from his cigarette. He tries to feel only the very real physical sensations presented to him, the things he knows are caused by the real world around him.

Neighbors coming home for lunch or leaving for work come up and down the steps and he says hello to all of them. The head maintenance lady, Leonor, comes to sit and smoke a cigarette; they chat for a while, Leonor telling him about her dog.

"I don't know what it is about Kerrin; you've lived her for how long?"

"Oh, just about a year and maybe a half," Emmett says.

"A year and some change, and she still won't come up to me."

"Yeah, it just takes time with her. She's a rescue dog so I'm not really sure what she went through before I got her. But just give her time—she'll warm up. And when she does, she's the sweetest dog."

"That's what it's like with my Missy; doesn't like anyone but me, she'll bark and bark at anyone who tries to get near me unless she knows them."

"Makes her a good guard dog I suppose."

Leonor laughs, "She's only about this big," holding her hands only about a sub sandwich length apart, and Emmett chuckles. "So I don't think she's going to be doing any damage any time soon."

"She'd at least warn you if anyone was coming," Emmett offers. "That's what Kerrin does—anyone strange comes into the house she's barking right away, letting me know they're there."

"You're right about that," Leonor says, taking a drag of her cigarette. Leonor is exactly the kind of person you want in a head maintenance person at an apartment building: hardworking, smart, doesn't take guff from nobody, and tough. Leonor looks like she's seen some things, and it only adds to her charm as the head maintenance lady, a sort of intimidation factor that probably works well with the homeless people she occasionally comes across who squat in the empty apartments in the basement.

Emmett and Leonor are still talking when Dad comes walking up the stairs; Emmett glances his familiar profile out of the corner of his eye.

"Hey homie," Emmett says, caught off guard by Dad, a little anxious about all the people who've passed by the stoop without him realizing it. Normally he's still aware of everyone who passes while he's conversing with people, but Leonor just commands his full attention.

"Hey Emmett. Hey Leonor," Dad says.

"Hey sweetie," Leonor says.

Dad laughs. "Where's Kerrinpuppy?"

"She's inside. Imma finish my cigarette and we'll go in and say hi to her," Emmett says getting up, taking a few last shallow drags on his cigarette before putting it out on the brickwork of the building. He always puts his cigarette out in the same blackened place. He figures it's better than having a bunch of blackened spots, and that the eventual rain or snow will wash it right off.

Dad opens the door.

"Thank ya, sir," and Emmett steps inside the entryway, enters the door code, and opens the door into the hallway, holding the door open so Dad can join him.

Kerrinpuppy is scratching at the door and they can see the doormat moving in and out as they near Emmett's apartment. Dad chuckles, "Oh, Kerrin."

They go in and Little Baby Kerrin scoots right past Emmett to say hello to her grandpa. Dad greets her to Emmett's choruses of "get down" and "no jumping."

Once they've settled inside, Emmett tells Dad about his psychotic episode and his little conundrum. Dad offers to take Little Baby Kerrin for a quick walk to go to the bathroom. Emmett counteroffers with the poop walk—up the street to the end of the block and then turn around, she usually poops when they're back in front of their building, and then they go inside. That way Dad is close at hand, and Emmett isn't just sitting at home with nothing to do but wait.

"Fine by me," Dad says, giving a thumbs up.

Emmett shuts off his desk lamp and locks the door behind him. When he's alone he wouldn't even bother, but Dad would say something, and Dad saying something might piss him off.

Why don't you lock the door, Emmett? Dad's voice rings in his head.

Because it's only down to the end of the block.

Still, someone could break in.

I don't want to lock the fucking door

Just lock the door.

I don't want to.

LOCK THE DOOR.

The scenario plays in his head, Emmett growing frustrated that he's an adult, free to make his own decisions about whether or not to lock the door, that he's already locked the door any- way and there shouldn't be any reason to have the discussion. It doesn't matter that the discussion hasn't actually happened; it's real-to-him, so he follows Kerrinpuppy and Dad down the hall, on the brink of seething rage, trying to calm himself by reasoning with an irrational mind that just wants to see him suffering today.

Emmett is quiet as they walk down the stairs, Dad seeming to sense that something is wrong.

"Everything okay, Emmett?"

"Yeah," Emmett says. "I mean, no. I mean, I don't know. Just don't talk right now. I have to work on something."

"Okay," Dad says. And Emmett almost snaps at him for say- ing something.

Emmett focuses on his breathing, on the wonderful day and how the sun is perfectly bright and the temperature just about ideal. Breathing in slowly through his nose, counting to five and exhaling suddenly through his mouth—an attempt to calm himself down as he'd learned from his CBT. He does this several times, reaching into his pocket to rub his lighter, which he's chewed the end of to make an indent with his teeth so he can feel the minute imperfections, taking note of them. Hopefully this will ground him to reality, keep him from floating away and dissociating.

By the time they come back in front of Emmett's apartment building and Kerrinpuppy has done her business, he's feeling a lot better.

If only he weren't so fucking unstable. Might as well call him Emmett "Powder Keg" Selv … ready to explode at a moment's notice.

Dad and Emmett walk down the hall, Kerrinpuppy scouting ahead, eager to discover newly sniffed-out treasures.

"Okay, we can talk now," Emmett says as he opens the door to his apartment, thankfully not reminded of the situation his head put him through as he had been locking the door. He goes into the kitchen, fills Little Baby Kerrin's food dish, and starts water boiling to make himself a cup of AeroPress coffee; there's still a good thirty-five minutes before Dad has to leave to be back at work. "Would you like some water?"

"Yes, I would."

"Small glass?"

"Small glass."

Emmett gets a small juice glass down, fills it with filtered water from the fridge, and walks it over to Dad who's seated in the chair in front of the computer closet. LBK has busied herself with trying to get Dad to play squirrel with her.

"May I?" Dad asks, head motioning to the expectant Kerrinpuppy seated on the couch, tail wagging.

Emmett hesitates, "Yeah, I suppose you can."

"Oh boy," Dad says, setting the glass down. "Kerrin, we get

to play squirrel!" Emmett tries not to take this as condescending, because he knows Dad doesn't mean it as such. Kerrinpuppy stands alertly on the couch as Dad takes the stuffed squirrel by its tail and tosses it up in the air. Kerrinpuppy turns around and catches the squirrel in midair and bites down on it, making it squeak. Then she shakes it from side to side and squeaks it again, in general killing it again and again until she takes it over to her grandpa and tosses it on the floor with a nod of her head (which always elicits a chuckle from Dad), waiting with tail wagging for him to toss it up into the air all over again.

Emmett's coffee is brewed and he sits down in his comfy chair and watches Dad and Little Baby Kerrin play their game. Emmett's version of the game is much the same, though he sometimes varies it by sitting next to Kerrinpuppy on the couch and tossing the squirrel toward the bookcase by the door—this gets her running and wears her out more. He fears she doesn't get enough exercise during the week and so has too much pent-up energy, which is maybe why she's such a picayune eater at their place.

Emmett remembers a song by Nas, "Life's a bitch and then you die," and how much he can relate to those words right now. But he can't share those lyrics with Dad right now. He doesn't like his status in the family of being the "one with the filthy mouth." But it's true; he's only heard Mom use the f-word once, and that was when he'd spray-painted his ceiling. He's never heard Dad cuss, and the worst he can remember Clarissa saying wasn't really even that bad—"ass" or something like that. But Emmett? It was probably just because he heard them all the time from the voices in his head that he'd inherited a filthy mouth. He tried to curb it, but it was hard; especially when no other word would do.

And the phrase "life's a bitch and then you die" sums up his view on life right now all too succinctly.

"How are you feeling?" Dad asks.

"Not really sure; I think the coffee is helping, though."

"I'm sorry, I should have offered to go and get you some."

"'s okay, sometimes making my own is grounding in and of itself."

"Really?"

"I dunno. I think it's more that I just want you around more than waiting for you to go and get me a coffee, you know?"

"Makes sense."

"I just wish I weren't so freaking unstable," glad he hadn't resorted to a more sordid word.

"I know," Dad says with a pained smile.

"It's maddening. I go through these scenarios in my head and the scenarios become real and it's like they've actually happened and they upset me like they've actually happened and I don't know what to do to make them not upset me. And I don't know how to explain them in such a way that people will understand what I'm talking about.

"People will say that they understand, but I know they don't," Emmett continues. "Because I didn't used to experience them before; they're not normal. People don't have hypothetical conversations with themselves and then think they actually happened, they don't actually get truly upset by them to the point that they want to cuss out the people they love. Shit, I wanted to rip you a new one just a little while ago, just yell and yell. I'm glad I didn't."

"Me too."

Emmett manages a smile. "I'm sorry I treat you like this, I know it's not fair. But I'd bet it bothers me as much as it does you ... maybe more. I don't like being moody—I want to go back to being happy and pleasant to be around. Like the little kid in that picture of me with the blue hoodie, just having fun at the park without a care in the world. I feel so far removed from that kid sometimes that he seems like a stranger, like I'm looking at a distant relative, rather than myself."

"It's still you, you're still that happy little guy. It's just your illness. You're still the happy, fun, Emmett I've known my whole life."

"Yeah, the illness is still me, though. It's at least a part of me—a fundamental part of me. A part I can't deny."

"Maybe so. But it also isn't you."

"All so confusing. No wonder people confuse schizophrenia with multiple personality disorder so often."

Emmett and Dad sit in silence for a little while. Kerrinpuppy gets down from the couch and goes over for some head scratches from Emmett before going to eat some of her lunch. Then, onto Emmett's lap for some quality snuggling.

"Do you want me to stay a little while longer?" Dad asks when the clock reads one-thirty.

"I'm not sure. I'm feeling a lot better, but I'm also a little… what's the word? Pensive, maybe?"

"I can stay as long as you need me."

"How 'bout just one more cigarette and we'll see how I'm doing?"

"You gots it," Dad says with a thumbs up. He takes the apron off that he'd donned in case Little Baby Kerrin wanted to get in his lap and hangs it up on the nail in entryway of the kitchen.

Emmett gets Kerrinpuppy's leash from its hook behind the bathroom door and the procession goes down the hall to the stoop for a cigarette which leaves Emmett feeling largely right-as-rain. Or as close to right-as-rain as one can get when saddled with such a weight.

Chapter Thirty Three

"Life's rough sometimes," Lacey says in her calm voice, barely above a whisper.

Emmett looks down at Kerrinpuppy sleeping on his lap and is silent for a number of long moments. Finally he says, "Yeah. I suppose so. And I don't know as if there's anything I can do about it."

"We can at least honor how far you've come."

Emmett's eyebrows arch. He nods his head. "I suppose so. I just didn't think life would be so ... mundane when I finally gained my freedom."

"What did you think it would be like?" Lacey asks.

"Oh, I don't really know. I don't think I put anything concrete to it because it seemed like such a pipe dream, such an impossibility. But I didn't think I'd be spending most of my time draining the battery on my phone and then worrying about how I've drained the battery on my phone even though I don't go anywhere, so who cares if the battery on my phone is drained?"

Lacey smiles at this; always the peculiar answers with Emmett. He smiles back. A pained smile, a smile that doesn't come easily. Sometimes Emmett's smile is the easiest thing in the world but other times it just refuses to come out and play.

He watches the janitor across the street slowly plod along; going from window to window with a squeegee cleaning the windows. It happens every Monday, Wednesday, and Friday while the weather is still nice. If it's been snowing, the janitor won't be out. Not that there's much likelihood of snow just yet; it's too early. Emmett has seen it snow as early as June, but that was probably twenty years ago.

My how time flies when you're waiting for it to snow.

That particular June snow had been exciting. Imagine—

building a snow fort during summer vacation. An eight-year-old Emmett had stayed by the window most of the day, dismay gradually taking hold as he realized the ground was too warm for the snow to accumulate. He'd abandoned his post at the window after a while and returned to his computer to play video games with his crushed expectations.

Emmett has never dealt well with crushed expectations, and this is especially true now as he sits on the stoop, waiting for pill time. 10:00 a.m. is still half an hour away and he doesn't know what to do with himself. Jayne had texted him earlier in the morning to let him know she wouldn't be able to get coffee with him because she wasn't feeling well. It's not that he's angry with her, it's just that now he doesn't know how to occupy himself. He isn't looking forward to taking his pills; he's looking forward to Mom's text message—she should be able to tell him what to do. Or maybe she'll just commiserate with him and tell him he ought to cook something. Mom always seems to want him to cook.

He sits and finishes his cigarette, content to entertain himself with the posts on his Facebook wall. He's already spent a good two hours on the site this morning—sitting out on the stoop, smoking cigarette after cigarette while the phone's battery he's so anal about steadily decreases; he'll have to charge it again when he gets back inside if he's going to expect it to make it through the day.

The phone is more a compulsion than anything; it's the most natural thing in the world to sit on the stoop, smoking a cigarette, with his phone out—those four inches of screen real estate becoming a reality unto themselves as he scrolls past posts ranting about the newest super food, pictures of people going to parties, pictures of those famous Colorado sunsets, posts of people talking about how amazing their life is, and posts of people talking about how miserable their life is.

Emmett knows Facebook isn't real, and he knows the danger of indulging in something which doesn't promote reality. Like movies, like television, Facebook can delude him, can remove him from reality, can stimulate that ever-familiar, ever-terrifying vague electrical humming which lets him know psychosis is imminent. But still he browses it, as though he feels he has to browse it.

People walk past his stoop, Emmett hardly noticing them, and this feeds his subconscious anxiety—to know that a threat could walk up to him and he wouldn't know it because he's so absorbed in this tiny world in the palm of his hand.

The phone is getting pretty hot by now from being used continually for so long. Has he really wasted his entire morning looking at Facebook? He looks out at the street he should be so familiar with by now…he's only taken breaks to roll more cigarettes and he's smoked maybe five or six, staring intently at his phone, reading every post and every article of every post. He gets obsessed with doing this sometimes. He remembers the meme of a bunch of folks his age walking down the street, every single one of them staring at their phone. "What's the point of being afraid of the Zombie Apocalypse when you're already a zombie yourself?" the caption reads. He fears he's turning into one of those people.

The clock on his phone reads 9:59 a.m. and the bells of the church down the street have started chiming. It's basically time to take pills. He takes one last drag on his cigarette and heads back inside, tossing the spent cigarettes into the trash can on his way back to his apartment.

Kerrinpuppy looks at him like he's a stranger as he feels his pocket vibrate. She's a sleepy puppy. He usually would have made the bed by now but he's been too busy keeping up with the world-in-his-phone to give the entropic nature of their apartment much attention, or to give Kerrinpuppy any kind of attention, for that matter. He apologizes to her and strokes her head. She closes her eyes. Emmett gives her a quick scratch behind the ears and heads into the bathroom. He swallows his pills with a movement familiar to him after who-knows-how-many-hundreds of times of taking his pills, and wipes the dripping water from his beard.

Mom will be texting soon. He plugs his phone into the wall and turns the ringer on so he'll hear it. He snaps his fingers and tells Little Baby Kerrin it's time to make the bed. She obliges and hops down so Emmett can make the bed and get his apartment looking like an apartment again.

It looks more like an office, actually. His drafting table with papers all over it, all the writing projects he's working on, and his laptop at the ready. Emmett had been determined not to let his studio apartment look like a dorm room when he'd moved in. It meant sleeping on a futon instead of a real bed, but the trade-off is worth it to him. The apartment feels much more adult, much less juvenile, even if it means it's not the most comfortable during the night.

By the time he's finished straightening his apartment, there's a ring-ding from his phone: a text message from Mom.

MOM:
Morning. I'm finishing up with the bulletin and will be ready for my lunch date with Mallory

EMMETT:
Good Morning. I didn't know you had a lunch date with Mallory.

A few minutes pass in which Emmett occupies himself with making some coffee, boiling the water in his electric kettle and grinding the beans.

MOM:
Yes I do. I think she gets lonely. So I've decided to
treat her to lunch once a month.

Mom is a sweet, kind lady. Mallory is a new teacher at the
church and school where Mom works, replacing the kindergarten through second grade teacher who'd been teaching there
since Emmett had gone there. Not much was known about
Mallory, but Mom has taken it upon herself to take her out to
lunch so she'd feel more welcome.

The water finishes boiling so he pours it into the AeroPress,
stirs the liquid around with a spoon, and presses the coffee down
with the plunger. At least he's made coffee; that's always a start.

Chapter Thirty Four

"How's your mood been?" Lacey asks.

Emmett thinks about it for a minute. "Ohhh, I would say not exactly the best."

"How so?"

"Well I suppose it's at least nice that I'm not depressed or suicidal or anything, but I've got this new friend I like to call my rage monster," Emmett says.

Lacey looks at him with a 'go ahead' look on her face.

"The rage monster is always there, and his job is to boil rage. Exactly like a restaurant, he has to provide more rage than there are customers so there's plenty to go around. So he comes up from my heart every so often to a place slightly above and right behind my eyes and begins boiling his rage, and I have to suffer the consequences. He's not exactly the best cook; oftentimes the rage boils over, and he has no clue about portion control—he'll make a whole cauldron full of rage for just my Dad and then expect him to eat it all. He's got a sign above his cauldron that says 'eat until you cry.'"

"That's quite the elaborate story for explaining your anger. How long have you been thinking about that?"

"I came up with it just now," Emmett says, his smile coming a lot easier this time.

And Lacey smiles back.

Emmett is occupied with a project on his computer. It's total nonsense; he's trying a different method to get the fonts on his Linux machine to display better. It means editing a lot of text files and logging off and on again to see the progress he's made. He sort of lives for this kind of thing; it can keep him occupied for hours. But he always feels as though he's wasted that time when he looks back on what he's done with himself at the end of the day. One thing he likes about Linux is how you can make it do just about anything if you're clever enough. He'd stumbled across the new font-rendering script by accident on some forum he'd been browsing. After reading the post, his own fonts looked as though they weren't really the best, so he thought he might as well give it a shot, just to see what kind of improvements he could make.

To Emmett, a computer isn't really all that interesting unless it's broken. He doesn't get attached to a computer until he's fixed it. His shiny new Retina Display MacBook Pro isn't nearly as important to him as his six-year-old ThinkPad X201, even though pretty much everyone else would say the MacBook Pro is the superior machine (and from a technical standpoint, it is). But he hasn't done anything cool with the Mac. He has done tons of cool stuff with the ThinkPad, including replacing its entire housing after he'd gotten it. He also gets rather attached to any computer he's built, as is the case with the computer he's working on now. He's put love into this machine, not something you can say of a store-bought machine. He'd hand-picked the parts, he'd routed all the cables by hand, he'd built the thing from scratch.

There's a gentle knock at the door and Kerrinpuppy perks up. She does a seesaw stretch, first her rear legs and then her front legs, as Emmett calls out for Dad to come in.

"Kerrinpuppy!" Dad exclaims as she trots up to him and greets him in her usual way. "Hey Emmett," he says.

"Hey, Homie," Emmett replies "Sorry, I got wrapped up in a project."

"NBD," Dad says: No Big Deal.

Emmett gets up from his closet desk and gives Dad a hug, telling him he's doing all right. Dad calms Kerrinpuppy down, giving her butt scratches while Emmett goes into the kitchen to roll himself a cigarette. Then it's out of the apartment, locking the door, Kerrinpuppy bolting down the hallway to the entrance and then back again to Emmett and Dad.

They're both slow walkers. Whenever Emmett finds himself walking with someone else he always notices how quickly they walk, and he oftentimes struggles to keep up and still manage to have a conversation at the same time. People frequently pass Dad and Emmett on their walks, with one or the other having to move to one side to let folks pass, but they don't mind—you see more when you slow down, you experience more, and it's a lot easier to talk when you aren't out of breath.

"Comere you little goober," Emmett says to Kerrinpuppy as she dances around stomping her paws on the floor, too excited at the prospect of going outside to stand still long enough for Emmett to clip the leash on. He finally manages to clip her by grabbing her collar with one hand and clipping the leash with the other. He gives her a quick scratch behind the ear; "Good girl."

Out the door.

Then down the stairs and a turn to the left. Emmett suddenly feels himself get very empty; he's violated a golden rule.

They walk two blocks, Dad talking away about his day, before Dad seems to recognize that something is wrong.

"Everything okay?" Dad asks.

"I don't know."

"Should I keep talking or just shut up?"

"I don't know." Emmett doesn't know anything, except he knows on some level about his mounting anger and that it's because he'd been interrupted, but saying that to Dad is another matter entirely.

But why the delay? Why this four-minute waiting period?

Dad continues talking anyway, and Emmett's rage monster stirs.

"WHY WON'T HE JUST SHUT THE FUCK UP? WHY
DOES HE HAVE TO KEEP TALKING ABOUT BULLSHIT
NONSENSE THAT YOU DON'T EVEN CARE ABOUT?
WHO GIVES A FUCK ABOUT THE ECCENTRICITIES OF
HIS BOSS? WHO GIVES TWO FLYING FUCKS ABOUT
THE LATEST GOD-DAMNED PATHETIC DOCUMENT
HE'S WRITING? WHO GIVES A SHIT ABOUT DAD'S
PRECIOUS DOCUMENTS?"

Under normal circumstances, Emmett does, but he just gets in these moods. Not moods; choleric sieges—a bile surging up from him he can't contain, where anything anyone says to him is the dumbest thing he's ever heard. It doesn't happen with everyone. His rage monster only seems to show itself to those whom he loves the most. It's a sad, twisted kind of honor for Emmett to direct his rage monster at you.

The rage monster can lead to lashing out at Dad, to sometimes even reducing him to tears. The rage monster can be the harbinger of psychosis. Emmett begins to think of exit strategies, thinking it'd be best if Dad just kept going and he and Kerrinpuppy turned around. If anything bad happens, Kerrinpuppy will lead him home.

Kerrinpuppy breaks the nice walking pace they've set for themselves and starts sniffing in the grass. Emmett can tell by the way she's walking and sniffing that she's looking for a place to poop. Finally, she finds one.

There's something in the almost embarrassed, completely self-effacing way she squats in the middle of a stranger's yard that snuffs the rage monster out almost completely. Kerrinpuppy's way of looking behind her, completely exposed, apologetic and yet rebellious. A certain morose self-consciousness that comes with being a domestic dog—made to live in a human world, on human terms, made to ignore thousands of years of instinct. Tied to a leash and allowed to wander only so far away, made to poop only at certain times and in certain places. So many rules and so many instructions and so many odd customs, completely alien to the code that is dog. And Emmett sees all this on LBK's face, her opinions on the absurdity of it all: the squeaky toys, the thermometer up her butt, the fact she has to wear sweaters when the weather gets cold, the same food for every meal, absurd commands whose purpose she doesn't understand like "shake" and "high-five" which bring so much praise; everything laid bare on her face as she squats there pooping. And the rage monster vanishes.

Total reversal. His dog taking a dump can make Emmett's mood do a one-eighty.

"It's that I feel I haven't been doing anything," Emmett admits as he and Dad and Little Baby Kerrin sit on their usual bench at Governor's Park.

"Well, what have you been doing this morning?"

"I browsed Facebook for about two hours and then I got obsessed with the font rendering on my Linux machine and occupied myself with that until you came over."

"Hmmm. Do you have any projects in your queue that would make you feel as though you've accomplished anything?"

Emmett thinks about it. "I've been meaning to get Plex up and running on my Mac Mini so I could experiment around with it."

"Well there you go," Dad says. "That's what you can do when you get home."

"I don't know. I just … it's just that I want to work on something substantial, I want to do something important. Plex just doesn't seem that important," Emmett says. "I'm sorry. I sound like a whiny little brat."

"No you don't. I think I can appreciate why you feel that

way," Dad says.

"Yeah? How so?"

"Well, I just picture myself when I was unemployed," Dad begins.

"And it was like you didn't have any purpose, anything to do, or at least, nothing important to do."

"Exactly," Dad says. "I had the stone project, but that was just to pass the time."

"Yeah. I suppose being on disability is a lot like being unemployed. I don't really have to do anything if I don't want to. I can sit around and make my computer render fonts differently and it's not going to effect my income."

Then Emmett adds, "But it's not like I really care about money. I don't have much but I don't need much, either. I just need to think of something to do with my time that'll make me feel as though I'm doing something important," Emmett says.

"What about your blog?" Dad says.

"The blog? Oh, it's coming along nicely. I've been wondering if I shouldn't increase the number of times I post to it each month. I've got a backlog of articles that means I could not write anything for like two years and still have material to post every month."

"Impressive."

"Yeah. I don't know how much of it is any good, but it's a bunch of words that I've written, at least. I think the initial charm is wearing off, like I've gotten used to the grind so I'm not so enamored, not so obsessed."

But their time at the park is up. Emmett feels like he's chasing something. Not paper, like most people. Something insubstantial but with more perpetuity. He wants to leave a life's work behind, is what he should have told Dad; he wants a legacy. He wants his life to have meant something, to have had value.

Kerrinpuppy is reluctant to come with them as there's a squirrel close by that needs to die. She whines and whines and strains against the leash, twirling around as though that will break her free of her bonds. But Emmett keeps a tight grip on the leash, wrapping the leash around his hand at least once so she won't get away. His worst fear in life is that something bad will happen to his Little Girl—her getting stolen, hit by a car, running away, or falling sick. Kerrinpuppy is his strongest tool in helping him with his illness, but she's also his greatest weakness; absolute love of someone will do that for you.

Working on the Plex server doesn't sound all that interesting, but Dad reminds him that it could end up being useful: he could stream his movies to pretty much anything connected to the Internet—his phone, tablet, computer, a Roku box—anything with an Internet connection. Dad seems really interested in the idea since he's just started converting their movies into digital format for viewing on a computer, the grand plan being having Emmett build a home theatre PC with all their movies on it. Emmett is less interested. He doesn't watch movies or TV shows anymore.

Movies and TV shows have a tendency to remove him from reality; enough that, when he watched The Walking Dead, he'd started carrying a huge knife with him everywhere he went. He'd felt as though he'd needed to be prepared—there was a threat out there he needed to be ready to defend himself against. He didn't think it was a dangerous thing for him to be carrying; lots of people carry knives. But few people carry six-inch Marine-issued tactical knives. He'd eventually come to his senses and opted to carry a folding knife in his pocket, a compromise, mostly for opening up boxes, though it'd also come in handy for prying open the fireplace and for tightening the screw on his infernal toilet seat.

Emmett and Dad reach the front steps to his apartment. Dad checks his watch but there isn't any time for him to come inside.

"Drink some water when you get back," Emmett tells Dad.

"You too," Dad says.

Then up the stairs and down the hall.

"Go, Kerrin. Go!" Emmett says to encourage her to run down the hall. She picks up her pace to a trot but isn't into it. Emmett wonders if it isn't because she's used to Dad coming in with them. She keeps looking back, as if expecting her grandpa to come through the door any second now.

Chapter Thirty Five

"You know, in all the time we've been meeting, you've only called me once," Lacey says.

"Really?" Emmett says. Then he adds, "Is that a bad thing?"

"No. At least, not as long as you're getting the help you need. It's just interesting to me."

Emmett cocks his head to the side.

"You're one of my sickest clients. I don't deal with a lot of clients with severe mental illnesses. And it's just funny to me that you call me the least, given how many years you've been coming here."

Emmett smiles, "Yeah. I think I just don't want to bother people."

"I would agree. That's hallmark Emmett-like behavior: you don't want to be a bother."

"Is that a bad thing?"

"No worse than any other character trait," Lacey says. "It's only unhealthy if you're suffering and don't ask for the help you need because you don't want to bother anyone."

"Understandable. I don't think that's how I roll, though. I totally believe in the slippery slope argument as it applies to mental illness."

"What do you mean?"

"Just that it always gets worse if you don't address it."

Emmett and Kerrinpuppy get inside and Emmett checks Kerrinpuppy's water. It's still halfway full, but he doesn't remember the last time he'd changed out the water. He runs the tap for half a minute to make sure the sediment that builds up in the faucet has washed out and fills her bowl with cool water.

He sets the bowl down and calls her over, snapping his fingers near the bowl, telling her to "drink up." She takes a short, polite drink of water and goes over to the futon to pass out. She still has food left over from that morning; in fact, she's barely touched the food. Emmett isn't going to get her back up to eat; it'd been more important that she drink water.

He goes into the bathroom for a washcloth soaked in cool water. He's still sweating profusely, despite the cooler weather, though it isn't as bad as mid-August. He soaks his face and stands there, staring at his image in the mirror. The reflection staring back at him is a foreigner. He remembers himself being much thinner, his cheeks not quite as puffed out, his chin much closer to his jaw. This is the price he's paid for his sanity—this extra weight, this auslander staring back at him. He remembers sitting in Dr. Bogsdaughter's office saying he'd rather be fat and happy than thin and miserable, and, while he's not exactly happy, he at least wouldn't describe himself as miserable.

Cooled off, he sits down in his chair to relax for a few minutes before getting to work on the Plex server.

He soon loses interest.

Kerrinpuppy hops up in his lap and he scratches her for a few minutes before turning his attention to his phone. Instagram first and then Facebook.

Jayne has posted a picture of her riding bikes, with the caption talking about some cycling term he's never been exposed to. Jayne is a hardcore cyclist, not the kind of cyclist Emmett had been back in the day. She's the type to wear spandex and measure how many watts she's produced with a bike computer. She's the type who tries to push herself to her physical limits—riding all over the mountains, sometimes riding a hundred miles a day. Emmett had just used bikes as his preferred method of transportation; he'd never had a custom-made bike frame, he'd never worn spandex (refused to, in fact), and he'd never been interested in comparing his feats of athleticism with his fellow cyclists. "Bike kids," they'd called themselves—folks who just liked to ride and ride without turning it into so much of a got-dang production.

What catches Emmett's attention, though, is that Jayne was supposed to have been sick today. But here she is posting pictures of a bike ride she's been on. It makes Emmett's heart sink into his stomach. He's incensed. She could have just told him she was going to go on a bike ride instead—it would've hurt, he supposed, but not so much as her blatantly posting pictures of her bike ride on Facebook. He likes to think they're close enough that they can cancel on each other for stuff like this. He doesn't really understand why someone would want to spend four to six hours riding their bike with no particular destination in mind; but he would've appreciated the idea. He cares about Jayne so he cares about the things she's interested in, regardless of how little he understands them.

Should he text her to ask? If he does, he might cause a needless confrontation. She'll of course deny it, tell him it was a ride she'd been on earlier. If he doesn't, it'll eat away at him, he'll obsess over it and it probably won't be any good. What would Lacey say?

He doesn't call his therapist too often; only when it's an absolute emergency. He can only remember one time when he's called her: when SAR had insulted him by doubting his explanation as to why SAR was getting poor Wi-Fi reception in the basement and accusing him of setting up his router incorrectly. SAR had said some cruel things and Emmett had gone on a walk with Kerrinpuppy where he'd become convinced SAR was going to blow the house up. He'd calmed himself down by reasoning he had Kerrinpuppy with him, so he had everything he needed in life. But still, he'd called Lacey to have her help talk him through the obviously irrational reaction. Who blows up a house in reaction to a disagreement over poor Wi-Fi reception? Because SAR can read Emmett's mind, of course, so he'd do it just to spite him.

This situation has the same kind of potential for bad things happening. He's just about to hit the call button when a text message appears on his phone's screen.

JAYNE:
Hey love! I was just wondering if you wanted to hang out tomorrow.

This calms him down. She still loves him. She says that he's like family to her, that he's her best friend. Memories, not even his own but manufactured from a mythos, come flooding back upon reading the phrase "Hey love!" He feels foolish for not having pursued Jayne. But she hadn't even been eighteen yet and Lauren, a year older than him, had been right there. A twenty-two-year-old and a sixteen-year-old wouldn't be the best kind of relationship, regardless of how mature Jayne might act.

EMMETT:
I think I would very much enjoy that :)

He includes the smiley face mostly for his own benefit. He doesn't know if he's seething mad or what, but he also loves her like family, he supposes. He doesn't really have feelings of his own, not in a conventional way. Spend any amount of time severely depressed and you get used to not having stable, everyday feelings; everything is just mud. His so-called logical brain isn't always trustworthy. If Jayne says they're family then they're family—he has to trust her at her word, is kind of forced to.

JAYNE:
Awesome! Where do you want to meet?

EMMETT:

I'm down with wherever. Dynamo maybe?

JAYNE:

Perfect! I'm free around 2

EMMETT:

So am I! Do you wanna say 2:30p? gives me time
walk there and so forth

JAYNE:

That's perfect. I'll see you then!

Emmett has calmed down now; his week will have the proper balance of social time. He opens the calendar on his phone and puts Jayne in for tomorrow. He schedules it for two hours, his standard amount of hanging-out time. He looks at the weekly view of his calendar, color coordinated according to activity— red for pills, blue for walks with Dad, purple (his favorite color) for time with friends—he can look at his week and get a sense of whether it's balanced, and this week is finally balanced.

Thoughts of calling Lacey slip out of his mind as his frustration at Jayne recedes. All he'd wanted was to see her, and that had resolved itself.

Chapter Thirty Six

◇◇◇

"I don't know, maybe I'm just a fool," Emmett says, a finality in his voice.

"I wouldn't say a fool. I would say 'loyal,'" Lacey offers.

"Loyal. That's definitely a more ambassadorial way of putting it," Emmett says, bitterness tinged in the sentence. He sighs and reconfigures himself in the chair. "No. I can understand loyal. Probably loyal to a fault."

"What do you mean by 'fault?'"

"Fault, from the Latin 'fallita,' meaning shortcoming or failing. So I suppose loyal to a fault meaning it will be my downfall."

"That's a pretty weighty thing for you to consider, a downfall."

"Yep," Emmett says, resigned, sighing. "The last downfall was pretty bad, and if I can help not going through it again, I will."

◇◇◇

Emmett gets home from his usual walk with Dad and changes into fresh clothes. He oils his beard again and combs his hair. He thinks about brushing his teeth but figures the toothpaste would just ruin the taste of coffee.

He fills his bag with his laptop, a sketchbook, drawing supplies, and a water bottle, and refills his pouch of tobacco with fresh tobacco from the can so he can smoke to his heart's content. It's a hot day again, so he takes his Pendleton hat with him to shade him from the sun. He says goodbye to Kerrinpuppy, who looks heartbroken, like she's never going to see Emmett again. He appreciates the look for its sincerity, though it kind of breaks his heart, too, to know that she loves him so much and doesn't understand that he'll be coming home again in a couple hours. "It's okay, Kerrin, I'll be back in a couple hours.

You be a good girl," he always says. But still she sits there, like it's goodbye forever.

He leaves at 2:00 p.m. and reaches Dynamo Coffee Bar at 2:30 p.m. Jayne is inside waiting for him, a partially drained cortado next to her. Emmett walks up to her and she looks up from her book and says, "Hey you!" and gives him a hug. Jayne feels impossibly small when Emmett hugs her. She's a good head shorter than him and probably weighs less than half of what he does.

"I'm gonna go get myself a drink," Emmett says, putting down his bag next to the seat across from Jayne.

He goes up to the barista and orders himself a cortado, figuring he'll drink the same thing as Jayne. He waits for his drink, chatting with the barista about what she's been up to. He takes his drink, wishes her a pleasant afternoon, and sits down across from Jayne.

Jayne's busy tapping away on her phone, something important, given the intensity of her scrunched-up face. She's always doing that, and it's increasingly bothering Emmett, who gets paranoid that she's texting her friends to talk about how bored she is hanging out with him. She frequently does this with Emmett—saying how she wishes she were hanging out with him because whoever she's with is so painfully boring. He's asked her to stop, but all she's ever done is apologize, promise to "try to stop," and keep doing it anyway.

"So I got a new job," she says, putting down her phone.

"What happened to your old job?"

"I still have it. This is just another job."

"Cool," Emmett says, wondering if Jayne having three jobs is really a good idea. "What is it?"

"My old teacher, Stacen, has bought a house. A huge one, really expensive. I'm actually kind of suspicious how he can afford it on a teacher's salary.

"Anyways, he's renting the house and the Airstream in the back yard on Airbnb and wants me to take care of cleaning it after people visit as well as welcoming new guests and getting them acquainted with how the house works." She goes on to explain that she runs errands for him and gets his mail, and does pretty much whatever he asks her to.

"Interesting," Emmett says. "So ... you're ... his personal assistant?"

"Pretty much."

"Cool," Emmett says. This is a bad idea. Stacen has a history of trying to manipulate her. She really needs to stay away from him. He wants to sleep with her pretty badly, but is the type of guy whose theory on seducing women is treating them like garbage one minute and then adoring them the next—throw them off balance and pretty soon they'll stumble into bed.

"Yeah, it's kind of a bullshit job. But the money'll be worth it. I'm broke as a joke right now, it's just ... " Jayne doesn't finish her sentence, pausing to tap away a message on her phone.

"Maybe you'll get to meet some interesting people?" Emmett offers. "I'd like to see this place."

"I'll take you over sometime, it's not too far away from here, and ... " she trails off, again tapping away on her phone. The phone doesn't even ring or vibrate. The screen just lights up and she's right there, the most overprotective phone-mother on the planet.

"What kind of house is it?" Emmett asks, feeling like he's the only one participating fully in the conversation.

"I suppose you would call it modern, loft-like. It's really open and spacious, I think you'd like it."

"Cool."

They talk for about ten more minutes, continually interrupted by Jayne's need to tend to her phone. She's so distracted that she has to start asking Emmett to repeat himself. If it were Mom or Dad asking him to repeat himself, even if it's just because they hadn't been in the room when Emmett was speaking, he'd be furious. But he doesn't get angry with Jayne; he just calmly repeats himself as the back of his mind urges him to tell her he has to go home. He asks her what she's been up to, and she tells him she's been doing pretty much nothing, that she's wasting her days and it's really frustrating. Emmett can definitely relate. But how could one be wasting away doing nothing with three jobs? Does she save all her so-called work-related-texting for when she hangs out with him?

They hadn't even been there for half an hour when Jayne announces, after looking at her phone, that she has to go. She gathers their empty cortado glasses and puts them in the bus tray. Emmett rolls himself a cigarette while she packs her things and they walk outside together.

"Sorry love, I rode my bike today. Otherwise I'd totally give you a ride," Jayne says.

"No worries, it's not too far of a walk." Emmett says, thinking of the ratio of walk time to hang out time: two-to-one.

They hug and Jayne tells him how good it was to see him and that they should see each other soon. She promises to text him on Saturday so they can hang out. She disappears around the corner on her bike and Emmett puts his hat on, lights his cigarette and starts walking back home. Two-to-one, he keeps thinking.

Chapter Thirty Seven

Emmett sits in the waiting room of Lacey's office. He remembers coming here so many years ago for his first visit with her. There'd been different decor but the paintings have remained the same. He remembers filling out the sheet of paper with insurance information, contact information, his emergency contacts, the reason why he was coming in the first place.

He'd written that the doctors were telling him he was going to die soon if they didn't figure out what was wrong with his digestive system. That he was there to face the existential crisis of dying before doing anything substantial with his life.

Sitting here now in her waiting room, having faced death in a much more real, much more substantial way than the abstract notion that he might starve to death in a year or so, he feels protected by a certain armor. Nothing can touch him. Except Jayne.

By the time his appointment with Lacey rolls around the next week, Emmett is feeling despondent about Jayne. She hadn't texted on Saturday when he'd planned his entire afternoon around hanging out with her before Dad picked him up to go back to Aurora at 5:00 p.m.

"She never does what she says she's going to do. Not once has she actually texted or called me on a day she said she would," Emmett is explaining to Lacey. There's been a lot of sighing in this session.

Emmett goes on a rant about how he can't trust Jayne at her

word, how she's constantly on her phone even though he's asked her multiple times not to do it because it makes him paranoid. He finishes his rant by explaining about how she'd cancelled on him and then posted pictures of a bike ride the next day.

"That was certainly a lot to get off your chest," Lacey says.

"Yeah, sorry."

"Don't apologize. That's what this time is for."

"I suppose so. I feel a lot better, so … " Emmett says, not finishing his sentence.

"Good," and Lacey pauses while Emmett looks at the floor. Lacey continues: "One theme that I've noticed with her is that she's really inconsistent. She says one thing and does another; she makes a promise and then breaks it. And you've always valued people whose word you can trust. You need people whose word you can trust."

"I've always figured that, at the end of the day, your word is pretty much all you've got."

"Exactly. It's important to you. Do you know why that might be?"

"I think it's because Lauren promised me when we started our relationship that she'd always be there to support me. And then she left me."

"A hard thing to go through."

Therapy with Lacey doesn't work like therapy in movies does, where the therapist tells the client exactly how to solve a particular problem. Lacey's style is to gently nudge Emmett toward his own conclusion. "What do you want to do about it?" is a question she asks frequently.

He comes out of the appointment, walks up Logan, Kerrin-puppy in tow, composing an email to Jayne in which he'll try to be as candid, as vulnerable as possible—explain the paranoia, explain the deep, ugly truth of paranoiac and delusional thinking. Maybe that will make her understand. Or maybe, like any ultimatum, like any existential imperative—and really, what was this email he was composing if not an ultimatum, an existential imperative—it could pull the thread that would unravel the weave.

It's complicated with her. In many ways, he's in love with her; and in other ways, he's outgrown her (or perhaps, she's outgrown him). He's slowly beginning to realize, however unconsciously, however dimly, she's all style and no substance. That it's one thing to tell someone you're like family and quite another to actually treat them like family. People often want the title without the work—they want to attain the status of surrogate family without actually earning it, without being there for their friends when things are at their worst. Jayne certainly hadn't been there for Emmett when he'd needed her during ECT; she'd been living her little life and enjoying herself while Emmett was driving himself insane with loneliness and despair, an utter hopelessness that the word "hopeless" seemed hopeless at beginning to describe; having to start his life over again from the beginning. It's left a bitter tinge in the back of his throat, and the thought enters his mind that maybe he's projecting an air of hostility on Jayne because of how much he resents her abandoning him, how much he resents her only being around when he was doing well.

Emmett needs more than just fair-weather-friends; he needs friends who'll be with him while he drags himself through the muddy, disgusting fields of mental illness. Was he perhaps asking Jayne to be more of a friend than she was prepared to be?

Chapter Thirty Eight

◇◇

"What are you thinking about today?" Lacey asks.

"Memory. And memories, I suppose," Emmett answers.

"Wanna tell me about them?"

Emmett sighs and says, "It seems to me we place too much value in memories, too much of our identity in memories. We think that without our memories we are nothing. But I don't think that's the case."

"Why not?"

"My brain might as well be Swiss cheese with all of the memories I've lost, and I don't feel any less myself for it. I feel largely fine. About the only thing that bugs me is when people mention things or people of which I have no memory."

"Like Lauren?"

"Exactly."

"Tell me about it," Lacey says, and Emmett knows this isn't just an expression of agreement; Lacey wants to hear more.

Emmett looks down at his Little Girl sleeping in his lap, and he sighs again. Then he says, "I wrote her an email after I'd moved out of my parents' house for the last time, into SAR's house. I just wanted to know her side of things: what happened, why she left me, if I did anything terrible to her, that kind of stuff," and then Emmett pauses.

"Go on," Lacey says.

Not a sigh this time, but a deep purposeful breath. "Well, first off she said that no one had the tools to deal with my illness. I'd kind of like for her to see me now, to see how I've changed in the five years since everything fell apart; I'd like for her to see my level of mastery over my illness. But that's not all she said. She also basically lied to me—said that she came over for dinner all the time, that she went to many of my ECT appointments. My parents deny that she did, and I believe them over Lauren; they have no reason to lie.

"She also made it sound like my illness was a major inconvenience," Emmett continued. "My suicidal tendencies, my urgent calls to her for help made her cancel appointments with her professors, which damaged her reputation, blah, blah, blah. Almost like I could help being suicidal and was doing it to be vindictive or something. She said I was the reason she failed French; just, in general, blaming me for the dissolution of her academic career."

"How do you feel about that?"

"That? Oh. It's bullshit. I was just trying to survive the best I knew how. I make zero apologies for trying to preserve my life. Not that it doesn't remain a sore subject at times."

"I feel as though you haven't said your entire piece," Lacey says.

"Yeah," Emmett says. "It's just that she's this kind of insubstantial vapor in my life now. I don't remember what she looks like or sounds like or smells like. She's like this phantom that enters my consciousness occasionally."

"I'm sorry you have to go through that," Lacey says in a gentle voice, full of empathy and concern for her client of nine years. It's really all anyone could say about the situation; there was no trick to get out of it, there was no mindfulness exercise that could heal this. Time would just have to do the mending for Emmett, like it'd been doing all along.

Emmett sits across from Jayne for the last time, her train of thought interrupted by her phone, such that she's completely lost track of her point. She busies herself with her inane contraption, tapping away with a certain kind of fanaticism until, satisfied it had been appeased for the moment, she puts it down and asks him how he's been doing.

"Oh, I suppose life has been a little hard lately," he admits.

"I'm sorry, love. What's been going on?"

"I've been having … a terrible new kind of psychosis lately. I don't know. It's hard to explain. It's nightmarish. It's painful. It feels like it's chipping away at my ability to cope with things."

Jayne picks up her phone and taps away, a new demand from the hunk of metal and plastic.

"That must suck," she says simply.

"Yeah. It does," and Emmett gets up to go refill his water. He rarely talks about the exact experiences of his illness with her. Jayne has never seen him sick—he goes home as soon as he feels it coming on, even if it means a very dangerous walk home on the brink of psychosis. But he's asked her to edit his speeches and later on his blog posts, maybe to make sure that she'd read them so maybe she would understand. She'd told him that the speeches brought her to tears, and said the same with some of the blog posts. But then she'd stopped sending him feedback and Emmett had had to learn how to edit his stuff on his own.

"I don't know. I guess—" and he cuts himself short as he sees Jayne once again involved in her phone.

"Do you suppose we could move over there?" Jayne says, pointing to an empty table near a power outlet.

"Sure thing."

They transfer their stuff and Emmett puts their empty cortado glasses on the bus tray. Jayne takes out her charger and plugs her phone into the wall.

Jayne is talking to her old high school friend, a kid who now calls himself Sysco, which makes Emmett think of the networking company Cisco, whose equipment Dad is so fond of.

"He's just a privileged white boy. He doesn't know anything about real life, or being broke. He always has Mommy and Daddy to fall back on," Jayne says between bursts of blurry thumbs.

Sysco had started out as a bit of a hipster with his Holga camera, studying who-knows-what at some college on the west coast. But somewhere along the way someone had introduced him to anarchism and crust punk, and he was doing pretty much the same thing Emmett had done in college, only much more hardcore. His anarcho-punk ways came replete with a punk house, traveling on coal cars, polyamory, and a marriage that meant nothing other than getting him and his now-wife-of-convenience residency so they could get in-state tuition. His parents were quite wealthy, having an enormous house in Cherry Hills.

"Well, I think just about any white male from the suburbs is pretty well privileged," Emmett says, suddenly recalling the numerous rants he'd heard about the subject while dating Lauren during their more radical phase together. He was very much a white male from the suburbs.

"I know. I know. It just irks me. He has everything provided for him; he doesn't have to really work, he doesn't have to worry about money, he doesn't even really have to go to school—his parents pay for everything."

"Well I don't have to go to work, or worry about money, or go to school either. Well, I suppose it's more like I can't. But I think you get my point."

What Emmett really wants to say was that she's just as privileged as this so-called Sysco kid, it's just that her parents live in a less-expensive neighborhood. Jayne doesn't have to pay her own rent; she doesn't have to pay for her college education or her phone bill or her Internet connection. She just has to pay for her groceries and other minor expenses, which means she works a few days a week at a coffee shop. She'll always have a roof over her head and a nice, quality education to fall back on.

But still, Jayne often compares herself to Emmett, which he finds offensive, even degrading—it completely ignores some rather harsh realities about his existence. The facts of Emmett's current existence were the roughly same: his parents pay for almost all of his expenses too, the government pays for his rent, he's on his parents' insurance, and his parents are paying off his school debt. But the biggest difference is that Jayne is a completely healthy and capable individual, whereas Emmett has a severe, debilitating mental illness which renders him incapable of working or going to school. He'd tried working, he'd tried going to school, and he'd ended up paying for it dearly—with his sanity and very nearly his life. Hospitalizations, psychosis day after day, suicidal thoughts and ideas, untold suffering, not to mention ECT. He'd lost nearly everything: his job, his home, his memories, his friends, his skills, his hopes and dreams, his fiancée, even his beloved cat. His entire life had fallen apart, and Jayne has just conveniently forgotten all that. He'd tried and tried with school and work until Lacey and Dr. Bogsdaughter had finally convinced him to give up and apply for SSDI. Now he was living just above the poverty line. And though he didn't lack for anything, he'd certainly never own a house or be able to support a family on the pittance he received from SSDI, which had to be supplemented by his parents so he could live in Cap Hill.

"It's different, though," Jayne says, picking up her phone once more and tapping back a message. Emmett can't help but feel a little jealous of her; he used to be that popular, people texting him all the time … but his phone hardly buzzes these days. And, when it does, it's never particularly exciting, never anything pressing or important. Just Mom wondering if he was up, or Dad wondering if he wanted to go on a walk. Texting Jayne was probably the best part of being her friend; she almost always replies immediately. He can count on Jayne more as a texting buddy than as a real-life friend. It's almost as though she takes words on a screen more seriously than a face-to-face conversation.

Jayne doesn't complete her thought. And Emmett excuses himself to go smoke a cigarette. He knows Jayne won't go with him; she never goes with him, though it's important to him that his friends come out to smoke with him, even if they don't smoke, to brave the cold or the absurd heat and chat with him while he relaxes from the relative oppression of a semi-crowded coffee shop. If they're inside waiting for him, he feels rushed, and the whole point of the cigarette is moot.

But he doesn't care so much now. Jayne is plenty entertained talking to Sysco, plenty occupied being glued to her phone; she doesn't need him in there and he doesn't need her out here. She'd probably be more entertained, more satisfied if he stayed outside smoking and they just texted each other. He sits outside, takes his own phone out but puts it back because the sight of it makes him feel disgusted—he'd have gotten rid of it in that moment if he could.

Chapter Thirty Nine

"You know, I think I saw you one time on your bike," Lacey says.

"When was this?"

"Oh, a long time ago. Maybe three or four years. I thought about saying hi to you but thought it might be awkward for you."

"Ah. Was I weaving in and out of traffic like a madman?"

"No, not that I remember. Did you often ride your bike that way?"

"From what I can remember I did. Get me on a bike at that time and I'd go full-out, as fast as I could, as hard as I could. Didn't seem to give two flying craps about safety. I'd blow through stop lights with minimal concern for on-coming cars, just sort of slow down to make sure there weren't any coming and speed right back up."

"I wonder if that wasn't some kind of subconscious desire to kill yourself."

Emmett had never thought of it that way. "Huh," he says. "Maybe. I've always just thought it was because I was being young and stupid."

◇◇◇

"Ugh," Jayne says. "He's so frustrating."

"Who's frustrating? Sysco?" Emmett has just returned from his cigarette break to find Jayne still tapping away at her phone.

"Stacen, he wants his pillow back."

"That sounds pretty reasonable," Emmett says, not following. "Where's his pillow?"

"In the back of my car," Jayne says, setting down her phone and readjusting her hair tie.

"Ahh," he says, not knowing if he ought to ask how his pillow got in her car.

"He wants it back now. Says that his neck has been hurting because he doesn't have his stupid fucking Tempur-Pedic pillow."

Jayne is busy tapping away on her phone, Emmett thinking about another cup of coffee. He'll probably have to get it to go, in which case he might as well just go to the coffee shop next to his apartment—he has a free coffee on his punch card. He checks his watch. Why does Jayne insist on meeting at Dynamo if she's just going to bail on him after twenty or thirty minutes? It's quite a way for Emmett to walk, a mile's worth of a walk. He doesn't mind if they're going to stay for a while, but hanging out with Jayne lately, it feels like he spends more time walking than he does hanging out.

Exercise, he tells himself. You desperately need exercise. And God is teaching you to be thankful.

He takes his pouch of tobacco out of his shirt pocket and starts rolling, figuring this is the end of their hangout session. He can't really walk and not smoke, can he? It's like peanut butter without jelly. Sacrilege. The two just go together.

He has Dr. Bogsdaughter's blessing to smoke. His quirky psychiatrist had heard a lecture on how a cigarette can be the best part of the day for someone with schizophrenia (and by extension, someone with schizoaffective disorder). So, when Emmett had announced that he was a smoker a few years ago, Dr. Bogsdaughter was all for it, had calmed Emmett's mother down and brought both of Emmett's parents on board with the filthy habit. Everyone was so on board with Emmett smoking that Mom and Dad paid for his tobacco, considering it part of Emmett's treatment, just like medication or doctors' appointments.

He always especially craves cigarettes when he's anxious. He doesn't feel especially anxious at the moment, but he probably is. He has this tendency to run on autopilot, just rolling cigarettes, going through his whole anti-anxiety routine without being consciously aware of being anxious. The brain-in-the-gut, his reliance on intuition, is a key factor in how he handles his illness. Just floating along like an accident, doing what he feels he needs to be doing, rarely fighting what his gut tells him he ought to be doing.

He wonders if things have always been this way with Jayne. He's known her for eleven years, though lately it feels like he barely knows her. She made mention of how she hasn't ever had a friend for that long. Jayne goes through a lot of friends— she sees the negative in everyone and is probably one of the most cynical people Emmett knows. He already recognizes that Jayne brings out the cynic in him, that unhealthy mistrust of people that prevents one from treating people as people, that hides deep in the recesses of any person, but which for some reason both Jayne and Emmett pass off as an endearing sort of "get off my lawn" grandpa-type behavior. It's a removal from the optimistic kind of realist Emmett naturally is.

He finishes rolling his cigarette, licking the gum and folding the paper over before pinching off the excess tobacco at either end, something he's done he-doesn't-know-how-many thousands of times, figuring he and Jayne will be parting ways soon, when she announces, "Okay, I have to go and give him his precious pillow. Wanna come with me?"

Caught off guard; she rarely invites him along on these little errands of hers. He really doesn't like this Stacen guy and Jayne isn't the best driver, possibly a recipe for a bad time and an even worse time upon getting home later that afternoon. But she's his best friend, at least by title, and if Emmett is anything, he's loyal. Loyal to a fault. So he accepts her invitation, tucks the freshly rolled cigarette behind his ear, and they collect their things and put their water glasses on the bus tray. They wave goodbye to the barista and head toward Jayne's car.

Every car Jayne has driven has been a "piece of shit," but

this is the only car where Emmett disagrees with the sentiment. It's a late model Volvo something—Emmett doesn't know, he knows next to nothing about cars. Why would he? He doesn't own a car; he hasn't driven a car in something going on ten years. He isn't even allowed to have a driver's license. The seats are quite comfortable; it has an engine that doesn't make any funny noises, a stereo that works well, and windows and locks that function without eccentricity. It's much flashier than Dad's car, which is just a plain, no-frills Toyota Camry. Jayne's yellow Volvo has different driving modes depending on the situation and tons of stuff Rob had gone on and on about but which Emmett didn't really understand.

Emmett scoots the seat back as far as it will go. The interior is a little cramped, definitely not designed for someone six feet tall, two-hundred-and-forty pounds with bad knees, but he can manage; they're just going downtown.

"Do you know where the Y is, downtown?" Jayne asks.

"The YMCA?"

Jayne nods.

"I didn't even know there was one downtown." He gets his phone out, pulls up the map and tells her the cross streets, Sixteenth and Lincoln.

Jayne starts the car and pulls out, her phone clutched precariously in her left hand as she tries to balance it and turn the wheel at the same time. She puts the car into drive and switches her phone to her right hand. She drives down the street, looking one second at the road and the next second at her phone. Emmett isn't about to get into a car accident or have Jayne hit a cyclist or pedestrian, so he snatches the phone away from her. Jayne shoots him a look but doesn't say anything; how can she?

Emmett looks out the window.

It's amazing how quickly Denver can change in just a few blocks. The change isn't as drastic on foot, but zooming down the street in Jayne's nimble little car, the transition from one neighborhood to the next is wholly remarkable: one moment they're in the clean, newly developed neighborhood Emmett only knows as North Cap Hill, freshly gentrified and full of yoga studios and gourmet pet food stores, the next they're in the weird chaos and sure-to-bring-(unwelcome)-adventure of Colfax. A couple minutes later they're in downtown, a bike messenger flying by, cars surrounding them on all sides on the impossibly broad streets, and that foreboding echo of cars and the high heels of business executives in A-line skirts echoing off the high buildings surrounding them on all sides, tall enough to block out the sun.

Lost in thought, Emmett watches a bike messenger approach the intersection, pause momentarily at the red light, and then dash across at break-neck speed, mere yards in front of an on-coming car which blares its horn. The bike messenger yells an obscenity and continues on. Jayne sees it too, and lets out a tiny gasp as the messenger speeds away on his errand.

Emmett makes no sign of having seen the near-accident, he's lost in a memory which the scene has churned up from the recesses of his ECT-fried brain. There'd been a time when he'd ridden his bike as recklessly as that bike messenger just had. A time when suicide had seemed a welcome end to his life, and had spoken to him sweetly from a distance while he pedaled; calling him home as he'd weaved in and out of traffic, her siren's song beckoning him to ride head-long into oncoming traffic. She'd sung of the glory of it, of a memorable and tragic exit, but mostly she'd sung of an end to his suffering.

It'd seemed to him he'd been made to suffer, such was his lot in life. The siren's adjuring voice had comforted him, and in the end Emmett was forced to a crossroads, what Dr. Romero later termed his Existential Imperative; the ultimatum which brought him before the mercy of the good doctor's electrocut-ing paddles. And in that place where life and death existed on such equal footing, Emmett had chosen life. He doesn't regret his choice.

Even today, now and then, the sweet seduction of the siren's voice still haunts him. While it had failed to lure him onto the rocks of his destruction, its song entices him with promises made but never specified. He feels a certain affinity toward his illness. Here lives art. Here lives solace. Here lives genius, the siren seems to sing. The nobility of suffering. The romance of a tragic ending.

Looking back on his surviving of those deadly shallows, he can see clearly the deceit and treachery together with the platonized attraction. He knows all too well how sweet the song is, and he can't deny the appeal of relinquishing himself to the fatal embrace of his own twisted head. But. At the same time. He knows that surrendering to the song would pull him onto the shoals of despair; to a destruction from which there may be no return.

Emmett is brought out of his reverie as the car suddenly stops. Jayne's found a parking spot a block and a half away from the Y.

Jayne turns off the car and Emmett hands her phone back to her. She taps away at it while they walk down the sidewalk toward the intersection that will take them past the YMCA, Emmett watching out not only for himself but also for Jayne, fearing that she'll walk headlong into an oncoming car.

This is a totally different Denver than the almost small-town Cap Hill Denver Emmett is used to. The funny thing is that Emmett can see the high rises of this version of Denver from his stoop during the fall and winter when the leaves have fallen from the trees. Downtown is only a half-hour walk away from his apartment, but he almost never comes here. It occurs to him that he rarely strays beyond the confines of his neighborhood—only every other week when he walks to Lacey's office on Seventh and Grant; technically the Alamo Placita neighborhood, but Google Maps still calls it Capitol Hill.

They're crossing Broadway, which is an order of magnitude wider than the streets Emmett usually walks on. On Pennsylvania Street, it's an exercise in precision to have to squeeze past a car going the opposite direction (and good luck if you drive one of those ridiculous Ford F-450s), and he's glad that he doesn't have to drive on them. This stretch of Broadway, on the other hand, is four lanes wide and traffic speeds down it with impunity. Not a section of town where you want to cross against the light.

Emmett remembers biking downtown Denver when he was still going to school. It had been exhilarating, weaving in and out between the cars. He'd climbed hills as if they were nothing, a feat he can no longer reproduce since he feels his heart protest just walking up the relatively mild incline on their way up to the Y, embarrassed to remember having read that Denver is actually one of the flattest cities in the country. He'd been borderline-irresponsible on his bike, blowing through red lights and generally sprinting to his ultimate destination with hardly a thought to his safety. It was totally different now, overwhelmed by all the cars and the noise and the pedestrians making their way home after work …

Electricity hums in his head and he wishes there were some sly way he could pop a couple ziprasidone without anyone noticing. But without water they'll just get caught in his throat and then the capsule will disintegrate and he'll cough and the fine powder of the medication will come poofing out and it'd be the worst taste in his mouth imaginable, all without any of it getting into his bloodstream.

All he can hope is that this won't take long.

They reach the YMCA and Emmett assumes Jayne has texted Stacen. But she hasn't so much as really glanced up from her phone, so there's no way of telling.

"He says he'll be out in a few minutes," Jayne says. They stand there, Emmett absorbing downtown Denver as though it were some alien planet, trying to enhance his calm, running an inventory on his various body parts, grounding himself; Jayne oblivious, her eyes and thumbs absorbed in the four inches of screen about six inches away from her face. A few minutes later Stacen comes out of the entrance, showing off his hairy body with fashionably short shorts and a tank top showing a not terribly unattractive body—the guy obviously takes care of himself and has something to show for the effort. He has a kind of saunter to his stride that suggests (to Emmett, at least) he's planned the whole thing so Jayne could see him in this outfit.

"Hey Jayne," he says.

"Hey. Here's your pillow," Jayne says, handing him his pillow. "Do you remember Emmett?"

"Yeah, I do. How's it going, Emmett?"

Emmett says he's doing fine, polite and neutral. Stacen regards Emmett for as long as is polite and goes back to ogling Jayne in her short skirt and tank top and asks her if she'd kept the pillow because she wanted to smell him while she slept, to which Jayne declares a disgusted, "No."

"Yeah, right," Stacen says, with a mocking laugh. "How are you guys doing?"

"We're doing fine," Jayne answers for Emmett. "We were just getting coffee when you texted."

Stacen doesn't seem the least bit concerned by this, that he may have interrupted their coffee date in order to get his precious pillow back. They stand there awkwardly for a few moments, Jayne on her phone and Emmett, who's standing further back toward the curb, thinking it might be a good idea for him to pull his own phone out, while Stacen stands there, obviously trying to think of something clever to say. Emmett is glad he's come; Stacen probably hadn't planned on Emmett coming.

Jayne finally says that they need to get going and Stacen offers her an awkward hug, promising her he isn't sweaty yet. She refuses as politely as she can. He laughs uncomfortably, says goodbye to Emmett, and goes back inside while Emmett and Jayne go on their way.

"So … he's pretty creepy," Emmett says.

"Yeah, he really is."

"Why do you hang around him then?"

"I don't know. Probably because he pays me, and I could really use the money right now."

"Better ways to make money than that."

Jayne doesn't say anything back.

They head back down the direction they'd come. "Rob works in that building right there," Jayne says, pointing to a golden glass building in front of them.

"Ah," Emmett says.

"Would you mind if we waited for him to get off work so we can give him a ride home?"

"Not at all," Emmett says. He rather enjoys Rob. Rob is down-to-earth and very practical; he likes fixing things like Emmett likes fixing things, the only difference being that Emmett fixes computers and Rob fixes bikes.

Emmett produces the cigarette from behind his ear and lights it while Jayne wanders around to find a place to sit, still staring at her phone.

Chapter Forty

◇◇◇

"Are public sightings frequent?" Lacey says.

"Well. I wouldn't say they're infrequent. I think it's just kinda depends on what my brain feels like doing."

"Understandable."

"What do you mean?" Emmett says.

"Well, psychology isn't really an exact science—"

"That's the impression I've gotten from reading Jung," Emmett interrupts.

Lacey chuckles, a smile in her eyes. Emmett, always with his quips at the exact right moment. "So I don't really need to even explain, do I?"

"No, I suppose not. Not at all," Emmett says. "The more I find out about life, the more I realize that expectations don't match reality. Even simple expectations."

"What do you mean?"

"Well isn't that one of the greatest causes of suffering for me? That reality doesn't match my expectations? It's like John Malkovich's character in Art School Confidential."

"I'm not familiar."

"It's a great movie if you ever wanna know what art school is like. But anyways. This character's only real bit of teaching in the entire movie is this: 'Don't have unrealistic expectations.' And, to me, that about sums it up—mental illness is largely about managing expectations, albeit not the mundane, every day sorts of expectations that tell my Dad today he'll have a peanut butter and butter sandwich for lunch … No, I mean the real kind of substantial, life-changing expectations."

Lacey writes something down in her notebook as Kerrinpuppy lets out a sigh from Emmett's lap. Lacey puts down her pen and looks at Emmett, that same smile in her eyes. Her I'm proud of you eyes.

◇◇

A nd now they are here, a pair of them walking down the street toward Emmett.

Naked with pale yellowish, sickly flesh. Their bodies grotesquely disproportionate—bellies being sucked in and blown out by their laborious breathing, breasts sagging down near their belly buttons; and penises from which brightly colored tubes hung. The tubes, turquoise and red on one of the creatures and teal and cobalt on the other, are being dragged from down the block as far as the eye can see. They walk awkwardly so as not to step on the tubes, pained as though their joints had been worn down such that it is bone grinding against bone—not so much limping as much it is that their every movement is an operose process. Their heads are bald, as the rest of their bodies are hairless, and they wear dull, greasy, metallic masks that hide their faces. They have no eyes; the holes cut into the masks where their eyes would be only look into darkness, though occasionally he can see a glowing orb in one of the cavities. They lack mouths, just two narrow horizontal slits for them to breathe through, under where the eyes would be; he can hear them sucking in air and expelling it as though the process is like vomiting to them. The fingers are long and spindly like spider legs on the one and short and swollen, segmented like a fattened, maggoty insect on the other one. Both pairs of hands end in thick, brown fingernails.

These are the hands that had searched him in the night— had tried to abduct him, had tried to take him some place he couldn't even begin to imagine the horrors of. These are the hands that violated him, that shoved their way inside of him and grabbled around and then pulled and pulled until there was nothing left to pull, tossing his innards aside when they'd proved boring playthings. The pain had been excruciating and its aftereffects had lasted for days. He'd winced every time he'd sat down, reminded of the terrible pain they'd inflicted, of the nightmare episode in which he'd felt, with vivid detail, the sentience of having his intestines ripped out through his anus.

They ignore him just now, as they always do in broad daylight; —they are just patrolling the periphery; testing the boundaries, letting him know they are there.

Sometimes a pack of huge wolves would come and drive them away, snarling and snapping and circling them until they turned back. Sometimes he only knew the creatures were nearby because he caught glimpses of the wolves down the block, dancing to protect him. He wondered why they never came inside to protect him while he slept, when he needed them the most. The creatures had never made a move to hurt him, not in public.

He'd drawn these things almost exclusively since he'd started seeing them, or maybe he'd started drawing them and then they'd appeared; as though his tortured imagination had granted him his wish like a twisted Harold and the Purple Crayon. His sketchbooks are full of drawings of them in different poses. Emmett had always been frustrated with the results of his attempts to draw his hallucinations; they always paled in comparison to the real thing.

He's fully aware they aren't real. But that never stops his visceral reaction, the wrenching gut, the creeping skin. He watches them lug their bodies down the street, wondering if they are coincidence or omen.

"What are you looking at?" Jayne asks, looking up from her phone to see Emmett staring at an empty street.

How could he tell her? How would she understand? How could he get her to understand their horror?

"Oh, me? Nothing, I suppose; —just being fascinated by my brain." Best to just brush it off. People don't understand what it is to be haunted in broad daylight.

Jayne makes a noise to indicate that she's heard what he'd said and goes back to her phone. Soon Rob comes out, wheeling what looks to be a really nice road bike of a brand Emmett doesn't recognize. "Hey Emmett," Rob calls out, and the two of them embrace. "How're you doing?"

"I'm doing pretty adequate. Err...adequately. Or is it adequate? I don't know. Either way, I'm doing just fine and it's good to see you."

Emmett often wonders if he and Rob would be friends if Rob and Jayne ever broke up. They certainly got along well enough, though they'd never been alone, just the two of them, long enough to really tell if they would be friends if Jayne weren't always there. Rob doesn't seem as into the image of being a cyclist as Jayne is. Rob seems to just be a nerd about bikes, endlessly and innocently passionate about them like Emmett is about computers. Jayne is almost too aware of the implications of being into bikes—the lifestyle it entails, the quirks it brings out in a person, the whole culture surrounding it and what it means to be a cyclist.

Emmett drags on his cigarette as Jayne and Rob greet one another with a kiss, the tiny Jayne on her tippy-toes, and then heads to the car. Jayne gets into the back seat, and Emmett stays outside, —trying to get as much nicotine as possible before having to get into the car, Rob securing his bike to the rack on top of the yellow Volvo.

"So how's your lady friend doin'?" Rob asks when they get into the car. He's referring to the barista at a coffee shop up Thirteenth that Emmett has a crush on.

"Oh, I'm not so sure about her," Emmett replies.

"Yeah? Why not?"

"I was drawing there this past weekend and a couple walked in, one of those annoying couples who're overcompensating by being really cute in public, carrying shopping bags from the Sixteenth Street Mall, talking about how much money they'd spent and so on. Anyways. They got on the topic of the pills they'd done that weekend and my so-called lady friend chimed right in, talking about all the different kinds of drugs she's done and how much fun they were, and in general giving me the impression that she wouldn't be the type of person I could depend on."

"Well ... haven't you done a lot of drugs too?"

"Yeah, I guess. But I'm over it now. I think recreational drugs are something for the young, and this girl is older than me, as old as my sister maybe. Just doesn't seem like a good fit for me. I definitely need someone who isn't so much into pills. You know, so I don't have to worry about her stealing mine."

"Why didn't you tell me anything about this?" Jayne a little incredulous from the back seat.

Well, one, because you were on your fucking phone the entire time, Emmett thought. And two, because we weren't hanging out long enough for me to get to it. But instead he says: "I dunno, just didn't come up, and we were talking about other things."

Emmett can't see her reaction but knows she's gone back to her phone. Rob drives down Broadway and up 14th, turning right onto Emmett's favorite street in Cap Hill. Emmett hugs them goodbye, Rob seated in the driver's seat, Jayne getting out of the car to give him a hug. She tries to put a lot into her hugs, but they always seem to lack something; they're unsatisfying. Empty like diet soda. Jayne tells him that she loves him. Emmett loves her too, wondering if those words were diet soda too.

He's hollow on the inside, someone having excavated his brain out of his skull, slipping the gelatinous mass gently through his nose like the ancient Egyptians had done when mummifying their pharaohs. He needs to get some food and some drugs into his system.

He hurries across the street and up the steps of his stoop, down the hallway and into good ol' number seven. Kerrinpuppy is ecstatic to see him, beyond barks with how glad she is he's finally come back home. She extends her paws up in the air and Emmett catches them and starts to scratch underneath her armpits. Eventually Emmett lets her down and goes into the bathroom to wash his face, an act which sometimes works to at least temporarily fill a cavity between the ears. He looks at himself in the mirror, not really recognizing the person looking back at him. He remembers the mirrors back in Dr. Brains's office; he hasn't been able to handle mirrors at times like these for a number of years now.

Finished with his face, he goes into the kitchen to scrounge up some food for himself and Little Baby Kerrin.

Chapter Forty One

"It's been a little hard, ya know?" Emmett says. "It's like moving out was almost a mistake."

"A mistake?" Lacey says.

"Yeah. Sometimes I wonder if it was worth it, with how often my parents have to come and pick me up. It seems like once a week sometimes. Like I just can't handle being by myself."

"Emmett, I think you're forgetting how miserable you were at your parents' house."

"Yeah. I suppose so. I'm almost wishing for SAR's house again. At least then I wasn't being picked up so often, I had people to talk to, there was something going on."

"Maybe go back and read your journals from that time. From what I remember it was a rough time for you."

"Yeah. You're right," Emmett says. "There's no sense in wishing for a past that's not going to repeat itself. I guess sometimes I just feel resigned to the fact that I'm going to be miserable for the rest of my life."

Sitting down. Emmett chokes. Something grabbing onto his throat. Threatening to strangle the life out of him.

Little Baby Kerrin in bed. Sleeping away the evening like she sleeps almost every part of the day away.

Such a strange evening.

Everything more and more empty as time goes by.

Emmett filled to the brim with absolutely nothing. That Nothing causing him a lot of trouble.

Pill won't help. No prescription medication will fill a vacuum.

Lacey has taught him something, though. The Jedi Mind Trick.

Sitting in his chair, Emmett calms himself.

Breathing in and out.

Slowly.

Gathering himself as he visualizes the vacuum inside of his chest. The vacuum steadily growing, encouraging the choking. A spheroid the size of a grapefruit, spinning and globular and sucking the life out of him the more he waits.

But he has to take his time. If he doesn't do this right …

He closes his eyes and surrounds the spheroid with his consciousness, visualizing it moving outside of his body, being sucked through his chest and floating several inches in front of him. He can feel it resisting, the confines of his flesh parting to the mass of the void as he slowly draws it outside of himself. It's a sloppy sensation, like slowly blowing his nose through his chest. The spheroid is a deep dark crimson, as though bloodied. It seems to be leering at him, as though daring him to mess with it. He reaches out and pops it, the orb-like mass of a void deliquescing without ceremony, and he feels instantly better.

He puts his reading glasses on and picks up his book and begins reading distractedly, wondering what to do next, foreboding telling him more is coming.

The void starts growing again, as though he has a slow leak somewhere. It makes room for itself by shoving aside vital organs—his heart, lungs, diaphragm, stomach—until he has more of a void than he'd had before.

He looks at his watch.

Four more hours until pills.

He's already eaten dinner and fed Kerrin. Perhaps a podcast? Or an album? An album is a better idea; —music doesn't seem to affect him the way a podcast might. Music is predictable; he has a plethora of playlists for any kind of mood he might be in. He turns on his TV, more just a monitor for the Mac Mini hooked up to his stereo, takes the mouse and keyboard out from the drawer in the coffee table, and sets about to find the perfect mix.

He settles on a mix that starts with the introduction to Mussorgsky's Pictures at an Exhibition and transitions perfectly into Blackalicious's Blazing Arrow. It's perfect in his mind—a nice relaxing classical piece to calm his angsty body down and then an ingenious transition into one of his favorite hip-hop groups. He takes the mouse with him over to his chair and gets his headphones ready. He sits down and starts the mix, trying to envelop himself in the music.

Mussorgsky's music puts him into a kind of trance that he doesn't want to end. But the track is only one minute, forty-nine seconds long, not nearly long enough. The transition he thought would be perfect disrupts his calm. It's a trick that works when someone is ready for a pumped-up mix, as it lulls them into a false sense of security, but a horrible choice for someone who needs to fill an empty void, a void constantly expanding and threatening their very existence.

Emmett tears off his headphones in frustration and turns off his stereo receiver. So much for that idea. He's at a loss for what to do.

"YOU PATHETIC LITTLE FUCK," *Myra purrs into his ear.* "YOU PATHETIC LITTLE, OVERLY SENSITIVE, WHINY ASS FUCK."

Emmett doesn't have the patience for this. He switches his stereo receiver back on, switches the output to the speakers and throws the volume way up. Blackalicious is still playing. He turns the bass knob all the way up in an effort to drown Myra out. But she has an inordinate power to speak above even the loudest music.

"SHE DOESN'T GIVE A DAMN ABOUT YOU. NO ONE
GIVES A DAMN ABOUT YOU. IF YOU DISAPPEARED
FROM THE FACE OF THE EARTH, NO ONE WOULD
NOTICE. YOUR FUNERAL, IF THEY EVEN BOTHERED
WITH ONE, WOULD BE THE MOST PATHETIC AFFAIR
IMAGINABLE. NO. ONE. GIVES. A. FUCK. ABOUT.
YOU."

Nope. Full of shit. Myra's wrong. Always wrong. Everyone
always says so, and everyone is always right. Emmett turns the
music down, not wanting to disturb his neighbors with his loud
music if he doesn't have to.

"OF COURSE IT'S TRUE. YOU KNOW THAT I ONLY
SPEAK THE TRUTH. I COME FROM THE DEEPEST
RECESSES OF YOU, THE WISEST PARTS OF YOU. IF I'M
SAYING IT, IT'S WHAT YOU KNOW IN THE CORE OF
YOUR BEING TO BE TRUE."

No, I'm diseased. I'm not well. I'm sick. I can't trust those
parts of myself, Emmett speaks silently back, collapsing onto
the floor with his back resting against the coffee table.

Myra continues to tell him all that he knows to be true: he's
pathetic, worthless, deserving of nothing, a pissant. He's better
off dead; it would have been better if he'd never been born,
because then his family wouldn't have to suffer him. Not even
his best friend gives a damn about him; she's more interested in
whatever is on her phone than in what he has to say and, really,
she's right—nothing he ever said was interesting or important
or worth listening to. Jayne was just being honest. She's his only

honest friend; everyone else is just too fucking polite to tell him how fucking pointless everything he says is.

Myra is always right. And, in the end, Emmett knows she's right. And he knows what's coming next—he looks at an object in his apartment, and Myra tells him how he could kill himself with it. Taking all the books and piling them in the middle of the room and setting them on fire. Removing the power supply from his server, drawing a bath, and then introducing the power supply to the water while it was turned on. She has this uncanny ability to figure out ways for him to kill himself. Strangely, she never suggests the knife he carries with him, and she'd stopped suggesting he overdose on his medication since he'd actually tried it a number of years ago; Dad stopping him just before he swallowed a possibly lethal dose of dextroamphetamine is why he owes Dad his life.

Emmett ends up reaching for his phone. He dials the number he knows so well and holds the phone up to his ear.

"Hey Emmett," Mom's voice sounds brightly through the receiver.

"Hey, Mom." His own voice was empty, full of despair.

"Not doing so well?"

"She's back. And she's telling me such awful things."

"She's a liar, honey. She doesn't speak the truth. Do we need to come get you?"

"I just want it to end. Just please make it end," Emmett pauses in his broken-up speech and says, "It won't end. Just make it stop, make it stop. I don't want to hear this anymore."

"Emmett, listen to me. Can you hear me?"

"Yeah."

"We're going to read some Psalms. Dad and I just need to get into the car so we can come get you. Would you like to pray the Lord's Prayer with me?"

"Yeah," Emmett manages. Empty, hollowed-out, but hopeful too. He has one hope: that Mom and Dad can come and make it stop. He's powerless; it had been everything he could do to dial these numbers, and now help is coming.

Mom starts: "Our Father in Heaven. Hallowed be your name," and then Emmett joins in, quietly, almost imperceptibly, and with all his courage: "Your kingdom come. Your will be done on Earth as it is in heaven. Give us today our daily bread. And forgive us our sins as we forgive those who sin against us. Lead us not into temptation, but deliver us from evil. For the kingdom, the power and the glory are yours now and forever. Amen."

Emmett feels better; he feels the hot, stinging promise of tears coming to his eyes—relief. Little Baby Kerrin comes over to him, kisses his face and lets him know that she's there for him. She settles down next to him on the floor and curls up into a ball. Emmett switches the phone in his hands so he can pet her reaffirming fur.

"Are you doing any better?"

Emmett nods. Silent.

"Emmett, are you there?"

"Yeah. I was nodding."

"Okay. Good. Dad and I are in the car and we'll be there in about forty minutes. Will you stay on the phone with me while we drive?"

"Yeah," he says, nodding again.

Mom reads him Bible passages, mostly from Psalms. Psalm 91 is among his favorite, and when she gets to it a few tears do flow, and it seems to him the only time he's ever cried in the past five years is when he's been scared-out-of-his-mind psychotic and Mom is reading the Bible. He has a tattoo on the base of his left thumb which reads Psalm 91:11. "For He will command His angels concerning you, to guard you in all of your ways."

He recites that part out loud when Mom gets to that verse, that verse being a great comfort to him. His life is one battle after another. He understands perhaps better than most the Bible's references to war … because that's what he does every day; he fights a war. He'd gotten the tattoo because he'd been haunted by a particular psychotic episode every night for weeks on end. He was still living at Mom and Dad's house then, and Mom would come into his room when he'd cry out in the middle of the night, terrified when those same insidious creatures tried to take him, and Mom would recite that passage to him. It had been such a comfort to him that he decided to get it tattooed someplace where he would see it all the time. After he'd gotten the tattoo, the psychosis had ended for a while.

But it reappeared, because psychosis, mental illness, is a fire that cannot be quenched. It only ever simmers, can only ever be reduced to smoldering coals. Mental illness is inevitable, as inevitable as the coming night. The smoldering is made fire, and all he can do is cling to the knowledge that he's protected—that regardless of where on his body those fingers make purchase, whether they tear organs out of his body or merely try to take him someplace unspeakable, he's protected, he can't be touched.

Forty minutes later, Dad parks their car in the parking lot outside the coffee shop. Mom stays in the car while Dad goes inside Emmett's apartment building. Emmett's feeling much better, but is still in a weakened state. Any little thing can bring Myra back again, and if that happens she will have her claws dug even deeper into him than she did the first time she showed up. It's best to take Emmett back to Aurora to be with Mom and Dad.

Dad comes in the building, walks down the hall, and gently knocks on the door.

"Come in," Emmett says, much too softly for Dad to hear

through the door. Dad creaks the door open and Kerrinpuppy greets him excitedly. Dad greets her more reservedly than he normally does, respecting the severity of the situation. Emmett says goodbye to Mom on the phone and gets to his feet. He hugs Dad more tightly than he had during their walk that day and goes over to get a tissue to blow his nose with.

"What do we need to take?" Dad asks.

"Oh, I don't know," Emmett says quietly. He always speaks softly when he's just gone through psychosis, his usual commanding voice replaced with something more private, more intimate.

"You'll need some clothes, and your pills, and stuff to do tomorrow before Mom takes you home."

"Okay," Emmett says, and looks about the apartment as though he were just seeing it for the first time. He goes into the closet and pulls out new underwear, socks, a tee shirt, and a button-up shirt. He stuffs these into a Vasari Oil Paint tote bag. Next, he gets the collection of books he's reading, as well as the latest issue of Maximum PC magazine and a National Geographic in case he needs something lighter. These also go into the tote bag.

He packs up his laptop, being sure to run the rsync scripts he's written to make sure the data on the laptop is up-to-date so he can do work in the morning. He places it in his black messenger bag along with a collection of file folders, his headphones, and the laptop's power adapter.

Dad is giving Little Baby Kerrin butt scratches. Emmett suggests he get Kerrinpuppy into her harness. Dad obliges.

Last thing he needs, the most important, is his pill case, which Mom had made him to fit the absurd amount of pill bottles he's accumulated. It's about the size of a hatbox and has a zipper that goes around almost the entire perimeter, so the top lays flat when open, exposing the inside completely.

He checks to make sure he has enough clozapine in case he needs to stay a few days—the pharmacy will only fill the clozapine when it gets his blood test results and, while he has a backup supply, it's his hardest-to-come-by drug and also one of the most essential; not having enough would mean bad things.

Little Baby Kerrin leads the way to the entrance and Emmett and Dad plod along, Emmett deep in thought about nothing in particular.

They reach the car and Emmett has Kerrinpuppy hop up into the back seat where she waits on the console for her grandpa to get into the car. Dad is putting Emmett's stuff in the trunk and Emmett has to wait, bent over into the car, holding Kerrinpuppy so she can give Dad a quick few kisses before settling down into her bed and getting clipped into her seatbelt.

They don't say much at first. Emmett feels good looking out the window, experiencing the world outside of his 350-square-feet of life. He thinks about Jayne: how she ignores him, how her phone seems more important than he is. He finds it interesting that he thinks more about the phone and less about the people she's inevitably using the phone to talk to. It's doubly insulting that it doesn't ever beep or vibrate; she just checks it obsessively—hovering over her phone like a hawk, always looking for the next message, ignoring him, her best friend, right in front of her, ignoring the person she supposedly loves and considers family. He's told her on multiple occasions how much it offends and even destabilizes him, how it makes him paranoid, and she just does it anyway. Then there was her depression. If there's anything he was good at, it's having a mental illness—she'd come to him for help and then completely ignored his advice to see a therapist. There's an underlying issue that needs to be addressed, and having three jobs is about the dumbest way to go about treating it Emmett can think of. Her posts on Facebook talk about how happy she is, but Emmett knows she isn't, he can sense it: there's something she isn't addressing, and he feels powerless to help her. But he also knows denial is just a phase in accepting life with a mental illness.

He knows there's nothing he can do except tell her how he'd come to recover, how he'd come to live at peace with his particular demons; by being tenacious, by refusing to surrender, by facing his demons head-on. By being brave. Please, Jayne, you have to be brave, he wants to plead with her. But it has to come from her ... no amount of pleading, begging, whining, or tough love will convince her otherwise; —it has to come from her.

Chapter Forty Two

"I've thought some more about my parents' house." Emmett says, sitting down.

"Oh yeah? What about it?" Lacey says.

"I think it's one of those 'rarity is the zest of life' things. Because I'm gone from their house, it's become a place of refuge, a place to relax. It's no longer a prison."

"I think that's a good point."

"I'm just worried that my own home will soon become a prison, that I won't be able to handle living there."

"What would need to happen for it to not be a prison?" Lacey says.

"About the only thing I can think of is to live in a larger place—a place with more than one room. But that's not going to happen any time soon. Not with the way rent in Denver has been headed."

After they get home, Emmett finds himself in Mom and Dad's backyard. It feels good to be there; he enjoys the cool autumn evenings in their backyard, mostly because their backyard is Kerrinpuppy's favorite place in the whole wide world. Plenty of space to run around and replete with squirrels and bunnies and birds to chase out of the yard. Occasionally the neighbors' dogs come out and she'll bark at them and tell them everything she's been up to since the last time she's seen them—the butts she's sniffed, the places she's walked, the new territory she's marked, the cheese she's eaten. There's much excitement to be had in the dog world; all of it glorious, all of it seeming to be good news. Emmett wishes he were a dog.

Thoughts of Jayne and how much he loathes her attachment to her phone, her attachment to people other than him.

A general dislike of the always-on, always-connected nature of his generation is starting to take root. When he pictures her in his head, he always sees the top of her head bent down over the tiny screen, both hands poised on the screen to tap out replies to whomever it is who's more important than he is. Maybe she has a good reason for always talking to someone else, and maybe she does it to everyone else. But he thinks he can expect a certain amount of decorum out of her; not this, always-on-her-phone-never-quite-participating-in-reality version of Jayne who's been coming out to play lately.

Jayne is driving him crazy. He remembers sitting on this very porch with Dad having two very different kinds of conversations with him. Sometimes he would be ranting about how Jayne is his best friend and how one really ought to be with their best friend, that he ought to declare his love for her or otherwise bide his time and wait for her to break up with Rob. And other times he'd be almost whining about her: criticizing her for petty things like her expensive fleece jacket that doesn't do a good enough job of keeping her warm so she could keep him company while he smokes during the winter. Or the more legitimate complaints like when she invites him over for dinner and then says she's too tired and has to go to bed as soon as there's a lull in post-dinner conversation or else that she has to go to the grocery store, which Emmett suspects she does knowing he can't go along, since grocery stores are such strong triggers for him.

Back and forth Emmett has gone, never finding a resting place for his feelings toward Jayne. It was classic bipolar behavior and Emmett is kind of mad Dad hadn't picked up on it. But Emmett has a way of making his illness seem so reasonable and well thought out, and sometimes what he thinks is crazy is actually just perfectly normal. Because normal is oftentimes crazy, too.

Today could have been bad, Emmett thinks on his third cigarette, the sun nearly set. He'll be seeing Lacey soon; not soon enough, but soon—something needs to be done. Soon. Soon.

Chapter Forty Three

◇◇

Emmett sits across from Lacey in the same chair he's sat in he-doesn't-know-how-many times. She's looking at him like she's looked at him so often in the past: a mixture of tenderness and perhaps pity. He doesn't want to use the word "pity" because it suggests he's perhaps pathetic. But maybe he is, and that's exactly what the look means. He sits there, his head cocked to one side, Lacey sitting across from him with an encouraging smile that beckons him to say more, that smile that wants to know what it is that's going through that head of his.

"It gets lonely up there, doesn't it?" *she finally says.*

"Up there in my head you mean?"

"Yeah."

"I suppose so. I think it gets lonely just about anywhere. I suppose I just wish that there were someone out there who understood. But right now I'd settle for someone who at least wanted to understand, so ... " *Emmett's voice trailing off.*

"You don't think Jayne is that person?"

Emmett looks down at Kerrinpuppy who's sleeping so comfortably in his lap, oblivious to the conversation going on around her; he's jealous of her ability to just sleep through these appointments. "No, not at all, not in the slightest. I tried telling her about the worsening psychotic episodes and she didn't seem the least bit interested in them—said something along the lines of "that must suck" and then went on with that stupid phone of hers."

"What did you want her to say?"

"I'm not really sure. I never really have it planned out what I want people to say. People can say what they want to say. But to say nothing? To just pick up your phone and tap away at it? Bull. Shit. She couldn't care less. That freaking phone of hers," *Emmett says.*

Emmett looks up off the spot on the floor where he was staring and his eyes find Lacey's; he immediately goes back to staring at the same spot on the floor.

"For the past several months I've been hearing you talking about Jayne," *Lacey begins, speaking slowly, softly.* "Sometimes it's good stuff and other times it's *not so good stuff. More and more, recently, it's talking about how crummy of a friend she's being. I think it's about time you meet her where she's at."*

"Meet her where's she's at?"

"Yes."

"So, what do you mean?"

"You've been putting so much time and energy into being a good friend to her, putting so much effort into your friendship, that it might just be time to let her take the lead, let her have control for a little while to see what happens."

"So … have her contact me to hang out kind of thing?"

Lacey nods, "Mmhmm."

"What do I tell her?" Emmett asks.

"Don't tell her anything. Just wait."

"Sounds simple enough."

◇◇◇

The air is cool as Emmett sits on the grass outside of Lacey's office and rolls himself a cigarette. He puts his earphones in and selects some music—a mix that he'd made Jayne a long time ago, before she'd moved to California. It starts out with All Apologies by Nirvana before transitioning to Over Here, Over There by Dr. Dog … all in all, a mix with a lot of good transitions, a good walking mix. He lights his cigarette, puts his iPod in the pocket of his jean jacket, calls for Little Baby Kerrin to follow him on her leash, and heads down the street toward Logan.

He huffs and puffs up the hill near the Governor's Mansion, thinking about all the homeless people at Governor's Park not even a block away. Last fall he'd kept track of how the Broncos had been doing so he could have short conversations with a homeless man who was always at the park. The man had said the games were the only thing he had to look forward to. Emmett had brought him extra batteries for his radio. But then the Broncos went to the Super Bowl and royally screwed it up and

Emmett had never seen the homeless man again.

It's cool enough to have to wear a jacket, but warm enough that he still comes home sweaty. Such is the paradox of being poikilothermic during fall in Colorado. Or perhaps it's the extra pounds he's gained that cause him to sweat so much. Either way, it's a little ridiculous. He goes into the bathroom and washes his face with a cool washcloth and then heads outside to smoke a cigarette with Little Baby Kerrin.

Into the coffee shop for an iced latte, LBK patiently waiting by the benches outside. Just the kind of thing to cool him off today. Feeling a little embarrassed for still being covered in sweat despite the cooler temperature outside. Thankfully the barista doesn't say anything.

Back on the stoop with his iced latte and Little Baby Kerrin, Emmett rolls another cigarette, smokes half of it, and then heads back inside his apartment.

Sitting in his chair waiting for his phone to ring-ding with a text from Jayne proves to be pretty boring, though, so he retires to goofing off on his computer, reminding himself that it might be a while before Jayne even thinks to text him. Emmett thinks about the collective unconscious and how people often have the same thoughts at the same time.

Has he really been investing as much into the relationship as Lacey had suggested? Is he really a good friend to Jayne? Doubt is a perennial entity in his life. He seems so bound to the unconscious, acting automatically, from his gut, where logic and language are largely abandoned—Jayne might just see their relationship in a very different way. It occurs to Emmett that she might be purposefully pushing him away, trying to give him little hints that she doesn't want to be friends anymore. And his stubborn self just keeps wanting to hang out with her and her polite self is too nice to say no.

Chapter Forty Four

◇◇

"Fear is a powerful motivator," Emmett tells Lacey.

"What do you mean?"

"A human's most basic instinct is the fight or flight response, always, or almost always, brought on by fear. I think people make some of the most powerful decisions of their lives under the influence of fear," Emmett says.

"Are you speaking about murderers?"

"Yeah. But also people like me. I got ECT because I was afraid. I was afraid of dying. And I was afraid of going to hell if I killed myself. ECT flavors everything I do in my life these days—it's almost like my mental illness itself in how many aspects of my life it's touched."

"But not everything is fight or flight. You've come a long way," Lacey reminds him.

"Certainly not, but ECT seems to loom over a possible future, and I want to do everything I can in order to avoid that future."

"And that's a totally valid fear," Lacey says.

◇◇

Lacey is right; Jayne doesn't text right away. It takes a few days. A few days in which Emmett has to call Mom and Dad at night—not to have them take him back to Aurora, but just to chat so he has some human contact.

It's probably refreshing for them to have Emmett call and it not be a dire, life-or-death emergency where every minute counts and they don't know who or what they'll find when they arrive at his place. Just an Emmett who's a bit bummed because he hasn't been talking to anyone all day.

Emmett tries texting other friends too, but they don't have

the rapidity of Jayne, the immediate response Jayne has always provided. And Emmett misses this. She may have been a terrible person to hang out with face-to-face, but she was a great texting buddy. Maybe he could negotiate the terms of their friendship such that they would just text each other, never meet face-to-face, their only contact being through their phones.

No, that would probably be terrible if Emmett were to go through another anti-technology phase.

Shortly before ECT, Emmett had wanted to get rid of all of his computers. He was working at a computer repair shop at the time and he saw them as the root of all evil, a crutch on which people depended too much for entertainment and information and work, the fulcrum on which their lives pivoted and, as such, he was going to get rid of all of his computers because he wasn't going to be dependent on anything. He would have no fulcrums.

He'd started selling off his computers and got as far as selling his black MacBook (something he still regretted to this day) before Dad offered to take his computers from him, store them so Emmett didn't have to look at them. Emmett agreed, letting Lauren borrow his gaming computer with the enormous (at the time) twenty-four-inch monitor so she could do school work on it. So Emmett lived in an apartment where he only had his iMac to watch movies on.

He would ultimately try to get rid of that too and live in his apartment with nothing to do but read, listen to music, and paint—the only things he thought were worth doing, totally ignoring the fact that it was important to relax and blow off steam, and that one didn't have to be working all the time. Looking back on it, Emmett sees an immature version of himself with a mental illness, completely unaware of how to deal with the realities of schizoaffective disorder. But he also recognizes the same trends within himself even now. It wasn't that much of stretch for him to give up something completely because he saw perceived dangers in it, because he saw it as a threat to him being productive—was he doing the same thing with his gaming machine by relegating it to Mom and Dad's house, only playing on the weekends? "The work week is for work; all I can do is work, work, work!" Wasn't he just chasing after that Spartan lifestyle again under the guise of saying games are a danger to him for their tendency to dissociate him? Wasn't he just chasing this kind of military discipline whose success was measured in productivity? How did he measure productivity anyway?

It's funny how we repeat the same patterns over and over again in our lives, Emmett muses; how our subconscious can take the helm without our realizing it. How much useless second-guessing can occur if we let it happen. The issue of the gaming machine is a curious one: on the one hand, it makes sense that Emmett ought to have it at Mom and Dad's house, especially if playing too much makes him dissociate. Playing video games is such a fun thing for him to do, such a good way for him to unwind; it even helps with cognition and memory. But it's also a dangerous tool; if he isn't very deliberate about taking a break every hour (instead of the usual every two hours), he tends to dissociate. Having his gaming machine at Mom and Dad's house means he can more easily regulate the amount of time he spends playing, plus he can get help if he accidentally does spend too much time playing. On the other hand, couldn't the whole Spartan lifestyle argument also be at least part of the truth of why he doesn't keep his gaming machine at home, if only a small part of it?

Emmett recognizes within himself the desire to live in extremes, which makes sense given that the "affective" part of schizoaffective disorder refers to having bipolar disorder. The very nature of bipolar disorder is to live, to one degree or another, in extremes. While most of the time he felt relatively calm, relatively at peace, there was a time of day, usually in the evening when the pills were wearing off and he just didn't have the energy to sustain the ruse anymore, that he was beside himself, and this was a dangerous time. A half-hour to an hour-long window where the world seemed to teeter on the edge of destruction, as though Atlas himself were about to heave his heavy load off of his shoulders.

This is the state of mind that produces the Spartan thoughts—not thoughts about how to be more Spartan but worry over being too Spartan. Everything is a precarious balance, like those cartoon movies featuring a man riding a unicycle while balancing spinning plates on the ends of sticks: one misguided move and the whole operation comes crashing down. Plates have fallen off on numerous occasions, but he was well-practiced at getting new plates spinning; he was even getting good at seeing when plates were about to fall and correcting them, at getting them spinning properly again.

ECT, which had seen every plate come crashing down in spectacular fashion, meant Emmett had had to start completely fresh, almost as though he'd been reborn. He'd forgotten almost everything: how to paint, how to fix computers, even how to read. Dad had had to read to him every night before bed like he was a little kid because he hadn't been able to read himself. He could understand the individual words—he could understand the notes Mom left him in the morning, the notes that said *Coffee! Text me when you get up! <3 Mom.* He'd been able to read and understand text messages and the IM conversations he had on Facebook ... but not books. He just couldn't make sense of the more complicated arguments made unless he had the context of someone tailoring their statements with him in mind. So they'd read a Beatles book and had gone through all of Douglas Adams's Hitchhiker's Guide to the Galaxy series and a number of other books over the course of several months before Emmett finally had the confidence and capacity to read on his own.

After ECT, he'd started out sleeping in Mom and Dad's bathroom—too afraid to sleep on his own or in his own bed. Too afraid of the monsters that would get him. They hadn't yet appeared to him or made their presence known; they were more an ominous threat, more just him being aware of their existence and their intentions rather than them actually acting on those threats. It'd been the start of a life of terror, of torture at the hands of his infinitely creative mind. He went to bed feeling as though he were walking to death's very doorstep.

Without knowing what it was that brought him to ECT in the first place, it was hard not to blame ECT for all of his problems, for his life falling apart. But he knew he needed to shift his attitude toward thinking, toward knowing, that ECT was the start of him putting his life back together again. Dr. Romero had called his march toward completing suicide an existential imperative—a kind of crossroads where he either chose ECT and life or else chose his eventual death. It seemed like an obvious choice. Though sometimes, especially when he was in the pit of the black overwhelming nothingness at having to start over fresh with his life, it didn't seem like it was such an obvious choice after all; it seemed like he'd chosen a different kind of death.

He'd slowly rebuilt his life. He'd gotten new friends; he'd met Marta Lee; he relearned how to draw and paint and tried to do it the right way, fixing bad habits he knew he'd gotten into because no one had taught him how to draw in the first place. His art was much different this time around: he chose a neutral palette, not so many bright colors. The figures he painted were darker, more foreboding, less whimsical. He painted the figures that haunted him, that followed him around wherever he went, though he wasn't quite conscious of their existence at the time.

He'd moved out of his parents' bathroom, into his studio/bedroom, sleeping on the floor on a camping pad Mom had bought on Amazon so his back wouldn't hurt so much. He'd started going to Tag and Rag Church again. He was out of the house more and more, was less isolated, and was around people his own age who shared his own beliefs. But with these changes came more frequent psychosis, the near-constant reminder of how different he was from his peers and having to be picked up by Mom and Dad, who were gracious enough to park a few blocks away, by ten o'clock, waiting in the car with a bottle of water and a cup of pills so he could take them as soon as he got in so he wouldn't be off schedule.

Emmett was given a taste of hope, given a taste of success while taking a math class during the summer semester, getting a ninety-eight percent, the highest of anyone else in the class. It was the first time he'd ever gotten the highest grade in a class that he could remember, especially a math class. He'd tried not to fool himself—told himself that it'd been the only class he was taking, that it was math he'd done in high school so it was just a refresher, that it didn't predict a future of success; but he couldn't help his optimism. So he looked forward to getting his PhD in computer science, dreamed of the house he would buy, how he would show them all, how he would lead a successful life despite his severe illness, how ECT would have been worth it, how the pain of putting the pieces of his life back together again would have been worth the pain and suffering and embarrassment. It was essential to have that hope.

But God had other plans for Emmett. He got to his first computer science class and didn't even make it to the midterm before old problems started popping back up. The textbook didn't make sense, the programs he wrote didn't work, he didn't understand a lick of what he was doing, he started getting psychotic every night; the same signs of sanity-killing-stress appeared. And Dr. Bogsdaughter recognized the early signs of what had brought him to ECT in the first place and told him to drop the class and apply for SSDI. Lacey told him the exact same thing.

No more school. No more PhD. You'll have to show them

some other way. You'll have to do something else with your life. You'll have to tear this structure down and start fresh yet again.

It's not so bad, it's not even half-built, you haven't even finished the foundation, he'd told himself. You can build a new one, it'll come to you. Mom told him to be patient. "God's got a plan," she said over and over and over again. Each time he'd come to her with a new crisis she repeated the mantra, a mantra he wouldn't adopt as his own until years later when he finally realized the wisdom of the statement.

Because God really does have a plan.

He'd applied for SSDI and all he could think to do was to get out of Aurora, the place that held him down ... that place of captivity.

And now so many things were falling into place and Jayne was maybe going to fall out of place and he had no idea who was going to take her place.

Chapter Forty Five

"Jayne and I had a conversation a while ago about how I'm a Ludditic nerd," Emmett says.

"Ludditic nerd?"

"Yeah, from Luddite—someone who's opposed to new technology."

"I can see how you'd describe yourself as that, you're very old school." Lacey says.

"Thank you," Emmett says, pitching his voice higher. *"Anyways. I wonder if that's part of the reason why she frustrates me so much."*

"Because your Ludditic tendencies make you resent the technology she's using?"

"Exactly. Though it doesn't quite fit. I'm just as much a fan of my phone as she is—the only difference is that I'm not glued to it, ignoring the people actually in front of me, while I'm using it. I usually use it out on the stoop when there's nothing else to do." Emmett says.

"Interesting. Do you think this is triggering anything for you at all?" Lacey says.

"You mean like a hardcore rebellion against technology?"

"Yeah," Lacey says.

"Shit. I don't know. I hope not. I think I panicked my poor Dad when I went through that phase, and not only because I sold off a lot of nice hardware for much cheaper than I should have."

To which Lacey can just smile, enjoying Emmett's sense of humor in the face of his illness.

E mmett sits at his drafting table, his little black notebook open flat before him—the notebook itself in rather rough condition. It's spent every day of the past few months in his back pocket, bending and half-submitting, half-resisting his sitting in various chairs in all the places he'd taken it, the paper with grooves and hills in it.

He has a beat going, talking about how maybe he was suffering because he was loyal to a fault.

Loyalty is such an interesting concept, he writes. *The notion that we ought to stick around merely because we've stuck around in the past, so we ought to continue sticking around. What is the nature of loyalty anyway?*

Lacey always grows excited when the philosopher in him comes out; she seems to take it as a sign he's getting back to his old self. He writes about Kerrinpuppy and her loyalty to him, how she seems to exist to do nothing else but please him.

… but that's a dog's loyalty … embedded in her DNA, it's a trait she's been bred for. I'm loyal to Jayne because I've assumed she's always been there for me. That she always would be there for me. But she hasn't been. Lauren left me in January, halfway through ECT, and Jayne says she never visited because Lauren was being territorial, she wouldn't let anyone near me. What about after? February? March? April? I'm loyal for no reason. I'm loyal to vacuous words. Jayne has no substance. Soldiers are loyal to their country because their country means something to them. Kerrin is loyal to me because I have substance, because I mean something to her. What does Jayne mean to me? I feel as though she's largely a stranger, and maybe I'm a stranger to her. I really get offended when she tells me I haven't, we haven't, changed in the ten years we've known each other—because I know I've changed an awful lot. I'm not the same kid I was in high school; going through the things I've gone through, you can't help but change. ECT changed me in a fundamental, substantial way, and I go back—

And then his phone next to him, so wonderfully and contentedly silent a moment before it gives a jerking buzz and lets out a ring-ding.

He has a text message. It's Jayne.

His blood heats just seeing her name pop up on the screen as he glances at it. Just when he's getting to the good part in his little essay, trying to process his thoughts about her. His thoughts had been capitulating into something, something—a conclusion, and it had all vanished with the little ring-ding of his phone. And now all he can do is look at the screen and see her name and the first few words of her message to him.

It's been a few days since he's last talked to her. It'd been a tough first day; he seemed to be just waiting for his phone to go off, willing it to give its ring-ding like a bicycle bell, letting him know he had a text message. And then he'd grown used to his phone's relative unobtrusiveness, though seeing her presence on social media had pained him. A big part of him had been wishing for her to text him, for her to ask him to hang out, an unexpected coffee date, an impromptu dinner invitation; but the part of him that had come to relish the silence was growing.

He picks the phone up. Jayne doesn't want to get coffee, isn't inviting him over for dinner, isn't apologizing or wondering if he's doing okay, like he once asked her to, to check in on him every day. She's starting a blog, an online magazine of sorts, and she wants him to do the illustrations. "And of course I thought of you," she says. Of course. Of course. What?

How many times has he explained to her that he's a fine artist? Not a fucking illustrator. He doesn't make art at the behest of someone who simply lacked the skills. He isn't a trained monkey. He's an artist.

Emmett knows that if he responds now, their relationship will probably be over; —it would be a long-winded lecture on just that—he's an artist and not an illustrator, someone who makes art and not advertisements.

Off the stool, where his thoughts had been capitulating into something resembling a conclusion, and onto the couch, Kerrinpuppy perking up from her bed upon detecting his presence on the couch. She gets to her feet and stretches, hops up on the couch, and snuggles down beside him.

Three days without a text message and this is how she contacts me? To see if I'll do trained monkey work? She knows very well that I'm terrible at that kind of work. I'll make whatever image I want, and if they want changes they're out of luck.

Emmett knows nothing of Photoshop; if they want anything changed he'll have to make the image all over again, a time-consuming process and more a waste of his time than anything. Reason upon reason piles up in his head as to why it's very stupid for her to ask him to do these illustrations in the first place.

He stays seated on the couch for a long time, trying to calm himself down to the point where he feels he can respond to her text without yelling at her.

Finally, he gets up, Kerrinpuppy looking up from her curled up little ball, perhaps a little hurt that he's ended their cuddle session to go and get his phone. He knows how she feels.

He composes a message. Not saying no, but also not saying yes. He asks for more information. Perhaps she just wants to use the animal drawings he's already done. He asks what sizes she needs, how many she needs, what types of scenes—all of the practical questions a professional artist might ask. He channels Dad; best to get all of the information before making a decision.

And he waits for a response.

Chapter Forty Six

◇◇

"It's a shame, in a way, I suppose," Emmett says.

"About Jayne?" Lacey says.

"Yeah, or maybe the whole situation. The way we were holding onto each other for perhaps no apparent reason."

"'No apparent reason?'" Lacey says back at him.

"I dunno. Maybe I'm just one of those people who needs to see purpose in my friendships. Like a 'why are you in my life?' kind of thing."

"Do your other friendships have purpose?"

"This is where you enter tricky territory. Because of course they have a reason—any number of reasons which might be expressed at different times on different days. To speak the reason is to betray the friendship."

"I'm not sure I agree."

"I'm not really sure I do either. I just don't like the idea of saying to one of my friends, 'this is the reason we're friends and without that reason we wouldn't be friends.' But that's exactly what happened with me and Jayne."

◇◇

Jayne never texts back. Would never text back. That's the last Emmett will hear from her.

"What a crummy way to end a friendship," Emmett says when he admits to Marta Lee that he hasn't talked to Jayne in a month and doesn't think they're friends anymore.

"No kidding, I'm sorry."

"So it goes," Emmett says, twisting his body to display his knuckle tattoos for ML to see.

She laughs. "But I'm not too surprised."

"Yeah?"

"From what you told me, she goes through a lot of friends."

Emmett thinks on it for a bit. "You know, you're right. I just thought that things were different with us. That she wouldn't just give up like that after ten years."

"Yeah … " Marta Lee says, letting the word trail off.

"But you're right. Thinking back to what I can remember of our friendship … there was, like, this constant parade of other friends. People who would stick around for a little while and then disappear. I'd meet them once, twice if I was lucky, and then I'd ask about them and she'd say something about how they were mentally unhinged or did something not even particularly awful but annoying and they weren't friends anymore. I just never put two and two together because I'm no good at math in my head."

Marta Lee laughs again. "Gotta put that down on paper."

"Tell me about it. Maybe I learned a lesson, though."

"What's that?"

"I remember Lauren telling me one time that I ought not tell her I love her all the time, because it cheapened the word. I thought it kind of offensive because I felt as though I demonstrated the love, too. But I think with Jayne it was one of those instances where she didn't mean what she said—she was always saying stuff like 'we're going to grow old together' and 'you're my best friend' and 'I love you' and so on, and I believed it. Because I take people at their word. Maybe I ought to be a little more discerning about looking at people's actions more than what they say."

"Yep," and Marta Lee leaves it at that.

They sit in silence for a few minutes, Emmett smoking and looking out at the street.

"So tell me about this Owen guy," Emmett finally says. Marta Lee has recently met a guy whom a girl at Tag and Rag had set her up with. The boyfriends Marta Lee's had since he's known her haven't been the greatest, always so peculiar. But this Owen guy seems like he might actually be a decent person.

"Oh, he's kinda weird. But, like a good weird," Marta Lee says, smiling. "He actually asked me if he could kiss me."

"Sounds like something I would do, actually. All those years spent in anarchist circles talking about getting consent makes a guy really wary of just pushing himself on a girl he's attracted to. He's not an anarcho punk like what's-his-face who moved to Fiji, is he?"

"Oh no, no. Not at all. He's actually kind of nerdy. Really sweet. When he found out that I don't like ice in my water, he proceeded to take his spoon and scoop out all of the ice from my water glass."

"That's pretty adorable actually, I think I kind of like him. What kind of music does he like?"

"I'm not sure yet," Marta Lee admits.

"It's pretty important," and Emmett pauses. "Actually, it's only really important to me. And you've got such terrible taste in music that as long as he's not into something unbearable like the last guy, I think y'all will get along."

Marta Lee gives him a look.

"I'm serious! I've always been honest with you, and at least I haven't let it get in the way of our friendship," Emmett defensively jokes. "Some people just have bad taste in music. My sister likes the Jonas Brothers and I love her to pieces. I figure if I can get around a person's—i.e., your—," Emmett says, flashing her his best charming grin, "poor taste in music and still ride in the car with them for an hour and a half to go to Manitou Springs, then they must be pretty dear to my heart."

"Emmett," says Marta Lee, dead serious.

"Marta Lee," Emmett says, mimicking the tone.

"You brought along music."

"Oh yeah," Emmett's entire argument deflated. "But!" with refreshed gusto, "your CD player didn't work, so we had to listen to your radio stations anyways."

"Still doesn't count."

"Yeah, but … "

"Uh-uh."

"But—"

"Uh-uh."

"Okay," and Emmett hangs his head in mock shame. "Guess I'm just a lousy friend."

"Oh you're not," Marta Lee says, her Midwestern accent showing through.

"So when do I get to meet this Owen?"

"Whenever you like. He likes The Walking Dead too, so maybe he and I could come over and we could all watch."

"Hmmm, maybe. I was thinking about that and it kind of puts me in a vulnerable position. Not sure if I want to do that upon first meeting a person. I think that might have been a mistake with the last one."

"So maybe someplace more neutral?"

"Well we can still meet at my place. Just no promise of The Walking Dead…just in case I'm not feeling up to it. It's just a little awkward without him knowing about me, ya know? Unless, did you already tell him about me?"

"I did, and he actually works at a children's home for kids with mental health issues," Marta Lee says.

"Ah! I think you told me that. Sorry, that whole memory thing again."

"No worries."

Marta Lee and Emmett head back inside after Emmett finishes his second cigarette. Kerrinpuppy greets them at the door and, being a polite dog, greets Marta Lee first before greeting Emmett. Emmett is old news, she sees him all the time. Marta Lee is a treat and Kerrinpuppy absolutely adores her.

Emmett remembers when Kerrinpuppy first met Marta Lee. He'd only had her for about a week and a half, maybe two weeks, so she wasn't quite adjusted to living with Emmett. She also hadn't met any of Emmett's friends yet. Marta Lee had made the typical playing-motion that one makes with dogs, a short pounce on the ground with legs bent and arms extended and a triumphant "ha!" and Kerrinpuppy had started running all over Mom and Dad's house, like she'd lost her mind. Kerrinpuppy stayed out of the room where they were talking and would periodically come in to bark at Marta Lee before running off again. By the time she came back for a second visit, Kerrinpuppy was in deep puppy-love with Marta Lee and smothered her with attention, licking her all over her face until Emmett finally had to tell her to get down so Marta Lee could have some room to breathe.

Kerrinpuppy adores, just loves all of Emmett's friends to death. With the possible exception of Jayne. Months later, as he thought back to how his dog had interacted with Jayne, he remembers that his dog hadn't been particularly fond of her. She would go up to give a polite greeting to Jayne, but it wouldn't be the kind of greeting where Emmett would have to yell at her not to jump, but just a polite greeting to acknowledge that she was there. Maybe it was telling, maybe Emmett should put more stock in Kerrinpuppy's reactions to people. He remembered a picture from Pinterest that said something along the lines of: *If our dogs don't like you, chances are we won't either.* Emmett found the statement a little standoffish and rude, but there was probably some truth to it. Dogs can tell the good ones from the bad ones.

Saying goodbye to Marta Lee, Emmett realizes that the lack of Jayne in his life has been an overall improvement. He never finishes the essay he'd been writing when Jayne texted him the question that seems to have ended their friendship. He couldn't go back and finish it if his life depended on it—the thought train has left the station for good. But the essay doesn't much matter anymore.

What is the nature of loyalty? As usual he sought answers in his thesaurus. Language can reveal so much about the nature of questions, particularly when that question rests on a single word.

Loyalty: Fealty, faithfulness.

The latter sounds a lot like marriage and the former sounds a lot like the feudal system of government, like someone pledging to support King Joffrey in Game of Thrones, an obligatory gamble. It doesn't matter how much you hate the king or mistrust the king, how evil the king is, or how big of a boob the king is: you must swear fealty or risk your life. The king doesn't put up with people who don't support him; he chops off their heads.

So does loyalty stand at the cusp of these two? Between sacred oath and obligatory political gamble? Perhaps. Or maybe I'm overthinking it, Emmett thinks. He sits down on the stoop, smoking the cigarette he rolled while walking Marta Lee to her car. His loyalty to Jayne had carried with it the dangers of his mental health regressing, the steady wearing away of his defenses until finally the careful rebuilding of his life came toppling down. Or maybe that's just a slippery slope argument, the kind of postulate that gets more and more outlandish, a fool's argument because pretty soon you're predicting nuclear holocaust and the end of the world. But then again, the one time the slippery slope argument applies is with mental illness—the first electrical hum always begets psychosis which always begets something worse if not treated. Mental illness never gets better on its own; it only ever gets worse.

Did Lacey catch something before it got too big? Was his loyalty to Jayne going to tear his life apart? Was his loyalty to her a part of a slippery slope? The slope is just slippery. It's not inevitable that things fall apart, it's not a given that you're going to fall down—just highly likely. Loyalty to the wrong person can be dangerous. Emmett sometimes calls his illness the perfect friend filter, and Jayne has just been filtered out. Perhaps because she just couldn't take it anymore. Or perhaps because Lacey had orchestrated it in a way, because she knew if Emmett stopped making an effort, so would Jayne, and it would be for the best. Emmett was getting sick every single time he hung out with her. Psychosis begets more psychosis, and if that cycle happens long enough it begets something much worse.

He's looking at his phone now, looking at Jayne posting about how happy she is, how perfect her life is. It's making him sick. Not quite literally, he supposes. He can't bear the thought of unfriending her, but he can't bear the thought of seeing her posts, so he deletes the app from his phone. First Facebook, then Twitter, then Instagram.

We treat them as surrogate realities, Emmett thought, as replacements for the world in front of us, and he is sick of it. He needs things that ground him; he needs real conversations. He needs relationships, friendships with substance. He figures he won't be missing out on very much—memes and cat videos, inane and pointless political rants from people who won't take it any further than Facebook. He'll look at the people passing in front of his stoop from now on, thank you.

So much of his experience with schizoaffective disorder has been his brain attempting to remove him from reality—why should he help his brain do that? Dr. Bogsdaughter and Lacey talk to him about the importance of making sure he remains grounded, and social media always leaves him floating three feet off the floor. Seeing Jayne post about how happy she is, knowing, just knowing she isn't (how could she be?), makes him finally realize social media allows us to present only what we want to present. He does the exact same thing: he never mentions his mental illness, never once posted when he wasn't feeling well. He's sure most people have no clue. Where's the humanity in that? What's the point in interacting with people if you aren't vulnerable on occasion? If you aren't yourself?

Emmett wants ties that bind, not ties that deceive—he wants love and support and companionship, he wants mutual affection. Not the mere appearance of such. So he pockets his phone and observes his neighborhood for perhaps the first time.

Chapter Forty Seven

"You know," Emmett says, his voice half an octave higher than usual. "I think Jayne made me human again."

"How do you mean?" Lacey asks.

Emmett sits in silence for a few moments, collecting his thoughts. "I think it's because she got me thinking about love again. She was the first non-family-member to tell me she loved me after ECT. So, from a certain point of view, she was the first."

"You don't remember Lauren ever telling you she loved you?"

"No. Not directly. I don't remember much of anything prior to ECT. Not in the sense of them being memories. I know that such and such a thing happened to me, but those 'memories' feel like they happened to someone else.

"Anyways," Emmett continues. "I don't think I ever thought about love prior to Jayne's declaration. Maybe it messed with me, maybe it tarnished things because I couldn't hack it." Emmett pauses to collect his thoughts again. "But love is the essential human emotion. I feel like maybe I was just going through the motions, an automaton, prior to Jayne reminding me it exists."

"There's something you need to honor in that," Lacey says.

"Absolutely. Even though it fell apart. It's like … she helped me turn into a person again."

Emmett has done this he-doesn't-know-how-many times before, but this is the first time he's done it in his own apartment. Sitting across from someone, telling them his life's story with mental illness as they take notes and ask pointed questions for clarification. He isn't quite sick of telling the story yet, but it's getting a little old, a well-worn path in his head, as he tells Owen about the troubles he'd had in high school, the drugs he'd abused early on in college, the day he'd been diagnosed, the early years ignoring his illness, his engagement to Lauren, the pill rebellions, ECT, the whole story: symptoms, psychotic episodes, his semi-abusive roommate, all the way up until the present.

Owen is in school to become a psychologist and is writing a paper on schizoaffective disorder, and with the paper comes needing to act like he has schizoaffective disorder—coming up with a narrative and list of symptoms so that another student can practice diagnosing him with the illness. Emmett wishes that he could be there to see what the other students think Owen has. He's letting Owen borrow his sketchbook—his psychosis journal, the one where he draws his especially bad episodes to document them. He'd had plans that it'd ultimately become a graphic novel, but that particular plan had kind of fallen apart as he'd been overwhelmed with the sheer number of psychotic episodes he was having. Which ones to draw? Which ones to immortalize? The drawings took so long to do and the episodes just kept coming such that he couldn't keep up with the drawing, so he'd just stopped with the project altogether.

Emmett hopes that Owen will be the best-prepared person in the class; it'd been especially endearing to him that Owen had jumped so quickly at picking schizoaffective disorder so as to make sure that he did it justice, so as to make sure it was done right.

Marta Lee was right; Emmett has taken an immediate liking to Owen. It seems like they've known each other for a long time, even though it's only been two or three months since they'd first met. They both have an affinity for video games, and they both share a quick wit, their senses of humor similarly leaning toward the absurd; Emmett can see a lot of himself in Owen. They'd hardly met each other when they'd begun jabbering on about the most inane, most ridiculous things—like how Emmett would start a business wherein he would airdrop a sperm whale anywhere in the world within six hours were he to suddenly find himself a billionaire. Owen hadn't batted an eye, hadn't called him weird, had instead embraced the idea and made it better. Emmett wouldn't have normally let his weirdness show through with anyone except Dad, but with Owen he felt comfortable, almost immediately showing this weirder, truer side of himself.

Whereas previous boyfriends of Marta Lee's had been clingy or aloof, Owen was appropriately affectionate, exactingly endearing; he held her hand but not in a desperate fashion. He seemed comfortable with Marta Lee being good friends with Emmett, something that previous boyfriends hadn't been too comfortable with (and Emmett always remembered with a particular smirk one of Marta Lee's boyfriends who'd just shook his hand, looking deadpan into his eyes but not offering up his own name or any kind of indication that he was meeting a fellow human being who also happened to be goofing his way around planet Earth).

It was one of his favorite quotes from Vonnegut, that he was just goofing around like everyone else in Indiana and all of a sudden "stuff came gushing out"—he had no control over it, it just came out. It was the kind of image of the artist that Emmett most easily identified with: you don't choose it, it chooses you. You're simply the medium by which the art bursts forth into the world.

Emmett's relationship with Owen is in blindingly stark contrast to his relationship with Jayne, where they'd been so cynical, so miscreant, so nearly-bitter about things. Emmett now feels so much more himself.

Maybe that's the key differentiation to avoiding this theme of unhappy endings in his life. Doing an occasional or perhaps scheduled audit of how much he feels like himself around the people in his life.

"Emmett? You with me, buddy?"

"Yeah, sorry. Just went off on a thought tangent," Emmett says.

"No worries. Just thought I'd lost you there for a minute. Doin' all right?"

"Yeah, I think I just need some coffee. Would you like some?"

Owen rubs the tops of his thighs with his hands. "Yeah, that'd be great."

Emmett gets up and heads into the tiny closet excuse of a kitchen. He puts water in his electric kettle and turns the kettle on. He prepares the first AeroPress and gets the beans ground for a second AeroPress, all the while thinking to himself about the Christmas movies Mom will be watching in a few weeks while busying herself in the kitchen.

A few minutes later, he comes out of the kitchen with two steaming mugs of coffee; one black and the other with a minuscule amount of cream in it.

"You like it black, right?"

"Yeah, that's perfect. Thanks."

"You're welcome."

Owen takes the hot mug of coffee and takes a sip from it.

"You look a little off, you doin' all right?"

"Just following a thought train is all," Emmett says.

"Care to share?"

"Oh sure," Emmett says. "I was just thinking about how the relationships in my life don't tend to have happy endings."

"How do you mean?"

"Like when I was diagnosed and told all of my friends about it, how the vast majority of them just stopped talking to me—no closure, no goodbyes, just silence, just stopped answering my text messages and emails and IMs and phone calls. And the same thing happened with Lauren. Well, kind of."

"What do you mean 'kind of?'"

"Well, if I could remember the end of our relationship I would have closure, but ECT erased all of that, so it's just one big mystery to me. I actually emailed her a few months after I was done with ECT and asked her why our relationship ended but didn't get very good information; just lies about how things were. I don't think she really realized that I had, that I *have* no clue how it ended. I don't know why she left me; I don't remember if I did anything terrible to her or hurt her in any way. There's just no closure from my end. It's like she just left."

"I'm sorry, buddy."

"So it goes," Emmett says. "And now the same has happened with Jayne—but it's been a good thing, really. I'm psychotic less often, for one. Which is really good. I'm spending more time with friends who are a lot better for me. I'm a lot more productive, having gotten off of Facebook and the like, getting more writing done and spending more time doing better things than staring at my phone for hours on end. I'm also a lot less anal about my battery, and the less anal I can be, the better." Owen is nodding his head and sipping at his coffee. "But it's also a little weird; it's just a strange ending to a friendship. You'd think there'd be some kind of exchange after ten years of friendship, that we'd honor it somehow, that we'd at least acknowledge we've been friends for a long time and it kinda sucks that it's over now."

"Do you really expect someone to do that, though?"

"Lauren did it," Emmett says.

"She did?"

"Yeah," Emmett said, chuckling. "All I remember from her breaking up with me is that I asked her if she wanted to get some lunch with me. So we biked to Suki's and I ran into a parked car on the way there and broke my collarbone."

"Shit," Owen says.

Emmett lets out a laugh, thinking about the ridiculousness

of the situation. The last word he remembers Lauren uttering is "Jesus!" as Emmett ran into the parked car; after that, everything goes black again. He knows that they went to Suki's and he ordered his usual sesame tofu and then called Mom and told her what happened and asked her to come and pick him up. He knows that he ignored the pain in his shoulder for several days before going to the doctor to get it x-rayed.

Is it significant that the last words he heard Lauren utter were a plea to God? What does it mean to cry out God's name anyway? He supposes it's a plea, a supplication, something done out of desperation. More likely it's just something she learned from her parents or from her friends when her mind was still a piece of putty forming in the trammels of her skull.

"I don't know," Emmett begins, resetting his mind to factory defaults. "I suppose it's just that one thing I've learned in my life is happy endings are a luxury. I was thinking that in a few weeks it'll be Thanksgiving and it'll be the start of my Mom's favorite time of year; Hallmark and Lifetime will start showing their stupid Christmas movies and they'll be playing nonstop when I go over to my parents' house on the weekends. They always have a happy ending and she always says that she loves, even needs, a story with a happy ending.

"I'm not like that," Emmett continues. "I'm not particularly attracted to a happy ending. They don't seem realistic to me. Maybe because there isn't really an ending in the conventional sense—you're born, you grow up, you die with so many loose ends left untied. And it's so rare that you get to reach a conclusion, that you get to say goodbye in a proper way, that you get to 'achieve' (if that's the right word) your so-called happy ending."

"I can see that," Owen says. His phone makes a vibrating noise on the coffee table and he sets his coffee down and picks up his phone. "Marta Lee is here."

"Oh good," Emmett says, brightening up. "I'll go get her."

Emmett and Kerrinpuppy head down the hall, Emmett walking his slow, steady pace—keys jingling from their usual place where they hang from his belt, Kerrinpuppy running up and down the hall. Marta Lee walks into the entryway and stands there, bent over making excited gestures at Kerrinpuppy through the glass door.

He opens the door and his Little Girl goes bursting into the entryway and jumps up at Marta Lee, Emmett calling at her to get down. Marta Lee gives him one of those hugs that reassures him everything is okay, that he is loved, that he is safe.

They walk down the hall and into Emmett's apartment.

Owen had told Marta Lee that Emmett is close to his heart shortly after meeting him and this is on Emmett's mind as he closes the door after saying goodbye to them. He can create such connections with people, they seem drawn to him, but they also seem to abandon him so readily. But Owen and Marta Lee are fundamentally different. Lacey has always told him he can trust his gut and his gut tells him they're made of different stuff than Jayne, that they'll always be there. He feels he'd been ignoring his gut with Jayne, the myriad signs telling him she didn't care. Never again. He's going to listen.

He walks back down the hall, back inside his apartment. He selects Terror Twilight by Pavement from his collection of records and sets it on his turntable. He sits there, Kerrinpuppy on his lap, headphones atop his head, enveloped in the music, sorting his thoughts as best he can.

Acknowledgements

I'd like to thank Neil at High Prairie Press for agreeing to publish my book; without him, his guidance, and his enthusiastic encouragement I wouldn't even have a novel to publish. I'm indebted to my Aunt Mary and my friends Taylor and Kelsey, for reading early drafts of my novel. My editor, Erin, did a wonderful job and was a sage guide in helping me shape the text of this novel. I'd also like to thank my parents, and the rest of the folks who, over the past few years, have been gently encouraging me to write a book. I'd especially like to blame my Mom for the existence of this book, it was her idea that I start writing in the first place.

Mostly Just Like You

This has been the first book in the Mostly Just Like You series by Chris Feld. Book two is planned for late 2018 or 2019. To find out when the next book is released, please sign up for the High Prairie Press newsletter at HighPrairiePress.com.

If you liked the book, your feedback and review would be appreciated on Amazon or elsewhere. High Prairie Press is a small indie publisher that thrives because readers and fans of the books we publish refer friends online in reviews, through social media, and via that old fashioned thing called personal interaction, which we're a big fan of by the way.

Your referral not only helps new and upcoming authors like Chris Feld gain the attention they deserve, but also introduces stellar new talent--that the traditional publishing machine is unaware of--to your friends, family, and your network of social contacts (on line and off.)

Thank you for supporting the growing indie revolution by reading this debut novel by Chris, and we look forward to sharing his next installment, which is coming to life through his fingertips and within the bits and bytes of his trusty Mac as I type these words.

About The Author

Chris Feld has been passionate about writing since he was a child. From entering and winning story contests in middle school to being named the Ivan Turgenev recipient for excellence in writing in high school, the praise surrounding his talent seemed to suggest an educational pursuit revolving around literature or manuscripts in one way or another. So everyone in his life was surprised when he instead chose to pursue a degree in painting upon graduated from high school.

His plans of artistic glory suffered a blow in 2007 when he was diagnosed with schizo-affective disorder, a combination of schizophrenia and bipolar disorder. A consummate optimist, he refused to let such a serious weight drag him down. But in 2009, the weight of the diagnosis caught up with him and his life disintegrated. He embraced electro-convulsive therapy (ECT) in order to save his life, but its effect on his brain was devastating, leading to near total memory loss and the loss of many abilities he once took for granted.

His innate stubborn tenacity helped him to slowly rebuilt his life. He now leads an independent life that he often describes as idyllic in an eclectic Denver neighborhood with his service dog Kerrin. He's traded his paint brushes and canvases for a keyboard and word processor, and has dedicated his life to helping people understand what living with a severe mental illness is like.

Chris regularly shares his unique and remarkable insights into mental illness in blog posts at MostlyJustLikeYou.com. He also speaks to NAMI Family-to-Family classes, sharing his experiences, guiding those with family members who are afflicted with a mental illness, assuring them that the affliction is not a death sentence.

The example Chris paints every day with the life he lives inspires us all that it's possible to lead a rich and fulfilling life despite the heavy burden of mental illness. His writing translates that inspiration into tangible storytelling that moves readers to rare and wonderful insights.

Discussion Group Questions

What are some ways that our culture deals well with mental illness? Are there examples in the story that bear this out?

What are some ways that our culture deals poorly with mental illness? Are there examples in the story that bear this out?

Are you aware of other cultures that deal with mental illness in a healthier manner than our culture does? If so, how are they healthier? How about historical examples/cultures?

Are there cultures who deal with it in a less healthy manner? If so, how are they less healthy? How about historical examples/cultures?

What are the hidden costs (financially, morally, and culturally) of not dealing well with illness, either mental or physical?

Did the story change your perspective on ECT in any way? If so, how?

Emmett doesn't actively resist Myra and her cadre. Does the story do a good job of describing this choice? What is your perspective on the choice he has apparently made?

Emmett describes his mental illness as a "twisted sort of blessing." Do you see any ways that Emmett does or could benefit from his mental illness?

Consider the difference between the way Emmett's dad treats Emmett when he's not feeling well and the way Jayne treats him at those times. What's your impression on the way these differences might affect Emmett?